Joanna Hines

Joanna Hines was born in London and studied at Oxford
and the LSE. For over twenty years she has lived and
worked on the Lizard, Cornwall, with her Canadian
husband. She has a step-daughter, a daughter, and a son.
This is Joanna Hines's fourth novel. Her earlier books are
the contemporary suspense novels *Dora's Room* and *The
Fifth Secret*, and *The Cornish Girl* and *The Puritan's Wife*,
novels of seventeenth-century Cornwall. All are available
from Coronet.

SCEPTRE

Also by Joanna Hines

Dora's Room
The Cornish Girl
The Fifth Secret
The Puritan's Wife

Autumn Of Strangers

JOANNA HINES

SCEPTRE

Copyright © 1997 Joanna Hines

First published in 1997 by Hodder and Stoughton
First published in paperback in 1998 by Hodder and Stoughton
A division of Hodder Headline PLC
A Sceptre Paperback

The right of Joanna Hines to be identified as the Author of
the Work has been asserted by her in accordance with the
Copyright, Designs and Patents Act 1988.

10 9 8 7 6 5 4 3 2 1

All characters in this publication are fictitious and any
resemblance to real persons, living or dead, is purely coincidental.

A CIP catalogue record for this book is
available from the British Library

ISBN 0 340 65369 8

Typeset by Palimpsest Book Production Limited,
Polmont, Stirlingshire
Printed and bound in Great Britain by
Clays Ltd, St Ives Plc

Hodder and Stoughton
A division of Hodder Headline PLC
338 Euston Road
London NW1 3BH

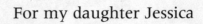
For my daughter Jessica

$\int$

An afternoon like gossamer. Blue shadows blurring into infinity, even the insects seemed half-asleep. From a high point of land nearby, the village appeared to be floating, an island of rooftops and tidy gardens adrift in a pale sea of stubble fields and grasslands. Animals and trees weighed down by the drowsiness of late summer heat.

Time played tricks in the shimmering stillness.

Lydia, gazing down at the village from Raven's Beacon, wanted the afternoon to go on for ever. That evening, dinner loomed. Dinner at the Manor. Conversation as starched and unyielding as the napkins, and the kind of welcome which only emphasised her not-belonging.

The elderly lady who would be her hostess fiddled unnecessarily with a bowl of sweet peas and gypsophila she had finished arranging an hour before. In theory, having reached the final years of her life, she had run out of time, yet on afternoons such as this, she felt she was wallowing in a surplus.

Not far away her daughter Caro, as usual, seemed to have exhausted all the hours available that day and was simply flying here there and everywhere, in a sweat of heat and irritation, simply to keep up.

Only the small boy in the lorry, waking from a troubled sleep and shouting to be heard above the shake and roar of the engine, was blissfully unaware of time, still lost as he was in the endless present tense of childhood.

'Is this the place we're going?'

'Yes.'

'What's it called?'

'Briarswood.'

The name meant nothing to him. Not yet.

Sated with the September heat, it was the canine residents of Briarswood who noticed the intrusion first. Suddenly there was a darker texture to the gauzy hum and buzz and drone, a distant sound, as gently ominous as summer thunder, but approaching all the time.

It was Suzie who saw them first. Ambling along the road with her elderly labrador, Bumpkin, she was finding that time weighed very heavily indeed. Because she was only fifteen, people were for ever telling her she had her whole life in front of her – kindly meant, obviously, but a truly appalling prospect, when she had a hard job knowing how to fill a single afternoon.

And then the vehicles appeared.

The car at the head of the procession had once, long ago, been red. It was struggling to pull a bouncing, old-fashioned caravan. Behind that, as Suzie observed through her screen of fair hair, came a lorry with windows at the side and a curious little chimney. Behind that a van, and behind that a small lorry towing another caravan. And still the ancient vehicles came over the hill.

A cold finger of apprehension touched Suzie's spine.

As the red saloon car came closer, there was a grinding screech of brakes. The two human occupants of the car had noticed Suzie at the same moment that their dog, huge and white and out of control, had spotted Bumpkin. Letting rip with a frenzy of barks, it hurled itself like a crazed ghost against the dashboard, obscuring all else from view. Even above the roar of the engine and the barking of the dog, Suzie could hear the yelled curses of the temporarily blinded driver, and the even louder yells of the passenger as he fought to bring the dog under control. The car swerved towards Suzie. Bumpkin raised his hackles and growled a warning. Suzie froze. Just as the car was about to veer off the road, the dog was overpowered. A woman's face surfaced once more above the steering wheel and the vehicle crunched to a halt. Disaster had been avoided by inches.

The passenger, a young man of devastating good looks, leaned out of the side window and called to Suzie, 'Is this the way to Ted Sedden's farm?'

For once in her life too shocked even to be self-conscious, Suzie shouted back, 'Through the village and first left after the fire station.'

'Cheers!'

The grin that accompanied the young man's thanks was doing extraordinary things to the pit of Suzie's stomach. He was darkly handsome with black hair that was cut short on the crown of his head, but long at the sides. His companion was plain by comparison – anyone would have been plain by comparison, Suzie thought – but she threw Suzie a warm smile and made a thumbs-up sign before flinging the car into gear and setting off once again. The pale dog was still barking excitedly, but through the rear windows, at the caravan which bobbed and swayed behind them.

With a roar of danger and exhaust fumes they were on their way, followed by the lorry with the funny windows and the little chimney and the whole cavalcade of geriatric, protesting vehicles.

Good heavens, thought Suzie, when she was left standing once more by the roadside in silence. And to think that a moment ago I was telling myself that nothing interesting ever happens in Briarswood.

As the unusual convoy was passing in front of the wrought-iron gates of Briarswood Manor, Suzie's grandmother, christened Veronica Jane but known for more than seven decades as Twinks, was getting, as she would have said, into rather a state. No one observing her would have detected this fact, since she maintained at all times an enviable poise. Impossible therefore to imagine that the elderly woman with the once beautiful and always serene features was in the throes of a crisis. Certainly her husband had no idea of her inner turmoil: George's ignorance concerning Twinks' true feelings had remained constant through nearly fifty years of marriage.

She touched the double strand of pearls at her throat as if they were prayer beads, and therefore calming. 'You invited Wyndham Sale? Here? Tonight?'

'That's right.' If George had possessed a tail, he would surely have been wagging it now, as he gazed down at her with his usual bluff affection. He was a tall man and remarkably unaffected by the years, though his jackets hung a little more loosely from his shoulders than they used to, and he was troubled by all manner of annoying pains that he would have scorned to mention, even to his wife. 'Knew you'd be pleased,' he added.

'Pleased?' Twinks' voice was a merest echo. 'And why would I be pleased?'

'Knew you wanted to have the fellow over for a meal. Bumped into him on the road. Perfect opportunity.'

Twinks' pale green eyes had acquired a strange lustre, but George had not observed the transformation. She was momentarily at a loss. Recently, she had felt that she was losing a certain amount of peripheral vision, as though a kind of mental fog were closing in on her world. But through the fog she saw quite clearly that George had sabotaged her once again.

'One would have liked,' she told him serenely '—one would have *preferred* to have had a little more warning, George. One might then have been able to arrange a proper dinner party. One could have chosen the guests and menu with proper care.'

'That's just it.' George, having hung his cap on its peg, stooped down to pat his dog Hamish, a younger, coal-black edition of Bumpkin. 'Knew we had people coming tonight already.'

'Caro and Suzie. Jim. Lydia Fairchild.' Twinks dropped the names into the conversation with infinite distaste, like soiled items of laundry into a basket.

George, undaunted, had begun towelling Hamish vigorously. 'Just the job eh? Charming ladies, family atmosphere. What the fellow wants after losing his wife.'

'Wyndham Sale,' she pronounced his name with particular emphasis, 'is the new owner of Haddeley Hall.'

'Monstrous old pile. Poor bugger, wonder what he'll do with it.'

An uncomfortable simmering sensation in her chest decided Twinks in favour of a tactical retreat. Leaving George to tend his dog, she passed into the front part of the house, moving at all times with the gliding motion learned many years before, and, deciding on a little detour, she crossed deep carpets to the drawing room, and the comfort of the drinks cupboard. Never for one moment did it occur to her that she might be angry with her husband. Like George, she believed they were well-suited and wholly compatible. Besides, discord was vulgar. Nor was it possible she might be unhappy. How could she be, when she had so much to be grateful for?

The tokens of her good fortune were everywhere: the fine family paintings on the walls and the cabinets filled with delicate and much loved objects in silver and porcelain. And the grand piano, hardly ever used these days, but still polished and tuned regularly. In her young days, Twinks had been much praised by her music teachers, and throughout her adult life she had found a solace that went deeper than mere pleasure from her playing. About five years ago the increasing stiffness of her hands made it pointless to continue. She did not permit herself to indulge in regrets: she had so much else to be thankful for; but it was since then that the first tendrils of mist had begun to cling about her head.

She was no longer even aware of being disturbed by George's impetuous invitation. She would ring Sandra and tell her to come up an hour earlier than planned, and Mr Gee could always be roped in at short notice. She must also phone Caro and warn her of the altered plan. But first she decided to treat herself to another little 'bucker upper'. A small tot of sherry or gin did so help one to view things more clearly again: her doctor would surely have advised it as medicinal, had he known

Some little while after her unexpected brush with the traffic, Suzie wandered in through the back door of the Lodge to find her mother busily washing large quantities of plums under running water. Keen to avoid being roped into any harvest-type activity, Suzie wandered out again almost immediately and went to sit on the swing seat at the bottom of the garden, where she could contemplate the memory of the youth with the remarkable dark eyes without fear of interruption.

Caro had seen Suzie materialise briefly with Bumpkin at the back door and then vanish again, but she was in such a rush that there had been barely even time to say 'Hello'. The heaped-up Victorias with their magnificent bloom of reddish-purple had been so beautiful in the farm shop as she drove past that afternoon that she had been quite unable to resist the temptation, even though she had heaps of other things to do before going to the Manor for supper that evening, and Victorias as she well knew were notorious for spoiling if not dealt with straight away. She softened the fruit in the preserving pan, and had just added the sugar and was stirring it carefully, when the phone rang. As usual, no one else in the house seemed even to hear the wretched thing, which left Caro with no alternative but to seize a towel and, still wiping her hands, simply sprint into their tiny hall and grab the phone, shouting out to the silent household, 'It's all right! I've got it!' As if anyone even cared.

'Caro.'

Caro's voice dropped. 'Oh, hello, Mummy.'

'Something's cropped up,' announced Twinks. 'Your father ran into Wyndham Sale at lunchtime and he's invited him to dinner.'

Caro grasped the gravity of the situation at once. 'Can't you put him off?'

'We'll manage somehow. Sandra says she can stretch the lamb. Just make sure that Suzie and Jim are presentable. I only hope poor Lydia can rise to the occasion.'

'Lydia . . . oh heavens.'

'Please make sure your bunch are all on time. For once.'

The line went dead before Caro had a chance to protest her family's unfailing punctuality.

Still smarting from that undeserved 'for once', Caro turned to knock on the door of Jim's study to pass on news of this latest crisis, but then she heard a hideous roaring, hissing explosive noise coming from the kitchen. Uttering a wail of despair she sped back the way she had come, entering the kitchen just in time to witness the laval flow of hot fruit and sugar as it erupted over the side of the preserving pan, poured down over the cooker and plunged in a joyous tide towards the floor.

Jim Lewis, gazing at but not really bothering to read the book that was open on his desk, had heard the phone and then his wife's agitated but mercifully brief conversation. From her anxious, good-daughter tone he assumed she must be talking to Twinks, but he did not judge it necessary to intervene until he heard her final howl of anguish. Over the years Jim had grown so accustomed to Caro's constant hum of activity that he no longer even noticed it unless, as now, a transition was indicated from normal rush to abnormal crisis. Since he had long ago decided that life would be intolerable if they both maintained the same frenetic momentum, Jim had opted to be the calm eye at the centre of Caro's domestic storm. It was a role he had perfected to such an extent that he was sometimes in danger of grinding to a halt altogether.

Now he rose slowly from his chair, closed his book carefully and strolled in a leisurely fashion the short distance from study to kitchen. There he paused for a moment in the doorway and surveyed the scene of devastation with a smile of practised tolerance. Caro was on her knees, frantically mopping up the sticky mess on the floor while yet more descended in reddish-brown blobs from the cooker rim.

'Oh dear,' he said. 'What a mess.'

Caro glanced up at him, her face red with exertion. 'Mummy's on stage one alert,' she announced. 'Daddy's taken it into his head to invite Wyndham Sale to supper tonight.'

'That's all right then. I thought it must be a real disaster – Mr Gee giving in his notice or something. You've both been wanting to meet this Sale character ever since he bought the place.'

Caro simply couldn't be bothered to explain to Jim that a pot-luck family dinner was hardly the ideal introduction for the new owner of Haddeley Hall. She only said, 'We simply must be punctual. Mummy needs us there by seven.'

'I can be ready in five minutes.'

'Well I can't. And we've got to be smart.'

'You're never anything else,' he said.

Compliments always caught Caro unawares. She stopped her mopping and looked up at him with a startled smile which transformed her appearance at once. She had a no-nonsense sort of face, capable and straightforward, but with none of the femininity or elegance that had always been her mother's great asset. She pushed back her hair, which she still wore in the long bob that had been fashionable in her youth, and said, 'Oh Jim.' And then, 'Look at this. Aren't I a clot?'

But at least she was smiling. Jim loved to see her smile, that shy, self-deprecating smile that he still found endearing. Especially as it indicated he might now safely return to his book.

Before he left he said, 'If you clean the stove first, it won't keep messing up the floor.' He seldom offered practical help, his efforts having been so often rejected in the past.

Wyndham Sale, fielding simultaneous calls from Minneapolis and Hong Kong in the panelled downstairs room at Haddeley Hall which he had chosen for his temporary office, was unaware of the turmoil precipitated by his acceptance of George's invitation to dinner at the Manor. In fact, he had forgotten all about it.

'Idiots,' he commented, but without rancour, as he punched the off button and disconnected a frantic voice in Minneapolis. 'Their problem. Let them sort it out.'

And to Hong Kong he said briskly, 'Have the figures ready by tomorrow at the latest, or it's no deal.' The shrill voice at the other end of the line leapt up an octave, but Wyndham said mildly, 'That's my last word, I look forward to your call tomorrow,' and then Hong Kong was silenced in the same manner.

'Right,' Wyndham turned to his secretary, a man of indeterminate age who was wearing a vibrant salmon-coloured tie, 'what next?'

'That about wraps it up,' said Mark. What he most liked about this job was the economy of his present boss's style. Wyndham Sale ran a hugely efficient business operation with an absolute minimum of fuss. Not for him the tantrums and dramas with which so many tycoons bolstered their insatiable egos. He could be ruthless when necessary, but his manner was so relaxed – distant, almost – that by the time his associates detected the danger they were in, it was far too late for avoiding action.

'Are you sure?' Wyndham looked irritably at his empty in-tray. From his own point of view, the main disadvantage of his famed efficiency was that it often left him with not enough to do. He gazed hopefully at the fax machine, as though willing it to spew forth a problem.

Mark gathered up a couple of papers. 'I thought we might

walk down to the Bird in Hand for a drink and a bite to eat. It's a beautiful evening.'

'Is it?' Startled by this unexpected nugget of information, Wyndham stood up and crossed to the window. He stared for a few moments at the long shadows cast by the enormous oak trees dotted around the park. His venerable trees, his rolling acres of park. 'So it is.' He sounded mildly baffled by the intrusion of the natural world, but he realised, as he looked out over his newly purchased domain, that the view had a cardboard appearance, like a painted backdrop. People always said nature had a comforting effect, but since Annabel's death landscape views invariably assumed this oddly stagey character, and offered no consolation whatsoever.

'Damn quiet,' he muttered. The workmen who were installing a seventy-foot pool in what had once been the orangery, had packed up and left half an hour before.

Mark was watching him. Medium height and solidly built, Wyndham Sale was in his early forties, but could have passed for younger. He had neat, precise features which habitually hid much more than they revealed, and he was saved from any possible hint of blandness by an air of energy reined-back, like a man constantly hungering for fresh activity to stimulate his interest.

Mark admired his employer, and relished time spent in his company, as if he hoped he might grow more like him and end up equally successful and wealthy. He said, 'It's Indonesian night in Briarswood, apparently.'

'Really?' Wyndham was far from enthusiastic. The prospect of an evening in the company of his secretary was not appealing, but nor did he wish to pass another evening alone.

With relief Wyndham remembered that he did after all have other commitments. 'Another time, Mark. I'm going to be launched into the heights of Briarswood society this evening.'

'Does such giddy splendour exist?' asked Mark, hiding his disappointment behind a smile.

'Apparently, yes. I met a cheery old buffer this afternoon down by the church. He suggested it was time I started to fraternise with the locals and invited me to supper. George Cartwright. He lives at the Manor.'

'That pretty house with the iron gates? I've seen it from the road.'

'The very one. So it's another lonely pint for you, Mark, I'm afraid. There won't be any reply from Milan till tomorrow, so that's about it for now. I'm off to get ready. My host looked the type who's a stickler for punctuality. I don't want to be late.'

'That would never do,' agreed Mark.

In the event it was Lydia Fairchild who was late for supper at the Manor. Punctuality was among the minor virtues that had apparently deserted her since her arrival in Briarswood. The reason for this was a complete mystery, as for once in her life she had all day and every day to suit herself: no deadlines, no commitments, no pressure of any kind. Rose Cottage was only a ten-minute walk from the Manor. Yet she was invariably late.

She could hardly explain to her no doubt fretting hostess that she had been absorbed in the contemplation of several goldfinches feasting on the thistle heads at the end of her garden and that she had forgotten everything else. Nor could she imagine Twinks lending a sympathetic ear to her latest theory, which was that time ceased to abide by normal rules in the country, so that hours stretched and shrank in an altogether unpredictable way.

After all, she had only intended to stay at Rose Cottage for a few days, a week at the most. It was to have been a brief respite, a chance to pull herself together and make some definite plans for the future. That had been more than two months ago. Not that she had ever made any actual decision to extend her visit – it was hard to remember the last time she had made any kind of decision – rather that tomorrow always seemed like the best time to contemplate knotty problems. Never today.

Exactly how she had filled such a succession of todays was another mystery, since she had always thought of herself as someone who had to be fully stretched to avoid feeling restless. Perhaps she had needed this bucolic interlude to convalesce from the trauma of the spring. Perhaps. But then again, these eight rustic weeks seemed too separate from the rest of her life to have any real relevance. A city dweller, she was learning to scale down her perceptions to accommodate the immense detail of the countryside: the way the hedgerows were just now acquiring a first dusting of russet and purple as the berries coloured; the infinite variety of chatter among the swallows as they gathered on the telegraph wires; those enchanting, late-making goldfinches.

This very afternoon, returning from her walk, Lydia had noticed a new sound among the usual repertoire of agricultural noises. It seemed to be coming from an area known to the local people as the Hollows, which was about a quarter of a mile from her cottage. There had been much roaring of motors and that exasperated noise engines make when the wheels to which they are attached are spinning without getting anywhere. She was not unduly curious. She had been in the country long enough to know that farmers got up to all sorts of strange activities about which it was best not to enquire, since the answers tended to be long and complicated and, ultimately, not all that informative.

She had ceased to notice the noise from the Hollows. The goldfinches had arrived. She had gone into the garden with her sketchbook. If only she could capture their hectic assault on the thistles. Lydia had always found it easy to 'draw what she could see' and her talent had been useful. But now she longed to reach beyond mere replication and capture the essence of objects, the unique swoop and glide of those birds. A charm of goldfinches. She saw now how they had come by their collective name. And while she was struggling with this impossible challenge, another afternoon had evaporated, like all the others.

Lydia was aware that she spent long hours avoiding necessary tasks. Like not sorting out her life in a sensible way. Like not answering Gordon's letters.

His most recent had arrived that morning, and lay on the kitchen table. Already it was printed with brown half-moons where she had set her coffee mug down to prevent its blowing away. Uniquely among doctors, Gordon had handwriting that was glaringly legible. Lydia wished it wasn't, since every phrase was loaded with reproach: '—understand your need for privacy, but this ridiculous secrecy has gone on far too long—' and '—surely we can talk this whole thing through like sensible adults—'

Well, actually, no. Not yet, Gordon. Not a chance.

Lydia had no difficulty constructing brilliant answers to all his queries – but only in her head. Alone in her dilapidated little cottage she explained time and again exactly what she was doing here, precisely why she couldn't yet tell him where she was, and why she still had to use her sister as intermediary.

It was just that she never got around to committing her thoughts to paper.

Tomorrow. Tomorrow, for sure, she would buckle down and write the kind of rational, let's-talk-this-through-like-grown-ups sort of letter that Gordon loved.

Today, before the noise from the Hollows and the goldfinches distracted her, there had been the urgent problem of what to wear for supper at the Manor. As she had arrived two months earlier with only one small suitcase, she was hardly spoiled for choice. But the clothes she had left behind would not have been much help either. Lydia had always favoured items which were either hunted down on antique market stalls or of such instant high fashion that they were useless after a season. If the effect was a bit tacky, so much the better. With her slim height and her strong features, she could carry off a little vulgarity with ease. She had opted to wear a small black skirt and a shiny red halter top. The only drawback, apart from its total unsuitability for supper at the Manor, was that she had worn the same outfit on her two previous visits.

The hell with it, she thought, I don't care.

But she did care. Maybe the feudal atmosphere of Briarswood had undermined her self-confidence, maybe it was the fact that George and Twinks were letting her stay at Rose Cottage for hardly any rent, maybe she was simply tired of being odd one out. Caro, who was attractive in a big-boned, scrubbed kind of way, was sure to be wearing something classic – last time it had been a navy linen dress, simple, but expensively cut – and as for Twinks, she was the most stylish old lady Lydia had ever encountered. Hard to believe she must be well over seventy. She still looked terrific in her floating blouses of silk chiffon or exquisite dresses in shades like creamy almond or gentian blue. Not that Lydia had ever been a classic navy linen sort of dresser, still less the silk chiffon blousy type.

Heaven forbid. Suddenly aware that she had left herself barely any time to get ready, Lydia raced up the narrow stairs of the cottage and tore off the jeans and shirt she had been wearing all day. She ignored the clothes she had chosen and instead she pulled on a pair of tight black trousers, a skimpy lace vest top and cropped jacket. There was just time to pull a comb through her tangle of dark hair, dab on a few touches of make-up and find her favourite earrings, before racing barefoot down the grassy track that led from the ramshackle charm of Rose Cottage to the comfort and elegance of Briarswood Manor.

Lydia frequently spent a great deal of time making decisions which were then overturned on a last-minute whim. She had a deep-rooted belief that life is fundamentally random, and that the best of plans will always be thwarted. Experience had taught her that hard work leads merely to frustration and disappointment. It therefore made sense to act contrary to plan whenever possible, so as to catch fate on the hop.

Pushing open the little gate that led into the Manor garden, Lydia paused to slip on a pair of sandals and stroll across the wide lawn to the front door. An unfamiliar sports car was parked on the forecourt beside Jim and Caro's Range Rover.

Intrigued, Lydia pushed open the front door and went in.

2

To Twinks' dismay, it was Suzie who effectively derailed her dinner party that evening. The girl had made almost no contribution to the conversation throughout the first two courses, but Twinks did not expect lively debate from any of her guests, and certainly not from her granddaughter. All she required was that the proprieties be observed. Lydia's bizarre outfit clearly left a good deal to be desired, and there had been an anxious moment during the mushroom soup, when Lydia began some nonsense about people being either burrowers or nesters, and had the bad manners to describe Rose Cottage as the archetypal English burrow. Jim had been perverse enough to encourage her in this folly until Twinks was obliged to intervene. Apart from this lapse, conversation drifted gently over such reliable subjects as the keeping of dogs – always a favourite topic of George's – and the arrangements Wyndham was making for domestic help at Haddeley Hall. On the whole, Twinks was favourably impressed by Wyndham Sale: there was nothing brash about him – far from it – his voice was soft but authoritative. One or two of his remarks led her to understand that Haddeley Hall, though large, was by no means his principal residence. A potentially awkward moment, when Wyndham brought his late wife into the conversation, had been bravely defused by Caro, who had said how sorry they had all been to hear of her death. Little more was required of the other guests than murmurs of vague agreement, and Wyndham had nodded and said, 'Thank you,' in a fairly brisk way, which was all just as it should be. And now, just as Twinks had instructed Mr Gee to clear away the dishes and bring in the pudding course – one of

Sandra's stand-bys, an apple-marmalade tart with cream – Suzie presented them all with this. George had been inadvertently to blame because he had sought to draw her into the conversation by asking her about Bumpkin. Talking about her labrador had reminded Suzie of their walk this afternoon, and that had led to this present statement.

'What?' croaked George

'What?' repeated Caro.

The shock of being catapulted so suddenly into the lime-light was such that Suzie's blush covered her face at twice its usual speed.

She said again, 'I saw this sort of hippy convoy thing coming into Briarswood this afternoon. At least, I think it was a hippy convoy.' She smiled shyly as she spoke, as though to defuse the impact of her statement.

'Where?' demanded George.

'Yes, where?' echoed Caro.

'Near Bellings Wood. They were coming into the village.'

'A convoy?' queried Twinks faintly.

Suzie nodded towards her grandmother across the expanse of polished wood, the ornate Georgian candlesticks and a profusion of pale sweet peas in the blue and white tureen.

'How many were there?' asked George.

'Oh, I don't know, I didn't count. About six. Maybe more. It could have been ten.'

'Ten? Ten people?'

'Well, vehicles, actually. Vans and lorries. And a couple of caravans, you know. But it might have been only six.'

Twinks straightened her back and smiled serenely, her time-honoured response to any catastrophe. 'It's almost incredible,' she remarked to Wyndham who, sitting on her right, had so far remained impassive.

As ever, Caro was determined to look on the bright side. 'I expect they were only passing through, Mummy,' she soothed.

'Oh no,' said Suzie. 'At least, I don't think so. They asked for directions to Ted Sedden's farm.'

This final piece of information galvanised her grandfather into immediate action. 'Great heavens, the poor fellow,' exclaimed George. 'I'll get on to him right away, see if he wants help heading them off. What a frightful business. Just as well I've still got my gun. Jim, go down and make sure the front gate is shut and bolted. Did you come in the Range Rover? Good man, best park it across the entrance just to be on the safe side.' He strode from the room and could be heard in the hallway, calling for Mr Gee.

Jim refilled his glass. 'At last,' he addressed George's empty seat, 'the Range Rover's hour of glory has arrived.'

'I can move it, Jim, don't worry.' Caro had been observing her husband with increasing anxiety. Jim seldom drank to excess, and almost never in the company of her parents, but the rare occasions when he did were usually unpleasant, especially for her. She had no idea what had brought on this particular lapse, but there was no doubt that his normally gentle and sensitive expression had been overlaid by an ominous coarseness. His flushed face contrasted unpleasantly with the faded ginger of his hair, and his eyes had that watching, cynical glint she had learned to dread. Caro had never discovered a way to cope with Jim when he was like this: she suspected that her artificial brightness only goaded him to greater excesses, but she was rendered incapable of careful planning by her panic. 'No need for you to bother about it, dear.' She beamed at him across the table, at the same time trying to indicate with a secret frown that he had imbibed enough.

Jim observed his wife's facial contortions with interest.

'Nonsense, Caro,' he declared. 'A man must defend his family.' And he stood up so suddenly that he nearly knocked his chair over, before following his father-in-law from the room.

Caro hoped he would take his time so the fresh evening air might work some sobering magic. She smiled at those who were left.

'There now, Mummy,' she said, 'I'm sure it's all a fuss over nothing.' She cast around for a change of subject, but Twinks was already engrossed in passing on to Wyndham some of the more lurid reports from the newspapers concerning the personal habits peculiar to people who travelled in old vehicles. That only left Lydia. 'Well now,' Caro said to Lydia, 'what a to-do.'

Lydia merely raised a single eyebrow and said, 'Yes, indeed,' which for some reason left Caro feeling both foolish and cross.

She could never quite decide what to make of Lydia. She had been anxious at the beginning of the evening that Jim's former student must be feeling distinctly out of place in such an unsuitable outfit. She might have blamed herself for not ensuring Lydia understood the kind of dinner it was to be, except that Lydia appeared not in the least discomposed, quite the contrary in fact. Caro would have died rather than be seen with a tatty little piece of old lace stretched across her chest and those too-tight trousers, but she could see that in an odd way Lydia was managing to carry it off. It helped, of course, that she had kept her youthful figure – having no children probably helped there – and Lydia did have legs that seemed to go on for ever. Caro herself was wearing a beige striped dress and jacket which she had bought for a wedding a couple of years ago and which still looked reasonably smart, even if the sailor-suit collar did accentuate her bosom somewhat. She was puzzled by Lydia's lack of dress sense. She was sure Jim had said she'd been married to a doctor, and Caro had always found doctors' wives to be quite elegant.

She was still trying to think of something to say to Lydia, when Jim returned. As far as Caro could see, the fresh air had only been a partial success, for he announced with a too-loud jocularity that the Englishman's castle was now secured. Lydia, who had glanced up briefly at his return, was now abstractedly pushing her slice of apple and marmalade tart back and forth on her plate.

'The marmalade is home-made,' Caro told her brightly. 'It makes all the difference.'

Lydia looked up at this statement with some surprise. Her mind had not been on marmalade. She said politely, 'It's delicious, anyway,' and Caro smiled back her gratitude. Jim was pouring himself some more wine. From the hallway, George's voice, which had been rising in volume ever since he picked up the telephone, stopped abruptly.

He came back into the dining room, a stupefied expression on his face and lowered himself slowly into his seat. 'I just can't believe it,' he breathed.

'What?'

'Did you get hold of Ted Sedden?'

George nodded. 'He's letting these people stay at his farm. He's *invited* them, can you believe?' This news was greeted with general incredulity, but George insisted, 'I know, I know. The fellow must be off his chump.'

'Why the hell did he invite them?' asked Jim.

'God knows.' George loosened the knot on his tie. 'Plain bloody-mindedness if you ask me. He actually had the nerve to tell me that he'd met a bunch of these New Agers at some market or other and he told them – he actually *told* them – that they could park at his farm.'

'For the night?' Caro suggested hopefully.

'Longer.' George's deep voice was resonant with gloom. 'For the winter. Indefinitely. He wouldn't say.'

'That's it then,' Twinks laid her hands in her lap and spoke with quiet emphasis, 'a total disaster.'

'Oh come now,' said Wyndham, and since he had not spoken on the topic before, everyone was suddenly attentive. 'Surely the situation is not as bad as all that. There must be any number of ways of getting them to move on.'

'Quite right,' said George. 'Trouble is, they take time. And meanwhile we've got to be on our toes. Lydia, you can't possibly sleep at Rose Cottage on your own tonight. You must stay here.'

Lydia laughed, 'I'll be fine, don't worry.'

'No, no,' Twinks insisted, 'we wouldn't sleep a wink for worrying about you. Ted Sedden's farm is quite close to Rose Cottage, much better to stay here.'

'Please,' Lydia's smile faded as she realised their invitation had been in deadly earnest, 'you really mustn't worry about me. Besides, I insist on staying in my own place.' In an effort to deflect attention from her refusal, she asked Suzie, 'What did they look like?'

'Oh.' Suzie frowned and hooked her hair behind her ear. 'I did notice one couple. The ones at the front who asked the way. They looked sort of . . . different. Very scruffy. A bit scary, actually, but kind of jolly too.'

'Simply frightful,' breathed Twinks.

'If you won't stay here, Lydia,' said George, 'I'll lend you a shotgun. No need to know how to use it, just wave the thing about if you feel nervous.'

She stared at him in horror. 'A gun? Are you serious?'

'It's for the best,' Twinks told her. 'You've really no idea what these people are like.'

Lydia shook her head. 'I can't believe I'm hearing this. A bunch of youngsters turn up in a few old trucks and everyone starts carrying on as if the French Revolution has just broken out. It's outrageous.'

Lydia always looked her best when anything struck her as outrageous, especially after a couple of glasses of wine. Wyndham and Jim were both watching her with interest. Her dark curls bobbed with animation and her eyes flashed, as she regarded her fellow diners with mingled disbelief and contempt. Mistaking their silence for a readiness to listen to her argument, she went on, 'No one has even set eyes on them yet – apart from Suzie, of course – but already they've been condemned out of hand. Surely you can wait and see what they're like before you have to start all this talk of guns and moving people on?'

'That's all very well in theory,' agreed Wyndham, 'but in this instance you're probably wrong. I have always found it better to deal with this kind of nuisance before it's had a chance to take root. It saves everyone a lot of trouble in the long run.' As he finished, Wyndham seemed to relish the furious look which Lydia threw at him.

'Their dogs,' said Twinks, 'kill sheep.'

Jim grinned. 'Since when did you and George start keeping sheep?'

His mother-in-law regarded him sternly. 'This is no joking matter, Jim. Briarswood is a small place. If one landowner suffers, then all are affected.'

'Quite right,' agreed George.

'Still,' said Jim, 'look at it another way. Unwashed youth on the rampage is the modern rural blight. Now it's Briarswood's turn. Maybe we should just be grateful we've been lucky until now. We'll just have to endure them for a bit.'

'Don't even suggest such a thing,' said Caro with feeling. 'Why should poor old Briarswood have to put up with them? No one wants them here.'

'No one wants them anywhere,' said Lydia.

'Then they should just go away.'

'Where?'

Caro ignored this question. 'One feels so horribly powerless,' she lamented. 'There ought to be a law.'

Lydia said, 'There are. Masses of laws.'

Twinks leaned towards Wyndham and said in a conspiratorial voice, 'They have No Lavatories. They Do Not Wash.'

'So I hear,' he said with a smile, for Twinks still evoked gallantry in men of all ages. 'Isn't it frightful?'

'Oh for heaven's sake,' exclaimed Lydia, 'I've never heard such blatant prejudice in my whole life.'

'Give it a rest, Lydia,' Jim told her. 'No one wants to hear your pat little opinions. You're not in the student union now.'

She flinched, as though she had been hit, then glared at him as she said, 'I'd have thought that you, of all people, would have agreed with my position. Since when did sticking up for people's rights become a pat little opinion? Do tell me, please. I'm longing to know.'

He shrugged off her sarcasm. 'You're an outsider here. Things are done differently in the country – Briarswood is different. Don't meddle in what you don't understand.'

Lydia began to say, 'I think I understand a case of—' but Caro intervened swiftly.

'Oh, don't let's argue about this, please. We simply must stick together. No one's got anything against these people as individuals, Lydia. I mean, we don't even know them, as you say. And I do so agree with all that business of standing up for people and all of that, heavens, yes. It's just that they don't belong in a place like Briarswood. They won't have the first idea how to fit in. I'm sure they'd all be much happier among their own sort. Proper sites, and that sort of thing.'

'Less talk, and more action,' declared George. 'Please excuse me, everyone, I'm going to make a few phone calls. Start rallying the troops.'

Throughout the debate, Suzie had sat slumped in her chair. Never before had any words uttered by her created such a sensation. She might have felt more gratified if everyone hadn't seemed to have forgotten about her entirely. She twiddled a strip of hair between her fingers, and her grandfather patted her fondly on the head as he left the room; he treated both grandchildren and dogs with identical tokens of affection. One day, thought Suzie crossly, he'll forget entirely and offer me a bone.

Twinks was aware of anger and tension in the air. The sound of raised voices was always so distressing, whatever the cause. She remembered her first and favourite piano teacher, dear Miss Finn, suggesting they practise a rousing duet to drown out the noise of her parents shouting in some room not far enough away. 'Play the piano, Veronica Jane, play, play! Music will never let you down.' Twinks' fingers moved restlessly over the polished wood of the dining table, but the comforts of music were no more.

'We'll take our coffee in the drawing room,' she announced, 'and I think under the circumstances we might treat ourselves to a little tot of brandy.'

Wyndham had been diverted by the brief flare-up between Lydia and Jim. He now decided that the most entertaining part of the evening was probably over and he could use the advent of the travellers as an excuse to cut his visit short without fear of offence. His announcement led to renewed concern from Twinks and Caro that Haddeley Hall was in imminent danger of being overrun.

'I hope they don't try to break in,' said Twinks.

'Why should they?' Lydia's question was scornful. 'They're Ted Sedden's guests.'

'Rogue elements,' said Jim provoking her.

Wyndham rose from his seat and moved to stand opposite Lydia's position at the table. Watching her as she struggled against the social tide, he had noticed first that she had a long and attractive neck. He saw now that she had finely arched eyebrows, one of which was slightly higher than the other, and that her eyes were hazel-green and most expressive.

'You believe everyone has overreacted,' he said.

'Damn right I do.' Lydia caught his gaze as she answered, and there was a brief moment of recognition: two outsiders at a family gathering who might – or might not – have more in common with each other than either had with the home team.

'Then I hope you don't have cause to regret your optimism,' he said smoothly. 'This particular group may turn out to be a convoy of Mother Teresas, but I'd be very surprised. Their fellows have earned themselves a terrible reputation. Sometimes even the newspapers get it right, you know.'

Lydia continued to stare at him, not softening her appraisal with a smile. She had not paid much attention to him through dinner, dismissing him as just another of the Cartwrights' not particularly interesting friends. Now she saw that Wyndham Sale's substance was based not just on wealth, but on a shrewd intelligence as well, and that he would enjoy the cut and thrust of arguments as much as she did; she saw – and this made perfectly good sense to her just then – that if he had been the sort of man she found attractive, she would have found him very attractive indeed. As it was, all she said was, 'Better to trust people and be proved wrong, than never to trust them in the first place.'

'Oh bravo,' said Jim. 'Lydia the eternal idealist.'

Wyndham smiled at her then, distancing himself from Jim's attack. 'As I said, I hope you are proved right and that I am wrong. In the meantime, don't dismiss all the things people say.'

'That's right,' said Jim. 'No smoke without fire.'

Caro beamed at them to mask her growing despair. 'Heigh ho, everyone, let's all go to the drawing room for coffee. No need to let these wretched people completely ruin our evening.'

It was the signal for them all to stand up. Wyndham made his excuses to Twinks and went into the hall to find George and say good-bye to him. Suzie, Caro and Twinks left the room together. As she passed through the hall, Twinks stumbled on the corner of a rug and Caro reached out her arm to steady her.

'Good heavens,' Twinks giggled as Wyndham went past, 'what a business. Thank you, Caro dear, I think I must be a little squiffy.'

'Oh, Mummy.' Caro's reproach was softened by indulgence. No one carried off mild inebriation quite like Twinks. She became yet softer and more feminine, her little weakness making her more approachable and loved. No one would ever use the word 'drunk' to describe Twinks at the end of a social evening. She herself had a whole fistful of words to describe her condition, like nicknames for a favourite child: tiddled, pie-eyed, a little bit fuddled. It was others, coarser and less favoured, who became drunk.

The trolley bearing coffee and cups, and pushed by Mr Gee, could be heard rattling over flagstones in the direction of the drawing room. Jim had remained in the dining room to pour himself a last glass of George's claret. Lydia hesitated in the doorway and turned to regard him for a moment.

'You're different,' she said, 'here.'

'I'm older. We're all different.'

'You know what I mean.'

'Yes.'

Suddenly his face was stripped of cynicism and malice, and seemed close to despair.

Lydia said, 'I preferred the younger version.'

'So did I.'

'Then why the change?'

'Life is never as simple as you pretend.'

'I disagree,' she said coldly. 'You have always made it unnecessarily complicated.'

Jim raised his glass of wine, but did not drink. He seemed to be on the verge of saying something important, but then Wyndham appeared behind Lydia in the doorway and said he hoped he would meet them both again, and Lydia departed for the drawing room, and coffee.

Unusually, that night, Lydia found it difficult to sleep.

For the first time since her arrival in Briarswood on a warm afternoon at the beginning of July, she was conscious of the fact that Rose Cottage was set back quite a way from the road and that she had no neighbours within calling distance. She refused to admit she was afraid; she remained convinced all the others had been overreacting horribly.

But still, she could not sleep.

She had the city dweller's mistrust of silence. And this September night was so quiet she could hear the blood pulsing through her ears – or whatever that internal whooshing noise was that she had never noticed until now. An occasional lorry hummed along the by-pass, nearly two miles away. Then silence again.

Except for those too-loud snaps and creaks and scuffles that punctuate the country night. She had never been bothered by them before, falling each night into the stunned sleep of the convalescent. They bothered her now.

In an effort to distract herself, Lydia concentrated on a review of the evening. She had long ago discovered that it was difficult to feel angry and afraid at the same time, and she preferred to be angry. She remembered the way Caro kept squinting at her clothes, as if she had made some terrible sartorial faux pas, like prancing around in a fake leopard-skin jump suit. This thought was instantly cheering: maybe next time she was invited to the Manor – if indeed she was ever invited to the Manor again – she should hunt one down. Or find a fringed cowgirl jacket and thigh-length boots.

Not that she had any real desire to upset Caro. Nor George and Twinks, who had been generous to a fault – besides, she liked them both. Everybody liked them; they had many admirable characteristics, like kindness and courage and the best kind of old-fashioned courtesy. She had not meant to be critical of them over the travellers, since she would not have expected them to hold any other view. Her scorn was all for Jim. Of him she had expected much more.

It was more than sixteen years since she had met Jim first. At that time he had been a youngish lecturer, radical enough to be popular with most of his students, and Lydia had been one of his brightest pupils, with time and energy for almost any cause except that of her own work. They had begun working together to organise a protest over the threatened deportation of an African student. Now she found herself wondering if his present pose was a careful camouflage necessary in the company of his wife's family, or whether the idealistic young lecturer had been the pose all along. Was it possible for someone to change so much in a mere fifteen years?

When the ritual of coffee drinking had been concluded, Jim had driven her home. With their usual solicitude Caro and George had forbidden her even to consider walking alone down the grassy track between the two houses in the dark. Jim had been instructed to make sure that 'everything was all right'. He had waited while she hunted through various piles of junk for the front door key. He asked her if she had a phone by her bed, and was duly appalled when she pointed out that there was no phone line to Rose Cottage in the first place. Lydia felt herself wrong-footed by his demonstrations of concern, with its implication that she was not only vulnerable but too naïve to appreciate her present danger.

The most infuriating part of the whole rigmarole was how effective it was. By the time Jim had finally departed and she had bolted the back door, locked the front and checked all the windows, she had become downright jittery. The very act of barricading herself in, far from making her feel secure, only emphasised the dangers that were lurking out there in the September dark.

Maybe she had been wrong. She had so often been wrong in her estimation of people in the past, it was quite probable that she was wrong again now and that the group of people whom Suzie had seen were every bit as undesirable as everyone assumed. She could hardly blame Twinks and Caro for their anxiety: no one in their right mind would want a sudden influx of outsiders who shared neither their lifestyle nor values. Maybe Ted Sedden's visitors were just another bunch of drugged-up misfits with a deep-rooted grudge against people like her who lived in proper houses and appeared to have every advantage. Maybe they had no respect for other people's property, no respect for other people at all. Someone had to be responsible for all the crime and mugging and burglaries that were reported all the time – so why not them? Even if reports of their activities had been exaggerated, chances were, as Wyndham said, that there was some basis for their unpopularity in fact.

She lay very still in the bed.

She remembered an incident from her honeymoon with Gordon four years earlier. They had been walking through an Italian hill town one afternoon of white, dusty heat. The place was apparently deserted, all the inhabitants sensibly taking their siesta behind sun-blistered shutters. An old dog had ambled round a corner and Lydia, glad of any signs of life, even canine, had said, '*Ciao*, dog,' and walked over to greet it. 'Leave it alone, Lydia,' Gordon had advised in his government-health-warning-voice. 'It could be rabid.' She had brushed his concern aside, and said, only half-joking, 'No need to worry about me, Gordon.

Didn't you know I've got a way with animals?' and had stooped down to pet it, whereupon the dog sank his few remaining teeth into her hand.

She had made light of it at the time and had shrugged off Gordon's attempts to make her have a series of anti-rabies shots. When she returned to England she entertained her friends with a graphic account of the consequences of her folly. 'I've got a way with animals,' became Gordon's automatic response when he thought she was about to embark on a reckless enterprise. She had always been the first to join the laughter at her own expense.

But that had been a different Lydia, a Lydia who had confidence in her ability to bounce back, no matter how painful her fall. Someone who really did believe you could make the world a better place if you just fought hard enough.

What had happened to change her into the kind of woman who was intimidated by a dinner party and then lay awake half the night listening for the crunch of footsteps on the path outside her cottage?

A lot had happened. Too much had happened. That was what she had come here to forget.

No smoke without fire, Jim had said.

Just before she fell asleep, a phrase floated into her mind. She must have heard it in some old film, or a history book . . . or somewhere.

'The barbarians are at the gate.'

A light wind had sprung up, rattling the old windows in their frames, and she pulled her covers closer round her shoulders. As if a duvet could make you safe.

Barbarians at the gate: it was a fear as old as time.

3

Caro was aware of tension in the air, the moment she stepped out of the house.

Whenever possible, Caro tried to make time to walk the quarter mile from the Lodge to Peggy's shop in the middle of the village. Quite apart from the value of the exercise, it was good to be reminded of what a perfect place Briarswood was. Especially on a fine September morning like this, when everything smelt deliciously crisp and clean, and the shadows were long and muted, and there was that beginning-of-autumn sense of frailty and impending change. Caro drew in deep breaths and reminded herself, as she often did, to count her blessings. In spite of all their many setbacks and tribulations, she and Jim really were incredibly fortunate to have found sanctuary in a place like Briarswood – or rather, in Briarswood itself; it was a form of disloyalty to imagine any other village might possess quite Briarswood's charms. This thought was especially strong as she passed the village church where Sir John Haddeley, the Jacobean adventurer who had built Haddeley Hall with riches from the Americas, lay in marble splendour with his wife. Caro allowed herself to pause for a moment and drink in the beauty of the ink-dark green of the two cedars planted in the mossy churchyard and the crystal-pure blue of the sky. As usual, a couple of jackdaws were pottering around the rim of the spire. Who could fail to be moved by such a sight?

'Have you seen them?' Peggy asked Caro, as she had asked all her customers that morning.

'No, I hear they've gone to Ted Sedden's place.'

Peggy nodded. 'The Hollows. I don't know what it's all coming to.' Peggy spoke in her flat Birmingham accent, a voice made hoarse by long years of smoking. No one knew quite how old she was, no one dared to ask. It was rumoured that she had been a chorus girl in her youth, but no one quite liked to ask about that either. She was hard-working, generous, formidable and well-liked. Whenever the inhabitants of Briarswood were accused of being insular and unwelcoming to outsiders, they would point to Peggy in triumph: there had been murmurs, years ago, when she took over the shop. Now it was impossible to imagine Briarswood without her.

'The police have been down to see them already,' Peggy reported.

'Gracious me, whatever for?'

'To keep an eye on them. And they'll be on the look out for drugs. I do wonder if Ted isn't going feeble-minded.'

'Poor man, I hope not.'

'It's his wife I feel sorry for. Poor Norma won't know which way to turn with that lot dumped on her. And she's the one will bear the brunt.'

'Let's hope they move on quickly then.'

'I have heard they're here for the winter,' said Peggy darkly. She appreciated that, apart from the supply of butter and stamps and last minute gifts, her role in the village was to dispense gossip. She also knew that bad news makes much better gossip than good. 'And once they're dug in, it's a terrible job to shift them. I tell you, if one of my grandchildren took up that way of life, I'd die of shame.'

Caro left the shop briskly, feeling disturbed by her conversation with Peggy, disturbed in some fundamental way that was quite different from the alarm and outrage of the previous evening. This was more like a kind of violation, a churning nausea beneath the diaphragm. Beneath the surface beauty of Briarswood a sinister presence had intruded. Crude visions of crime and drugs and sex and raucous music and outlandish clothes rose in her mind. Suddenly this village that she loved appeared desperately vulnerable. Everything that she held dear, everything she so often took for granted, could be smashed by an unwelcome group of outsiders. It simply wasn't fair. She had struggled long and hard for her present modest contentment, and she didn't see why it should all be threatened now.

As she drew nearer to her home, her pace quickened until she was almost running. Her previous generalised fear was focusing into a precise anxiety for Suzie. The girl was so immature for her age, and so vulnerable. Of all her four daughters, her youngest seemed least equipped to deal with the perils of modern life. When Jim took early retirement, Caro had been delighted to bring Suzie into the country for these difficult teenage years, and now, look, the ghastly pollution of the city had pursued them even here. She could almost see the danger, like a noxious smoke, curling round the walls of the Lodge, invading the precious sanctuary of her home. For some time now she had been meaning to have a serious talk with Suzie along the general lines of being careful and not doing anything foolish: it had been delayed long enough. She must speak to her that very morning.

She pushed open the front door, flung down her shopping and called out, 'Suzie! Suzie, I must talk to you!'

No reply.

The terrible fear sprang into her mind that Suzie wasn't even home.

Knocking, but not waiting for his reply, Caro entered Jim's study and startled him as he did battle with a couple of small round aliens on his computer screen. She was too preoccupied even to notice.

'Where's Suzie? Have you seen her?'

Jim automatically wiped the game from the screen. He was nursing a mild hangover, but managed a patient, 'As it is only ten o'clock, I would hardly expect to see the child. Her capacity for sleep at present is well nigh infinite. I suggest you check her bedroom before we consider alerting the police.'

'Oh. So you didn't hear her go out?'

He shook his head. 'Is anything the matter?'

'Yes. No. I don't really know yet. But I want to talk to her.'

Jim nodded, as if this was an excellent idea, then glanced pointedly at the book which lay open beside his keyboard. Feeling slightly foolish, Caro closed the door quietly behind her and proceeded up the stairs.

He was right, of course. Jim so often was right. It was wonderful being married to a clever man, but sometimes Caro did get a bit fed up with always being the one who got into a flap over trifles.

Anyway, there was Suzie, sleeping like a baby all burrowed down under her duvet. Her mouth was half-open, a strand of fair hair trailed across her forehead, her cheeks were flushed. Caro's brief moment of tenderness and relief lasted only until she remembered she herself had been up for nearly three hours. Really, she would be glad when term started again next week. As usual it took ages to rouse the girl, and even then she was more asleep than awake, so Caro had to postpone their talk until Suzie was in a more receptive state.

As Caro went down the stairs and picked up the bag of shopping which she had left in the middle of the hall, it dawned on her that she didn't have the first idea what she intended to say to her daughter.

The problem, as so often with teenagers, was how to warn her of the frightful dangers of the outside world, without planting ideas in her head that hadn't been there in the first place.

Watching George depart after breakfast, Twinks felt herself enveloped in a sense of foreboding. He looked so old and frail, and so horribly determined, as he jammed on his hat, picked up his shotgun and strode out towards the garage. Her suggestion that he should at least wait until Jim, or Mr Gee, were free to accompany him, had elicited a typically vigorous reply.

'Stop fussing, for God's sake. Got to grasp the nettle, y'know. Can't just sit around and do nothing, can I?'

That was exactly what she would have liked, but she said merely, 'Of course not, George. All the same, if you would only wait—'

'What for? Jim's no use to anyone. Wyndham's a newcomer. It's up to me, you know. I've got to talk some sense into old Sedden. Can't let him get away with this.'

He was enjoying himself, of course. A chance to demonstrate proper leadership, to show the younger men how this kind of situation ought to be handled, a chance to forget that he was nearly eighty and suffering with prostate problems and arthritis in his hips and knees.

Twinks went to the window of the morning room and watched him reverse the BMW out of the garage, narrowly missing a granite mushroom and a newly-planted magnolia, before setting off down the driveway and turning carefully into the road.

Too anxious to have any idea how to fill the time until he returned, Twinks crossed the hall to the drawing room. Instinctively, she drifted towards the grand piano and ran her fingers over the smooth wood. To her amazement, it was often the early scales that she missed the most. She had been so thrilled as each one was mastered and could be played with rippling ease. 'Excellent, Veronica Jane. What nimble fingers you have my dear.' In those days she had lived for a word of praise from Miss Finn. Now one must resort to other forms of consolation. She had just closed the door of the drinks cupboard and was straightening once again, her cheeks slightly flushed, when Sandra came in wielding hearth brush and duster.

'I passed Mr Cartwright on the drive just now,' she said cheerily. 'Where's he off to so early in the morning?'

'Ted Sedden's farm. He thought he'd try to talk some sense into him. About these terrible traveller people.'

'Good luck to him.' Sandra was on her hands and knees, sweeping out the grate, and the scent of warm ashes filled the room. 'I passed a couple of them just now. Filthy they were, and their dogs looked vicious. I wouldn't want my David tangling with that lot.'

Twinks raised her chin slightly and graced Sandra with a dignified smile. 'Heavens above, I'd never waste my time worrying about Mr Cartwright,' she said softly. 'He's always been well able to look after himself.'

Only a slight tremor in her hands betrayed her continuing anxiety, and Sandra was far too busy to notice that. It never for a moment occurred to Twinks that she might confide her fears to Sandra, or to anyone else. Hiding all emotion had been second nature for so long that she would not have known how to appeal for sympathy even if she had wanted to.

With no real idea of where she was going, or what she intended to do, Twinks made a stately exit from the drawing room, leaving Sandra's image of her employers unimpaired.

When Sandra left the Manor a couple of hours later, George had still not returned, but unlike Twinks, Sandra felt no anxiety for the elderly gentleman. As far as she was concerned, Mr and Mrs Cartwright were both immune from the worries and dangers which afflicted ordinary folk. She was both impressed and irritated by their apparent exemption from the everyday grind of trying to keep one's head above water.

She liked working at the Manor and she was glad of the extra cash. She had been lucky to be taken on. Her father, Mr Gee, who had helped out there for some years as handyman, butler, gardener, chauffeur or whatever else was needed, had recommended her a couple of years ago and, as this had coincided with one of David's occasional periods of unemployment, she had accepted at once. Her husband worked for a local builder and though he was good at his job, he always seemed to be one of the first to be laid off when business was slack. When he was in work they could just about manage to pay the mortgage and the bills. The months when he was out of work were an agony of worry. They tried to avoid money arguments, but these inevitably flared up sometimes. At the moment, however, he had been in work for almost a year, their debts were nearly paid off and she was making plans to redecorate the children's bedroom and even, after Christmas, think about installing some decent kitchen units.

As she emerged between the wrought-iron gates that led on to the road, she paused. A car was approaching which she recognised at once as Wyndham Sale's. It was low and sleek and a pearly grey colour, and of a make so exotic and expensive she had never even heard of it before. She watched the car glide past her towards the village. There had been a glimpse of Wyndham Sale himself, looking every bit as debonair and masterful as he had done when she had peeked through the pantry window and saw him arrive the previous evening.

She set off walking once again, absorbed by topics of much greater interest than decorating or kitchen units. Men had always found her attractive; she had a stunning figure and her face wasn't bad either. She had seen a film recently on television in which a middle-aged tycoon had made friends with a much younger couple who were deeply in love (like her and David) but in financial difficulties (another similarity). The wealthy business man, who happened to be extremely good-looking (as was Wyndham Sale, in her opinion) had offered the young husband a million dollars to sleep with his wife for just one night. At the time Sandra had considered the film a bit far-fetched: the millionaire didn't look the type to pay for sex, but Wyndham Sale had recently lost his wife and might not want to make the effort involved in dating. And, having only just moved in at Haddeley Hall, he probably didn't know many attractive women in the area yet.

A night of torrid passion followed by a shopping spree that need never end. It was in many ways the perfect fantasy.

Wyndham Sale had not in fact recognised Sandra as she stepped on to the grassy verge beside the main road, but a little further on he did notice Lydia Fairchild. She was wearing jeans and a checked shirt and carrying a plastic bag of shopping. For a moment he considered slowing down and offering her a lift, but then he thought better of it and pressed his foot down on the accelerator. He was late already for his meeting in town and, besides, he had no idea of where she lived, nor any desire to know. He had registered her the previous evening as an attractive woman and one whom, in different circumstances, it might well have been diverting to pursue. But not at present. Since Annabel's death he had found his interest in other women to have dwindled almost to nothing. By one of life's cruel ironies the fickle husband had been transformed into the faithful widower. Annabel dead inhibited him in a way Annabel living had never done. What he had appreciated in Lydia first had been the haughty way she held her neck, like a dancer. Long ago, Annabel had trained as a classical dancer, and held her head in that same proud manner. But Lydia's hair was dark and curly and cut in a short bob, whereas Annabel's had been brown and straight and pulled sleekly back from her forehead. Lydia's features were strong, attractively irregular, whereas Annabel's beauty had been in her quiet delicacy. Lydia's manner was forthright, tending almost to brashness, Annabel had been at all times refined and self-effacing.

These comparisons he found endlessly irritating, yet somehow impossible to avoid.

The death of his wife had affected Wyndham in all manner of unexpected ways. They had been married over fifteen years, but after the first few years he had not been aware of any great bond between them. She was beautiful; he was proud of her. He was sorry that she was so obviously unhappy, but he put that down to the lack of children, and she never told him any different.

During her final illness, Wyndham had, as always, behaved impeccably: the best doctors, the most lavish care, trips to the opera or her favourite hotels whenever she was strong enough. And she herself remained dignified to the end.

'Will you miss me?' she had asked, a few weeks before she died.

'Of course I will,' he told her gently. Afterwards he had wondered if it were true. And on the day she was buried, he felt sadness, but also the easing of a burden.

It was only in the following weeks that her absence began to trouble him. Not that he was aware of missing her, particularly. He wondered if his symptoms were merely coincidental. He had trouble sleeping, he lost weight. Concentration was occasionally a problem.

But he was determined to get through. He shook himself back into the here and now: Haddeley Hall in Briarswood, this idyllic corner of the country where they had chosen to make a home.

As he left the village he saw, on the road ahead, a small group of what must surely be travellers. Half a dozen youths who looked like extras from a film set during the Irish potato famine, complete with ragged clothes and verminous dogs, were attempting to manoeuvre a hand cart down the middle of the road.

Glad of any distraction from the thoughts which plagued him, Wyndham slammed his fist down on the horn and accelerated, causing them to scatter in satisfying panic, and narrowly missing the handcart and a large, pale and extremely energetic dog.

*　　*　　*

'Where are you going with all those?'

Caro pounced just as Suzie was carrying an armful of books out of her bedroom.

'Just tidying up,' Suzie mumbled.

Caro peered at the spine of the top one. 'Oh look, all the Pippa books. How you used to love those. Such nice stories, weren't they?'

'Oh, Mum.' Suzie was mortified. 'That was years ago.' Not even to her mother would she admit that only last week she had been enjoying a furtive and nostalgic trot through *A Palomino for Pippa*. She was in agony at the thought that Caro might mention this social dysfunction in front of Mina.

Mina was Suzie's friend from as far back as she could remember. Mina was coming to stay. Mina still lived in the town where Jim used to teach. Mina was smart and sophisticated and had probably outgrown the Pippa books at the age of five. And Mina was not one to hide her scorn: her vocabulary contained twenty derogatory words for each one of approval.

It occurred to Suzie, as she tidied her room and removed any item that might arouse Mina's withering contempt, that she might well be doing all this clearing for nothing. Mina had been promising to visit for ages, but each time they arranged a date something else came up and Mina had to cry off. Suzie didn't blame her: the first time Mina had gone to a rave in a derelict brewery; another time a really close friend had overdosed and Mina had to go and visit him in intensive care, and on the last occasion Mina and some friends had decided to hitch down to the coast for a couple of nights sleeping on the beach. No wonder it had been thumbs down for Briarswood.

And no wonder Suzie's eagerness to see Mina again was tinged with anxiety. Their friendship had always been an attraction of opposites, but Suzie was afraid they would no longer have anything in common at all. While she passed her days taking Bumpkin for walks and mooching about doing nothing in particular, Mina had catapulted into an altogether more exotic existence. What on earth could Briarswood offer that might compete with the scandals and dramas of their home town?

Still, Suzie was determined her bedroom was not going to let her down. Hence the censorship: Pippa and her succession of interesting equine friends definitely had to go. Like an addict, Suzie could not leave them in the spare room without glancing through one or two first. In a matter of minutes she had drifted into another world. Pippa was her secret vice, as shaming as anything she could think of, just about as shaming as those totally unmentionable things. All that tacking up and rubbing down and rising to the trot. In her heart of hearts Suzie often wished she was Pippa, with that cheerful, slightly snub-nosed face, two no-nonsense pigtails and an unchanging uniform of 'jodhs'. Flying over hedges and streams, faithful sheepdog at her heels, Pippa coped in a simply wizard fashion with any problem she encountered. Suzie's attempts to ride had never come to anything: she had left it too late and had no talent for it at all. But she continued to ride like a champion in her dreams.

Caro sat at her dressing table and fussed with the pots of cream and powder. Anxiety niggled through her, like toothache. She could hear Suzie bustling around in her room, which was a good thing, but soon they would have to go and pick Mina up which meant a further postponement of their little talk. In fact it was in danger of joining all the other sensible talks Caro had intended to have with her daughter but for which there never seemed to be the right moment. Not that Suzie ever seemed to have much to do. It distressed Caro no end to see her slumping about the place as if she carried the burdens of the world on her shoulders, when anyone could see she was an extremely fortunate girl. A secure home, parents happily married, a mother who still made sure she was in the kitchen with the kettle on when Suzie got home from school. Not like those poor latch-key children you heard about, children from broken homes, children who never had any attention. But still . . .

It was no longer possible to ignore the fact that Suzie's long-delayed adolescence was upon them. Not for the first time, Caro found herself on the verge of wishing she could simply skip over the next few years and be waving her youngest away to . . . university, secretarial college, her first job, an early marriage – anywhere, really, so long as it was away. She checked herself just in time. It was all wrong to go wishing these last few precious years of family life away. Suzie was only fifteen and so wouldn't be leaving properly for another five years and then Caro would be *sixty*, goodness gracious. She just couldn't help being lazy about it, that was the trouble. She'd done the adolescent thing already, done it three times and that was enough, surely. Polly's had been a lengthy melodrama, Kate's the sneering, sarcastic kind, and Emily's all door-slamming fury. One summer, when the three girls were being simultaneously impossible, a friend had startled her by saying, 'Not much longer now, Caro, and your life will be your own again.' It was the 'again' that flummoxed her. It implied a halcyon era when she had been independent and in control of her life, but she was pretty sure such a time had never existed. If it had, she had somehow failed to notice it. She was still puzzling over that 'again', when she discovered she was pregnant with Suzie.

Of course she'd been thrilled to bits once the shock wore off. There'd been a few tearful moments, but that was just those pregnancy hormones, everyone knew about them. And Jim had been a bit strange about it too, to begin with, but the moment Suzie was born, everyone just loved her. Their little fair-haired blue-eyed late baby. A late baby keeps you young, that's what people told her, though most of the time she was too busy to know if she was young or a hundred and one. No point in fussing, anyway: one simply got on and made the best of things.

Caro leaned her cheek on her hand and gazed at her reflection in the mirror. It was a broad, straightforward face that gazed mournfully back at her. A face that, when young, had been attractive for its fresh-skinned vitality, a typically English peaches-and-cream complexion with a disarmingly open expression. Now it had grown into a face which radiated a kind of competent benevolence, a face which led people to assume she was longing to organise fête stalls and rotas and take care of people's pets when they went on holiday. It was the face of someone who invariably made the best of things.

But sometimes, just occasionally, she felt completely worn out with the effort of always making the best of everything. She had never expected to reach her mid fifties and still be struggling to keep up appearances. She knew it was wonderfully kind of her parents to let them live at the Lodge, and it was a decent enough house in its way, but there was only one bathroom between three people, and no dining room at all.

She sat up very straight and frowned at her reflection. She had been on the verge of sliding into self-pity. Worse still, her thoughts might have degenerated into disloyalty towards Jim, and that was out of the question.

Caro didn't recognise Mina at first, as she told Jim later that evening when the girls were tucked up in bed. She'd dyed her lovely black hair a hideous shade of pinkish red and was wearing so much make-up you could barely see her face and a terrible old skirt which looked as if it had come from an Oxfam shop. But underneath it was still the same old Mina, thank heavens, bright as a button and talking nineteen to the dozen.

She'd hugged Caro enthusiastically, and then she and Suzie had greeted each other like long lost sisters.

'Where's your case, Mina dear?' asked Caro.

'Oh. Travelling light.' Mina indicated her woven shoulder bag which, Caro observed with dismay, was not large enough to hold more than a pair of underpants and a toothbrush.

'I'm sure Suzie can lend you anything you need.'

'I always wear other people's stuff,' giggled Mina. 'Saves on laundry. This is Rupert's T-shirt and Mum's skirt.'

'How is Jean? It's ages since I saw her.' Caro went to open the boot of the Range Rover, then remembered Mina didn't have any luggage, and went round to the driver's door.

'Fine. She sends her love, by the way.' Mina got into the front seat and Suzie sat in the middle at the back and leaned forward so as not to be left out of the conversation. 'She's much more together since the divorce came through.'

'When was that?'

'Oh, May, sometime.'

'Heavens, that was quick.'

'Well, Dad wasn't contesting and they wanted to keep it civilised.'

'That's good,' Caro pulled out of the station car park and into the light, early afternoon traffic. 'Very sensible.'

Mina chattered on, 'I mean, obviously it was hard for Mum to begin with, but now that it's all, like, definite, she's much better about everything. She's socialising again and really beginning to get her confidence back.' Mina's schoolgirl treble had somehow become overlaid with an accent that sounded rather common, Caro thought, as if she had grown up in one of the poorer areas of South London. Caro blamed television.

'Poor Jean, after all those years.'

'Mm. She says she's glad now really because it's forced her to take stock and reevaluate and it's given her the chance to make a fresh start. She's planning to get a career going soon.'

'Well done her. And how is your father?'

'Oh, he's OK. And Sonia and I get on all right, sometimes it's just like having an older sister and we have loads of laughs together. I go over to their place quite a lot.'

'And how's school?'

'Fine. Well, we don't go back till next week. But work's a doddle, really. I took a couple of GCSEs early and the others are mostly course work. I thought I might do sciences at A level, but it's hard to decide.'

'Sciences, gosh. And how's Rupert doing? He must have just had his A level results, hasn't he?'

'Mm. Well. There was a bit of a muddle up over the exams,' Mina giggled. 'Not his fault at all, everyone agreed about that, but it meant he didn't do as well as he was expected to. I mean, everyone had him down for three As and just because the school got the day wrong on one paper he didn't get graded *at all*. Jean said the school should do something, but of course, they never do. So anyway, he'll probably go to a crammer. He'll resit in November and then he'll do a year abroad. You know, good works in Africa. Or India. Somewhere like that.'

'How exciting.'

Suzie had been listening with especial attention to the update on Rupert. He was totally unlike his younger sister in looks, tall and fair and languid where Mina was small and dark and dynamic. Suzie had always been interested in tales of Rupert, ever since he was a conker-wielding eight-year-old who used to sneak up behind her when she was watching TV at their house and pull her plaits. Secretly, she had even enjoyed the plait pulling.

'Wow. Country air. Just what I need. Town sucks.'

Pleased with Mina's appreciation, Caro decided to overlook her rather odd way of expressing it.

Mina was looking out of the window, now that they were approaching Briarswood. Two youths, one with shaven hair and the other with dreadlocks, were walking in the direction of Ted Sedden's farm. 'New neighbours?' she asked, craning her head to keep them in view.

Caro's expression changed instantly. 'Dreadful, isn't it. They turned up yesterday. For some reason one of the local farmers took it on himself to give them the use of one of his fields. Can you imagine? Sheer spite, obviously. He wanted to build himself a hideous bungalow to retire to, and various people quite rightly opposed it. But they'll soon be gone. My father's been on the phone since crack of dawn trying to sort it out. They simply can't stay here, it's quite outrageous.'

'Yeah, I bet.' Mina slid Suzie a conspiratorial grin. 'Briarswood's waking up then, eh?'

'It's wonderful the way poor Mina's adjusted,' said Caro to Jim as they settled into bed that night. 'I was afraid she and Rupert would be badly affected, but Jean and Bob seem to have handled everything frightfully well. Such a nice child, Mina, even if she has dyed her hair that ridiculous colour. I've always thought she was a good influence on Suzie. Such a lively girl, and so interested in everything.'

'Come on, hop in Sooz, there's loads of room. Just like two lessies. Ouch, watch out for my boobs. There's this terrible dyke takes us for CDT sometimes and she used to fancy me to death. Always gave me As and Bs even when I did really crappy work. Insisted on calling me Wil-hel-mi-na just so she could savour every syllable. Ugh, she gave me the creeps, so I started skipping school on those days. No one even noticed, so I skipped lots of the other days as well. School's a stupid waste of time anyway, if you want my opinion, no one's ever going to give you a job so why bother, just to check out goods in Tesco's. No thanks. In the end some stupid moron came round to complain to Mum, but she was going through one of her can't-you-see-my-husband's-left-me-for-a-younger-woman? psychodrama phases so she didn't get much joy there. Then a welfare officer came round and he was young and gorgeous looking, or so Mum thought, and they started going together and now she acts as if she's just found the secret of eternal youth or something. She's so busy going out all the time I don't think she's cooked a meal in months. Not that I care about food anyway, but Rupe got really mad at her once. He said he didn't mind about no meals but how about she *bought* some food once in a while. And she went like totally nuts and told him he was a parasite and she'd had enough of everyone draining her energies and she owed it to herself to lead her own life for a change. All the usual crap, but she's got a point. Rupert doesn't think so. He was really screwy for a while, but he was doing loads of drugs so he was just out of it most of the time. Two of his exams he never even managed to get there. Mum wants him to go to a crammer, but she doesn't have any money, and Dad's getting into loads of debt because of taking sexy Sonia to Prague and God knows where and buying her red lacy underwear with holes in all the wrong places – ugh, he's such a creep these days, and Rupe just says, "Hey, what's the big deal?" anyway. Oops, watch out, I'm going to have to climb over you, Sooz. I've got this kind of infection thing which means I have to pee all the time. When I went to the doctor he just asked me all these really naff questions about sexual partners and I thought, hey, you dirty old man, I'm only fifteen, it's none of your business who I go with. And when he said he'd have to examine me I was like out of there before he could come near me. No way. Sorry Sooz, did I tread on your knee?'

'No. It's all right.'

Suzie listened to Mina pad briskly over the landing to the bathroom. She had been wondering about sexual partners too, but hadn't known how to ask.

4

'If that bugger sets foot on my farm again, I'll set the dogs on him.'

Norma Sedden listened to her husband's statement with dismay. She had overheard the gist of his conversation with George Cartwright, so she understood his anger, but still, she dreaded the consequences. She knew Ted himself was startled by the strength of the reaction to the travellers. He had expected it to create waves, but not on this scale. George Cartwright was only one of several local worthies who had seen fit to give him a piece of their mind this morning. Norma was in despair. All she had ever wanted was to be liked, but, having married a man who cared nothing for other people's opinion, she spent much of her time attempting to pour oil on waters deliberately troubled by him. Her only moments of real happiness were when she was able to get out of her work clothes and put on a skirt and sit with her friends at a coffee morning or jumble sale or some other village activity. Now, once again, she feared she would be blamed for Ted's behaviour and she did not think she could bear it.

She said none of this to him. Unlike George Cartwright, Norma Sedden knew that her husband relished opposition. He would deal with this as he had dealt with all the other reversals a lifetime in farming had thrown at him, from investigation by the Inland Revenue to an outbreak of fowl pest: he climbed up into the cab of his Massey Ferguson and carried on as if nothing had happened. There was plenty of farm work to keep him busily trundling up and down a twelve-acre field while the radio played love songs and told him news of traffic blackspots on roads he would never see.

*　　*　　*

When Norma Sedden ventured into Briarswood later that day, she found the village awash with rumours.

Not since a young anglo-catholic curate had run off with a retired schoolmistress old enough to be his mother, had the speculation flowed so freely. The nine vehicles Suzie had seen arriving on the Friday evening were said to be merely the advance guard. New Age travellers preferred to be in groups of at least fifty, and the rest were expected any moment. They were planning to hold a rave which would mean continuous loud music for at least a week. They had been forced to leave their previous site because of an outbreak of diphtheria. There were four convicted criminals among them, one of whom had escaped from an open prison before finishing his sentence and was now on the run. They had a large number of dangerous weapons such as hunting knives. The leader of the group was a notorious drugs dealer. One of their dogs had already savaged a child, but they had spirited the animal away so the police wouldn't put it down.

The local farmers and landowners had reacted to the crisis with a speed and ingenuity borne of desperation. By lunchtime on the Saturday, two days after the vehicles arrived, every gateway within a five mile radius of Briarswood was blocked to fend off the expected invasion. Some with giant bales of hay or silage in black plastic bags, some with large items of machinery, one or two with huge boulders or a hastily-ordered mound of gravel. One farmer filled his dung spreader with slurry and kept it fully-primed and ready to spray over any traveller foolhardy enough to approach his farm. Teenagers were forbidden to go anywhere near Ted Sedden's farm and younger children were kept close to home. Peggy at the village shop was torn between fear of the travellers and the realisation that a few extra sales might bolster her declining profits. She decided on a compromise: the travellers would not be banned outright from her shop, but they would only be allowed in two at a time so she could keep an eye on them.

'I lose quite enough through shoplifting already,' she told Norma Sedden, who took the statement personally, and already felt she was being held responsible for Peggy's ruin.

*   *   *

Jim sat at his desk and tried to concentrate.

This room, his study at the Lodge, was really the dining room, and it was a measure of Caro's dedication to his career that she had insisted when they moved here just over a year ago that it must be his workroom. He would have been content with one of the bedrooms, but she wouldn't hear of it, even though it meant they had to eat their meals and even entertain guests in the kitchen, which in Caro's eyes, he knew, was a social embarrassment on a par with only having one bathroom. He was gratified by her support for his career, but also found it exasperating. Especially now when it was effectively over. If he were to install his PC in a library the size of a tennis court, his career would still be over.

But Caro didn't see it like that. She believed that his early retirement last year – he'd been laid off, really, the result of his department having to make drastic cuts – was a career move that could be turned to his advantage if only he played his hand right. Nothing would budge her from her belief that he was working on an important paper which, when published, would have faculty heads all over the British Isles phoning up to offer him jobs. The longed-for professorship at last.

Poor Caro, she had so desperately wanted to be a professor's wife. He thought it quite ludicrous that she should mind so much – and then found himself minding about it almost as much, just because of her.

From his own perspective, his career had been meteoric as it was. His father had been a local government clerk and his grandfather had been a station porter. Jim felt he had been extremely fortunate to spend his working life amidst books and ideas and reasonably interesting people. When he tried to explain this to Caro she just said how typical and sweet of him to be so modest but he owed it to himself to fulfil his potential. It would have been so much simpler to ignore her hopes had they been selfish ones, but they weren't. Caro was not, thank heavens, one of those wives who try to piggyback their way to success on their husband's careers. She wanted the best for him, for his own sake, because she was a loyal wife, and that was what loyal wives did.

He could hear her now. She was shunting chairs and side

tables back and forth in the sitting room and asking someone, Suzie and Mina probably, what they thought of the various arrangements. Caro had been fiddling about with the furniture ever since they arrived at the Lodge, and there was no prospect of an end in sight: the house was far too small for the effect Caro was after, but she laboured on regardless, convinced that if she just shifted the sideboard an inch or two, adjusted the standard lamp, so . . . then the place would miraculously double in size.

Jim frowned and tried to concentrate on the page. Scale was not something he and Caro had in common. He was intrigued by the way the Lodge grew and shrank depending on perspective. Returning from a visit to his widowed mother, in the tiny terraced house she had lived in for over fifty years, the Lodge appeared vast and airy . . . but it collapsed back to almost dolls' house pokiness after a few hours at the Manor.

And because they spent much more time at Briarswood Manor than at 24 Fidelity Row, it was the claustrophobic aspect which predominated. And for which Jim couldn't help feeling in some way responsible. If he had been a better provider . . .

From the moment he and Caro married, his salary, which he considered almost embarrassingly large, had never covered their outgoings. It was impossible to accuse Caro of extravagance since she agonised over every purchase and seemed to spend next to nothing on herself. For over thirty years, month by month, their household accounts had never balanced. In secret desperation, Jim had taken out a loan or two, then a second mortgage. Then the property market slumped.

So that when he ceased work, the future was looking distinctly bleak. Enter George and Twinks, with the offer of the Lodge, pretty well rent free. Whatever its drawbacks, Jim and Caro had no real option but to accept. Caro saw it as a temporary solution; Jim was resigned to staying there for ever.

Even here the expenses mounted. They had to have two cars, apparently, because now they lived in the country. And one of those had to be a four-wheel drive, again because they lived in the country, though as far as Jim could see the roads here were no worse than in town and they hardly spent their days trekking over open moorland transporting bales of hay to starving sheep. But he had voiced his opinions *sotto voce* and with little expectation of being heard: Caro was country born and bred and therefore knew more about such essentials than he. And Bumpkin thoroughly approved of the Range Rover and tended to sulk now if he had to travel in Jim's Metro.

So it seemed churlish of Jim not to share Caro's vision of their future.

Through the half-open window came the sound of voices – Suzie and Mina wandering over the lawn towards the front gate. He watched them for a moment. Not for the first time Jim wondered what they could possibly still find to say, but he had long ago decided it was better not to know. So often it was the banality of teenage conversation that shocked, rather than anything outrageous. But still, it was good to see Suzie looking mildly content. Of all his daughters, she was the one who reminded him of Caro when he had known her first. That same long-boned awkwardness which he had always found more attractive than poise. The same straight blonde-brown hair with a tendency to flop over the eyes. The same hesitant and charmingly toothy smile.

Not that Caro's smile, hesitant or otherwise, had been much in evidence recently. The loss of status on returning to the parental home, empty-handed and dependent, had deepened the anxious lines around her mouth and eyes and made her a still more ardent champion of her husband's shamefully neglected talents.

And maybe she was right. Maybe this article was to be the start of his academic renaissance.

'. . . The role of highwaymen in eighteenth-century social mythology was twofold. Their capture, trials and punishment served to reinforce society's values and rules, while their colourful defiance and their often heroic escapades provided a vicarious outlet for a people who were themselves constrained . . .'

He was unhappy with that sentence. Too wordy, somehow. Lydia would have been swift to criticise. When he had been a youngish teacher of social history, hers had been exactly the kind of intelligent iconoclasm he relished. Now her arguments felt like an irritating attack, rather than a welcome challenge. Perhaps he had altered more than he realised. It was a far from cheering thought.

He frowned, pushed back his chair and walked over to the window. Suzie and Mina had vanished from view. His argument with Lydia two nights before had left a sour taste in his mouth. Clearly, she assumed he had abandoned the ideals he had once taught her, which was an altogether ridiculous notion. He had perhaps refined them to meet present day realities; nothing wrong there. He had no time for rigidity. Besides, what would have been the point of arguing with George and Twinks? Lydia should understand that the apparently privileged are as much deserving of tolerance as society's down-and-outs. She ought to realise . . .

Suddenly impatient with arguing with Lydia in his head, he decided to pay a visit to Rose Cottage, and tackle her face to face.

'Let's spy on them.'
'Who?'
'The travellers, of course.'
'Oh.' Suzie considered this for a moment. 'Why?'
'It's better than doing nothing, isn't it?'
'Mm.'
'And they might sell us some dope.'
'There's lots of other things we could do.'
'Like what, for instance?'
'Oh. You know . . .'
'Go on Suzie. You know where they've camped, don't you?'
'Of course I do.'
'Come on then. We can put leaves in our hair so they won't see us. It's years since we've done all that Birnam Woods stuff. It'll be a real laugh.'
'All right then.'

Suzie took Mina on the scenic-loop way to Ted Sedden's farm, hoping that while they were getting there she'd have a brilliant idea for some less hazardous means of entertaining her guest, or that Mina would get tired of walking and want to go back to the Lodge, but neither of these happy diversions occurred.

Lydia was seated on the step at Rose Cottage. One knee drawn up close to her chin, and her dark hair flopping over her face, she was a study in concentration as she painted her toenails a lurid maroon. She wore a flimsy sundress in a particularly vicious shade of green. Unaware that she was being observed, she had achieved a pose of almost childlike grace.

Jim, approaching Rose Cottage from the road, happened to catch sight of her over the hedge. The thought flitted into his mind that never in a thousand years would Caro perform such an intimate task in full view of a public highway. Nor dress with such vulgar elegance.

'Hello, Lydia.'

'Damn. You've made me jog it.' She frowned intently at the nail now in need of rescue and did not even glance up at his approach. His shadow fell across her bare legs. He sat down beside her on the step.

He said, 'God, what a revolting colour.'

'I know. Isn't it brilliant?'

'It looks like a joke vampire kit.'

She appeared pleased by this comment, and five nails winked up at him maroonly. Lydia dipped the tiny brush in the glass bottle, gripped her left foot in her left hand and said, still without looking at him, 'I assume you're here to apologise for being such a prat the other night.'

'By no means,' said Jim stoutly, though he had in fact been intending to do just that. 'If you must get up on your high horse—'

'And a damn lonely high horse it was too. I thought you at least would back me up.'

'I might have done if you hadn't begun spouting such infantile rubbish.'

'That's rich, coming from you.'

Silence.

Jim mentally awarded himself a 'could do better' grade for bridge-building. Lydia, however, appeared to be totally absorbed by her toes.

'It's all a question of judgement,' he heard himself say, 'of what is appropriate in a given time and place. George and Twinks hold opinions which on the whole I disagree with. I do, however, respect their right to hold those opinions and I would consider it a betrayal of hospitality, not to say a complete waste of time, to cause them offence by attacking them.'

'Meanwhile,' said Lydia, who had reached toe number ten, 'George is free to mobilise every landowner for miles around to make life difficult for the poor travellers and terrorise the farmer and his wife into evicting them.'

'Do you mean "poor" in the sense of impecunious or "poor" in the sense of unfortunate? And if you had ever met Ted Sedden you would know that a whole battalion of Georges couldn't terrorise him. Which brings me back to what I was saying just now about appropriateness. George's family have been in Briarswood for aeons, Caro and I have been here for just over twelve months and you, Lydia dear, are a mere visitor. Neither you nor I are therefore in a position to pontificate—'

'That's just a cop-out.'

'Fact. Plain fact. As a historian, I prefer to assemble all relevant facts before leaping to conclusions.'

'Bollocks.' Lydia clenched her fist around the tiny bottle of nail varnish and looked as though she would like to hurl it across the garden. She let out a slow breath, controlling herself, then set the bottle carefully to one side. 'Pure, unadulterated bollocks. And you know it.' She leant back on her elbows and stretched her legs out in the sunlight. For the first time she turned to look at him, and Jim was shocked by the glare of rage in her eyes. 'If something is wrong, then it is wrong no matter where.'

'OK,' said Jim unexpectedly, 'let's drop the whole subject.' At that particular moment, sitting in the sunshine at Rose Cottage, Lydia's feet assumed far more importance than the rights and wrongs of a few outsiders. He was seized with a startling urge to play 'this little piggy' with her ten wiggling toes. He smothered the urge.

She shook back her hair. 'So long as you admit you've been a total creep.'

He grinned. 'Total is a bit harsh, don't you think? Can't we settle for just creep?'

'I'd offer you a drink or some tea, but this lot have to dry first.'

'Fine.' They sat in silence for a few moments, until Jim asked cautiously, 'Are you OK here, Lydia?'

'When you say "OK",' she mimicked, 'do you mean "OK" in the sense of contented or "OK" in the sense of simply getting by?'

'Either. Both.'

'Getting by OK, I guess. Contented would be a tad ambitious, in present circumstances.'

'Do you have any plans?'

'Of course. Everyone needs plans. There's a pretty tasty shade of yuk orange I thought I might try out next. But after that, it's hard to say.'

'I'm sorry. I shouldn't have asked. I was just anxious you might be bored here, or restless . . .'

'Oh but I am. All the time. Restless without wanting to go anywhere, bored without wanting to do anything. It's bloody pathetic, really.' Suddenly there was a catch in her voice and she sat up very straight and said in a different voice altogether, 'How about you, Jim, how are you adapting to life in the sticks?'

'Hush, keep your voice down.' Jim pretended to scan the horizon to make sure the coast was clear. 'If any of the natives hear you calling Briarswood "the sticks", then I'd be no longer able to vouch for your safety.'

For the first time she smiled, and raised one eyebrow in the way he remembered so vividly. If anything, she seemed to have perfected the gesture in the years since she had been his favourite student.

'Danger? Here?'

He nodded. 'You might be refused service in the shop.'

'No!'

'Excluded from the Bird in Hand. Cut dead in the street by Colonel Brinshaw's border terrier—'

'Oh, horrors, I can't bear it!'

'*Blackballed by the WI.*'

'I repent. I give in. I can't take any more. Let me rephrase my question: how have you adjusted to this rural idyll, this little piece of heaven, this corner of our sceptred isle, this ever blessed spot?'

'Quite well, actually. I am at present occupied by a piece for a book on the role of outlaws in English history.'

'Really?' There was a sudden twist of mischief in Lydia's smile.

Recognising its cause, Jim said lightly, 'I'm sure you'd find it riveting, Lydia. I focus on one or two of the more notorious highwaymen of the eighteenth century and show how they were simultaneously feared and reviled villains and icons of popular mythology. I explore the way a settled and fairly rigid society both needs and condemns the safety valve represented by those who contravene its rules.'

'Better and better,' gloated Lydia. 'You will, undoubtedly, be penning this with your well-known air of detached amusement at the foibles of those less tolerant folk of long ago. Can we even look forward to a modern-day comparison?'

'Only if I think it's relevant. And, yes, Lydia, I do see the irony of the situation. But I would say that to draw any parallels between an eighteenth-century rogue with the panache and intelligence of Tom Fanshaw and those wretched no-hopers at the Hollows is sheer romantic claptrap.'

'Obviously this statement is based on observation. I take it you've been to the Hollows and met them yourself.'

'I hardly think that is necessary.'

'Facts, Jim, what happened to your precious regard for facts?'

'I was simply trying to say—' Jim caught himself in time. He was about to get angry, very angry indeed, and he had no wish to do that. This had been intended, God forbid, as a peace mission. He said, very calmly, 'But this is a waste of our time. We are simply quibbling over terms. Now, how about your happy band of toenails, are they dry yet? And more importantly, do you have any beer in the house?'

'I'm a poverty-stricken runaway wife, remember. I don't do beer.' Lydia too was forcing herself to move into a more neutral gear. 'But yes, they are dry and I'll make you a cup of tea if you're good. I still think you're a creep though, Jim. A total creep.'

'Damn. We should've brought binoculars.'

Suzie, Mina and Bumpkin were at the edge of a small piece of woodland that led down to the stream marking the boundary of Ted Sedden's farm. Scattered on the lower part of the field beyond the stream was an assortment of vehicles – caravans, lorries and vans, in varying states of decrepitude. A few strangely-dressed figures were lounging in the sun or moving between the vehicles. Half a dozen dogs were prowling around. Suzie recognised the ghost-pale sheepdog who had barked at Bumpkin two days before. Her anxiety intensified.

'I wish we'd left Bumpkin behind. He's sure to bark or do something awful. Sit, Bumps. Don't even breathe.'

Bumpkin dropped his rump on the leafy soil and gazed up at her obligingly. Then, a random thought swimming into his mind, he twisted round and began to scratch his neck vigorously with his hind leg. His chain collar jangled loudly.

'Do stop it, Bumpkin. *Please*,' she hissed.

'We need to get closer,' said Mina. 'I can't see properly.'

'Can't you?' Suzie affected surprise. 'I can see fine.' Her sole wish was to head for the safety of home, not go even closer. There was something strange and unnerving about the scene they were watching, like looking down on a little tribe of Ancient Britons. Spying made her feel like their enemy.

She saw the girl with dark hair who had been driving the red car at the head of the procession. She was wearing a coloured skirt and a black sleeveless T-shirt and there was something odd about her hair. She emerged from one of the caravans – which had already sunk so low on its wheels it looked as if it had been in the field for years and would be impossible to budge – and looked around her. She seemed to be calling to someone, though at this distance it was impossible to make out the words. She cupped her hands around her mouth and shouted again, then went up to someone who was sitting in the open doorway of one of the vans. He shook his head.

'We must get closer.'

'I'm staying here.'

'We can creep forward on our bellies. Like commandos.'

'I'm not moving. Oh, look.'

The white dog was moving towards the stream, followed by the darkly handsome youth Suzie had noticed on the day the travellers first arrived. Mina gripped Suzie's arm in imitation horror. 'Oh no! They've seen us!'

Suzie's horror was anything but simulated. 'Let's go.' Her

terror was that Bumpkin would give them away, but luckily he was peering down his nose at a large black beetle.

'Nonsense, Suzie. We'll go and introduce ourselves. He looks quite cute.'

'I thought you couldn't see,' hissed Suzie. 'I've seen him before. He's not cute at all. You don't know anything about him. He might be dangerous. He might be a mental case from all the drugs he's taken. He'll be furious if he finds we've been spying. He might—'

'Stop fussing.' Mina still had her hand on Suzie's arm. 'Look, there's something really weird about that dog. He's limping, or something.'

'Looks like he's crippled, poor thing. And what's that on his neck?'

'It's all kind of green looking.'

'Maybe it's paint.'

'Why would anyone paint a crippled dog green?'

'Could be some kind of disease. You know, gangrene, or rot. They obviously don't care about it at all.'

The white dog had crossed the stream and the black-haired youth followed. He was carrying a large implement. They could hear twigs snapping as he entered the wood. The white dog woofed once or twice and Bumpkin forgot about the bug and rumbled the beginnings of a growl.

'I'm off,' said Suzie.

'Wait, he's digging a hole. Maybe he's going to hide some drugs or – Oh!' Mina turned to her with an expression of sheer delight as she whispered, 'OK, let's get out of here. He's come into the wood for the *loo!*'

Giggling and stumbling, they hurried up the slope away from the stream. Bumpkin trotted along beside them, his tail held high.

At the edge of the wood, just before the stile that led into a field of stubble, they stopped. A small boy with dark hair and a pinched and dirty face was standing beside the path. He held a pointed stick in his hand and was glaring at them.

'Hi,' said Suzie nervously.

'Piss off,' said the boy.

Mina smiled at him. 'Fuck you too,' she said, and then the

two girls scrambled over the stile and ran giggling most of the way home.

After Jim had left, Lydia sat down at the kitchen table and tried to continue with a letter she had begun the previous day. It was to her friend Charlotte who was running a sea-food bistro in Minorca. Charlotte wanted her to come out during the winter and help decorate the walls with fishy murals. Lydia had worked for a firm of decorators for a while, and it was the kind of commission she knew she would enjoy. So far, however, inertia and an inability to make decisions kept her in Briarswood. She had got as far as, 'Keep sending your recipe inventions – Squid for the Squeamish sounds mouth-watering,' but then her mind emptied of words and the letters appeared to dissolve on the page. A familiar angry energy was fizzing through her. She made an effort to ignore it. 'I can imagine a whole new direction for your cooking skills,' she wrote. 'Octopus for—' but then she put down her pen in disgust.

She couldn't imagine anything of the sort. In fact she couldn't imagine anything at all. All she could think of was how bloody unfair life was.

'Damn Jim,' she declared, her voice exaggerating the silence of the house. 'Damn, damn and double damn him.'

She stood up and paced out into the garden. 'Damn,' she said to the trees and the sky.

He had made another feeble attempt to convince her that his views were fundamentally the same as the ones they had once shared. She had reacted, inevitably, with angry disbelief.

'Don't take everything so personally, Lydia,' he had said as he was leaving. 'You lose all sense of proportion.'

'But it is personal,' she had told him, 'I happen to know what I'm talking about. For you it's all just convenient theories.'

And she had slammed the door on him before he had a chance to ask her what she meant.

What did Jim know anyway?

She knew. Had known for a long time.

'Oh, damn them all,' she muttered, pulling on a pair of battered sneakers and setting off down the road that led away from Briarswood, away from human habitation.

Hers had been an unremarkable family. A mother, a father, an older sister and a younger brother. Lydia had always felt she was the odd one out. From an early age she liked different television programmes, different music, different books. They thought she was a snob, and she believed them and was miserable. She dreamed of escape. And then she met Grace. Grace's father, Michael, was something in films. Grace's home was full of books and they had original paintings on the walls. Grace's family had large noisy suppers and argued and laughed and swore at each other and made Lydia wonderfully welcome. Lydia, aged twelve, would have lived at Grace's house if she could, and for a few months she practically did.

One morning Grace was missing from school. The teachers said she had been withdrawn: her father was in some kind of trouble, but no one would say what the trouble was. Lydia returned home in an agony of anxiety. She tried to phone Grace's home, but the phone was off the hook. The next day it was in all the papers. Lydia's family tried to keep them from her, but she spent half an hour in the newsagent's on the way home and devoured ten different versions of the same story. Grace's father had been accused of having sex with under-age girls whom he lured to his home with the promise of stardom and fame. He had been arrested and might be sent to prison for years. That evening, while Lydia was in the bath, there was a ring at the door. Lydia knew at once that it was Grace. Dripping wet and flinging a towel around her, she raced down the stairs, but the front door was closed and a taxi was driving away. Her father was blocking the doorway.

'That's the last we'll see of her,' he said in a satisfied voice to Lydia's mother. 'I never liked her anyway.'

'What did you say to her?' Lydia wailed.

They had told Grace Lydia no longer wanted to see her. Lydia made frantic attempts to contact her, but the family had fled to a secret address. Two days later Lydia read in the papers that the accused man's thirteen-year-old daughter had taken an overdose and been rushed to hospital. She survived, but only just. Lydia never forgave her parents for what they had done. Worse, she had never really forgiven herself. Surely, even though she had been only twelve, there must have been some way she could break through the parental barriers and the secrecy and tell Grace she was still her friend? At the time she had not found one. Six months later, Grace's father was cleared of all charges, but by then the family had moved away. As Grace's mother said in a magazine interview just after the acquittal, 'We have lived through a nightmare, but at least we learned who our real friends were.'

Lydia Allen had not been one of them.

She had been a difficult teenager, punishing both her parents and herself for what had happened. She set her sights on escape, despised them all, studied as hard as she could. She had made her getaway and gone to university, but had not completed her degree. Later, she had gained a place at art school, but never finished that either. Like tin cans tied to a cat's tail, the sense of unworthiness had clung to her always. She could never allow herself to be successful. Just as she began to make her mark in any field, she found a reason to change direction. She craved the clean slate, the urge to prove herself anew.

And she was always broke. She could never convince herself that she deserved to keep money. When she was earning, she wasted it, spent it, didn't pay her taxes so the bills came in and plunged her into crisis.

Sometimes, now, it seemed to Lydia that the impetus of her escape had never ceased. The energy and anger required to release her from her suffocating family was driving her still.

Without having noticed her route, Lydia had walked a good distance from Briarswood. The signpost, now she paused, said three and a half miles. She had been climbing for some time and, looking back she could see the village, or parts of it, tile roofs and green-topped trees tranquil in the afternoon sun. She found she was hungry, and very thirsty. She wondered what it would be like to belong there, what it would be like to belong anywhere.

In her early years she had found the passion and drive necessary for escape. She sat down wearily on the grass verge and hugged her knees. It seemed unlikely, now, that she would ever find a way back to any place that felt like home.

5

Howls of glee from the girls' room that evening. Mina had discovered a copy of *Pippa's Pony Days* amongst Suzie's school texts.

'Oh, this is hilarious! Just listen to this, Suzie – "Golly, Mrs Turvey, those sandwiches were scrumptious!" *Scrumptious*! And listen, here she says the *cake* was WIZARD. Where did you find these? They're priceless.'

Suzie had turned away to hide her embarrassment. 'Oh, I think my sister Polly used to read them.'

'She would, I can just see dopey Polly lapping this up. Oh no, listen to this bit: "Pippa spoke severely, 'If you don't look after Blaze better than that, Monique, everyone will just assume you're the gruesome depths.'" The *gruesome depths*! Suzie, this is classic!'

'I know.' Suzie was rolling around on the bed, apparently helpless with mirth. She would have opted to be trampled to death by a herd of stampeding pony club members rather than admit she'd been engrossed by *Pippa's Pony Days* only a few weeks before. Why on earth hadn't she spotted the wretched book when she cleared her room out? Now she'd never hear the end of it.

'Oh look, the daft cow wrote heaps of the bloody things,' Mina was reading the title page with genuine awe. '*A Pony For Pippa, Pippa's Pony Adventure, Pippa and the Perfect Pony, First Past the Post for Pippa* – likes her Ps, this woman, doesn't she? This lot sounds like a tongue twister. Pippa's pony picked a peck of pickled piddle!'

Suzie's laughter was genuine now. How ridiculous it all sounded! She'd only enjoyed them because they were so funny, she could see that.

'How about this?' Mina bounced on the bed in her enthusiasm. *'Pippa's Pony Pops his Clogs*! – or *Pippa Potters Past the Post*!'

'Ooh hooh!' Suzie was clutching her sides. She was laughing so much it was beginning to hurt. It was ages since she'd laughed like that.

Later, Mina asked, 'You haven't got any others, have you?'

'I don't think so. I could look.'

'Can I take this one then? Rupe will kill himself laughing.'

'Take it,' said Suzie with hardly a qualm. The Pippa books had died for her, anyway.

Although it meant heaps of extra work, Caro secretly relished Sandra's off times because then she had the kitchen at Briarswood Manor to herself. She loved all of the house, but in many ways it was in the kitchen that she was happiest. It was a comfortable blend of ancient charm and up-to-date convenience. A massive solid fuel oven had replaced the old range, but the Victorian cupboards and dresser remained, as did the slate flags on the floor and the huge table, its pine surface worn to a pale and grainy loveliness by over a century of use. There was a large cool larder, a proper utility room and several walk-in cupboards, and from the huge sink in the scullery one now had a glorious view across smooth lawns to the kitchen garden and the orchard.

Perhaps because her parents were doing her an enormous favour by letting them live in the Lodge rent free, Caro worked on the principle that her parents were incapable of looking after themselves and would probably starve on Sandra's days off if she didn't cook for them and bully them into proper meal times. Twinks and George were both quite happy to go along with this fiction, and indeed, after a year of being worried over by Caro, it was turning into reality.

When she had fed Hamish, Caro set the cottage pie and apple charlotte in readiness on the table and covered each with a fly guard.

As usual at this time of day her parents were to be found in the drawing room, George with a whisky and soda, Twinks sipping a gin and tonic.

'Supper's on the kitchen table,' Caro announced. 'Just pop it in the oven for ten minutes when you want to eat.'

Normally Caro would have given George and Twinks long and complicated instructions about how to warm up each dish, before she rushed home to complete the preparations for her own family's supper, but this evening she had more pressing matters on her mind.

'Daddy, you really must promise me you won't go near Ted Sedden's place again. Not on your own at any rate. I can't think what you hoped to gain from it.'

'Tut, Caro. Had to give the fellow a piece of my mind.'

'But anything could have happened.'

'I was all right. Had the gun with me.'

'Crikey, that makes it ten times worse. Supposing you'd bumped into one of the travellers?'

George, who had been looking remarkably self-satisfied during this conversation, now looked even more pleased with himself. 'And who said I didn't?'

'What!'

'Just a bit of a ding dong. Nothing I couldn't handle.'

'You never told me that.'

'You never asked.'

'What happened?'

'Bumped into a couple of the loathsome females. Getting water, or some such thing. The most ghastly pair of harridans you ever saw. Soon put them straight. At least they know what to expect if they set foot on any of my land.'

'Oh Daddy, what did you say?'

'Mm. Can't remember the exact words now.'

'I hope to goodness they didn't threaten you or anything.'

George frowned. 'Bloody rude. And they smelled disgusting.'

Twinks had stood up and gone to pour herself another drink. She was wearing a light wool skirt of soft heathery blue and a cashmere sweater in a deeper shade of hyacinth which accentuated the pallor of her pearls and hair.

'No point trying to make your father back off once his mind is made up, Caro dear,' she said, dismissing her daughter's concern with a little laugh. 'He's a law unto himself, always has been. Luckily he knows how to get results.'

'Let's hope so. Heavens, Mummy, that's an awful lot of gin.'

'My hand slipped. No, it's all right, there's tonic in it, so

I can't pour it back. I'll probably throw most of it away later.'

Caro cast around for something she might have forgotten which would save the elderly couple from the consequences of their isolation, but she could think of nothing.

'Well, if you're absolutely sure you're going to be all right, I'd best be getting back. There's still the troops to feed at home. Promise me, Daddy, no more gadding off to tackle the travellers single-handed.'

'I did not gad,' said George huffily, then he added with a frown, 'Still, we'll have to find another way to put pressure on the fellow. He's obviously not going to listen to the calm voice of reason. In the meantime, I'm planning one or two little surprises for that lot, just in case they're thinking of coming this way.'

'Good lord, what sort of surprises?'

He only smiled. 'You'll see. Soon enough.'

It had been such a lovely day, the last of the summer perhaps, that Caro had walked from the Lodge to the Manor, even though it took an extra five minutes and she had a hundred and one things to do at home. Hurrying back down the drive, and then across the lawn to the side gate, she allowed herself the luxury of a moment's pause. Caught in the last rays of the dying sun, the Manor looked so beautiful that Caro felt a kind of fullness in her upper chest. Sunlight touched the upper windows with bronze. The shadows fell like spilled ink across the stripy lawn. Everything about the place was just as it should be.

Her elder brother William, who hardly ever visited, was naturally going to inherit the Manor when George died. He would also get the Lodge and Rose Cottage and a couple of other properties that had always belonged to the Manor. As George said, no point in breaking the place up. William worked for a merchant bank. He had an ex-wife, Felicity, and three grown up children, and now a new wife, Laura, whose parents had property in Norfolk. He and Laura had two boys at prep school. They had a house in Richmond and a cottage in Normandy and Felicity kept the house near St Albans where she and William had brought the first family up. Obviously that all meant tremendous outgoings, and Laura was always complaining about how hard up they were. When George died, William and Laura would have the five Briarswood properties as well, and Caro and Jim would be their tenants. Sometimes, thinking about this gave Caro an odd sensation, but she was not aware of feeling any resentment. William had always been treated differently, but she had always adored him and she liked those she loved to be happy, so that was all right. She had never had much time for all that women's lib stuff – literally, no time, because when it was in all the headlines she was up to her ears looking after her three little girls and trying to keep an eye on Jim's career and making sure they had a lovely home even on his tiny income, so she could hardly go rushing off to meetings or sit around complaining the way some of the other university wives did. She had no patience with those women who tried to make you feel guilty for enjoying being feminine, as if it was some kind of crime, for heaven's sake. If anything, the discrepancy between her brother's prospects and her own filled her with a vague sense of failure; if she was ending up so badly off by comparison with William, then it was probably her own fault. Though she did sometimes think he and Laura might help out more with George and Twinks.

Now, however, as she looked back across the glorious sweep of lawn to gaze at the front of the house where a few of the wisteria leaves were already beginning to turn their lovely, buttery yellow, her main feelings were of affection and pride. The Manor represented all that was best in this life – stability and a sense of the past and doing things properly. Through Twinks and George she was able to feel a part of all that tradition.

Passing through the side gate and into the village street was always a jolt, bringing one instantly face to face with the modern world again: the council estates that had been built on the edge of the village, the busy main road less than half a mile away, a handful of tacky looking bungalows. And the Lodge itself, an unlovely box of a house if ever there was one.

On the road ahead of her she saw two people that she recognised at once as travellers. They had terrible hair, baggy trousers and heavy boots which gave them a distinct air of menace, as did the two lean dogs that loped beside them. Caro was relieved that she was practically at the Lodge and so did not have actually to walk past them. They were both carrying what looked like several packs of lager. Normally she would have been alarmed, but, still under the mellow influence of the Manor, she felt almost sorry for them. Poor things, they'd probably never in their lives set foot in a place like the Manor; they could never have lived in the kind of homes she had been lucky enough to grow up in nor had wonderful parents like Twinks and George. How dreadful not to have been brought up with the high standards she had always taken for granted. To them probably even a place like the poor old Lodge looked wonderfully grand.

Then she hurried into the safety of the Lodge. She had heard terrible stories about squatters and homeless people just barging in and taking what they wanted. She had a sudden fear that the two travellers might nip in ahead of her and stake a claim to her home.

Suzie drew the smoke cautiously into her lungs. She had smoked proper cigarettes once or twice before, but these roll-ups of Mina's were altogether more powerful.

'How about that moronic kid?' Mina shielded her eyes from the sun and sank back on the cushions. She had a round face, and no amount of make-up could ever quite disguise its youthful chubbiness. Fortunately for Suzie's experiments with smoking, the swing-seat on which they both reclined was out of sight of the house and, more importantly, out of range of Caro's smoke-detector nose.

'I wonder if he goes to school,' mused Suzie. Their expedition to the encampment at the Hollows had provided plenty to speculate about.

'Doubt it. No manners, anyway.'

'Mm.' Suzie took another drag on her cigarette. She was beginning to feel rather ill, but didn't care to say so. Nor did she feel inclined to comment on the way Mina had responded to the boy. She had an idea that you shouldn't swear at children, because of setting them a bad example, no matter how rude they had been to you first. Yet she had noticed that Mina and the boy seemed to share some kind of common base from which she, with her feeble friendliness, was excluded.

'It's the dog I'm really worried about,' said Mina.

'I know, all crippled and green. It's dreadful.'

'I mean, it's obviously got some dreadful disease like gangrene or something and they're just too mean and selfish to take it to a vet.'

'So cruel.'

'We ought to do something to help it.'

'Mm.'

'We've got to find a way to rescue it, they're obviously hopeless owners.' Mina thought for a while before saying firmly, 'I think we're going to have to kidnap it.'

'What!'

'It's the only way. We simply must get the poor beast away from there before it dies from its terrible injuries.'

'We can't just kidnap someone else's dog, Mina. Don't be crazy.' Suzie giggled, and then, because of what the smoking was doing to her stomach, wished she hadn't.

'Well, we can't just leave it to its fate either.'

'Why don't we phone the RSPCA or something. They'd know what to do. A sort of anonymous tip-off.'

Mina looked shocked. 'That's sneaky. Like telling tales on people behind their backs. We've got to be upfront about this and stick up for animal rights. The problem is, how?'

Suzie remembered Mina's love of daring plans from old. Nine times out of ten they remained in the realm of fantasy . . . but there was always the tenth time to watch out for. She began to feel butterflies of apprehension in the pit of her stomach. Or maybe it was the smoking.

'Maybe we could just lure it away,' Suzie suggested with no great enthusiasm. 'Tie a bone to a long piece of string and sort of jiggle it about and entice it through the wood.'

'The scent gets lost in the stream. We'd have to use something really smelly, like old liver. Then we could smuggle it to a vet.'

'It might work,' Suzie said, secretly grateful that this plan was too far-fetched for even Mina to think of putting into practice.

'Are you OK, Sooz? You've gone kind of green.'

'Fine.' One syllable was all she could achieve.

While she was being sick behind the *cupressus leylandii* hedge, Suzie did wonder if Mina had perhaps added something to the tobacco in her roll-up, and not bothered to mention it.

*   *   *

On Sunday it rained. It rained so much that Mina cooked up an excuse to return to town, and Suzie, who had no idea how to entertain her in the country in the rain, was mostly relieved to see her go. People began looking out their winter clothes and Bumpkin trekked large muddy footprints into the house after every walk. Little was seen of the new inhabitants of the Hollows, but what little there was, did not inspire confidence.

On Monday morning at Rose Cottage it was still raining and Lydia discovered three new leaks in the roof of her lean-to kitchen. Perhaps to drown out the sound of the rain drumming on the corrugated plastic and plinking down into assorted bowls and pans, she switched on the radio and heard a familiar voice.

'Hello, Vera. Dr Gordon here. Yes, Vera, this problem is bound to be embarrassing, I can see why you find it difficult to talk about it, and thank you so much for raising it now.' Lydia groaned, and pulled a face at the radio set; the voice continued, 'You're afflicted by a form of what we in the medical profession call stress incontinence. More commonly this is associated with sneezing, or coughing, but there are a number of women, like yourself, Vera, who find themselves . . . letting go, in this way, at the height of love-making—' Lydia let out a shriek and threw a bread pellet at the radio. 'Of course, it's bound to be distressing, but you're certainly not unique, Vera. At least, not in that respect!'

'Oh *yuk*,' exclaimed Lydia. 'Give the poor woman a break!'

'No, Vera, I regret to say there isn't any cure just at present, but there are one or two things you might like to try to make it less—'

Lydia leaned forward and flipped the knob, and there was only the steady tattoo of rain on roof. Thank you very much, Dr Gordon Fairchild, that's quite enough for one day. She lit herself a cigarette. Funny how listening to the good doctor brought on an overwhelming urge to light up a cigarette, to indulge in all those self-destructive and childish instincts that were always so alien to him.

She had only switched on the radio to remind herself of why she was here, in this draughty, leaky, lonely little cottage rather than in Dr Gordon Fairchild's solid Victorian house in South London. Her husband's voice could have been made for radio –

resonant and leisured, with a reassuring hint of a Scots accent: Dr Gordon, the radio doctor with a strong line in dealing with those problems which are too embarrassing to admit to face to face. Like a kind of aural deodorant, Gordon's voice sanitised all those unsavoury nooks and crannies of listeners' lives. It never ceased to amaze Lydia that some unfortunate had to confess all before an audience of millions in order to get their trouble sorted. Odd, the way the only real privacy now is in front of a vast public. Obviously, Vera (not her real name) was hardly going to stump into her local GP surgery and have her problems typed into their computer records for all to mock. This moment of broadcast reassurance might well be a turning point in the life of Vera (not her real name – but surely friends and neighbours would recognise her voice?) and her long-suffering husband. No doubt about it, Dr Gordon's radio slot met a national need.

It wasn't just the voice, either. He was an attractive man in a clean-cut traditional way. He was a man who deserved a decent wife, and a family. She twisted awkwardly on her chair. Always, listening to Gordon's radio slot reactivated the worms of guilt, but it wasn't an urge towards self-punishment that led her to tune in to his thrice weekly slot on a regular music programme. Perhaps it was simply to hear his voice, to know that in spite of everything he was carrying on, that he was healthy and functioning, that he had survived intact. Perhaps also it was to remind herself of what she had left, and why. There was luxury in being able to silence that brilliantly wise and reassuring voice. Oh, the relief of *not* having to listen to Dr Gordon's calm and measured tones. It was a relief so strong it was almost physical.

She smiled to herself and turned the radio on once more. '. . . going to have to talk this over with your mother at some stage, Gavin . . .' Click. He was erased. She had escaped the glue pot of his infinite reasonableness.

She leaned back on her rickety chair and listened to the rain. No doubt there was something productive and sensible she ought to be doing on a morning like this, but if so, she had no idea what that something was. The letter for Charlotte in her Mediterranean restaurant had become submerged by a half-read paperback and a few empty envelopes. 'Octopus for the Orderly,' she had managed, before grinding to a familiar halt. She wasn't even thinking, not properly.

Jim had stopped by on his way to Edleston earlier to tell her that George was arranging for a firm to come and install window locks and to see if she wanted anything in town. She had told him no. And she had turned down his offer to accompany him – to get out for a bit, which was shorthand, she knew, for not hanging around at Rose Cottage doing nothing.

She ought to be painting. She ought to be gripped by the challenge of doing something worthwhile. She ought not to be brooding about what might have been, about the life which had ended before it began, on 15 May that year.

It occurred to her, and not for the first time, that she might still be the resident Mrs Gordon Fairchild, but for the miscarriage.

Gordon put his own sorrow aside so he could support her. The grief she had expected, but it was the bursts of irrational rage that she found impossible to handle. It was then that Gordon's soft spoken sympathy added fuel to her already raging fires. How on earth could she carry on howling and smashing things when he insisted on being so bloody reasonable? 'No, no, darling, you cry, you'll feel better for it . . . not that there's any reason why you *should* feel better, I didn't mean that, not yet, anyway. No one's trying to pressure you into . . . oh dear, careful darling . . . well, never mind, just an old jardiniere . . . yes, I know it was an antique, you're absolutely right, OK then, an heirloom, if you insist on calling it that . . . but it's hardly important compared with . . .'

Lydia shook her head, like a spaniel that has water in its ears. If only she could switch off the remembered voice as easily as the radio.

Gordon had reacted with sympathy because he assumed she was grieving simply for the loss of the baby, but it went far deeper than that. The miscarriage had confirmed all her worst fears about herself: that she was fundamentally flawed and incapable of seeing any task through to its conclusion. Even that most basic of female activities, the creation of new life.

She'd bumped into Jim one June morning in the Tottenham Court Road. They went to have coffee together. Rather quaintly, Lydia thought, a legacy of all Jim's London visits with Caro, he had taken her to the coffee shop at Heals. There, among the women comparing swatches of tasteful linen union, Lydia had brought him as up to date as she could without either sobbing or hurling her cup and saucer against the nearest wall. Jim had sworn and said, 'Oh Lydia, that's bloody gutting,' and after a little while he had asked, 'Why does tragedy always make one feel so angry?' Lydia had felt no easing of her physical pain, but she had felt something lift. She had mentioned the need to get away for a bit. He had mentioned Rose Cottage. When she told Gordon of her plan, he had been so horribly understanding, despite his natural reluctance to be left alone in a house whose spare room was uselessly papered with bunnies and spring flowers, that she knew she had made the right decision. And hated herself all the more for doing it.

Now she was no longer sure whether any decision was ever right, particularly. Certainly she did not feel cured of anything. The pain had subsided to a dull ache. She had entered some wasteland of the spirit that was neither sickness nor health. Gordon would no doubt say that was a stage on the road to recovery. Mercifully, she did not have to hear him say it.

She had escaped from poor Gordon. Where now?

'I'm worried about Lydia,' said Jim to Caro that evening.

Caro glanced up from the interior decorating magazine she had been reading. 'Why? What's the matter with her?'

'I had to go down to see her this morning,' he said. 'George wanted me to arrange a time for the man to come and fit window locks. He's worried about security there. She seemed all right, I suppose. I can't put my finger on it. And the kitchen roof at Rose Cottage leaks terribly.'

'She ought to get it fixed, then.' Caro ringed one of the small ads. There was a firm that made antique style curtain tie-backs: they would let more light into these terribly pokey rooms and also make the curtains look more finished, or so she hoped.

'But Caro, she doesn't have any money.'

Caro looked at him sternly over the top of her spectacles. 'So? She is staying there practically rent-free as it is. She can hardly expect my parents to start a major overhaul just for her. I do hope she's not going to turn out to be one of those dreadful tenants who are never satisfied with anything.'

'You know Lydia's not like that, she never even mentioned it. But you could hear the rain pouring in through the kitchen roof all the time I was there.'

'Besides,' Caro pushed her glasses back on to the bridge of her nose and ringed another small ad, 'I can't understand why she pretends not to have any money. That doctor husband of hers must make a fortune.'

'Perhaps she doesn't want him to support her, now they're not living together.'

Caro, he could see, was genuinely baffled by this possibility. To her, Lydia's efforts at financial independence smacked of affectation and self-indulgence. Lydia was happy enough to take charity from George and Twinks in the form of cheap rent, so why turn her back on what her husband was prepared to offer?

'Have they separated?' asked Caro. 'I thought she just wanted a holiday on her own.'

'She needed space, I think.'

'I thought they had a big house in Dulwich.'

'Not that kind of space.' Sensing her growing lack of sympathy for Lydia's situation, Jim said, 'She's depressed, I think. Probably that's a natural reaction, after a miscarriage.'

'Of course she's depressed, sitting around moping all day long,' exclaimed Caro, who often confused cause and effect. 'Anyone would get depressed with nothing to do. She ought to stop brooding and get out more. She seemed to make quite an impression on Wyndham the other evening. Maybe we ought to have them both to supper here.'

'Why him? We hardly know the man.'

'Well, he lives at Haddeley Hall, Jim, we're bound to be sociable with whoever lives at the Hall.'

'I didn't particularly like him.'

'Though what he'll think of eating in the kitchen, I can't imagine. His dining room at Haddeley Hall is simply huge.'

'I can always shift out of the study for a bit,' said Jim. 'You could have a dining table in there.'

'Oh Jim, I wouldn't dream of disrupting you like that. If I

prepare everything the day ahead, I can clear the decks in the kitchen and it won't look so workish.' To Jim's relief, they were now back on familiar ground. He had been irritated by Caro for interpreting Lydia's leaking roof as an attempt to extract funds from George and Twinks and irritated with Lydia for having failed to be cheered up by a couple of summer months at Rose Cottage. The idea of Lydia as a permanent fixture filled him with gloom. When he had suggested the Briarswood retreat, he had expected her to be back with her abandoned husband by now. He rather agreed with Caro that Lydia did not seem to be making much effort to improve her lot.

'I'll go down and have a word with her,' said Caro later, while Jim and Bumpkin were doing battle over a worming tablet. 'Maybe she can do something at the school. Ann Robertson has been asking for help with the early readers. Much better than just sitting around and festering.'

But what with the rain and one thing and another, Caro didn't get around to visiting Rose Cottage, and Lydia was left to fester in peace for a few days more.

6

'Dear Caro,

Thanks a million for a great couple of days in the country. All that good food and fresh air, just what the doctor ordered! Can't wait to see you all again. Mum sends her love by the way and says do drop by when you're next in town,

Love, Mina'

'Dear Suzie,

Has your hair dropped out with boredom, yet, or have you managed to kidnap that poor dog and rescue him from his terrible fate? No sign of Mum since I got back, I think she's making merry with one of Rupe's friends in Wales, disgusting old cow. Thanks for introducing us to Pippa, by the way, I thought Rupe would die laughing when I showed it to him and he says please please PLEASE can you find some more, he wants to start a fan club. How about *Pippa Pulls a Pony Pervert*? Come and visit any time, there's loads of room and we're having a great time without Mum moaning about all over the place,

See ya, Mina'

Lydia was just emerging from the village shop with a tin of sardines, a small loaf, a bottle of cooking sherry and ten cigarettes, when she nearly ran into Caro.

'Hello Caro, how are you?' she said routinely, and prepared to continue on her way but Caro stopped her in her tracks and exclaimed, 'Lydia! Just the person I wanted to see!'

'Really?' Lydia managed a watery smile.

'I've just been chatting to Ann Robertson at the school. She's desperate for help with the children's reading. You were the first person I thought of.'

'Me? Why me?'

'Because you're so good with children, Lydia!' Caro knew she had launched into her mission far too fast: she had planned to bring the conversation round by subtle stages, but this chance meeting seemed such a heaven-sent opportunity that she had blurted out the core of her message straight away. She could tell at once that she had blundered by the way Lydia's smile had been replaced by a closed-off, frosty look. For some reason Lydia always made Caro feel clumsy and ill-at-ease, she couldn't imagine why – Lydia was not at all grand, so there was no reason why Caro should feel intimidated. After all, she was only trying to help. She rallied, 'I know you'll enjoy it once you get started. It's a wonderful way to meet people. I'd do it myself if I had the time. Just drop by at the school and ask for Mrs Robertson, you'll like her, she's terribly enthusiastic about everything.'

Lydia said coldly, 'It's not really my scene, Caro.'

'You can't say that until you've given it a try. Little children are always so good at taking one out of oneself—' Caro was off again. Lydia watched her with increasing dislike. She noticed a small patch of face powder on the side of Caro's nose that had not been properly smoothed in. She had recognised at once Caro's mission to get her to buck up and stop feeling sorry for herself, and she bitterly resented the interference.

Caro ended with a flourish. 'And you must come and have a meal at the Lodge. How about Friday? Just a family supper in the kitchen. Nothing grand.'

Lydia snapped, 'Is that supposed to put me at my ease?'

'What?'

Caro was startled into momentary silence. She must have offended Lydia somehow, though that was the last thing she intended. She began, 'I didn't mean—' then broke off, unable to apologise without knowing what for.

'It's all right, Caro, I'd love to come to supper. I'm just not sure about the teaching.'

Caro was frowning, still trying to work out where her enterprise had come unstuck. Then her vision widened and her frown deepened to encompass a couple of travellers who were approaching the shop. They were both wearing loose sweatshirts and baggy trousers. The man had spiky brown hair and glasses and the girl's mass of red hair was pulled back into a fat pony tail. A thin, lurcherish-looking dog loped beside them. They walked with a purposeful stride and avoided all eye contact. Caro put her hand on Lydia's arm and drew her to one side as they passed and went into the shop. The dog remained outside, sniffing the litter bin.

'Just look at that. Absolutely no manners. They never even said hello.'

Lydia removed her arm from Caro's protective grasp. 'Nor did we,' she pointed out.

'Did you smell them? Ugh, the sooner they leave the better.'

'Why? They haven't done you any harm.'

'Not yet. It's all very well for you, tucked away at Rose Cottage. Everyone else is worried sick. Still, my father thinks he knows how pressure can be put on Ted Sedden. With any luck they'll be gone soon.'

Lydia said, 'I'd better get a move on, then. I was planning to go and pay them a visit.'

'Who?'

'The travellers.'

'Whatever for?'

'Just to be neighbourly. And to see for myself what all the fuss is about.'

'What, just march up and introduce yourself?'

'If I have to. It does seem rather rude, but I'm hardly going to meet them at a dinner party, am I?'

Caro opened her mouth to protest, then lapsed once more into conspiratorial silence as the couple emerged from the shop. She watched them with suspicion. They carried a plastic bag full of groceries.

'Hello there,' said Lydia brightly.

The red-haired girl looked startled, then she registered Lydia's greeting, grinned and said, 'Hi,' before striding away beside the man, who had not spoken or looked at them at all.

'Fifty per cent,' said Lydia with some satisfaction.

Caro was not amused.

'I think you're mad to want to go and see them. At least promise you'll tell someone.'

'Why?'

'In case anything happens to you.'

'What do you think they're going to do, kidnap me?'

'People will do anything for drugs, Lydia. It makes them crazy. You read about it all the time. Don't wear any jewellery, or take any money. Leave your handbag at home.'

'I don't have a handbag. Look Caro, you don't have to worry about me.' She grinned suddenly, and added, 'I'm well known for having a way with animals.'

'What?'

'Just a silly private joke.'

'You mustn't touch anything while you're there. They have all sorts of diseases.'

'Caro, I'm going to Ted Sedden's field, not half way down the Limpopo and back. Stop worrying.'

But afterwards, as she walked home, Lydia herself began to worry. Why on earth had she told Caro she intended to visit them? The thought had never even occurred to her before. Now she had to see it through. But how to handle it? Was she supposed to march up to the first rusting van, bang on its door and say to whoever happened to be inside, 'Hi there everyone, my name is Lydia Fairchild. I just thought I'd pay you all a visit and see if you really are a bunch of homicidal, drug-crazed, psychopathic, kleptomaniac misfits and losers like everyone says you are'? She could imagine several ways she'd rather spend her time. It was all wretched Caro's fault.

Caro, driving the Range Rover up to the Manor with a jar of Marmite and half a pound of butter for George and Twinks before rushing back to the Lodge to be home when Suzie returned from school, was racking her brains to understand why Lydia had suddenly become so prickly. Generous to a fault, Caro hated the possibility she might have unwittingly caused offence.

An explanation occurred to her: she groaned out loud. How could she have been so tactless? There she'd been, extolling the joys of working with little children when the poor woman was supposed to be recovering from a miscarriage. Oh, poor Lydia. How stupid and clumsy Caro must have seemed. No wonder Lydia was annoyed.

Cheeks burning with self-reproach, Caro vowed to make it up to Lydia by pulling out all the stops when she came to supper on Friday.

The track that ran along behind Ted Sedden's farm was muddy after the rain earlier in the week. Lydia, whose left boot had recently sprung a leak just above the heel, picked her way carefully between the puddles. The air had a damp, autumnal smell.

True to her usual practice of acting contrary to plan, Lydia, having first decided to wait for a while before visiting the travellers, set off to see them the very next day. There were so many excellent reasons for not going to the Hollows that she knew she had to act at once, before the reasons overwhelmed her. After all, Briarswood was supposed to be a haven where she could lick her wounds in private; *not* getting involved was what this whole exercise was about. She ran the risk of opening a door she'd be unable to close again. If she showed sympathy to these travellers, what might they then expect of her? No one in their right mind would choose to live in a rotting caravan with no modern conveniences. The plumbing arrangements at Rose Cottage might be primitive, but they were infinitely superior to a bucket of cold water in the middle of a field. A picture formed in her mind that was anything but reassuring: a queue of unwashed travellers stretched down her stairs, each with one of her towels over their arm. And once they were scrubbed and clean, how could she possibly send them back to the soggy discomfort of their vehicles? They'd probably want to doss down for the night on her sofa. She imagined her floors littered with grubby sleeping-bag cocoons. Supposing things began to go missing? Most of the items at Rose Cottage weren't even hers, so she'd have to replace it all when her tenancy ended. In her present financial state, even the purchase of an electric kettle or a toaster would be disastrous.

Don't be insane, she mocked herself, why would someone

living in the middle of a field want an electric kettle? Or a toaster?

A voice in her head which sounded remarkably like Caro's said: 'To sell for drugs, naturally, they'll do anything for drugs.'

Lydia hesitated. Briarswood was nothing to do with her, the travellers were none of her business. She was only doing this out of pig-headedness. What was she trying to prove, anyway?

She didn't even bother answering that question. Maybe she had all the wrong motivations. So what? No one had ever been so susceptible to the words 'I dare you' than Lydia. She had told Caro she intended visiting the travellers, and so she would. She did not want Caro to think she was a coward. A spineless moper, maybe. But not a coward.

She reached the gate at the end of the lane, and stopped. She had arrived.

Her first impression was of a cross between a wrecker's yard and a girl guides' campsite. The cars and lorries and caravans which were dotted about the field looked practically derelict: hard to imagine how they had ever got there in one piece; harder still to imagine the convoy ever being sufficiently roadworthy to leave again.

Closer inspection showed signs of order among the disarray: several vehicles had piles of wood neatly stacked beside them; smoke was rising from one or two makeshift chimneys and some attempt had obviously been made to build a communal fire – there was a trapeze of slender branches and a large cooking pot hung from it over blackened ashes. Less encouraging were the prowling dogs.

Trying to erase the memory of a certain afternoon in a Tuscan hill village, Lydia smothered her anxiety and pushed open the gate. She was looking for the girl with the red hair who had greeted her outside the shop the previous day, but she was nowhere to be seen. Again Lydia felt a twinge of trepidation; again, she suppressed it. A couple of large, smooth-haired dogs loped over to investigate. They had an oddly springy stride; she noticed also that they did not bark.

A young woman with long brown hair was coming towards

her. She had a plain face and looked neither hostile, nor particularly friendly.

'Hi,' said Lydia. The woman gazed at her steadily but said nothing. 'I thought it was time I came round and introduced myself.'

The woman waited.

'I must be one of your nearest neighbours. I live at Rose Cottage, it's this side of the village.'

Still the woman did not speak.

Lydia said uncertainly, 'I hope you don't mind me dropping by.'

'Of course not.' The young woman had clearly reached some kind of decision. 'It's just that we don't get that many friendly visitors. Would you like a cup of tea?'

'Sure, so long as I'm not interrupting.'

'Not at all. Come on in.' The young woman treated her to an enormous and unexpected smile, before leading the way towards a green-and-white painted caravan and up a couple of boxes that had been positioned to form crude steps. Lydia noticed that this was one of the vehicles with smoke coming from a little chimney.

As she followed her guide, Lydia felt a spark of jubilation: Lydia Margaret Mead, she told herself in the quietly earnest tones of a TV voice-over, intrepid anthropologist, has successfully overcome the first barrier in her mission to win the trust of the wary Samoan traveller people.

The inside of the caravan was a mix of squalor and neatness. Patchwork curtains hung in the windows, a crocheted blanket covered the bed which took up all of one end and was partly concealed by a tie-dyed sheet. Four jars of home-made wine stood under one window, a geranium was flowering on a little shelf next to a row of battered paperbacks, but a good deal of Ted Sedden's soil had transferred itself on to the floor and there was a large pile of dirty crockery stacked in a red plastic bowl. A good-looking youth with long black hair and the red-haired girl Lydia had seen outside Peggy's shop the day before were sitting next to each other on what looked like a rolled-up mattress. Their clothes were none too clean, but despite that the only smells in the caravan were wood smoke, autumnal mud and the sweet, heavy scent that Lydia remembered from her cannabis-smoking days.

The girl said, 'This is Terry, and that's Kate.'

They all grinned at each other and said, 'Hi.' Lydia introduced herself.

'And I'm Hopi,' said her hostess.

'As in Hope, Faith and Charity, or the North American Indians?'

'Indians.'

'Weren't they the ones who were totally non-competitive?'

'That's it.' Once again Hopi's homely features were lit by a broad grin. 'My parents hated all that competition stuff. They just weren't into it at all.'

In that case, thought Lydia, their daughter's present situation must make them delirious with parental joy. Terry and Kate had shuffled sideways on the mattress and Lydia sank down on to the space provided.

Hopi pulled an old tea caddy down from a shelf.

'PG Tips?' she asked. 'Or would you prefer Earl Grey?'

While sipping her mug of Earl Grey tea, Lydia learned quite a lot about Hopi and Kate, rather less about Terry, who seemed younger, and shy in her company. Once they were satisfied that she was not an undercover Briarswood vigilante, they talked about life on the road and their reasons for living the way they did.

Hopi's parents were folk musicians who had led a rootless existence during most of her childhood. She said proudly that she had been travelling since she was a baby and could imagine no other way of life. She'd had little formal schooling, but considered herself better educated in the things that matter than many people who had exams and qualifications to their name but were utterly clueless when it came to anything practical. She had a low, gentle voice and a face that would have been plain but for her beautiful dark eyebrows. Her movements were slow and deliberate and there was something vaguely contemplative about her. Lydia found it easy to imagine her parents doggedly singing protest songs about her cradle.

Like Terry, Kate not only had several small earrings in each lobe, but one or two in her nostrils as well. She was far less serious than Hopi; she told Lydia she had grown up on a massive housing estate on the outskirts of Manchester and she had hated it. She had got on OK with her mother and brothers (apparently her father had disappeared when she was a baby and had never been seen again) but she had hated her home, her street, the whole environment for as long as she could remember.

'All that thieving and violence,' she chided, 'little kids couldn't even go outside to play. You're not safe to walk the streets at night. You're a prisoner in your own four walls. I hate houses, I do. I go back to see my mum once or twice each year, and I always get ill straightaway. It's so stuffy in her house, you can't hardly breathe. And the telly is on all the time. It's like being locked up.'

'Yes,' said Hopi, 'I went to visit an aunt last year. She's got a house miles away in the country, and she and her husband have everything they need right there. It's dreadful,' she went on, describing her aunt's comfortable home in a voice of shocked disbelief. 'It's as if they're sealed up in some kind of airtight box. All they know of the real world is what comes in to them via their television. It's like virtual reality, that place. You think you're experiencing life, but it's just an illusion.'

'On site, there's always stuff happening,' said Terry.

Kate nodded her vigorous agreement. 'This way, I'm free to come and go as I like. And on site everyone is your friend. We all help each other out. You never have to lock your stuff away. You're never lonely. It's great . . .'

'But what about people who cause problems? How do you stop the place from filling up with travellers who aren't like you?'

'It doesn't happen,' said Kate firmly. 'Everyone here shares our outlook on life.'

Hopi added, 'You see, if we started deciding who could join us and who had to keep out, then we'd be just as bad as all those people who try to stop us from parking in their exclusive little patch of countryside. And when people are free, and treated with respect, they respect you back. It's great.'

Lydia's mind was digesting all this information with some difficulty. She had expected the rumours in Briarswood to have been exaggerating somewhat, but she had never anticipated either Earl Grey tea or this deluge of cheerful enthusiasm.

Finally, in some desperation, she asked, 'Are there any things you *don't* like about travelling?'

Hopi considered this thoughtfully, but Kate said at once, 'All the hassle we get from people, that can really get you down. The day after we arrived here, this old fella turned up with a shotgun and started swearing at us and waving his gun around and threatening all sorts. We'd only gone up to the farm to get some water, Hopi and me, and he was marching around up there, ranting and raving and carrying on so bad we thought he might have a fit or a heart attack or something. So I said to him, "Watch what you're doing with that gun, old man, it's not a toy, you know."' Hopi and Terry were smiling broadly as Kate told her tale. '"You might hurt someone, you might. You could blow your own foot off and then where would you be?" And he started to go really mental on us. Then he started on about our dogs and how they ought to be put down. And he had this filthy great black dog with him, and Hopi asked him, all gentle and polite, "What's that you've got there then? A four-legged parrot?" And then he really flipped his lid, so we thought we'd better leave him to it before he spontaneously combusted or something.'

Hopi and Terry had keeled over in a fit of giggles. Hopi was the first to recover. 'People always assume we're thieves,' she said, 'that really gets me down too sometimes.'

'Right,' agreed Kate. 'All the local villains come out of the woodwork the moment we show up. As far as they're concerned it's open season. They know we'll get the blame.'

'Some shops won't even serve us,' said Hopi, 'and that's not fair because we always pay for what we want.'

'Pubs too,' Terry spoke with sudden feeling. 'Most pubs won't even let us in, not once they know we're travellers. If you just go into a strange place and they don't know, they serve you, no problem. Or if you're with friends who aren't on the road. But once they know you're a traveller, forget it.'

'It's not right,' said Kate.

'It's discrimination,' said Hopi. But neither seemed especially bothered by it.

Lydia was struggling to make sense of all of this. She remembered Wyndham's 'no smoke without fire' and she asked, 'So why do you think people are so hostile to you?'

Kate chipped in at once, 'It's the media – the papers and TV. They make up all these stories about us. They go on about how we kidnap people and eat babies and God knows what. I think people must think we're all Satanists or mad black magic witches or something—' Terry and Hopi were once more convulsed with laughter at the notion of their diabolic reputation. Kate was enjoying herself. 'They just write lies all the time. We don't like speaking to media people any more, they never print what we say, only the bad stuff.'

'Like we're all cannibals,' exclaimed Terry.

'Then people go on about how dirty we are and how we don't have any lavatories and just go anywhere. And that's not right because we're really careful, and anyway we're not the ones polluting the environment with chemicals and putting superstores up in the middle of fields.'

'Or building roads no one wants,' added Terry. 'And cutting down loads of trees all the time. We don't do that. We live in harmony with nature.'

Hopi had become thoughtful again. Frowning, she raised her eyes and gazed very directly at Lydia. 'That's all part of it,' she said sombrely. 'But mostly I think people hate us because we're different.'

A figure appeared in the open door of the caravan. It was the man Lydia had seen visiting the shop with Kate the previous day. He looked older than the others, perhaps in his late twenties or early thirties, and he had a thin, serious face and deep-set eyes. His brown hair was long and unruly and he had the beginnings of a beard. He wore small narrow-framed glasses that gave him the appearance of a nineteenth-century radical, someone who might have plotted against the Tsar and been sent to Siberia in chains. Or who might just have suffered in an attic with TB.

'Hi Mal,' said Kate. 'This is Lydia. She lives at the cottage across the field. She just came by to see if we're all as bad as people say.'

Still enjoying the joke, Terry said, 'We told her to come back at the full moon and we'll have some stolen babies to sacrifice.'

Mal was grinning at Terry's remark. 'Hello, Lydia,' he said but he spoke with a formality that made her feel ill at ease for the first time since she had entered the caravan. Almost as though she ought to stand up and shake him by the hand, but she stopped herself: such an excess of courtesy would have been ludicrous in this hobo encampment.

So she just said, 'Hello, Mal,' and smiled. She seemed to have been smiling a great deal since she arrived, and the muscles around her mouth were beginning to register this unaccustomed exercise.

Mal asked, 'Has anyone seen Saul? I thought he was with you, Kate.'

Kate shook back her tawny hair and her cheerful, freckled face registered sudden annoyance, but Lydia had the impression she was reluctant to allow any hint of disharmony in front of their guest. 'He was,' she said flatly, 'but then he got bored and went off. He'll be all right.'

Hopi said, more soothingly, 'Saul often goes to the wood.'

Lydia assumed they were discussing one of the dogs.

Mal appeared far from reassured. 'I'll go and look there,' he said, and then to Lydia, 'See you again, then,' and he withdrew.

'I should be going too,' said Lydia. 'I've taken up plenty of your time.'

'Don't worry on our account,' said Kate. 'We've got all the time we need.' She giggled. 'When we aren't working, that is.'

'You work?' The question was out before Lydia could stop herself. She realised at once how rude it sounded, but no one seemed to mind.

'Of course we do,' said Kate. 'Everyone just assumes we're dole scroungers, but we work really hard when there's any about. In the spring we'll go down to Cornwall for the flower picking, then on to Lincolnshire maybe, or Somerset for the season there. Mal and the farmer negotiated some stuff that needs doing round here, for rent, like. We only go on benefit when we have to, when there's no work.'

'And there's always masses of stuff to do on the site,' said Terry. 'Cars to fix, that sort of thing. And wood to chop. I hate just sitting about doing nothing all day long.'

'It's hard, living the way we do,' said Kate. 'Not many people

could hack it. I'd like to see all those people who go on about
how lazy we are, try living like this for a couple of weeks.'

Lydia digested this for a moment, then, feeling she'd had
enough surprises for one afternoon, she stood up. 'Thanks for
the tea. It's been good to meet you all. There's been such wild
talk in the village, I wanted to find out for myself.'

'I'm glad you did,' said Hopi earnestly. 'Maybe if more people
took the trouble to talk to us, they wouldn't be so hostile all the
time.' She stood up also. 'I'll walk with you to the gate.'

'Come again any time,' Kate was irrepressibly cheerful to the
last. 'There's always someone about to make you a cup of tea.'

'Yeah,' said Terry. 'See you around.'

As soon as Lydia and Hopi had left the caravan, there was a
noise from within of ring pulls being removed from cans of beer.
Lydia was amused that Kate and Terry had been so conscious of
their public relations role that they had confined themselves to
tea drinking in front of her. Glad that she had not let her anxiety
about the dogs put her off, Lydia strode boldly towards a group
of two or three, but Hopi caught her by the arm.

'There's one or two you want to be careful of.' She was guiding
her away from a thick-set mongrel. 'Usually they're all right, but
they can be unpredictable with strangers.'

Lydia was about to say she had a way with animals, then
thought better of it.

Hopi added, 'And they go crazy if there's any arguments, or
fights. They hate violence.'

Fights? thought Lydia. Violence? So maybe all was not entirely
sweetness and light in Dingly Dell after all.

Mal was sitting on the steps of a lorry. Near him stood
a boy who could only be his son: that same narrow, sensitive face, those same deep-set, brooding eyes. The same thick
dark hair. Only the expression was different: the little boy was
scowling.

'Oh good,' said Hopi, 'you've found Saul.'

Lydia did not think this looked a major cause for celebration.
As well as being so cross-looking, the child was teasing a large
white dog by holding out a biscuit and then snatching it away
each time the dog reached for it.

Mal had been observing the child. Now he said, 'Don't tease

him, Saul. That's not fair. You wouldn't like it if it was you being teased.'

'I don't mind,' said the child, snatching the biscuit away once more. Lydia gritted her teeth.

Mal said, 'Give him the biscuit and then you can help me finish working on the engine.'

'No,' said Saul. But then he gave the biscuit to the dog anyway, and followed Mal into the van.

Hopi, with the air of a society hostess apologising for an eccentric family member, said, 'Saul used to live in a flat with his mum. He's only been travelling with Mal for a couple of months.'

'Are there many children on site?'

'Only three at present.'

'Do they go to school?'

'Sometimes. Depends on the school.'

They had reached the edge of the field.

'See you around,' said Hopi, her homely face lighting up once more with that broad and engaging smile. 'I'm really glad you came.' Then she turned and walked away.

Lydia glanced back at the Hollows before setting off down the track towards the village. The sun was beginning to go down behind ominous, pewter-coloured clouds and the air was bright with stormy orange light. The little cluster of caravans and trucks, some with threads of smoke escaping from little chimneys, looked oddly harmonious within the shelter of the hedges and the wood beyond the stream. Not so much wrecker's yard or scout camp after all. More Raggle Taggle Gypsies, O.

The evening sounds of birdsong and a small breeze moving through the leaves was abruptly shattered by the noise of two or three dogs snarling and snapping in fury. Human voices joined in, a torrent of foul language hurling abuse and threats.

Why is it, Lydia wondered as she trudged up the muddy track and past Ted Sedden's farm, that one is never allowed to enjoy one's illusions for more than the briefest of moments?

But then she realised that in over an hour she had not thought of Dr Gordon Fairchild, nor her own misfortunes, once . . . and for that much at least she was grateful to the travellers.

7

George was so delighted with his brain wave that he followed Twinks and Sandra up the stairs and into the bedroom.

'Can't imagine why I didn't think of it before!' he puffed. 'It's the perfect way to put pressure on old Sedden.'

'How, dear?'

'Wyndham Sale, of course.'

'Why, George? What does Wyndham have to do with Ted Sedden?'

Twinks had very little interest in the answer to this question, but she was anxious to get on with the serious business of sorting through her clothes with Sandra, and she knew that George, in this state, must be listened to before he would leave them in peace.

'Borwick Farm!' he exclaimed. 'It belongs to the Haddeley estate. Ted Sedden's daughter and son-in-law rent it from Wyndham Sale. Have done for years. All Sale has to do is let Sedden's son-in-law know how he feels about the travellers. I'm sure the lease is about due for renewal. Sedden will have to think again if he wants his daughter to keep her farm. There'll be no problems there. And Sale seemed sound enough. He'll be glad to do it.'

'Excellent, George. I knew you'd come up with something.'

George had been hoping for greater enthusiasm, but obviously this was all the praise he could expect. Twinks was already opening the doors of her built-in wardrobe and Sandra had taken up her position nearby.

'Right-oh then,' said George, 'I'll phone him now.'

'Excellent,' said Twinks again, and when his footsteps had

pounded down the stairs she said to Sandra, 'Men. What a fuss. Now, Sandra, let's see if any of these will suit.'

It was on the way to becoming a twice-yearly ritual. Some time towards the end of May Twinks sorted through her winter clothes; in September, the summer garments were culled. Sandra's presence had become a crucial element in the ritual.

'This is a lovely frock, Sandra, but I don't think I'll wear it again.' Twinks had taken from the wardrobe a lawn shirtwaister which was covered in an exquisite pattern of tiny blue and gold flowers. 'It's wonderfully cool in hot weather, nothing lets the skin breathe like good quality lawn. I'm sure you'll find a hundred uses for it.'

Sandra stared at the dress with disbelief. 'It's very nice, Mrs Cartwright, but—'

'I'd pass it on to Caro, but she's much too tall. It will do you very nicely, Sandra.'

'That's very kind of you, Mrs Cartwright, but it would never fit me, not in a month of Sundays.' And Sandra squared her shoulders as she spoke, thereby thrusting forward the part of her torso which most clearly made it impossible for her to wear Twinks' clothes.

'But we're the same height,' Twinks insisted. 'And you can always let the seams out, if you must.' She lowered her head, slightly, like a small and exquisite bird dipping into a bowl of seed, and peered down the neck of the dress she was holding. Emerging triumphantly she declared, 'Just as I thought. Generous seams. You can always rely on this manufacturer for generous seams. Ah yes, I bought this one at the same time.' She laid a second dress on the bed beside the first. This one was patterned in muted, gauzy shapes of clouded blues and greys and was undoubtedly beautiful. 'With these two dresses you'll never be at a loss on special occasions – garden parties, that sort of thing. Feel the fabric, Sandra, light as air. And it's just your colour.'

Sandra gazed wistfully at the two dresses. All her powers of observation and common sense told her they could never be made to fit, but already she was being seduced by the almost maternal intimacy of this interlude in Mrs Cartwright's rose-pink bedroom. Sandra's own mother had died when she was in her teens, leaving her to care for her two younger brothers. She had always missed these kinds of girlish moments, and for a short while she allowed herself the luxury of playing the part of Twinks' daughter, elegant and sophisticated in her designer clothes. And definitely flat-chested.

'It's no good, Mrs Cartwright—'

But already Twinks had moved on to the next item, a tiny sliver of finely-knitted silk in a shade that looked to Sandra like dingy brown but which Mrs Cartwright insisted on calling 'taupe'.

'It goes with everything,' Twinks caressed the fabric as she spoke. In fact her words were a kind of caress. 'Perfect under summer jackets. You'll find you never take it off.'

Sandra knew with absolute certainty that she'd never put it on, but her protests had ceased. Twinks only grew irritated if she continued to point out that although they were indeed the same height, Sandra's chest measurements were almost double those of her employer, and you can't fit a quart into a pint pot, no matter how generous the seams. Much simpler to play along with the pretence and enjoy herself.

It was only when she left the Manor at lunchtime, her new acquisitions ballooning the sides of a couple of smart carrier bags, that Sandra began to feel she had been taken advantage of. What really rankled was the knowledge that these useless gifts were Mrs Cartwright's excuse for keeping her wages down. 'My staff always stay with me for years,' she had overheard her say to a visitor. 'Sandra would probably work here for nothing, if I let her, she's so glad of the clothes I pass on.'

Caro's supper party at the Lodge that Friday was only a partial success. She had intended to prepare all the food the day before, leaving Friday free to transform their little kitchen into a room that might, under the benign influence of candles, be mistaken for a dining room. But in her anxiety over entertaining the new owner of Haddeley Hall – which was after all one of the grandest houses in the county – Caro decided to try out several impressive-looking recipes she had noticed in a magazine and which turned out to be masses more work than they looked on paper. Caro was still busy stirring and beating and sautéing at lunchtime on the Friday, so inevitably she was flustered and exhausted by the evening.

Luckily, neither Lydia nor Wyndham seemed to notice and she was able to leave Jim and Suzie to hold the fort while she did all the last minute preparations in the kitchen.

Caro had never found it easy to combine providing several courses with being a relaxed and gracious hostess. If they had had a dining room, she could at least have press-ganged Sandra for the occasion, but she could hardly expect the poor woman to lurk in the back porch while they ate. And of course, as the used plates piled up on the work top, the illusion that the room they were in was something other than a working kitchen was completely shattered.

Nor was the food quite as impressive as she had hoped: the croûte bit of the salmon *en croûte* had somehow gone simultaneously soggy and tough, and the avocados had all gone a horrible brown colour, even though she'd put masses of lemon juice on them. Jim started doing his maddening 'can't beat plain cooking' routine and never once said how nice anything was. While she was struggling with the salmon, he and Lydia indulged in an extremely silly conversation about the unparalleled joys of eating fish and chips out of newspaper. Even Wyndham joined in after a bit, saying the only fish and chips worth eating came from some obscure café in Hull, of all places.

But her main irritation was reserved for Lydia. After all, this whole evening had been laid on solely for her benefit, and she'd made absolutely no effort herself at all. She'd arrived wearing what looked like a man's shirt, black leggings and lace up shoes. When Caro had said not to be grand, she had not expected to be taken so literally: she'd have to be more careful in future. And then, just as Caro was relaxing with a cup of coffee, Lydia announced that she had, after all, gone to see the travellers at the Hollows.

'Really?' asked Suzie. 'What were they like?'

'Fairly scruffy. Very friendly. Definitely harmless.'

Suzie was intrigued. 'Didn't they mind you barging in on them?'

'Not at all. They were very welcoming and said it was a shame more people didn't take the trouble to find out for themselves what they were like. Considering all the flak they get, they were surprisingly jolly.'

'Hmph,' said Caro, who was by now feeling thoroughly out of sorts. 'They won't be jolly much longer.'

'Why not?'

'My father has found a way of persuading Ted Sedden to see reason. And a good thing too, if you ask me.'

'How will he do that?' Lydia asked.

Her question had been addressed to Caro, but it was Wyndham who replied. 'I think I may have something to do with this. Apparently his son-in-law is one of my tenants. I have been asked by George and several others to use my influence.'

'Blackmail?' asked Lydia.

'Oh, really!' exclaimed Caro.

Wyndham smiled. 'Nothing wrong with blackmail,' he said, 'in a worthwhile cause.'

When Lydia looked at anyone as she was now scrutinising Wyndham, her features had an almost hawk-like ferocity. 'And will you?'

'I don't see why not,' he replied calmly. 'No one has given me any good reason not to.'

'I could,' said Lydia, 'I could give you plenty of reasons.'

'Such as?'

But Caro burst in, 'Oh dear, I wish I'd never mentioned it, please let's not have an argument,' with such obvious dismay that the subject was buried.

Later, however, when the guests were leaving and Caro was resigning herself to the fact that her match-making efforts could not have gone more wrong, Wyndham said to Lydia, 'Would you like a lift home?'

'Thanks, but no. It's a lovely evening. I enjoy the walk.'

That's that, then, thought Caro.

Wyndham said, 'Why don't you walk over to Haddeley some time? I want to start doing the place up, and I could use a second opinion.'

And Lydia had said, 'Sure, I'd be pleased to. I love looking round old houses,' which came as an extra surprise to Caro, who had never seen Lydia as the interior decorating type at all.

'Tomorrow afternoon?'

'I look forward to it.'

Lydia had smiled at Wyndham then and Caro had suddenly seen that in spite of the oversized man's shirt and the lace-up shoes and the untidy hair, Lydia was really quite attractive. This discovery, for some reason, gave her a brief moment of disquiet.

Sandra tossed the sliver of knitted silk on to the bed.

'And what, I'd like to know, am I supposed to do with that?'

David picked it up. 'What is it?'

'Taupe,' said Sandra with disgust. 'For wearing under jackets, apparently. I'd never even get it over my head.'

He set it on his own head. 'How about a hat, then?'

'Oh, very droll.'

'It's got a bit of give in it.'

'Don't pull it about like that, you'll ruin the shape. Give it here. Look. Doesn't even cover my front.'

She held it over her generous breasts to demonstrate, but she was beginning to smile.

'I don't know,' he said encouragingly, 'it covers half a front. If you cut it down one side, you could wear it over one breast, like an Amazon, or something. And keep the other one exposed, you'd be a knock-out.'

'Oh, certainly. Just right for Briarswood.'

Sandra's irritation began to evaporate as various other possibilities occurred to them both, some of which were so outrageous that the fashion show quickly developed into a striptease and before they knew it they were making energetic love on the bedroom floor while the children played in the garden at the back of the house.

'Oh well,' said Sandra when they had finished, and she was removing a dove-grey chemise from David's buttocks, 'I suppose the old cow has her uses after all.'

The following day she packed all Twinks' clothes back in their carrier bags for the charity shops in Edleston.

'Well? How do you like it?'

'Are you fishing for compliments?'

'I simply asked a question.'

'The house itself is beautiful. You know that.'

Wyndham nodded. By any standards, Haddeley Hall was a magnificent building. Set in parkland that had been landscaped in the eighteenth century, it stood about a mile and a half from Briarswood. A high wall surrounded the grounds: there were tall gates at the entrance and a wide avenue of trees leading to the house itself.

An enchanted house, in an enchanted setting. But the moment Lydia stepped inside the doors, the enchantment ended abruptly. Lydia had meant to ask Wyndham about his plans for the travellers at the Hollows, but she was so appalled by the interior of Haddeley Hall that she forgot them entirely. Some time in the past the house had been decorated by owners with a passion for dark green gloss paint and wallpapers that would have done a Victorian funeral parlour proud. It was as oppressive and gloomy as a mausoleum. In one or two rooms a start had been made on the renovations, but as Wyndham explained, all work had ceased when his wife's illness was diagnosed. She did not have sufficient energy to supervise the work herself, and it distressed her too much if mistakes were made which she was not able to notice in time. He had moved her to the calm of their London house and the builders and decorators were put on hold. Since her death Wyndham had concentrated on his work, and ignored the house. So now it was part building site, part rabbit warren of dark, empty rooms, still coated in their heavy green mantle and bristling with half-finished wiring. Only the dining room and Wyndham's study, which she was shown, and the master bedroom, which she was not, had been completed. The rest was sombre chaos.

'There's a hell of a lot to be done,' said Lydia.

'You noticed.'

The conducted tour had brought them to one of the upstairs rooms, darkly painted and papered as all the others and, apart from a couple of packing cases in one corner, completely empty. But here afternoon sunlight was flooding in through the windows and patterning the oak floorboards with lozenges of gold. Wyndham was perched on the edge of a tea chest near the fireplace. He was dressed in what Lydia supposed counted as casual wear at a place like Haddeley Hall – fiercely-pressed slacks and a butter yellow cashmere jersey.

He was taller than she remembered from her two previous meetings with him and altogether more formidable. She wondered if he was one of those men who are only really comfortable when on their own territory. He had the precise features often found in the sons of beautiful women, but an intensity that was wholly masculine.

He said, 'Annabel spent years searching for the right place. As soon as she brought me here, I knew it was right.'

Annabel again. His late wife cropped up frequently in conversation, and in a manner so natural that Lydia almost forgot she had died and found herself wondering if they would come across her arranging flowers in one of the urns in the enormous entrance hall, or returning from a walk with the two spaniels.

She said, 'I can see why you fell for it.'

'It has what estate agents call "potential".'

'Bags of it,' Lydia agreed.

He nodded. 'That was what attracted us. Haddeley Hall is an object of great beauty, but it has been a sleeping beauty for far too long.'

'And you're the prince who comes along and wakes it with a kiss?'

'A kiss and a cheque book.'

'So what's the problem? You hire an interior designer, they do a wonderful job, problem solved.'

'With designers, one loses control. When Annabel was alive, we were an excellent team, but now—'

'I see. She was the artistic one, and you provided the cash.'

'On the contrary, Annabel's judgement was often appalling. She was capable of terrible lapses in taste, but she could always be relied on for ideas. My own were usually formed in response to hers. Now that the dialogue is missing, I find it . . .' he hesitated slightly before finishing, 'I find it less easy.'

'So whose opinion got the upper hand?'

'Mine.'

'Always?'

'Always.'

'Some dialogue?'

'The right decisions were made. That was all that mattered.'

'Hm.'

Lydia was thoughtful. Wyndham's description of his wife's role seemed heartless in the extreme, but she was beginning to think it would be a mistake to make any easy assumptions about Wyndham Sale. As his next question proved.

'Would you like to help me, Lydia? You said just now that you have had some decorating experience.'

The way he said the question, it did not sound like an appeal for help, exactly. She said lightly, 'You want me to suggest things just so you can tell me how wrong I am and go ahead and do it your way?'

He smiled. 'Maybe. Or I might like your ideas, you never know. Why not try some, and we can find out.'

Lydia decided it was best to treat it as a game. 'OK,' she said, then walked over to the window and studied the room carefully. It was a commission straight from heaven, she knew that, and the moment she began her imagination took flight. She said thoughtfully, 'It would be easy to play safe and do everything in period, fill it with antiques and that sort of stuff, but I think that would be a shame. Rooms like this one cry out for a more dramatic approach. Bold and theatrical, almost like a stage set. But very spare, a minimalist stage set.'

She paused. Wyndham was watching her impassively. He said, 'Go on.'

'Absolutely no clutter or fuss. Clean simple lines, but strong. For instance,' she had begun to move around the room as her ideas took hold, 'these windows. In their way, they are perfect. Almost anything you put with them would be a minus. But assuming that you want some kind of screen, if only for privacy, what can you do? Shutters might be in keeping. Or really beautiful curtains. But that's all a bit predictable. How about a great swathe of something really impressive and dramatic – garish, even – just looped over one end, like a theatre curtain that's much too large and falls in great heaps and piles on the floor? And then everything else could be totally minimal. Just a bed in the middle of the room, maybe a linen chest. Nothing else at all.'

She stopped. She could have gone on for much longer, but suddenly she was reluctant to play so readily into his hands. She waited for Wyndham's criticism. None came.

He asked, 'A four poster?'

'No. Much too obvious. An oriental one, perhaps. Or better still, something modern. You'd know it when you saw it.'

'And the walls?'

'Get rid of the wallpaper, for a start. Then plain paint. No pictures. No fuss. My own inclination would be to go for one of those old-fashioned cloudy paints, a light blue distemper, something like that. That would draw the eye to the panelling which is a work of art itself. You'd have to get all that paint and guk off and see what kind of condition the wood was in underneath.'

'How very decisive you are, Lydia Fairchild.'

The words were spoken without irony. Lydia was excited. She had forgotten until now how much she had enjoyed her work with decorators in the past, though, as in every other job, she had found a reason to quit as soon as she had learned enough to make any money at it. But all she said was, 'I'm what they call a Jill of all trades. Master of none.'

'Mistress,' he corrected. He was watching her intently, but Lydia was unable to decipher his expression.

She moved restlessly back to the window. 'There'd need to be one thing more in the room.'

'Like what?'

'I'm not sure yet. You can't decide just like that, but I think it wants to be something modern – a geometric rug, or a completely outrageous mirror. Or maybe something primitive.'

During the silence that followed, Lydia wondered if she had done a successful 'Annabel' and waited to be told exactly what was wrong with all her suggestions.

Eventually he said, 'When can you start?'

'What?'

He did not bother to repeat his question. He knew quite well she had heard. He said, 'Annabel's death put everything on hold for a while, but now I'm eager to begin. I've had a firm of decorators standing by for months. All you have to do is give the orders.'

Lydia was startled by her own reaction. Already she felt possessive about the room and her plans for it, and the idea of a troop of strangers marching in and attacking the precious panels with blowtorches was almost shocking. She said, 'I'm a hopeless delegator. More of a hands-on sort.' Unaware of what she was doing, she smoothed her palm against a patch of rough paint as she spoke. 'A room has to grow. It develops its own life. Only by doing each stage can you begin to understand what the next one wants to be.'

'Very well then. You do it. I'll pay you, of course.' He shrugged slightly, before adding, 'Money is not the problem.'

'Just this room?'

'To begin with, yes.'

'I don't know. My plans are pretty much up in the air at present.'

She moved back to the window and looked out across the park. Two energetic black-and-white spaniels were being taken for a walk by Wyndham's manservant: there was an obvious conflict of interest. The dogs wanted to streak across the grass at top speed, Miguel wanted only to lean against a tree and smoke a cigarette. Lydia Fairchild, she said to herself, don't even consider such a mad enterprise. You only came to Briarswood for a couple of days. You might want to move on again at any time. What about Charlotte and Minorca? A man like this would be an employer from hell, and you know it.

She said, 'I'd have to be paid by the hour. You can't rush a job like this.'

'You have all the time you need.'

She fidgeted, lectured herself sternly and then gave up and said, 'I'd have to charge seven pounds an hour.'

'Ten,' he insisted, 'and a bonus at the end if it works.'

There was a definite fizz of excitement. Apprehension as well. A contract had been established that went beyond the mere decoration of a room. There was a tension between them – or perhaps it had been there since that first evening at the Manor. She turned aside to one of the packing cases placed near the wall and lifted out a length of shimmering cloth.

'How come you have all this material here?'

'Annabel always liked to see the new designs and colours. They're sent from our factory.'

'You have a factory?'

'Several.'

'Here?'

'Hong Kong. Singapore. My grandfather started the business. We're up to five now.'

'We?'

'There's only me. Now.'

He was relaxed and easy under her questioning. He would never give away more than he chose. She asked, 'Are all the fabrics as beautiful as these?'

'See for yourself.'

She uncovered a length of poppy red silk. Draping it over one shoulder like a banner of flame, she moved across to the window, then threw back her head, twisting slightly so the sunlight would touch her hair and face.

'Well, how do I look?'

His eyes were on her face. 'I'd rather see you without your clothes.'

She stood very still, holding on to the length of silk, before turning slowly to meet his gaze. She asked, 'Are you always so direct?'

'Occasionally. When I'm flirted with.'

It was only the truth. At some stage since coming into the upstairs room, part of the protective shield that had marked Mrs Gordon Fairchild as unavailable to other men had begun to dissolve and slip away. She felt the first stirrings of sexual interest, but then answered him flatly, 'No thanks.'

Almost imperceptibly, he nodded. 'As you wish.'

'I'll do the decorating,' she said, as she shrugged the silk from her shoulders, 'but that's all.'

There was a flicker of movement below his eyes as his face registered emotion almost for the first time: it was annoyance. He said, 'There was no suggestion of any link.'

Now it was Lydia who felt a fool. She began folding the silk with extreme care. 'Of course not.'

'Keep the silk. It suits you.'

'Thanks, but I'd never wear it. I'm not really a silk sort of person.'

'People change.'

Again, Lydia experienced an unease that was far from unpleasant. Perhaps Caro's diagnosis had been right after all: she had simply been suffering from boredom. A job of work and some enjoyable flirtation and this whole business of recovery was suddenly quite straightforward. She said, 'I might look through this lot and see if there's anything that would be right for the window.' She wanted to get their conversation back on to more neutral ground. 'Some of them are stunning.'

'I'll have others sent down to you. The more garish the better?'

'Great.'

'My secretary Mark will see you're paid, and cover all your expenses. I have to be away a good deal, unfortunately.'

Lydia smiled. 'At least Caro will approve,' she said. 'She's been trying to make me get out and do more for ages.'

'I have no interest in Caro's opinions. She strikes me as a remarkably stupid woman.'

For the second time that afternoon, Lydia was shocked, not just by his words as by the manner in which they were uttered. More than cold. Cruel. What on earth was she letting herself in for? She knew nothing at all about Mr Wyndham Sale, except that he appeared to be quite remarkably wealthy and self-confident. And that his wife had recently died. How? Maybe he had murdered her? Maybe he had trampled on her opinions so many times that she had quite simply given up the ghost. Lydia couldn't understand why she liked Wyndham's company. Had her instinct for the wrong man led her unerringly to Briarswood's home-grown psychotic? Maybe she should simply cut her losses and say she had changed her mind, wouldn't be able to do any decorating for him after all. But then she ran her finger tip along the dado rail and glanced out of the window at the September light falling on the huge oaks in the park, and she knew she would never forgive herself if she chickened out of a project like this before she'd even had a chance to begin.

She said, 'Don't talk like that about Caro. She's kind.'

'Undoubtedly.' He looked at his watch and said, 'I'll run you back to the village. I have a conference call here at five.'

'Don't bother. I enjoy the walk.'

As they were driving back towards Briarswood, Lydia remembered the other reason for her visit.

'Have you decided what to do about Ted Sedden's son-in-law?'

she asked. 'Are you going to put pressure on him to get the travellers moved?'

'I haven't got round to it yet.'

'Are you going to?'

He did not look at her. 'I don't see why not.'

'How about blackmail?' asked Lydia cheerfully. 'Suppose I threaten to do terrible things to your panelling?'

Wyndham did not smile. 'Like you,' he said, 'I don't do bargains.'

'So, how do I get you to change your mind?'

'You might just try asking. People hardly ever think of that.'

She allowed a pause before saying lightly, 'Please don't do what George has asked.'

'OK, I won't. Not without a reason, anyway.'

They drove the rest of the way in silence. Lydia sensed that the time Wyndham had allotted for socialising that day had been used up. She also had the impression that he was pleased with developments that afternoon, and not the slightest bit put out by her rebuff earlier. Moreover, she had the odd sensation that she had performed correctly according to some prearranged plan of his.

An odd sensation, but not entirely unpleasant.

Late afternoon, Suzie stepped down from the school bus in the centre of Briarswood. About seven schoolchildren alighted at the same time, but anyone watching would never have guessed that she was acquainted with any of them. At this time of year the two first formers stood out a mile: their new clothes adhered to the uniform code in every detail and their schoolbags had not yet been antiqued by constant dropping and dragging and being sat on. The older pupils all demonstrated their contempt for uniforms by taking every opportunity to undermine the rules – socks the wrong colour, hair too long (or too short), skirts or trousers that were blue but not navy, and so on, in an infinitely ingenious variety of minor rebellions.

All but Suzie. From the very start Caro had made it absolutely plain that there was to be no swerving from the original rigorous standards. Suzie's doleful cry of 'But everyone else does it!' only reinforced her mother's determination. The crucial factor, as far as Caro was concerned, was that Suzie was not like everyone else, and if her daughter stuck out like a sore thumb then you only had to look at the riff raff pouring out of the school each afternoon to see what a thoroughly good thing that was.

It grieved Caro deeply that all her daughters had gone to state schools, but she had been trapped by an unbeatable combination of Jim's principles and their constant lack of funds. As Jim never failed to remind her, the state system had done very well by the older three. Yes, thought Caro, but circumstances had been different then. For one thing there had always been excellent schools in the university towns they had lived in and lots of the lecturers were of Jim's opinion so there was no shortage of well brought up children to mix with. Besides, Polly had always been so beautiful she had not needed that special boost a private education brings: her face was, quite literally, her fortune. Then Kate was so bright and Jim never seemed to stop teaching her things, and Emily had said once that if Caro ever dared to send her to a private school she would do all the most dreadful things she could think of until she got expelled, which Jim, for some reason, thought was hilarious.

Suzie, however, was different. Caro worried about Suzie. She had never done all that well at school and was not an especially good mixer. Even while they still lived in the university town, she had not made many friends, and here Caro could see there was an absolute dearth of nice children to mix with. She fretted mostly in silence: their ghastly poverty precluded any action.

Suzie could not fail to be aware of her mother's views, and sometimes she found herself sharing them. Pippa, in the brief intervals between riding ponies to victory, had apparently gone to a rather smart all-girls school where the teachers were all called Miss Something-or-other and were strict but fair. It sounded a lot more fun than the place she had attended for the past year. Daddy kept saying it would improve once she found her niche, and maybe he was right, but for the time being she was feeling distinctly nicheless.

And weary. Some afternoons she barely had the energy to amble the half mile from the bus stop to the Lodge. The other passengers all piled straight into the shop for bags of crisps and sweets and fizzy drinks, but Suzie knew Caro would be poised by the kettle, and watching the clock for her return.

Suzie wished for a lot of things that didn't seem all that likely to happen, but one of the things she wished for on an almost daily basis was that just occasionally Caro would not be hovering in the kitchen with her bright smile and her anxious, 'Had a good day, Suzie?' when she got home. What bliss it would be, just once, to slip unnoticed into the house, get something out of the fridge and slope off to collapse in front of the television for a bit before facing the inquisition.

'Well then and how was school?'

'Oh, it was OK, thanks Mummy.'

'Any interesting lessons?'

'Um. Not really.'

'What did you learn, then?'

'Nothing much.'

'Aren't they teaching you properly? Maybe I should talk to your father about some private tutoring.'

'It's OK, Mummy. You don't have to bother. School's fine, really it is.'

'Then I can't see why you refuse to talk about it.'

'It's just not very interesting, that's all.'

Instinct told Suzie it was best not to mention to Caro that Dawn Roper, who had once sat next to her in geography, was expecting a baby at Christmas, nor that a boy in the fourth year had been suspended for threatening the caretaker with a knife, nor that they had all been subjected to a long lecture on the perils of glue sniffing. Suzie would not have known how to sniff glue if she had wanted to. She realised that Mina would probably have made these incidents sound wonderfully dramatic, but Suzie just found school dreary. If she'd had a close friend, it might have been different. It was not that the others disliked her, or ostracised her, or anything like that: mostly they did not seem particularly to notice she was there.

When she was still about two hundred yards away from the Lodge, her footsteps developed that bendy, uncoordinated character that always happened when she was embarrassed or shy. Coming towards her was one of the travellers, the dark-haired youth who had asked her the way to Ted Sedden's farm on the very first day. Beside him walked – or rather, limped – the large white dog he had been struggling to bring under control, the one Mina had been so anxious to kidnap.

She hunched her shoulders and shifted her schoolbag. She knew she was beginning to blush. It was enough to make you agoraphobic, this inability to pass someone in the road without collapsing into a heap of mind-numbingly stupid embarrassment. But what were you supposed to do with your eyes? She couldn't look past him, because he might think she was staring at him; she tried glancing to the left, as if she had just seen an object of riveting interest in someone's front garden, but after a few moments that began to feel stiff and awkward so she had to turn her head to face forwards again to look at a point on the ground just in front of her feet. It was bad enough when it was someone ordinary coming towards you, like Mr Gee or Lydia, but about a million times harder when it was a traveller, and a young, male traveller at that. Even without looking at him properly she could tell by some kind of osmosis that in spite of his weird clothes he was really good-looking, with narrow hips and long legs and liquid black eyes. Mina had said he was cute-looking, and Mina was much more of an authority on the opposite sex than Suzie.

Another dilemma: the dog – like a large pale sheep – which was not even on a lead, had bounded ahead in its odd, three-legged way, to greet her. If she bent down to pat it, she might give its owner the idea that she wanted to talk to him, but if she just ignored it, she would seem like someone who didn't like animals. Also, she had been impressed by what Lydia had said at dinner the other night at the Lodge, that the travellers were quite willing to be friendly; it was the villagers who were so hostile.

Now the dog had reached her and the youth was only feet away. She stopped walking for a fraction of a moment and reached down to fondle the dog. Actually, she didn't have to reach down all that far, because it was a big dog, a collie type, but much whiter than most collies. And the big green patch that she and Mina had observed when they spied on the travellers from the wood had faded to a dull khaki.

The youth's boots had drawn level and stopped. Suzie straightened up and said, 'Hello,' in a distant sort of way, and began walking again at once. As she passed him her gaze kind of swept over his face without pausing for a moment in case she caught his eye. She noticed that he had a very peculiar haircut indeed, short all over the top of his head but long and stringy at the sides and his hair was very dark, almost like an Indian or a Spaniard. Also he had tiny silver rings in his nostrils and loads of earrings. But in spite of all these oddities he was even better looking than she had thought at first.

She heard him say, 'Hi there,' in a really mellow voice to her retreating back, and then, 'Come on, Misty,' to the dog, and then his footsteps started up again.

Suzie's heart was pounding as she walked the last few yards to the Lodge. She was in an absolute sweat of panic in case she had made a complete fool of herself for talking to him in the first place, or perhaps an even worse fool by not talking enough. Maybe she shouldn't have looked at him at all, or maybe she should have looked at him properly and been relaxed and friendly and sophisticated about the whole thing.

But as well as the panic, she felt a kind of fluttery excitement under her ribs. Already the scene was developing in her imagination. She might have said, in a really casual and confident manner, 'Hello there, nice dog,' and the youth might have said, 'He's really taken to you, I can tell. His name is Misty, by the way, I was just taking him for a walk,' and Suzie might say, 'Have you ever been to the top of Raven's Beacon?' And then a few awkward in-between stages were skipped over and there they were, just the two of them, gazing at the view from Raven's Beacon, while Misty and Bumpkin gambolled happily nearby. The handsome youth had his arm around her shoulders. They'd been kissing.

The soaring happiness of Suzie's daydream was abruptly intercepted by her mother's cheerful, 'Hello, Suzie! Did you have a good day at school?'

Suzie's wild bubble of daydream was shattered in an instant.

8

George was more relieved than he cared to admit even to himself when he turned off the dual carriageway and saw the familiar sign: Briarswood 4 miles. Driving a car on the public highway was another of those activities he had taken for granted for more than half a century, but which now, as his eightieth year drew nearer, had become increasingly problematic. George blamed the pace of modern life. He drove with the same steady courtesy he had perfected in his youth, when the roads had been mercifully empty, car engines had boiled on steep hills and passengers had to be wrapped in rugs and scarves against the cold. Now everyone was in such a tearing hurry all the time, they'd lost all sense of style. George was constantly being hooted at; other road users frequently shook their fists at him, or used bad language, with absolutely no provocation whatsoever. He never permitted himself to retaliate, but sometimes it was difficult to maintain a dignified silence. The truth was, the aggression and speed of other drivers flustered him but he couldn't bear to stop driving, not yet. That would be just another nail in the coffin of his self-respect. Another intimation of horrors ahead.

George had been brought up to meet every challenge squarely and old age was to be no exception. George wasn't proud of his stoicism: it was so much a part of him that he could no more have complained about his aches and pains than he could cut in front of the young lady in the small blue car who had been waiting on his left at the last roundabout, no matter how much the louts behind him honked their horns and yelled abuse as they swerved past him and nearly caused a very nasty accident. The joints in his feet and hands had been giving him trouble for years. Recently his knees had started to act up; sometimes the pain was so intense it pretty well made him forget where he was and what he was doing, for a couple of seconds. And now there was this beastly twinge – more than a twinge, often – in his upper chest.

He frowned and told himself not to be spineless. One didn't want to turn into one of those doctor-loving johnnies, for ever scooting off to some consultant or other at the first wobble. Mind over matter; the body soon put itself to rights if you just left well alone.

Nearly home now. He must have said the words out loud because Hamish, sitting on the passenger seat, peered through the windscreen in anticipation.

'Good fellow, Hamish.' George took his left hand off the wheel and laid it on the labrador's dark head. An old man's hands, joints swollen with arthritis, veins pushing against the skin like threads of grey wool.

A dismal business, getting old. This new pain, the one in his chest, was a particular nuisance. 'Better make the best of it, Hamish,' he said briskly. George's dog often received good advice concerning his master's problems.

Just as George was imagining the stiff drink he'd pour himself when he got home, he caught a glimpse of a scene which struck him as so appalling it was all he could do to bring the BMW to a reasonably controlled halt.

They had been in the wood for a couple of hours. To begin with, they had simply enjoyed themselves. Gentle sunlight was filtering through the canopy of beech leaves and every now and then the breeze sent a handful of orange leaves spiralling towards the earth. Kate had helped herself to a few blackberries, Hopi sat down on a fallen log and enjoyed a cigarette, Malcolm found some incredible cream-coloured fungus growing out of the side of a tree and wondered how you knew if it was edible or not. Hopi told him he should get a book from the library, the countryside was full of all sorts of free food, apart from blackberries, which everyone knew about. Kate meanwhile had discovered that elderberries were not at all pleasant and that sloes were more sour than lemon pith. For a while they all sat down beside Hopi on the log and chatted, and then they set to work. After half an hour or so they had a fairly respectable pile of logs stacked up and ready to load into Mal's lorry.

Then, 'Bloody hell,' said Kate, looking up from her task. 'Now what?'

Malcolm and Hopi, their arms full of logs, came to stand beside her.

'Oh no,' groaned Hopi, 'not him again.'

'You know him?' asked Malcolm.

Kate and Hopi exchanged glances. 'Yes,' said Kate, 'it's Psycho-Gramps.'

Mal saw a tall, well-built man climb out of the car. Although in his seventies at least he was upright and walked without a stick. He wore a tweed jacket, twill trousers and polished brogues. Just at this moment, he did not give the impression of a man at peace with the world.

'What the buggery d'you think you're doing?' the man roared. 'Get off my land this instant!'

Alerted by the stern voice of authority, a large black labrador put his head out of the passenger window of the car and watched.

'We didn't know this was your—' began Mal.

'Think you can just help yourselves, do you? Think you've got a God-given right? Put those bloody logs down before I call the police! How dare you!'

'All right, all right,' Mal was breathing heavily, but he laid down the logs he was carrying. 'There's no need to—'

'Look at this!' George spotted the logs stacked by the ancient van and was spurred to even greater fury. 'Bloody hooligans, I'll teach you to steal my wood, I'll—'

Kate pulled her woolly hat down over her frizz of red hair and squared up for a fight. 'Oh, for Christ's sake, shut up!' she yelled. 'We didn't know it was your bloody wood. You can keep it, if it's so damn precious. It was just lying about, you know, just rotting. Here, take it!' Still holding a couple of logs she marched up to the BMW and deposited them on the driver's seat.

'Don't you touch my car, you young hussy!'

'There!' Kate figured she could yell louder than him any day.

'Keep the lot! I hope you set fire to yourself and bloody burn to death, you miserable old bugger!'

George, unused to women shouting back at him, placed a frail hand over his upper chest and sputtered speechlessly for a moment.

Hopi decided it was time to intervene. She said in her placid way, 'We only took what was lying around. We didn't think anyone else wanted it.'

Mal blinked twice. With a nervous gesture he pushed his glasses up on to the bridge of his nose. His face had gone white and pinched. He said in a voice that was tight with self-control, 'There was no intention to cause any upset. We—'

'Go on, get off my land,' George had recovered from the momentary shock of being shouted at by a red-haired vagabond with three rings through her nose. His earlier anxiety had given way to triumph now that he realised he had them on the run. He said magisterially, 'If I see any of your lot round here again, I'll call the police, I'll have my gun next time, I'll—'

'Oh hell,' said Hopi as they drove away in the transit, 'all that lovely wood going to waste.'

'Yeah,' Kate agreed gloomily, 'stupid old sod. I bet he's got bloody central heating, and all.'

Mal, his knuckles white as he gripped the steering wheel, said nothing.

By early evening Kate and Hopi had already turned the incident into a joke.

'Would you like a puff of my weed, young hussy?'

'Oh, thanks ever so, old bean, don't mind if I do.'

Mal could hear them now in Hopi's caravan. Hopi was playing her guitar and Kate was attempting to play the penny whistle, but her inexpert notes set the dogs howling and the two girls kept collapsing with giggles. They were composing a song called 'The Ballad of the Irate Man'.

Mal envied them, but his sense of humour had temporarily deserted him. There was a fist of rage clenched in his chest that he could not budge. He had drunk more than a bottle of wine, but still the anger was eating away at his insides like caustic acid. He was angry with himself for drinking the wine. Since

Saul joined him he had been modest in his drinking, but this evening his self-control had vanished.

If there was one thing he hated, it was aggressive scenes. The sound of voices raised in anger was a knife twisting under his ribs. He hated, hated, hated any kind of confrontation. All he wanted was to live in harmony with the world, but oh God, sometimes that was so hard.

He poured himself another mug of wine and rolled himself a cigarette. His hands were shaking. He had long, thin hands – artistic hands, his mother used to say, with shy pride. At the other end of the lorry Saul was at last sleeping on the little bed that Mal had made for him six weeks before. His only solace was that Saul, who had that morning been attending school for about the third time in his life, had been spared the scene in the wood. More than anything in the world Mal wanted to protect his son against any hint of brutality. No one was ever going to raise a hand to his boy; no one would even shout at him. At the thought of how he might react if Saul were ever threatened, Mal felt a strange darkening behind the eyes. All thought blotted out.

There was little similarity between the well-dressed elderly gent who had been driving the white BMW that afternoon and Malcolm's father, Stanley Fraser. Stanley Fraser was a salesman who wore cheap suits and drip dry shirts, he was short and stocky and loud and sociable. And he was a bully. Both men were bullies. Mal hated, loathed, despised and utterly abominated bullies.

He was well into a second bottle of wine, but his rage was undimmed. He went outside, closing the door of his van carefully behind him, so as not to disturb the sleeping boy. The night was clear and the sky glittered with stars. He could hear the laughter coming from Hopi's trailer, could smell the wood smoke and the gathering dew. Peace, he told himself, be at peace with the world. Live in harmony with all things. Don't let one old man with an attitude problem get under your skin. Breathe slowly. Relax.

It was no good. Rage was hammering in his chest. In spite of all his best intentions, he was filled with an overwhelming urge to lash out and destroy. He wanted to bash and hurt and injure all those battalions of older men, fathers and teachers and policemen and angry landowners who thwarted him at every turn. He wanted to shift this terrible pain. He wanted to be tolerant and forgiving. He did not want to feel this way at all.

Behind him in the lorry a child's voice erupted, an incoherent cry of fear. Mal was by his side at once. Saul's eyes were open and his forehead was sticky with sweat.

'What is it, Saul?'

The child stared up at him with dark, unseeing eyes. 'Bastards under the sink broken . . .'

'What?'

''S obvious, moron,' the boy mumbled, and rolled back into sleep.

Mal shifted the small duvet to cover him properly. He wondered if he could make any sense of the boy's dream, but after a little while he gave up. He would have liked to be able to sing to Saul the way he had once heard Hopi singing to him, or tell him a story. It might help calm him after his bad dream, but Malcolm had no aptitude for singing or stories. So he just said, 'Sounds a bit of a jumble to me, Saul,' and decided to sit with him for a while.

At times like this, when Saul was sleeping, Mal felt so close to him it was almost uncanny. If Mal was strictly honest with himself he had to admit that Saul awake was more of a problem, since he was rude and difficult and found a hundred ways to wind Mal up. Asleep, however, he was different – innocent and vulnerable. Mal had a sudden strange sensation that the child lying in the little home-made bed under the stripy duvet was his own self as a child. That same long face, pale and anxious, even in sleep, the same deep-set and shadowed eyes, the same stubborn set of the mouth. There had never been any question about Saul's paternity.

Mal had met Saul's mother at a festival in Hereford about seven years before. She was with a man who knocked her about with dreary regularity, and at the end of the festival she had moved into Mal's lorry; they had travelled together for several months. Angie was a gentle, slightly lost person, but given to black moods and after a while they decided to go their separate ways. She had a tendency to indulge in whatever was on offer and was already an occasional crack user. Mal was becoming increasingly clear about his vision of life on the road, and hard drugs played no part in it.

The following year he had heard on the grapevine that Angie had had a premature baby and that she and her boyfriend had been housed by the council for the sake of the baby's health. He assumed the present boyfriend must be the child's father – Mal had never even considered the possibility that Angie had been pregnant when they split up. He had had a couple of other girlfriends since then. A year ago he and Kate had got together. He had pretty well forgotten all about Angie.

That Easter he had bumped into an old friend called Scottie, who had remarked casually, 'Your boy's the spitting image of you, Mal. D'you see much of him?'

Mal's world had changed entirely as a result of that conversation, though it was six weeks before he decided to try to see the child, and another two months before he was able to track Angie down. Kate had been dead against it from the start. 'It's nothing to do with you, Mal. Loads of kids have dark hair and brown eyes. You can't go feeling responsible for all of them.'

'I'm just going to see them,' he told her, 'nothing more.'

Angie was living in a fourth-floor flat on an estate outside Coventry. Mal felt the familiar suffocation of claustrophobia as he entered the bleak concrete world of the estate, but he told himself that it wasn't all that bad, there were plenty of worse places for children to grow up, he could hardly have expected the council to find Angie and her baby a nice thirties semi when there were so many families waiting to be housed.

Angie was neither surprised nor pleased to see Mal. She did not look as if anything had surprised or pleased her in a long time. She had put on weight, her pale hair was dirty and she looked generally as if she had let herself go since quitting her life on the road. Though the flat seemed no worse than thousands of others, there was an air of fetid gloom that disturbed him, as if Angie was some pale fish trapped in stagnant water where daylight never reaches.

He looked about the dingy room. Angie had flopped down into a battered arm chair and was lighting a cigarette. There was a toddler sitting on the floor. A little child with fair curls and his mother's blue eyes. Scottie had been mistaken. This child of Angie's was about three years too young to be Mal's. He was hugely relieved. He could chat for a while, then go.

She said, 'Fancy seeing you again. What do you want?'

'I bumped into Scottie at Easter. He said you had a child.' Mal sat down on the only other chair in the room and patted the child's curls. 'Nice kid,' he said. 'What's he called?'

'Vanessa,' she said. The child made no response to Mal at all. 'You've taken your time, haven't you?'

'Scottie said there was a resemblance,' Mal grinned awkwardly, 'so I thought . . . but he must have been—'

'Too bloody right there is. Well, there would be, wouldn't there?'

'But . . .'

'See for yourself.' She twisted her head slightly to shout into the next room. 'Saul! Come and say hello to the man!' She had to shout again to be heard over the frantic cartoon noises coming from the television in the next room.

Mal's immediate reaction on seeing Saul was to feel nauseated. What was this five-year-old version of himself doing with such a mother and in a place like this?

He stood up and said, 'Hello, Saul.'

The child just stared at him. His hair was brown and fell in girlish waves over his ears. Mal smiled in what he hoped was an encouraging way and crossed the room. He said again, 'Hello, Saul. My name's Malcolm.'

But when Mal raised his hand to touch his hair, Saul avoided his hand with an expert ducking motion, and dived back into the other room to hide behind the bed. Mal felt physically winded, as though someone had just slugged him in the stomach with an iron bar.

Tight with rage, he turned back to Angie. 'Who's been knocking him about?'

She shrugged. 'He can be a right bloody monster, that one. And lippy. I can't handle him when he's bad. Dan has to sort him out.'

'Dan? Is he your boyfriend?'

'Yes. Sort of.'

'And he hits Saul?'

'No need to get all high and mighty about it, Malcolm Fraser.

You don't have the bother of him all day. Saul's hyperactive, that's the problem. I tried to get the doctor to give him some medicine to calm him down, but he was bloody useless. The social worker says it's psychological anyway.'

'Social worker?' Shivers of anxiety danced up and down Mal's spine.

'Yeah. She says they can take Saul off my hands for a bit, give me a break until we get a proper house. They know I can't handle him, not since Vanessa was born. Saul's always causing problems between me and Dan. He can be evil, really bad.'

'You *asked* them to take Saul away from you?'

'Just for a bit. Until I get my strength back.'

'Angie, if you lose Saul now you'll never get him back, not in the state you're in. What does Dan do?'

'He's in business. Buying and selling, that sort of thing. It's a living. Dan's all right, but he's got a wild temper.' She brightened visibly at this last statement, before adding, 'Sometimes it gets too much for him, Dan can't help it. Saul's always winding him up.'

Mal could feel his whole life changing, while Angie spoke in her flat, listless voice. She said, 'The social worker says I've got post natal depression. It can be terrible here. You don't know what it's like.'

'I can imagine.'

'Well then, you're his dad. If you're such a bloody hero, you can have him.'

'I might just do that.'

Nothing had been further from his mind. He thought, this is ridiculous, what am I doing here? This is nothing to do with me. I should go at once. But the moment when he could still have turned away had slipped by him while he wasn't looking.

There was a presence at his side. Saul was fixing him with a pebble-hard stare.

'Are you my dad?'

'I think I must be, Saul.'

'My real dad?'

Mal nodded. He felt close to despair.

Saul asked, 'Do you live in a proper house?'

'No, Saul, but I've got a proper home. Only it's a lorry.'

'What d'you live in a stupid lorry for?'

'I like it. I like the freedom.'

The child was examining him closely. Mal wondered if the concept of 'freedom' had any meaning for Saul whatsoever.

'Can I come with you then?'

'For a holiday?'

Saul was frowning. 'To go with you in your lorry.'

'That depends.'

'Why?'

'Well, your mother probably wants—'

'She says I'm a bloody liability.'

'Only when you are, love,' said Angie hopelessly.

'I want to come with you.'

'Go on then,' said Angie, looking towards Vanessa who had begun to grizzle. 'You take him for a bit. I can't handle the both of them, not with Dan as well. You'll get fed up with him soon enough. Don't say I didn't warn you.'

Mal stood up. 'OK then,' he said. 'Let's get your things.'

All his life Mal had had his own powerful reasons for minimising the importance of genetics. The possibility that any part of him was due to the foul-mouthed and heavy-handed Stanley Fraser had always been abhorrent to him. But right from the first he felt a kind of animal closeness to his son. The moment Saul slipped his small, sticky hand into his own, Mal thought, we are one flesh, and he experienced a sudden flash of exultation, followed almost at once by a terrible panic at the hugeness of what he was taking on. This frail and damaged human being, who resembled him so minutely down to the tips of his narrow fingers, was his responsibility. He had lost five years of the boy's life already. From now on he could not afford to put a foot wrong.

Saul picked up a dirty, pink, seal-shaped animal but he seemed to have few other belongings. Mal went into the bathroom in search of a child-sized toothbrush. The toddler, Vanessa, had started crying in earnest and Angie fished under the sofa and extracted a filthy comforter which she tried to force into the child's mouth. Vanessa only cried more loudly. Angie grew impatient.

Mal wanted to be fifty miles away. He said, 'Have you still got my mum's telephone number? Ring her if you want to get hold of me. She usually knows where to find me.'

'Sure.'

Saul was standing near the door, carefully not looking at anyone. Mal told Angie they'd keep in touch, Saul could come back whenever he wanted, as soon as she was feeling better . . .

Angie did not show much interest.

'Well,' he said, 'we'll be off then.'

Angie stood up and came to the door. She looked down on Saul and for the first time there was an expression of tenderness on her face. 'So long, then. You be a good boy now. I'll see you around.'

Mal had parked his lorry at the edge of the estate. He and Saul reached it just in time to prevent a group of children from removing the wing mirrors. Saul climbed into the front seat without a word. Just as Mal had climbed in beside him, a shadow fell over the boy's face. He was watching a man with a thin pony tail and wearing a denim jacket cross the concrete walkway to the flats.

'Is that Dan?'

Saul looked away but did not answer.

'OK then. Let's go.'

The worst times, from Mal's point of view, were when he knew Saul was missing Angie. Not that Saul ever admitted this. He seldom showed emotion of any kind. In the two months they had spent together, Mal had never seen him either laugh or cry. Occasionally, when frustrated or hurt, he would rock back and forth and emit a strange high-pitched keening noise. The first time this happened, Mal was on the point of giving up in despair. Perhaps he had been wrong to remove the child from the place and people he knew; perhaps Saul needed more than even a father could give him.

Luckily Hopi had been present on that occasion. She just said, 'Show him you love him, Mal. That's all he needs.'

Mal was not sure if the feeling he had for Saul at that moment could accurately be described as love but he attempted to give the child a hug. Saul wriggled away and swore at him before running off.

'He'll come round,' said Hopi placidly. 'Don't worry.'

'How can you know it will work out?'

'He's with you now. You're his dad and he's got a real home. He just doesn't believe it yet.'

Kate was less optimistic. She had never thought that by moving in with Mal she'd end up caring for a small boy. Especially not a small boy who seemed to enjoy nothing better than the chance to start a row between her and Mal. Of course, she felt sorry for the child, but she also thought he brought most of his troubles on himself. She kept hoping Mal would tire of the whole fatherhood thing and send him back to his mother, where he belonged. On the evening that she and Hopi made up 'The Ballad of the Irate Man', she came back to the lorry and found Mal curled up asleep on the floor with his head on Saul's duvet. The boy's fists, tightly clenched even in sleep, brushed against Mal's stubble-dark cheek. She felt excluded and, annoyed, picked up a sleeping bag and went to spend the night in Hopi's trailer.

George was so excited by the incident at the wood that he forgot to brake in time and nearly drove across Caro's late-flowering asters beside the Lodge. Since Suzie had just got back from school he found them both in the kitchen, cosily drinking tea and discussing the day's events.

'Quick, quick, no time to waste,' he announced, 'get the Range Rover, Caro, hurry up, there's a good girl.'

'What is it, Daddy? Has your car broken down?'

'No, no. Car's fine. Need to get the wood though. Must get it all before they come back.'

'Wood? What wood? Do sit down, Daddy. Your blood pressure will go through the roof. I'll pour you a cup of tea and you can tell me what's—'

'No time for tea, woman. Can't you see? This is a crisis, for God's sake. I just caught a bunch of those frightful traveller people trying to steal logs from the Haddeley Wood. Can you imagine the sheer bloody impudence? I set them straight soon enough. Sent them away with a flea in their ear.'

'I'll phone Wyndham then. It's his wood. Let him deal with it.'

George's face broke into a grin of sheer delight. 'They think it's mine. I told them it was my wood.'

Caro asked, 'Why on earth did you do that?'

Suzie sighed and rested her head on her hand. She was frowning.

George said blithely, 'Thought it was the simplest way to get rid of the buggers. Now we must see it through, go back and get the logs. Bloody great pile of them. You might as well have them, Caro.'

'There's no room here, Daddy. We've just had a load delivered.'

Suzie asked, 'Why should we have the wood and not them?'

George and Caro both turned to look at her. Suzie could feel herself beginning to blush. She persevered, 'Why did you tell them it was your land, Grandpa?'

'Emergency situation, Suzie,' explained George. 'Must stop people like that taking other people's stuff. Couldn't let them get away with stealing.'

'But if we're going to go and take it, isn't that stealing just the same?'

'Of course not. Sale's our friend,' said George. 'Couldn't be more different.'

'But—'

Caro said, 'Suzie, do stop being difficult, there's a dear.'

George was staring at his granddaughter with affectionate bewilderment. He said, 'Buck up, Suzie. You can give us a hand.'

'No,' Caro spoke decisively, 'I'm sure she's got homework. I'll go with you to get the logs and then we'll take them to Wyndham. Suzie's right, the logs belong to him.'

'Damn fuss,' George was getting increasingly peeved that his coup had not been appreciated. 'You're both missing the point. The point is that Sale's a sensible chap and he wouldn't want a bunch of dropouts capering around on his land and helping themselves to his logs. Doesn't mean to say he wants the stuff himself. Can't understand why you don't see the point, Caro.'

George and Caro were still bickering as they went out to the garage and climbed into the Range Rover. Caro had to come back in again a moment later for an old blanket to protect the interior of the car from bits of bark. She found Suzie still staring moodily into space.

'Will you be all right here on your own for twenty minutes?'

'I suppose so,' she said, and then added, 'but it's not like Grandpa to be so mean.'

'Don't exaggerate, Suzie,' said Caro, 'Wyndham is sure to approve, so you don't need to worry about it at all.'

Silence enveloped the house as the Range Rover's engine faded into the distance. There's a different kind of silence in a house with no one else in it, Suzie thought. If her father had been working in his study, for instance, instead of out somewhere, the house would have been just as silent, but it wouldn't have felt so silent. This distinction had never occurred to her before.

Nor had it ever occurred to her before to imagine that anything her parents or grandparents did might ever be not completely right and admirable. She was so used to always being the person who forgot to clean out the bath, or write thank-you letters quickly enough, or say the right things at the dinner table, or do homework in time, that she'd barely had the chance to be critical of anyone around her. Not that she felt critical exactly just now. Rather, there was a feeling deep inside her that her mother and grandfather had gone off in a wrong direction. It made her feel lopsided and miserable. Being in the wrong had always been bad enough. To her surprise feeling that those you loved weren't in the right seemed almost worse.

9

A grey wash of cloud and the scent of mild autumnal air.

That morning, Lydia had woken early and opened her rickety bedroom window to watch the morning light fan out across the sky. The swallows were nowhere to be seen: had they migrated already, she wondered, or were they simply absent for a while on a practice run? No sign of the goldfinches either. Lydia realised she didn't know if they were migrants, like the swallows, or if they'd grit the winter out like loyal robins on Christmas cards. A large black bird – a rook, or crow, she assumed – cawed at her disapprovingly from a high tree. She thought, I bet you'll stay. You don't look the sort to head off for the self-indulgent pleasures of a southern winter. You'll stay and relish being miserable. The bird wobbled slightly on his branch, then spread his wings and flew away, still complaining hoarsely.

Good riddance, thought Lydia, closing the window against the morning chill. But then she realised that, unusually, she also was content to remain where she was. Her chronic restlessness had subsided to a level where it had become almost possible to ignore it completely. And she'd hardly been bored in over a week.

Not since she visited the Hollows; not since she began work at Haddeley Hall. She had forgotten the sensual satisfaction of working with her hands. Even the stages that others regarded as chores were for her a pleasure, especially in a room as beautiful and as perfectly proportioned as the room at Haddeley Hall. She had learned from Mark that it was known as the steward's room because of a ghost that was occasionally spotted flitting past its fireplace. Sadly, she had not yet been honoured with a sighting – sadly, because she could have used some company other than that of the almost silent Portuguese servant who brought a silver tray with instant coffee and biscuits at regular two-hourly intervals.

Once or twice, after a few hours' work on the panelling, Lydia had stopped off at the Hollows on her way home. She remembered her original fears that if she opened the door of communication to the travellers even a fraction she would be swamped by an avalanche of needy outcasts and she was amused by the turnaround in her expectations. It was she who sought out their company. She relished their easy-going welcome and their humour. And now that she was working at Haddeley Hall, she enjoyed moving between Wyndham's world of lonely splendour and the friendly chaos at the Hollows. It helped her to preserve the picture of herself as an outsider in Briarswood, at home with everyone but belonging nowhere. Yesterday she had estimated that at her present rate of progress she would be another month just preparing the woodwork. She had wondered whether to see if Hopi or one of her friends would like to help. She was intrigued by the idea of bringing two such different worlds together.

The only drawback to the present upturn in her fortunes was that one way and another she owed most of it to Caro. For a variety of reasons, Lydia preferred not to feel indebted to Caro.

She was still debating whether to go straight to Haddeley Hall or whether to enlist some help on the way, when the cowbell by her front door clonked a couple of times.

'Come in!' shouted Lydia. Bumpkin bounced into the room looking extremely pleased with himself. Having assumed it was Jim, Lydia saw with some surprise that her visitor on this particular morning was Suzie.

'Hi,' said Lydia, 'I thought school had started again.'

'We've got the day off. Teachers being trained. Hello, Lydia. I hope I'm not interrupting you.'

'Not at all. Coffee?'

'No thanks, I'm fine.' Suzie smiled at her uncertainly. She hooked a strand of fair hair behind her ears, then pushed both hands into the pockets of her coat and hunched her shoulders. She removed her hands from her pockets again and gazed hopefully towards the empty fireplace. Lydia observed that Suzie had reached that in-between stage where the features were moving towards adulthood, but the facial expressions remained child-like. She further observed that Suzie was showing distinct signs of having come with a purpose.

'Have a seat, Suzie.'

Suzie sat.

'Make yourself at home.'

But that, clearly, was too much to ask.

Suzie looked around. The room was sparsely furnished with items that had been discarded from other houses. Lydia's attempts to make it homely had only got as far as wild flowers in a glass jar, a few postcards on a shelf, and piles of muddle on every available surface.

Suzie caught Lydia's eye, watching her. She said politely, 'It's nice here, isn't it?'

'Suits me,' said Lydia, 'so long as it doesn't rain.'

Suzie gazed at Bumpkin, who had settled down by Lydia's chair. He was regarding Lydia who had a half-finished mug of coffee in front of her. Experience had taught him that mugs of coffee often led to biscuits.

Sex. The word popped up in Lydia's mind as a possible explanation for this visit. She's come to ask about something to do with sex. Her spirits sank. She felt a twinge of sympathy for Suzie, because she could imagine Caro being fairly uninformative on the subject, but she didn't know if she was strong enough for teenage sexual angst at this time in the morning. She said, 'Do you mind if we listen to the radio for ten minutes? Dr Gordon Fairchild. It's a kind of penance I do sometimes.'

'Penance?'

'For having married the guy. Or left him. I'm not sure which.'

'Oh, of course. Please don't let me interrupt. Oh dear, we've missed the beginning. Oh dear, it's all my fault. I'm so sorry.'

'Nonsense, Suzie. It's better this way. More surreal, believe me. Listen.'

Gordon's discreetly Scottish voice . . . 'Quite natural to want to have sex with your brother, Marigold, especially if you haven't grown up in the same house. You see, Marigold, there's such a thing as the incest taboo, but since you're only twelve it is a bit young to be thinking—'

Suzie was staring at Lydia with round eyes.

'Wow,' she said.

Lydia burst out laughing. 'Yes, wow's about it.' Well, thought Lydia, that should have paved the way for your average run-of-the-mill teen problem. At least Suzie didn't have any brothers.

Suzie asked, 'Are those real people?'

'All the problems are real, but occasionally they use actors' voices. I thought Marigold sounded a bit fake, didn't you?'

'What a name, Marigold!'

'That was made up. She's probably Petunia, or something.'

'Or Blossom.' Suzie smiled at Lydia, pleased to have been able to share the joke.

'That's enough for one day,' said Lydia. 'It does pall after a bit.'

'He sounds frightfully understanding,' said Suzie. There was a wistful edge to her statement.

Here we go, thought Lydia.

Suzie was frowning at Bumpkin again. As if the dog might be persuaded to put her worries into words for her. He wagged his tail obligingly. Lydia was beginning to become impatient, and she asked, 'Is something bothering you, Suzie?'

'Well, sort of.' Suzie twisted round in the chair in an agony of indecision.

Lydia heard the familiar words, 'Would it help to talk about it?' form in her brain and she bit them back just in time. No sense going to the trouble of leaving the good doctor if she was going to start repeating all his favourite phrases.

Suzie was launching herself anyway. 'Have you been back to see the travellers? Since that first visit, I mean.'

'Yes. A couple of times.'

'They're not as dreadful as everyone makes out, are they?'

'Not the ones I've met. I can't speak for all of them. Why?'

'It's just . . . well, you see, I just thought, I mean, I want to give them some wood.'

'Wood?' Having expected sex, it took Lydia moment or two to adjust to wood. Suzie was hampered in her efforts to explain herself by a laudable reluctance to be disloyal to her grandfather, but eventually Lydia got the gist of what had happened.

She said, 'How petty.'

'I know,' said Suzie miserably, 'that was what I thought, but

Mummy and Grandpa seemed to think it was all right because travellers don't count. It's not like Grandpa to be unkind at all. You know yourself what a super man he is.'

'To his own kind.'

'What do you mean?'

'Your grandfather's an old dear but he does have a few blind spots.'

'I think they ought to be able to keep their wood, that's all. I mean, it's not as if anyone else even wants it. Mummy tried leaving it at Haddeley Hall but one of the people who works for Wyndham said he only burnt oak or some really special wood like that, and the woodshed at the Manor is full. Now it's all piled up outside our garage and Mummy complains about it every time she has to get the Range Rover out because it's in the way. And it's all rotting and mouldy. I hate to think of the poor travellers being cold just because we've got their wood. It's not fair.'

'Damn right it isn't.' Lydia was beginning to think she had underestimated Suzie. The girl had a strong sense of natural justice, and that counted for a lot as far as Lydia was concerned. 'What does Jim make of it all?'

'I don't know. I wanted to talk to him, but then I was afraid it would be like going behind Mummy's back. You know, sneaky.'

'Mm. Difficult.'

'I thought you might know what to do?'

'Me?'

'I mean, my parents are going out this afternoon. I thought maybe you could tell your friends, and they could bring their van or whatever to the Lodge. I could be there to help them load it and then—'

'Suzie, if a bunch of travellers turn up in the middle of Briarswood and start taking logs from outside your mother's garage, they'd be lynched. What if George was driving by?'

'Oh dear,' said Suzie miserably.

'Don't worry about them, they'll find the wood somewhere else. They're very resourceful.'

Suzie did not speak for a bit, then she said, 'I was wondering . . . I mean, I don't want to be a nuisance but . . . well, if you were going to the Hollows any time . . . I mean, I'd like to come too. And meet them.'

'Sure,' Lydia was so relieved at being let off early morning Sex Education that she surprised herself by saying, 'I was going over there this morning to see if anyone wanted to give me a hand at Haddeley Hall. Why don't you come too?'

10 ∫

Suzie had been abroad several times. She'd been to France and Spain and Greece and done all sorts of interesting things, but never in all her life had she been anywhere that felt half so foreign as the Hollows on that morning when she visited the travellers for the first time. It was all just as strange and different and weird as could be, and yet after about twenty minutes it seemed like the most natural place in the whole world. And the most incredible part of all was that this exotic location was less than a mile from her own home.

No one seemed particularly surprised to see her, which was a relief. She was pleased too that Lydia had suggested she leave Bumpkin behind at Rose Cottage, because there were about half a dozen dogs, some of whom did not look all that friendly, though they did no more than sniff her knees. She was also glad she happened to be wearing jeans and an old sweatshirt, as even those clothes felt a bit prissy next to the travellers'.

She realised with a twinge of embarrassment that she had been half-expecting a scene of what Mina used to mockingly call 'depravity and debauch' – people stumbling about like total zombies because of all the drugs, and lots of evidence of No Lavatories. But it wasn't in the least like that. She did meet one chap called Biff who had very short hair and tattoos and smelt rather strongly of beer, but even he turned out to be all right. He gave her a friendly grin and said, 'Hi there,' and then asked Hopi if she wanted anything from Peggy's shop – which he called 'the offie' – because he was just going to the village for sausages and tobacco. She also met Kate who was bouncy and confident with a snub nose and a mane of gingery hair, and a young man called

Frankie, who had an oval face and a dreamy, placid expression. She was disappointed that Misty and his gypsy-looking owner didn't seem to be around, but her disappointment was swept aside completely in the pleasure of meeting Hopi.

Hopi was one of those rare beings who put Suzie at her ease at once. She wasn't at all glamorous looking, far from it, but she had wonderfully sympathetic brown eyes and great heavy eyebrows, and when she smiled her whole face lit up in a way that made Suzie feel she was really important. She seemed to radiate contentment. She was sitting on the ground in the sunshine while Kate and another girl called Donna braided her hair into hundreds of tiny plaits. Every now and then they added in a bead or a bit of shell with a hole in it, or a little twist of coloured ribbon. At first Suzie thought it looked distinctly peculiar, like those birds she had seen on a nature programme who decorate their nests with bits of broken glass and feathers to attract a mate, but after a while she began to look at it differently, and thought it quite distinctive.

Lydia seemed to be quite at home there. She wandered over to the three women and joined them on the grass and introduced Suzie, who sat down as nonchalantly as she was able. They chatted for a bit about nothing very much, and then Lydia said, 'Anyone want to give me a hand for a day or two? Paying work. For cash.'

'Doing what?' asked Kate.

'Decorating. The owner of Haddeley Hall asked me to do up one of the rooms. The preparation's taking for ever. I need some help stripping the wood panelling and getting rid of the wallpaper.'

Kate pulled a face. 'I hate decorating,' she said. 'One sniff of Dulux and I run a mile. Now, if it was mixing cement—'

'I'll help,' said Hopi, 'if you can wait till tomorrow. I've got a hair appointment today.'

'So I see. Tomorrow's fine by me. I'll just be glad of some help.'

'And I could use some cash right now,' said Hopi. 'Donna's spotted this brilliant sewing machine in a junk shop near here. One of those old treadle ones. It needs a bit of work, apparently, but Biff says he can fix it. Sounds like it's just what I need.'

'Do you do a lot of sewing?' asked Suzie, surprised.

Hopi turned to her with an expression that indicated she had never been asked such an intelligent question before in her life. 'I love making things,' she said, 'especially out of materials that are going to waste. It's great to create something beautiful out of other people's rubbish. There's a friend of mine who makes brilliant sandals out of worn out car tyres. They're amazing.'

'Wow, how clever,' enthused Suzie, trying meanwhile to imagine explaining to Caro that she would like some sandals made from old tyres. Her imagination was not equal to the task. In the Lewis household discarding objects had always been regarded as a virtue, and there were few enterprises that gave Caro more satisfaction than 'a good clear out'.

'You'd be amazed what people can make out of rubbish and stuff,' said Donna, 'I used to have this really great necklace made out of ring pulls, until someone pinched it.'

'Ring pulls?'

'You know, off of beer cans. It was brilliant.'

Kate had paused in her work and was rolling herself a cigarette. Suzie noticed that her finger nails were outlined with black. 'We're like dung beetles,' Kate said. 'You know, those bugs that survive off other people's rubbish. Dead useful, dung beetles are. They clean up after everyone else.'

'Speak for yourself,' protested Donna, 'I'm not a bloody dung beetle.'

'Ouch,' said Hopi, 'you're pulling my hair.'

'Sorry,' said Donna.

'It's going to look beautiful,' ventured Suzie, 'when it's finished.'

'Thanks,' said Hopi. She smiled at Suzie as if her opinion was more important than anyone's.

Donna smiled at her as well. 'I could do yours like this if you want. Your hair's long enough.'

Suzie swallowed hard before answering. 'That's really kind of you, Donna. But I think my mother would probably die of shock.'

'I can imagine,' said Donna with a grin. 'Mothers frequently do. You'd be amazed how quickly they come round, though.'

Not mine, thought Suzie.

'Not Hopi's,' said Kate. 'Nothing shocks your mum, does it, Hopi? She probably pioneered this way of doing hair.'

'Is that true?' asked Suzie.

'I don't know about the hairstyle, she was Afro for years. But she's not what you'd call a typical mother. Original sixties hippy stock, I am. I guess that makes me just another boring old conformist, carrying on the family tradition. It's my little sister who's the rebel. She works in a tax office and she and her boyfriend are saving for a deposit on a new home before they set a date for their wedding. My poor mum keeps wondering where she went wrong. Oh yes, and she's changed her name to Joan.'

'What was it before?' asked Lydia.

'Blossom. A much better name, don't you think?'

Suzie caught Lydia's eye and they both burst out laughing. 'I sure hope you don't have any brothers,' said Lydia.

'No, just me and Blossom – I mean Joan,' said Hopi, not really understanding the joke, but laughing all the same.

A small figure had moved up to join them. Suzie recognised the peaky-faced urchin who had sworn at Mina in the wood, and she felt rather guilty at the memory of how Mina had sworn back at him, but he didn't even condescend to look at her.

'Where's my dad then?' he said in an accusing voice to no one in particular. He made it sound as though he blamed them collectively for his father's absence.

Kate's normally cheerful face was shadowed with irritation. 'You know exactly where he's gone, Saul. Mal only asked you about a hundred times if you wanted to go with him and every time you told him to stuff it.'

Hopi was more sympathetic. 'I expect he'll be back soon. He's gone with Terry to get a new alternator for the van. They won't be long.' She turned to Suzie with a smile that seemed to embrace them both. 'This is Saul. He's got the day off school today.'

'Hello, Saul,' said Suzie politely, 'I'm off school too.'

'School's bloody horrible,' declared Saul.

'Mm. I don't care for it much either, but I suppose one has to go.'

'Why?' asked Kate. 'There's loads of stuff he can learn around here – how to fix cars and nature and making things. Much better than learning the names of all the rivers in Africa, for goodness' sake. I don't see why Mal has to make such a big thing of it.'

Hopi said gently, 'I think he wants Saul to have both kinds of education.'

'Waste of time, if you ask me,' Kate was adamant. 'I never learnt anything in school except how to skive off without being noticed. The other kids just pick on him anyway. He spends all his time bloody fighting.'

'Which class is he in?' asked Lydia.

'Infants,' said Kate, and then added, more vaguely, 'I think.'

Lydia watched the progress on Hopi's hair. Kate had finished her cigarette and began to plait three impossibly small strands. Unlike Donna, who worked with delicate skill, Kate's handiwork looked like frayed rope. When the job was finished it would be easy to attribute each plait. The reference to the other children picking on Saul had struck an old familiar chord. Right now he was muttering to himself and making jabbing motions with a small stick at an imaginary enemy. Lydia was beginning to find something touching about his lonely belligerence, and she remembered Caro's suggestion that she help with the younger readers at the school. She smiled wryly to herself: altogether too galling if she ended up following all Caro's well-meaning advice.

Saul flung down his stick and scowled in Suzie's direction. 'You go to school?' he asked.

'Yes.'

'What's wrong with you then? Aren't you a grown-up?'

'Not really. I'm fifteen.'

'Do you have to go then?'

'Afraid so.'

Saul was silent for a few moments, scrutinising this oversized schoolchild. Then he announced suddenly, 'I've got a Real Dad.'

Suzie was uncertain of the correct reply to this statement, so she merely smiled at him politely and nodded. Saul's frown deepened. He said, 'Me and my Real Dad live in a lorry-house.'

'Really? That sounds great.'

'It's like a proper house, only it's a lorry.' Saul appeared anxious that she might not have understood his earlier statement. 'It's better than a house, really, because you can move about and not get stuck in the same stupid place all the time. And I've got my own proper bed. He made it for me. Do you want to see it?'

Oh dear, thought Suzie, how embarrassing. She said, 'That's very kind of you, Saul. I'd really love to see it some time, only it would be rude to go into your dad's lorry-house without asking him first.'

The subtlety of this was lost on Saul. His frown deepened to an ominous scowl. Kate glanced at him and rolled her eyes, anticipating the worst. Alarmed that she might have inadvertently sparked off a temper tantrum, Suzie said quickly, 'But I'm sure there's something else nice that we could do.'

'Like what?'

'Well, let me have a think . . .' Suzie cast around desperately. She daren't risk suggesting anything like colouring or puzzles, because he might not have any of those refinements in his lorry-house. Inspiration struck when she remembered the stream that ran along the bottom of the meadow at the edge of the wood. 'We could play Pooh-sticks,' she said brightly, 'that's always fun.'

Saul reacted with scandalised contempt. 'Poo bloody WHAT?'

'Oh no, not that sort of . . . I see what you mean . . . oh help, I thought everyone knew.' She could feel herself beginning to blush horribly. 'It's what Winnie the Pooh did. It's a game you play with sticks. We ought to have a bridge, ideally, but I'm sure we could improvise. Winnie the Pooh and his little friend Piglet used to play it.'

Kate came to Suzie's rescue. 'Winnie the Pooh is a cartoon character, Saul,' she said. 'There's a film about him. He's a kind of bear, isn't he?'

'Well, yes, but it was a book first of all,' Suzie was unable to allow the error to stand. 'Quite a famous one, actually.'

'Yeah,' said Kate, 'but it was a film too. I saw it when I was little. Winnie the Pooh and this miserable old donkey character.'

'Eeyore,' Suzie supplied the name automatically. It had never occurred to her that there were children growing up in this country who didn't have Winnie the Pooh at bedtime. Was it perhaps possible Saul had never heard of Peter Rabbit either?

'I read it. Or maybe we had it on a story tape,' said Hopi. 'I think Bloss and I used to play Pooh-sticks too. It was quite fun. I'd forgotten all of that.'

'Dumb poo game.' Saul was jabbing the pointy end of his stick into the log Hopi was sitting on. 'That's rude.' But Suzie could tell he was interested.

Suddenly the child's face altered, and began to look almost radiant despite its abiding scowl. An old Cortina had lurched to a halt just inside the gateway, and two men climbed out. Suzie noticed with a little leap of excitement that one of them was the youth with the white dog. It tumbled out of the car behind him and began dancing around him and barking loudly. Several nearby voices were raised telling it to shut up. The second man was older, with little round glasses and the beginnings of a beard. He walked over to his son, who hid his pleasure by punching his father's knee and saying crossly, 'You fuckin' took your time.'

'Don't swear, Saul. I've told you before, it's bad manners. We've been going round the breakers' yards looking for a new alternator. You should have come with us. Hello, Lydia. Good to see you again.'

'Hi. This is my friend Suzie.'

'Hello, Suzie. I'm Malcolm.'

Suzie couldn't help noticing that the white dog and its owner had disappeared down the opposite end of the field. She wanted to crane her neck to see what they were doing, but was afraid that everyone would recognise her motive.

She was also anxious that Saul might remember his intention to show her his lorry-house, and though she was curious to see inside one of the strange-looking vehicles, she didn't want to appear nosy. But all the boy said was, 'Come on then. Let's go and play that pooey stick game.'

Suzie smiled weakly at Mal. 'Pooh-sticks,' she explained.

'Sounds great.' When Mal smiled, as he did now, his face became warm and approachable, and really quite good-looking, Suzie thought. He ruffled Saul's hair and said, 'You must have made a real hit with him. He's not usually friendly with new people. You're honoured.'

Suzie's pleasure at being praised wore off after a few minutes of playing Pooh-sticks with Saul. By then she had come to the conclusion that the only honour involved was that Saul had seen her as an easy touch. There was no sign of a bridge anywhere, so she devised a race from one stretch of the stream where the water gurgled along at a brisk pace, to a wider part further down where it slowed almost to a standstill. This should have made judging the winner fairly straightforward, but Saul, as soon as he had grasped the basic principles of the game, displayed an awesome determination to win at all costs, and if Suzie's stick showed any sign of moving into the lead he devised a way of holding it up, either by blocking its progress or removing it from the race entirely. Once he found another stick, similar in appearance to his own, and sped down the bank to place it near the finish ahead of hers. On another occasion, when her stick escaped all his best strategies and won, he claimed it was his own. All this was done with a stealth and lack of obvious emotion which would have done a poker player proud. After about five minutes Suzie was beginning to get rather fed up with being beaten all the time, and she thought that if this was how he behaved at school then it wasn't surprising the other children picked on him. She found herself wondering who his mother was. She didn't think it was Kate, or either of the other two, because none of them seemed to be obviously maternal, but then that might explain why he was such a difficult little boy. All in all, he wasn't much of an advertisement for bringing children up the traveller way.

'Six-nil to me,' said Saul. 'Let's do it again.'

'It certainly isn't six-nil, because you keep cheating. Just one more time, and this time, no interfering with the sticks. OK?'

Saul set off back to the start of the race with a gleam in his eye. They chose their sticks.

'One, two, three – Go!' said Suzie, but Saul had flung his stick in the water before she'd even finished saying 'one' and he whizzed off along the bank to wangle another victory.

Somewhat wearily, Suzie began to follow him.

'Hi, there.' A man's voice, just behind her shoulder.

Spinning round in alarm, Suzie came face to face with the owner of the white dog. She must have been so absorbed in her game with Saul that she had never noticed him approach the stream. The youth was carrying an empty bucket and the pale dog was at his heels.

'Oh, hello.'

Close to, he was even more handsome than she had first thought, with his high cheekbones and sallow skin and his extraordinary almond-shaped eyes. His wiry body was covered in a black T-shirt with some kind of writing on it, loose-fitting trousers and a heavy leather belt. Suzie smiled at him shyly and then put a hand down to pat the dog's head.

'Hello, Misty,' she said.

Misty waved the white flag of her tail and then, in that really embarrassing way dogs have, she thrust her nose into Suzie's crotch. Suzie twisted her body round and tried to push her nose away with her hand while disguising her defensive gesture as a firm pat, but just at that moment Saul's voice shrilled out from further down the stream, 'You've bloody lost again!'

'Don't swear, Saul,' said Suzie, for about the twentieth time. She had decided that if his father corrected him, then she should too.

'Nine-nil to me!'

'We're not keeping score, remember,' she explained patiently, 'until you learn to play the game fairly. Let's just call it a draw.'

'Nine hundred and ninety-nine!' insisted Saul.

'What's the game?' asked the youth.

Anxious to avoid another embarrassing misunderstanding, Suzie said, 'It's a kind of race game that you play with sticks in a stream.'

'Oh, like Pooh-sticks. I used to play that with my gran.'

'Really?'

'Aren't you supposed to do it under a bridge?'

'Well, ideally, yes, you would have a bridge. But we had to improvise. Did you have the *Winnie the Pooh* books as well?'

'I suppose so.' He sounded rather vague.

Suzie said, 'Your dog's hardly green at all now,' and then she began to blush, just a little bit, at the memory of how she and Mina had spied on him when he'd set off into the wood with his shovel, and how they'd planned to kidnap his dog.

'It looked terrible, didn't it?' he said. 'Poor old Misty, she had a bit of mange. There's been a lot about this summer, apparently. Hopi got me this flowers of sulphur stuff from the chemist. You have to mix it with Fairy Liquid to stop the dogs chewing it. I suppose they like the taste.'

'Does it work?'

'It's a bit slow, but yeah, it does work in the end. Better than putting all those chemicals on that vets give you. But it makes their fur go a weird green colour for a while.'

Suzie felt ashamed. So much for gangrene, she thought.

Saul had joined them and was tugging at her sleeve. 'Come on. Time for another go.'

'No, Saul.' If Suzie had learnt anything from being Caro's daughter, it was the vital importance of firmness and consistency. 'That really was the last race.' Out of the corner of her eye she could see Lydia stand up and look over in her direction. She had a helpless feeling, like trying to hold sand when it slithers through your fingers. 'I suppose I ought to go now, anyway.' The words sounded so final. She had to find something to say to this man. She might never see him again in her whole life, might never again meet anyone half so interesting and sensitive-looking and altogether remarkable. Here she was, with the one chance to say something that would change her world for ever, and her pathetic brain had gone completely and absolutely numb.

He said, 'I've seen you in the village, haven't I? Do you live there?'

'Yes, at the Lodge, actually. It's that rather ugly Victorian box right by the road.' That was how her mother always described their home to people, but it didn't sound terribly accurate, in this context. She was beginning to feel ill with misery at her own feebleness.

'I thought I recognised you,' he said, and smiled.

Suzie's heart skipped. He remembered their meeting. Their first encounter had been memorable. Maybe she had made some kind of impression on him after all. Maybe he had noticed something special about her that everyone else had missed until this moment. Maybe he had even thought about her afterwards, the way she had thought about him. Maybe he also had wondered if they would ever see each other again. Just thinking about the possibilities was the most incredible glorious happiness. She wanted this amazing meeting to last for ever, but she was so afraid of saying the wrong and stupid thing, like she always did, that she was in a panic to escape.

She said, 'Mm. Well, I'd better be going. I think my friend is leaving now.'

He nodded. Without doubt it was a friendly nod. 'See you around,' he said, and began to dip his bucket into the stream.

'Yes. See you around.'

Lydia and Suzie walked as far as Ted Sedden's farmhouse together. Suzie could hardly stop talking for excitement. When they reached the road where they had to go their separate ways, Lydia laughed at her enthusiasm and said, 'Don't go rushing to extremes, Suzie. Just because they're not the monsters some people make them out to be, doesn't mean they're a bunch of plaster saints. Just ordinary people. Like you and me.'

'I suppose so.'

Lydia could tell that Suzie was far from convinced. She raised a single eyebrow and teased, 'I see you met Terry then.'

'Mm,' said Suzie, then mumbled a hasty good-bye and thank you and headed off back towards the Lodge before Lydia could detect her giveaway blush.

Terry. So that was his name. She felt a great bubble of excitement growing inside her and pressing against her ribs.

Terry.

Never before, thought Lydia, had she had a job which was such a pleasure to travel to. She had a choice of routes: across the centre of the village and over the fields to the park, or round the little back lanes behind the church and across the cricket pitch, or, as this morning, the main road and the long, tree-bordered driveway. Besides which there was the work itself to look forward to, so many plans to consider, that she was lost in thought and did not notice the car until it pulled to a halt in front of her.

As usual, Wyndham was at the wheel: he had told Lydia before of his dislike of chauffeurs for everyday driving. She walked to the right hand side; the window sank noiselessly. Wyndham's face looked up at her. He did not smile.

'You're usually at work by ten,' he said coolly, 'I was beginning to wonder what had happened to you.'

'The deal was flexi-time, remember?' Lydia was annoyed by his implied reproach, 'Besides, regular working hours are a legacy of the industrial revolution and improvements in clock design. Both of which have probably done more harm to working people than good. I stick to my own routines.'

'I'm obliged to you for the history lesson.'

Lydia grinned. 'Actually my time this morning has not been wasted. I've been drumming up extra troops. Well, one extra troop, as it turned out.'

'You need help? You should have told me.'

'It wasn't critical. And Hopi has agreed to help out for a couple of days.'

'Hopi?'

'She's one of the group at the Hollows.'

The expression on Wyndham's normally impassive face was as eloquent as his silence.

'You'll like her, Wyndham.'

'There you are wrong,' he stated, 'for the simple reason that I won't meet her. I have to go east for a few days. I should be back the middle of next week.'

Lydia knew by now that when Wyndham spoke about 'going east' he did not mean Edleston, or even London. East was Hong Kong and Singapore.

He continued, 'If you run into any problems, Mark should be able to deal with them. In a real emergency, he always knows how to get hold of me.'

'There won't be any problems, Wyndham. Not with Hopi.'

'I'm sure you know what you're doing.'

'As a matter of fact, I do.'

'In future, however, you will check with me before making any decision affecting the work being done in my house.'

'This decision doesn't affect the work, only how long it takes.'

'I would have thought—' Wyndham began, then broke off, his thought remaining unexpressed. A flicker of annoyance danced around his eyes. He put his hand on the ignition key, then turned once more to look up at her, but this time, suddenly and unexpectedly, his face lit up with that rare and disarming smile. 'Too much shop-talk. How about supper when I get back?'

After their previous exchange, his question took Lydia by surprise, the more so because of the tentative way it had been voiced, as though he feared a refusal. Never mix work and social life, she told herself. She had had enough disastrous affairs with employers to last any woman a lifetime.

'I'd like that,' she answered, hoping she had made the words sound suitably non-committal.

'So would I,' he spoke with sudden sincerity. 'Good-bye, then. And don't work too hard.'

'Not much chance of that,' said Lydia with a grin.

As he drove away, Lydia found herself wondering about that startling shift to vulnerability. Given the satisfaction on his face as he bid her farewell, she suspected it was probably a strategy he had perfected over the years to wrong-foot the opposition.

Perhaps he used it sometimes with business associates as well. She could imagine it being highly effective in all manner of situations.

To her surprise, Lydia found she much preferred to think of him as manipulative, rather than sincere. It fitted her picture of their relationship. She was beginning to enjoy their cool, undemanding encounters. Wyndham was appealing in the way that cats are appealing; his charm was all of the aloof variety. You will suffice, he seemed to be saying, but only because you happen to be convenient.

After the emotional morass of her years with Gordon, Lydia was ready for a change of pace. She persuaded herself that Wyndham would have been quite unmoved had she turned him down just now. It meant she had no power to inflict injury on him; and if she could not hurt him, then it surely followed that he could not hurt her, either.

Joining the dual carriageway just beyond Briarswood, Wyndham placed a Bellini aria on the CD player and allowed himself a few minutes to analyse the question of Lydia Fairchild before turning his attention to more important business. Irrespective of whether she eventually became his mistress or not, he found himself pleased that she was involved, if only in a minor capacity, in the progress at Haddeley Hall. His staff were loyal and efficient, but they had not even begun to fill the gap left by Annabel's death. There had been no other sources of comfort or distraction, since Wyndham had, over the years, studiously cultivated an absence of either family or friends. Business associates he had in abundance, but closer ties he had always found messy and time-consuming, and therefore best avoided. He was most comfortable in relationships where there was a financial nexus. The fact that Lydia was in his pay was reassuringly familiar, but she had been a social contact before she became his employee.

On balance, he rather hoped Lydia would become his mistress. It would mark a stage in his recovery; the crippling legacy of bereavement had dragged on quite long enough. Lydia was endowed with an energy and irreverence which he found most attractive. He knew he would enjoy lavishing attention on her, taking her out for expensive meals, seeing her wear the clothes and jewellery he could buy for her. Most of all, he thought, it would be good to feel her bare arms around his back, press his flesh against hers and lose himself in her body, and thus wipe out that ache of absence which had gnawed at him for nearly half a year.

A possibility darted into his mind: maybe it had been longer than that. Maybe the emptiness had been there all along, but he had only just now become aware of it. This idea was so unwelcome that he dismissed it as yet another of those morbid fancies that had plagued him since his wife's death. Quite ridiculous. He removed the operatic CD, replaced it with some bracing Baroque strings and turned his attention to the business meeting he had set up for later in the day, and its intended outcome.

For Caro, it had been a morning of rare happiness.

A trip to London was always a terrific treat: a chance to whirl around the shops, have her hair cut by a first-rate stylist and catch up with her daughters. Or, as today, a chance to catch up with her eldest daughter. Kate and Emily were both busy working in obscure locations like Enfield or Wandsworth, but lucky Polly had a wealthy husband and was a lady of formidably-financed leisure.

One-thirty found Caro and her eldest daughter dining in a chic restaurant just off Bond Street. The initial euphoria that had sustained Caro through the morning was beginning to wear off and a little niggle of anxiety was making its presence felt at the pit of her stomach. She had downed a large sherry in an attempt to subdue her worries, but there was no getting away from the fact that this did seem to be a wildly expensive venue. Caro had suggested a salad in one of the large department stores, John Lewis, or Dickins & Jones, but Polly had dismissed this with a languid, 'Oh Mummy, don't be such a frump,' and had led her to this oasis of deference and luxury. 'After all,' Polly told her, 'we don't have the chance of a little tête-à-tête very often. Might as well spoil ourselves.'

Caro allowed herself the faint hope that this final phrase indicated Polly's intention to go Dutch, but knowing her eldest, this had to remain the very faintest of hopes.

Polly was a daughter any mother could be proud of. She had inherited all the best features from both sides of the family: Jim's slim build, Twinks' amazing pale green eyes, George's easy-going personality and – Caro allowed herself a little credit here – her own practical abilities. The only slight drawback to an outing like this was that Polly had a tendency – which Caro always forgot about the moment they parted – to make her mother feel like a somewhat overweight and foolish country cousin. Caro had dressed that morning with scrupulous care: a navy jacket, pleated check skirt and ruffled blouse, with a pair of court shoes that she knew she could tramp the shops in quite comfortably all day, an outfit that had seemed, at eight o'clock that morning, to combine style with timeless elegance. Now, sitting among these needle-thin girls in their designer neutrals, she felt florid and out of place, like a large and brightly-coloured dahlia plonked down amid elegant stems of willow.

To add to her problems, Caro didn't always know how to keep the conversation flowing with Polly, whose lovely eyes had a tendency to glaze over at the mention of the latest doings in Briarswood. It was much easier when they were actually shopping together because then there was always plenty to discuss. Already that morning Polly had bought herself a jacket costing over three hundred pounds because she thought 'it might come in useful, one can never have too many jackets', and Caro had been so awed by this carefree attitude that she had recklessly bought herself an aubergine wool dress which Polly told her was the sort of thing she ought to wear more often. It had been so expensive – though not, thank heavens, nearly as much as Polly's jacket – that Caro had tried to forget the price as soon as her credit card flew out of her hand, but now, as Polly was explaining to her, she would need to get a pair of shoes to wear with it. Classic courts, apparently, would destroy the effect. The worm of anxiety wriggled a little deeper. Over coffee Caro began hoping that Polly might offer to pay the entire bill. After all, her husband Angus was something important in film distribution and Polly could probably put it down to expenses. She remembered now that when Jim had dropped her off at the station that morning she had promised him she'd be positively miserly in her spending and Jim had said, with a relieved smile,

'Yes, do try, darling. We need to draw in our horns a bit.' Another hint that he was heading for one of his periodic fits of financial fussing. Of course it would have been unforgivably dreary to mention any of this to Polly.

Instead she ventured, 'I'm a bit worried about Suzie.'

Polly removed a pack of cigarettes from her bag. An ashtray materialised at once. Caro was always impressed by the limpet-like attentiveness that her eldest inspired in the most hardened waiters.

'It's her age, I suppose,' Caro continued, 'but she just doesn't seem to have much interest in anything. And she hasn't made any proper friends since we moved to Briarswood. Just mopes around all the time.'

'Oh,' said Polly. A tall woman had entered the restaurant and Polly was wondering where she had bought her black jacket and trousers.

'Sometimes I feel so aware of the age gap,' Caro was frowning. 'You know, being an older mother. It's hard to be on the same wavelength.'

Polly's gaze floated briefly across her mother's face and she said, 'Mm,' as though confirming Caro's deepest fears, then tilted her face to blow smoke towards the ceiling.

'And now she seems to have struck up a friendship with that old student of Daddy's. Do you remember her?'

Polly shook her head. She was watching a short, ugly, old man who was beginning to argue across a small table with the woman in the stunning trouser suit.

'Lydia Allen, I'm sure you remember her, she helped Daddy with that poor student who was going to be deported. Well, of course, she's Fairchild now, married a doctor who does radio programmes, only she's left him for some reason and come to Briarswood. She's all right, I suppose, but I wish Suzie would find some friends of her own age.'

Polly was suddenly examining her mother's face with such close attention that Caro wondered if perhaps she had some crumbs on her cheek. 'Lydia Allen? What's she doing in Briarswood?'

Caro patted her face with the napkin. 'Nothing at all, as far as I can make out, except complain about Rose Cottage, which is a bit rich considering she's hardly paying any rent.'

'You don't like her, then.'

'It's not that I dislike her, exactly. More that I don't see her as a particularly good influence for Suzie just now. She's one of those people who make a point of being different about everything. Like going down to visit the travellers at Ted Sedden's farm and then talking about it as if she thought everyone ought to do it.' Polly's attention was wandering again, but Caro struggled on, 'Which is pretty disloyal, considering we all think they ought to go and find somewhere else to live. I just don't want her filling Suzie's head with silly ideas.'

Polly heard the distress in her mother's voice. 'Why, has Suzie gone to visit these travellers too?'

'Heavens, no!' Caro laughed. 'Far too sensible for that.' Polly was stubbing out her cigarette. 'Actually, I thought maybe Suzie could come and stay with you and Angus for a few days at half term. I'm sure the change would do her good.'

'Mm,' said Polly. The argument between the very ugly man and his elegant companion had reached an interesting stage. She was wondering if he was going to punch her in the jaw or whether she would chuck her glass of champagne in his face first. 'Out of the question, I'm afraid. Angus would throw a fit.'

'Oh dear, it would be the last week in October. I thought maybe—'

'And, oh God, sorry, I just remembered, we've got decorators coming next week. So no spare room. Perhaps another time. I'm sure you don't need to worry about Suzie.'

'I expect you're right.'

Polly was congratulating herself on a narrow escape. She didn't mind her other two sisters, so long as she didn't have to see them too often, but Suzie was practically a stranger. Polly had already been on the brink of leaving home when her mother, with exquisite bad timing and lack of thought for others, had got herself pregnant. It was a period of appalling embarrassment for Polly who had just begun bringing boyfriends to the house, and suddenly there was her mother, large as a whale and flopping about the house in frightful flowered maternity dresses and endlessly complaining about heartburn. Polly had moved into her own flat as soon as she could, but on weekends when she came home for some looking after and good home cooking, all she got was sleepless nights and a mother far more exhausted than she had ever been. The whole business had been most unfair. Of course, Suzie had been a dear little thing and Polly had become quite fond of her over the years – but not to the point where she wanted her lolling about their Islington house over every half term. She had her own life to lead without doubling up as a surrogate mother to her youngest sister. Especially as Angus was going away during that week and she was hoping to see a good deal of Simon. Polly glanced at her watch with a sense of having had a narrow escape.

Trying not to let her disappointment show, Caro took the hint. 'Best be making a move, I suppose.' She waited for a fraction of a moment before saying, with greater cheeriness than she now felt, 'I'll ask them for the bill, shall I?'

'Mummy, how sweet of you.' Polly glanced towards the waiter, who sprang over to their table at once. She noted with some disappointment that the mismatched couple appeared to have resolved their argument, and did not see Caro's appalled expression as she read the bill.

Polly smiled at her mother kindly. 'Now, let's see about finding you some shoes, shall we?'

Caro was on the point of saying that she thought they had better leave that for her next London trip, when there was a sudden shriek from a nearby table, pandemonium as the small, ugly man was assisted by several staff all flapping napkins in the region of his groin.

'Oh, poor man,' exclaimed Caro, 'he's spilled his soup.'

'He's out of his league,' said Polly, with some satisfaction, as they emerged from the restaurant and she steered her mother firmly in search of the ultimate pair of shoes.

Sandra was on the point of handing in her notice. She could put up with being patronised, underpaid and, occasionally, overworked – but she drew the line at being electrocuted.

She had been dusting the drawing room, as she always did on a Wednesday morning. All had proceeded smoothly enough until she touched the ormolu clock that stood on the sideboard. The moment her finger tip made contact with its ornamented surface, she felt a ringing blow to the back of her head and she sprang into the air.

Twinks, who happened to have wandered into the drawing room at that precise moment to search for her reading glasses, observed her vertical take-off with astonishment. 'Whatever are you doing, Sandra?'

It was a moment or two before she received any reply. Sandra laid a hand across her heaving breasts and sank down into a pale blue chair. 'It's the clock,' she finally gasped. 'There's something wrong with the clock.'

Dutifully, Twinks went to peer at the innocently ticking clock.

'There must be a fault,' Sandra was insisting in a faint voice, 'I think it shorted on me.'

'Nonsense, dear,' Twinks reproached her. 'It's not an electrical clock, you know, not in the eighteenth century. I expect it was just your nerves.'

'But I know—'

Twinks laid a frail hand on the surface of the sideboard and prepared to be firm. Dealing with staff was something she had done all her life: irate cooks, hysterical maids, dishonest gardeners, uppity chauffeurs, she had coped with them all in her time. Now, on the whole, it was appliances that caused the most trouble – washing machines that refused to function, that sort of thing – but even a two-hours-a-morning girl like Sandra was bound to be fanciful occasionally.

'Now, look here, Sandra—' Twinks broke off abruptly. She had observed a curious wire emerging from the back of the clock, a wire she did not remember ever having noticed before. 'How extraordinary,' she murmured, 'I can't think what—' And then she fell silent, as slowly the veil of fog which so often enveloped her these days parted sufficiently for her to think precisely what . . . 'Just a moment, Sandra dear,' she said, quite gently now, and, leaving the drawing room she crossed the hall to George's study and entered at once. George, who was reading about a device for trapping moles, was not pleased at the interruption.

'The clock, George,' Twinks' voice was as serene as ever. 'What have you been doing to the clock?'

Prepared to be angry, George said at once, 'Like to have some peace and quiet in my own—' But Twinks interrupted him.

'Poor Sandra could have had a very nasty accident. What have you been doing to Aunt Anne's clock?'

'Ah,' said George. 'Yes.' He sat very still for a few moments and then turned aside to fondle Hamish's ears. 'Forgot about that.'

'Forgot about what? Really George, this is too bad, the poor girl simply shot up in the air like I don't know what.'

George stood up. 'Simple error,' he said. 'Should have switched the system off when I came down this morning. Just a few precautions I've been working on. Now that bunch have moved in at the Hollows, one can't be too careful.'

He wanted to find out from Sandra how powerful the impact had been, but when he saw how shaken she was, he decided it was better to say nothing very much just at present.

Twinks said, 'A little brandy, I think. This has been a frightful upset for both of us, Sandra.'

But it took more than brandy. Twinks had to promise to put up her wages, and George was supervised while he dismantled his entire system, which put him into an extremely bad temper. He felt secretly that Sandra's accident had provided him with valuable proof concerning optimum voltage but Twinks, with unusual firmness, would have none of it. That afternoon a home security specialist was contacted and the next day a young man came to the Manor and recommended an extremely complicated system of internal security alarms and infra red sensors which, Twinks realised with some dismay, would make coming downstairs in the middle of the night for a little something to help her sleep an alarmingly complex operation. Just to be on the safe side, she fell into the habit of taking a small bottle of spirits to her bedroom in the evening concealed in the folds of her cardigan or dressing gown. Since George was not always reliably sympathetic to her needs, she kept the bottles tucked away out of sight in her jewellery box and hidden among the moisturisers and anti-wrinkle creams in her vanity case.

'Better safe than sorry, Veronica Jane,' as dear Miss Finn always used to say.

12

Lydia was showing Hopi round Haddeley Hall.

To her surprise Hopi rather approved of the heavy dark paint and the subterranean gloom of the endless succession of rooms: her disdain for houses clearly did not extend to large Jacobean mansions.

In a room which had 'Library' printed firmly on the door, but not a book in sight, Hopi declared, 'You could throw a great party here.'

Lydia grinned. 'I don't get the impression Wyndham is much of a party animal, somehow.'

'So what's he going to do with it all?'

'I don't know.'

'He'll have to fill it with loads of friends. A place like this would be terribly lonely all on your own.'

Lydia had never heard Wyndham mention friends. She said, 'I don't think he minds being on his own. He told me once that he preferred beautiful objects to people.'

Hopi made no answer to this and, as the tour continued, Lydia began to wonder if it had been a mistake to ask Hopi to help with the work in the steward's room. So far the difference in their styles of living had not seemed to hinder their growing friendship, but perhaps that was because their previous encounters had all been on Hopi's territory. She hoped it wasn't going to be a problem, since she felt like company, especially today. The previous night she had been troubled with uneasy dreams, which she had forgotten as soon as she awoke, but a vague sense of discomfort lingered on. There was an ache, a kind of nausea, in the base of her stomach.

She felt it was important to keep busy, and cheerful. Today of all days, for some reason, she did not want to have to work alone.

To Lydia's relief, Hopi rallied as soon as they started work. Though not fast, she proved to be a steady worker, and also, somewhat to Lydia's surprise, a devotee of Dr Gordon Fairchild's radio slot.

'We're too late this morning,' said Lydia, as her portable radio filled the room with a steady thump of music. 'We've missed him.'

'He wasn't on,' said Hopi, scraping a stubborn strip of paint, 'I listened earlier.'

'It's one of his days. He should have been.'

'They said he was indisposed.'

Lydia felt the fist of discomfort clench a little tighter in her stomach. It occurred to her that she might have developed psychic powers since coming to live at Rose Cottage. Something had happened to Gordon and that's why she was feeling so peculiar. Then she told herself not to be so stupid, it was more likely something she had eaten.

'Did you listen on Monday?' asked Hopi. Absent-mindedly, Lydia shook her head, and Hopi continued cheerily, 'This really sad woman phoned in who thought her husband must have been a closet gay all their married life. Apparently she'd started taking pills which were making her grow a moustache and it really turned him on. Their sex life had never been so good. She wanted to go to a beauty therapist and have the moustache removed, but he wouldn't hear of it.'

They were both laughing when Mrs Miguel came in without a word and set down a tray with a cafétière, milk jug, two cups and a plate of biscuits. She was a woman of great beauty and shyness who appeared to speak no English at all; at least, no one had ever heard her utter a word of either English or Portuguese. She seemed so devoid of identity that Lydia had so far been unable to learn her name.

'You've got it made here,' said Hopi as she munched her third biscuit. 'Chocolate digestives, my favourites. I think you'll have to worm your way into this Wyndham's affections so he falls madly in love with you and you can stay here for ever. And throw lots of really tremendous parties and fill the place with your friends.'

'I could live happily ever after in my beautiful palace,' agreed Lydia, 'and have masses of servants and never, ever, ever worry about money again.'

'Waste of time, worrying about money,' said Hopi dismissively. 'You'd have to do something about that maid though. She looks horribly homesick.'

'Or frightened. Maybe Mr Miguel is a bastard to her. He looks the type, doesn't he? And you could get away with anything in a place this size. The flat they live in is miles away from the main part of the house, in that modern section at the back.'

'I never noticed any modern bits.'

'Eighteenth-century. Wyndham calls it the modern part.'

Hopi giggled. 'What does he call old then?'

They resumed work. In order to keep up a flow of conversation, Lydia asked Hopi about herself.

'Have you got a boyfriend?'

'Colin. Only he's in Spain at the moment. At least I think he's in Spain and I think he's still my boyfriend. But as I haven't seen him since June, I could be wrong on both counts.'

'You don't sound very bothered about it.'

'Yes, well . . . there's good and bad to Colin. You know the sort, when he's good he's very very good and when he's bad he's horrid.' Hopi was thoughtful for a while before adding loyally, 'But I do miss him, of course.'

Lydia was not convinced. 'I'd have thought Mal was more your type.'

'Mal? He's with Kate.'

'I know. But they don't seem to have all that much in common.'

'The problem is,' said Hopi thoughtfully, 'that Mal has changed since Saul arrived on the scene. The responsibilities of parenthood and all that. And Kate is still the same old Kate. She doesn't really understand what Mal's up to with Saul. But the kid has already changed out of recognition in the last couple of months. His mum had made a real balls-up of things.'

'What's she like?'

'I can't remember. I must have met her years ago at one of the festivals, but it's all a bit of a blur. From what Mal says she's been pretty useless. Saul's only just beginning to settle down and he's been with us for nearly three months. Angie's got another child now, apparently.'

'Would you move into a house if you had a baby?' For some reason Lydia almost tripped on the final word of her question. She frowned, and concentrated hard on her work.

'No way. Much healthier in the fresh air. Houses are bad for kids, I reckon. All cooped up and isolated – ugh! I'd like to have a family one day. But not yet. What I don't understand is why someone like Saul's mum keeps producing them and not looking after them at all. Still, Mal's doing great.'

Lydia felt a spasm of pain, and hardly noticed as Hopi moved on to talk about Biff, and his struggle to overcome various kinds of addiction. She spoke, Lydia noticed, with the enthusiasm of the moral crusader. By lunchtime Lydia was beginning to think she must have developed an allergy to the paint stripper, the discomfort she felt was making it hard to continue working. She threw open all the windows and announced, 'Down tools. It's lunchtime.'

Hopi complied at once. 'What happens now?' She was looking wistfully towards the door. 'A four-course meal on gold plates?'

'Only on Sundays. I brought some sandwiches.'

'I guess I'll have to rough it, then,' said Hopi with a grin.

'It could be worse,' Lydia consoled her. 'Cheese and lettuce and—' She broke off. A few words had separated themselves from among the blur of noise coming out of the little radio in the corner of the room and printed their unwelcome message on her brain.

Today, 8 October . . .

'Oh, hell . . .'

Hopi glanced across at her. 'Lydia, are you all right?'

Lydia had heard the question, but had no power at all to answer it and anyway, the question was pitifully irrelevant. October the eighth . . . What on earth was she supposed to do now?

She wrapped her arms around her stomach and leaned her back against the section of wall she had been working on that morning. From that position it was a gentle descent to the floor.

'Sorry about this,' she mumbled, her knees drawn up, 'I'll be OK in a minute.'

'You don't look it,' said Hopi, coming to squat beside her. 'You look terrible.' In spite of everything, Lydia registered a certain relief that it was Hopi with her at this moment. 'What's happened?'

Lydia tried to explain. 'It's today . . . it should have been today, but it isn't . . .' Hopi reached her arm across Lydia's shoulders, but Lydia shrugged her off. 'Don't . . . I can't bear it. Don't touch me.'

Hopi moved a little distance away. After a few moments she asked, 'What should have been today? Can you explain?'

'I am trying, damn you,' Lydia snapped. Then, 'I'm sorry, Hopi, but it's a bit hard to—' No, not hard, impossible to say the words. She tried a different route, cleared her throat and began, 'I had a miscarriage in the spring. Today was . . . today ought to have been—' She crossed her arms above her head, hiding her face against her knees.

'Ah,' said Hopi thoughtfully, and then finished the sentence for her, 'today was the day your baby was due,' and then she added in a low voice, 'oh Lydia, that's rough.'

'Damn right it is,' Lydia's words came out awkwardly. 'And for pity's sake don't start going all sympathetic on me. I don't think I could bear it.'

'Who says you have to bear it? What's wrong with just being sad?'

'Shut up, Hopi. You're beginning to sound like Dr let-it-all-hang-out Gordon bloody Fairchild. I came here to escape from all that.'

Hopi contemplated this appeal for a short while. Lydia was still sitting against the wall, her head buried under her forearms, so it was impossible to see her face, but every line of her body was taut with the strain of not breaking down. Eventually Hopi said in a matter-of-fact voice, 'Suit yourself. Do you mind if I make a start on lunch?'

'Go ahead,' came the mumbled reply.

When Miguel brought the next tray of refreshments, his worst suspicions concerning the two women were confirmed. The manservant disapproved thoroughly of Hopi. He had learned from Mark, who also disapproved of the new arrivals, that she was one of the tramps who had moved into the village and he was shocked that such a person was allowed to enter his employer's home.

Lydia was standing by the window and gazing into the distance with an expression of deep suffering in her eyes; worse, he thought he could detect signs of tears on her cheeks. Dramatics, when they should have been working. His outrage intensified. He vowed to be vigilant and keep his wife away from their corrupting influence.

When the door had closed once more behind his scandalised silence, Hopi ran the tip of her tongue along the edge of the cigarette paper before asking, 'Tea? Nothing like a nice cup of tea, you know, when you're feeling under the weather.'

Grateful for Hopi's flippant tone, Lydia came over to sit beside her.

'Fancy a roll-up?'

'No thanks. But I will have some tea.'

'How about a sandwich. I left you half. They were good, by the way.'

'You finish them. I'm not hungry.'

They sat for a little while without talking. The radio continued its cheery babble of music and chat, but Hopi and Lydia hardly noticed it. Legs stretched out before them, they leaned against the wood panelling, now almost completely stripped, and contemplated the round toes of their shoes. After some minutes, Lydia let out a long sigh and said, 'We ought to get back to work. Panic over. I'm OK again now.'

'Liar,' Hopi contradicted her amiably, 'you're a complete mess.'

'Maybe. But not that much more than usual.'

'I think work is over for today.'

'Don't be daft. We can get this section finished if we carry on.'

'Tomorrow. Or the next day. But today is different. Today is for you and your baby.'

'For Christ's sake, Hopi, I was just beginning to feel OK again.'

Hopi did not appear to have heard. 'There's a full moon tonight. It'll be perfect.'

'A full moon?' Lydia turned to look at her in horror. 'What are you, some kind of witch?'

'No,' said Hopi with a grin, 'though I've got a couple of friends who call themselves witches, and they're great. And I used to have a boyfriend who was a druid, but then he went kind of weird. Did you ever have a funeral for your baby?'

'Of course not. It was a miscarriage. You don't—'

'Then I think it's time to say good-bye.'

'And I think,' said Lydia as firmly as she was able, 'that is a totally despicable idea.'

'Too bad,' said Hopi.

Sometimes, when Lydia looked back on that long October afternoon, she felt embarrassed at having gone along with a pointless charade; sometimes she felt angry that Hopi had bullied her at a time when her own resistance was low. But more often she felt a kind of grudging relief, and gratitude.

They began by going back to Rose Cottage, where Hopi chivvied her into gathering up a selection of objects connected with the baby she had lost. At first Lydia protested that she didn't have any, but then she found a photograph of her parents, and an appointment card for an ante-natal check up in August which for some reason was still in her purse, and a postcard from her friend Charlotte in Minorca, congratulating her on her good fortune in being pregnant. 'Lucky you,' Charlotte had written, 'I intend lavishing all my own thwarted maternal instincts on your baby, so prepare the Bump for serious spoiling!' The card had a picture of an ancient-looking native American woman beneath a gaudy rainbow, and the words, 'We do not inherit the earth from our forefathers; we hold it in trust for our children.'

'How about this?' Lydia asked. 'It's right up your street.'

'It's beautiful,' agreed Hopi, either missing, or choosing to ignore, the sarcasm in Lydia's voice. She put the card with the other items in a cigar box which Lydia had kept for letters.

'Now what?'

'I was thinking,' said Hopi, in that gently emphatic voice that Lydia found both infuriating and a comfort at the same time, 'Last summer my friend Sasha had a baby on site—'

'On site? In a trailer? Isn't that dangerous?'

'It was a commer, actually. A commercial vehicle. Why should that make it dangerous? It's hospitals that are full of infections. You can get really ill going into hospitals.'

Lydia heard this statement with mute disbelief, and Hopi continued thoughtfully, 'Sasha had a really easy birth and the midwife was just great. She'd been doubtful to begin with and kept on about how Sasha ought to be in a maternity ward and all that, but after a couple of visits she really got into it and she brought loads of stuff for the baby. He was called Jade. We had a great party that night in Sasha's trailer, midwife and all, and the next day Sasha and I took Jade around the site we were living on and showed him all the things we thought he'd enjoy when he got older.'

'Terrific, Hopi,' said Lydia crossly as her eyes filled with tears. 'You certainly know how to cheer a person up. Just what does all this have to do with me? It might have escaped your notice, but I don't have a baby to show things to. That's the whole bloody point.'

'What I thought we'd do now is gather up some things that you would have liked to show your baby and put them in the box with the other stuff.'

'Then what?'

'Then we need to find a special, sacred place, perhaps under a holly bush, or maybe we could plant one, and lay the baby's box to rest.'

'What's so special about a holly tree?'

'The Ancient Britons saw the holly as a symbol of death and regeneration.'

Lydia groaned. 'Hopi, please. To my certain knowledge there has never been one single druid in my family.'

'Have you got a shovel? If not, we can go to the Hollows and get mine.'

In spite of her reservations, which were many and strong, Lydia discovered that she knew the exact place where she wanted the cigar box and its strange assortment of objects to be buried. Raven's Beacon was a height of land thinly planted with trees that overlooked Haddeley Hall and Briarswood.

As they were walking towards the Hollows, Lydia asked crossly, 'Where do you get all this stuff from, Hopi, all this junk about commemorating a birthday that never was?'

Hopi didn't answer straightaway and Lydia wondered if finally her scepticism had caused offence. Good riddance, she thought, then maybe we can skip the rest of the psychodrama. She was no longer certain, however, that she wanted to back out.

'We had a little brother, Blossom and me,' Hopi's voice cut into her thoughts, 'he was called Rowan and he died when he was six weeks old. It was terrible. I mean, bad enough just losing the baby, but my parents got loads of hassle from the authorities. Mum took me and Bloss to live with our grandparents for a bit because she was afraid we might get taken into care. Everyone was making out that it was our life style that caused Rowan's death, like my parents were irresponsible, or murderers. Then they did an autopsy and discovered he had some kind of heart defect and would have died anyway, even if we'd been living in Buckingham Palace. So we went back to Dad, but it was all too much for Mum. She got really depressed for a while and the doctor wanted to put her on tranquillisers or anti-depressants or something like that. But my dad didn't believe in all that chemical crap. Then on the day Rowan would have been a year old, Dad made a cake and a little wooden boat for a present for him, and he got Mum to find something, a rattle, I think it was. And he sent me and Bloss out to pick flowers. We just thought it was a game to begin with, except that Mum was so upset about it all. And then we had this celebration, kind of a birthday party and a funeral all at once, and Dad said stuff about birth and death and how close they are. It did seem kind of weird at the time, but Mum started to get better from then on. We carried on celebrating Rowan's birthday for years. I guess that's what gave me the idea.'

Lydia turned to Hopi, but she forgot her caustic comment when she saw that the tip of Hopi's nose had turned bright pink and her eyes were blurred with tears.

'Oh well,' she conceded, 'maybe it's not such a bad idea at that.'

They walked the rest of the way to the Hollows in silence.

Just as Lydia was becoming reconciled to the whole business, she discovered to her horror that about half the inhabitants of the Hollows were going to join in as well, probably because they didn't have anything better to do, and fancied a walk to the top of Raven's Beacon.

'Do they have to come along?' she whispered hoarsely to Hopi. 'It's turning into a circus. You never said you were going to involve all that lot as well.'

'Do you mind?' Hopi was genuinely surprised. 'Don't worry, it'll be better with more people.'

Lydia hugged her cigar box and said nothing. She was beginning to hope that none of her Briarswood acquaintances saw her among the odd-looking cavalcade which was setting off towards Raven's Beacon. On the way they paused so that Terry could dig up a small holly tree Hopi had noticed growing beside the track, and Lydia overheard Malcolm explaining to a puzzled Saul the purpose of their expedition.

'But why did the stupid baby *die*?' persisted Saul.

Good question, thought Lydia, and forgot Saul entirely until they had nearly reached the top of the hill, when she felt something sharp being pressed against the back of her hand.

'Ouch, Saul, that hurts. You shouldn't hurt people with sticks.'

'It's for the baby, stupid,' said Saul, 'for that baby box you're carrying.'

'I don't think—' began Lydia.

But Saul interrupted furiously, 'It's for things he would have liked to do, isn't it? Well, I would have taught him Pooh-sticks. It's a wicked game. Your baby would've fuckin' loved it.'

'Oh,' Lydia breathed. She felt too winded by the image Saul's words conjured up to be able to answer him straightaway and he stumped off, unsmiling as ever, to join his father.

They had reached the summit of the hill.

'How about here?' Hopi indicated a patch of rough grass a little distance from the trees.

'Fine,' said Lydia, 'anywhere. It really doesn't matter.'

'Good choice of place, Lydia,' said Malcolm.

'Good timing, too,' said Kate, her red hair flaming in the sun's brightness.

Lydia looked around. She had been so absorbed in her own thoughts that she had not been aware of much else. But she saw now that the sun which had been shining all day was huge and golden above a tiny ruffle of clouds on the horizon. A shiver ran down her spine and she gripped her cigar box tightly to her chest. Since the addition of Saul's Pooh-sticks, the lid no longer shut properly. Hopi was directing Biff to dig a hole while half a dozen dogs were dancing excitedly around a bramble thicket and barking with excitement. Their owners yelled at them to make less noise.

Hopi took up a position opposite Lydia on the far side of the freshly-dug hole and most of the rest formed a rough circle between them. Lydia began to feel distinctly apprehensive. She thought of putting the wretched cigar box in the hole and leaving them to get on with whatever form of mumbo-jumbo they had in mind, but she found she was unable even to contemplate giving up the cigar box. It felt welded to her hands. She glanced down at the lid in disbelief. My little Havana baby, she thought, full corona and extra fine, I don't want to let you go.

Hopi had begun talking in her usual low-pitched and slightly flat voice. 'We've all come here to say good-bye to Lydia's baby who should have been born on this day . . .' Lydia shut her ears to the rest and put all her energy into not breaking down. To her intense relief it wasn't very long before Terry began beating a slow rhythm on a drum, and someone else began a wistful tune on a treble recorder. She was aware that the moment had come for her to let go of the little box. The sooner you do it, she told herself, the sooner this whole performance ends. She didn't move.

Hopi was watching her. She took the hands of those on either side of her, Kate and Saul, and said, 'We all remember those we have loved who have had to leave us.'

Lydia stepped forward, the box was in the shallow grave and she watched through her tears as Hopi and Biff covered it with earth and set the spindly little holly into the loose soil, then stamped it down. Malcolm was observing her tenderly. His dark eyes were full of sympathy and he came over to offer comfort, but she moved away and said briskly, 'Well, that's that, then. Thanks everyone.'

The circle had broken up. People began calling their dogs,

when Kate exclaimed suddenly, 'Wow, everyone, just look at that.'

While the strange little ceremony had been taking place, the sun had been transformed into a perfect blood-red disc poised on a thin line of cloud. Reflected in its light, an enormous orange moon was rising behind the chimneys of Haddeley Hall.

'That's bloody fantastic,' said Biff.

'I reckon it's an omen,' said Kate, 'I've never seen anything like it before.'

'Harvest moon,' said Mal. 'It happens every year.'

'Not in towns, it doesn't,' said Terry.

'It's magic, whatever it's called,' said Biff.

Hopi said, a trace of smugness creeping into her voice, 'There's magic all around. We just don't see it most of the time, that's all.'

For a little longer they remained on the hilltop, noticing the way mist was spreading up from the streams in the valleys and the thin columns of smoke rising from one or two houses in the village and even from the vehicles hidden in the Hollows. But as soon as the sun had dipped below the horizon, the temperature dropped quickly.

'What now?' asked Kate.

Lydia was on the point of saying it was high time she headed back to Rose Cottage and a hot bath, when Hopi said firmly, 'Now I think we ought to have a proper wake.'

'A wake?' Lydia croaked. 'Haven't we done enough?'

'I mean,' said Hopi with her sudden and infectious smile, 'that we ought to go and get completely smashed.'

Kate whooped with pleasure. 'I've got some booze.'

'And I've got some elderflower wine,' said Hopi, 'I'm sure it needs drinking.'

'I'll drop down to the offie,' said Biff. 'They're open until eight o'clock.'

Oh well, thought Lydia, I might as well . . . She found she no longer felt all that sad, but surprisingly peaceful and more than ready for a drink, or several. As they set off down the hill she heard Saul complaining in adenoidal tones that he ought to be allowed more than just fizzy pop. Or he'd go and get his sticks back.

Terry, still beating his drum, was the last to leave. Alone of all the dogs Misty remained convinced that there was still a rabbit, or some even more exciting quarry, lurking in the bramble thicket.

'Time to go,' called Terry. Reluctantly, she began to follow him, but then she paused with a proprietary air to examine the newly-planted holly.

'Don't do that!' yelled Terry, but it was too late. An trickle of yellow liquid was sprayed with canine accuracy over the lower leaves of the holly, before Misty bounded over, a pale shape in the twilight, to join him.

'You filthy animal,' he said reproachfully, 'I bet you've bloody killed it. No boozing for you tonight, and that's a fact.'

Then he set off at a run with his dog to catch up with the others.

13 $\int$

A bright, clear morning after the full moon, and the air was sharp and autumnal. Jim and Bumpkin were walking along the lane that led from the Lodge to Rose Cottage. It was at moments like these that Jim felt more than reconciled to their enforced move to the country: Bumpkin had been all in favour right from the start.

Rose Cottage was looking every inch the rustic idyll: little windows peeping out from under a steep roof, a tangle of old roses growing over the door, even a late flower or two. Amid the clipped hedges and neat lawns of Briarswood, Rose Cottage remained, in Jim's opinion, a welcome oasis of disorder. Some houses, he decided, as he rounded the corner, were best suited to a state of casual *déshabille*. Like some women. He remembered surprising Lydia as she painted her toenails. But this morning there was no sign of life, the front door was shut, and curtains drawn.

Still, it was gone ten o'clock and Lydia was normally an early riser. Jim clonked the cowbell and Bumpkin scratched at the door. Just as he was wondering if Lydia perhaps had gone away for the night – he felt somewhat annoyed at not having been told – he heard footsteps on the stairs. The door squeaked open and Lydia, ashen-faced and wearing a baggy sweatshirt and leggings, peered out into the sunlight.

'Are you all right, Lydia? You look grim.'

'Compliments, Jim, at this hour.' She began to smile, then winced and said, 'I think perhaps I overdid things a bit last night.' Her voice was barely more than a croak.

'Do you want me to come back later?'

'No. I'm awake now. I'll make some coffee.'

Jim followed her into the cottage and looked around for signs of the previous evening's merry-making, but the living room seemed much as usual. He wondered, with sudden concern, if Lydia had perhaps fallen into the habit of solitary alcoholic bingeing, and blamed himself for not having spotted how lonely and unhappy she must be. He noticed a letter with 'ever yours, Gordon' scrawled in large, bold handwriting across the bottom, and instantly went and looked out of the window.

Lydia brought in two mugs, handed one to him and sank into a battered armchair. Bumpkin positioned himself beside a half-finished packet of biscuits, and signalled his readiness to be fed.

'It must have been quite a night,' Jim turned to look down at her.. 'What were you drinking?'

'Um. I lost track. It started with home-made wine and beer, but then it all got a bit out of hand.'

'I never knew you made your own wine.'

'Hopi,' she muttered, 'Hopi made the wine. I was down at the Hollows.'

'Oh.' Jim's relief that she had not been drinking alone would have been greater had her companions been more suitable.

'Your prejudices are showing,' she observed.

'I hadn't realised you were so thick with them, that's all.'

'It was a one-off. A wake, actually.'

'A wake? Did someone die?'

Lydia frowned. There was a memory of sitting in a circle round a fire, that sensation of burning hands and knees and face, and a freezing back which reminded her of childhood Guy Fawkes parties. A memory of smiling, happy and increasingly incoherent faces lit by the orange glow of the fire. A memory of something laid to rest. It wasn't so much that she didn't want to tell Jim about it, more that she doubted he would ever see it through her eyes. Normally she would have shared his cynicism, but just for today, she preferred to keep the memory private.

So she said, 'No one died. Just an excuse for a bloody good piss-up.'

'I'm glad you enjoyed yourself,' were the words Jim spoke.

His face said quite plainly, 'Aren't you rather old for that kind of thing?'

Lydia shielded her eyes with her hand. 'Stop doing the stern schoolmaster number on me, Jim. It might have been attractive once, but now it's just irritating.'

'Sorry.' Jim retreated to the window again, and some low-level humming. Lydia winced. Bumpkin stared hard at the plate of biscuits and then cast Lydia an adoring look. She ignored him.

She asked, 'How is eighteenth-century agrarian discontent this morning?'

'Coming along nicely, thank you Lydia. I'm just beginning to explore the links between activists on the ground and the contemporary theorists who were busy hammering out a more modern doctrine of civil liberties.'

'Very topical,' was Lydia's dry comment.

'I doubt it, somehow. I don't suppose your overindulgent chums at the Hollows would recognise a civil libertarian principle if it hit them in the face.'

'Maybe not. You should ask them yourself. Why not come down and meet them some time? You might be in for a surprise.'

'I no longer crave surprises,' said Jim, who was thinking that Lydia, like Rose Cottage, definitely was suited to the tousled, rumpled look. She pushed a thick tangle of dark hair back from her face and yawned.

'I need a bath.'

'Something your new friends could do with by all accounts.'

'No one's perfect,' said Lydia, 'or perhaps you hadn't noticed.'

'I'll leave you to your bath,' Jim wondered how his earlier mood of good humour had evaporated so rapidly. He began moving towards the door. 'Come on Bumpkin,' but the dog seemed incapable of wresting his gaze from the plate of biscuits. 'Damn, I nearly forgot why I came. We've got a bloody great pile of logs sitting in front of the garage. How it got there is something of a saga, but the point is, we don't need them. Yesterday Caro dented the rear wing of the Range Rover when she was reversing out. Poor thing was rather upset. Anyway, Suzie thought you might be able to use them. Interested?'

Lydia, still sprawled in her armchair, was suddenly smiling in spite of her throbbing skull. She said sweetly, 'Oh Jim, how kind of you. I'd love some logs. But I've no way of fetching them.'

'Don't worry about that. I'll bring them down myself later on. Suzie offered to help.'

I bet she has, thought Lydia. Well done Suzie. And to Bumpkin's immense delight she rewarded him with a celebration biscuit, a bourbon cream.

Denied Jim's services as an alarm clock, most of the inhabitants of the Hollows did not begin to surface on the morning following the full moon until nearly midday. Saul had mounted a determined campaign to pester people into activity since about nine-thirty, but had only succeeded with his father, and even that was only a partial success, as Mal sat on the steps of the lorry and held his head between his hands, too shattered even to go in search of coffee.

Eventually Mal asked his son, 'Do you know where Kate is?'

Saul's eyes narrowed. He knew exactly where Kate was, but since he had been doing his utmost to eject the hated rival from his father's life and lorry for months, he was not about to act as go-between.

'Nope,' he said, 'I haven't seen her.'

Mal sighed. Saul had the ferrety look which usually meant he was lying, but he didn't have the energy, or the motivation, to persist. He'd find out soon enough.

When Kate did finally appear, it was from Biff's commer. Mal was far from surprised, but he felt angry all the same. Yawning and stretching, she wandered over to the lorry. Her normally robust expression was haggard, and her freckled face was a sickly shade of grey. Endeavouring to hide all trace of rage, Mal shifted slightly to allow her in.

'Any coffee?' she asked.

'No, we've run out.'

'I'd better get my stuff, then.'

He could hear her moving around inside the lorry. Saul was watching proceedings intently from a distance. After a few minutes, Kate emerged with a sleeping bag and a mound of clothing.

'That's most of it,' she said.

Mal's heart was pounding but he nodded, and said evenly, 'Collect the rest any time.'

'See you then.'

Kate stumped away carrying her load. Mal clenched his fists. He tried to relax, but there were steel bands of tension around his chest and his head was throbbing. It seemed a weird end to a relationship that had lasted over a year. He couldn't decide whether they were both being brilliantly civilised and mature about it all, or whether it was just desperately banal. The writing had been on the wall for weeks, perhaps even before Saul appeared on the scene. At least there hadn't been any rows, he thought, though he was beginning to feel sick with the effort of reining in his emotion. He told himself he didn't even care. A small hand was creeping round the back of his neck.

'Yuk,' said Saul. 'Girls are just a load of crap, aren't they Dad?'

'Don't swear, Saul,' muttered Mal automatically, though for once he was half-inclined to agree with the boy's dismissal of the entire female sex. But then he remembered Lydia's taut expression as she clutched the little cigar box to her chest the previous evening, Hopi's soft voice bidding farewell to a child unborn, and he said, 'Not always Saul, not by any means.'

'Yuk,' said Saul again, and tweaked Mal's ear. Despite his present discomfort, Mal recognised the child's clumsy efforts towards sympathy and patted his shoulder. Saul took a swipe at his knee. 'I'm hungry, Dad.'

'Right. We'll walk to the shop and get something to eat.'

Obviously, in some ways it was going to be easier, now that he could give Saul his undivided attention, but Mal hoped fatherhood didn't mean he had to live like a monk for long. Especially not with winter coming on.

The wake which had been celebrated with such gusto on the night of the full moon had also been the catalyst for one of those periodic realignments which occurred every now and then on site. Kate moved in with Biff, Stella, who had been with Biff for as long as anyone could remember, moved in with Andy, and Hopi, who had been celibate since Colin departed for Spain, was startled on waking to find Terry in bed beside her.

Though any kind of mental exercise was made difficult by the throbbing of her skull, she contemplated this development as best she could while filling the kettle with water from the bucket just inside the door. She was fairly sure that technically this wasn't a development at all – not yet at any rate. As far as she could remember, they had keeled over into bed together the previous night for warmth and a primitive, bundling closeness, not sex. The state they'd both been in, actual sex would have been an unlikely outcome anyway. Terry had been Hopi's lodger for over two months, ever since he had left the city and come to live on site. As a lodger, he had the use of her caravan while he organised a place of his own. In return, he was supposed to take on the menial jobs like chopping wood and getting water. Sometimes he did, sometimes he forgot, but he was no worse than most lodgers and a lot better than some. Meanwhile, he had got himself a car, but showed no sign of even looking for his own living space.

Of course, if he became her lover, he wouldn't need his own space. But was that what she wanted?

Hopi cradled a mug of Earl Grey tea in her hands and curled up on the end of the bed. She considered waking Terry, and offering him some tea, but just for the moment she preferred solitude. Besides, he looked so tranquil, lying there, and beautiful, like an icon. He had the thickest, darkest eyelashes she had ever seen on anyone, man or woman, a finely chiselled nose, high cheekbones and a well-defined mouth. A perfect mouth. Hopi hadn't gleaned much information about his family in the time they had spent together. Contemplating him now, she saw how darkly foreign he looked. She might have been sharing her caravan all this time with a disguised Indian prince, a rajah perhaps, or maybe a Spanish flamenco dancer. It must have been some exotic lineage which had given him those dusky, aristocratic features.

Asleep, Terry looked even younger than Hopi knew him to be, which was nineteen or twenty. Nearly five years younger than her. Hopi was not at all put off by the age gap, in fact it quite appealed to her. Terry was in many ways immature, and probably would have found it difficult to adjust to life on site if she hadn't taken him under her wing. Taking people under her wing was a habit of Hopi's; she found it almost impossible to resist the appeal of anyone needy, or suffering. Her mother said it was her Achilles heel, but Hopi still saw it as a virtue. Terry's little-boy-lost aura worked even more in his favour than his good looks. If she could be sure that Terry really needed her, then Hopi might have been tempted to take him on.

If it wasn't for Colin.

Hopi frowned slightly, and pulled the blanket more tightly around her shoulders. She had been on the verge of forgetting all about Colin, but he was still technically her man. There was no mistaking his great need of her, which suited her just fine, but he had a tendency to demonstrate that need in all manner of destructive ways. He couldn't help it, she was sure of that. And she was equally sure that she could change him, given time.

Nevertheless, she had been mostly relieved when Colin suddenly decided to join a group heading south to spend some months in Spain, or France. Hopi had told him she couldn't leave England because of her father's health. This had usefully obscured the fact that the prospect of being exposed to Colin's violently irrational mood swings far from all the resources of her own country was distinctly unappealing. Besides, the friends he was travelling with were, as far as she was concerned, a bunch of losers she'd rather avoid. Since coming to Briarswood, Hopi had frequently found herself on the brink of hoping that Colin had found another tender-hearted female to lean on and forgotten about her altogether.

Terry awoke. It was something he did with startling speed, even on a hangover morning such as this. One moment he was lost in sleep, the next he was wide-eyed and fully alert – a condition that, today, brought problems of its own.

Sitting up, he pressed his fingertips against his forehead. He groaned.

'Like some tea?'

'Sure. Good party – ah.'

Hopi grinned. Terry had just absorbed the fact that he was in her bed, rather than on his futon mattress which was still neatly rolled up beside the salvaged car seats at the other end of the trailer; now he was avoiding her eye with quite comical embarrassment.

'It's OK,' she told him. 'Nothing happened.'

'Oh. Sure.' His face indicated relief, mostly. No, she had to be honest with herself, it was relief entirely.

Clambering down from the bed to make a fresh mug of tea, Hopi asked him, 'Do you have any Indian blood in your family, Terry?'

'Not that I know of,' he answered, easing himself over on to his side and patting the floor with his palm in a search for tobacco. 'My dad was a sailor. Mum said Italian, but my gran thought it might have been Arab. Mum wasn't all that hot on languages.'

Hopi poured hot water into a mug. 'Doesn't it bother you, not knowing?'

'Not really.' Terry had spied his tobacco on a little shelf just out of arm's reach; he was wondering about the degree of effort required to reach it. 'My gran always said you are what you make yourself. The rest is just bits of paper.'

Hopi was thoughtful. She had been hurt, just a bit, by his obvious relief. Also she realised that for all his waif-like charm, there was a core of self-sufficiency to Terry, something closed-off and secretive. She guessed he had never learned to trust anyone, and preferred to manage alone. Later, when he was setting off for the wood with Misty and the shovel, she said, 'It's time you got your own place, Terry. You don't need my help any more.'

'Sure,' said Terry easily. Which was what Hopi had been expecting him to say, more or less.

Terry was experiencing some difficulty keeping track of his mental processes that morning. At times like this it could be hard to maintain a grip on who he was and what he was supposed to be doing. Maybe it was that powerful cocktail of stuff he'd taken in during the wake, maybe it was the way Hopi suddenly asked him about his father, just like that, out of the blue and before he'd even had a cup of tea and a smoke. Usually he made something up about how his father had been a wealthy Indian who had been intending to marry his mum but had been killed in a car accident just before the wedding. It was Hopi coming straight out with the question when he was least expecting it that had tripped him into the truth, so far as he knew it. He was annoyed with himself; he might at least have said his father was a ship's captain, not just an ordinary sailor.

Anyway, he didn't mind Hopi telling him it was time to find his own space. Fact was, he agreed with her. He'd had a shock waking up in her bed that morning, had felt pretty sick. He liked Hopi fine – everybody liked Hopi – just not in that way.

The air was clean out here in the wood. Just him on his own with Misty. Pure fresh air and the branches making patterns over his head. When he had finished he filled in his little hole with the shovel, sat back against a tree trunk and lit a cigarette. The smooth bark was solid, pressing against his shoulders and spine. After a little while he began to feel as if the tree and his backbone had fused together: the tree was him and he was becoming the tree. He had a moment of anxiety – what would happen when he wanted to stand up again? – but then he relaxed. Trees were a force for good, he'd learned that much from talking to Hopi and Mal. And the trees in this wood were completely different from the pathetic, spindly, much pissed-on specimens they called trees in the piece of wasteland near his gran's house which was the nearest he'd ever known to a home. A real home, not a Home with a capital H which was where he went when his mother's nerves got too much for her and his grandmother was too ill to take him in. Still less a Foster Home where he was made to feel pitiful and the foster mum's eldest daughter kept coming into his bedroom at night and asking how did she look in her Wonderbra and why didn't he put his hands here, you could feel the uplift.

'Pushed from pillar to post, that boy.' It was his grandmother's voice he heard, coming from behind one of the trees nearby. He was not unduly worried. He often heard his grandmother's voice after a heavy night, and there'd been plenty of those since her death two years ago.

Pushed from pillar to post. He could feel the strength of the tree entering his spine. The tree was both pillar and post. Brilliant to be a tree, you never got pushed around. He imagined what it must be like to have roots, roots that went deep into the soil and anchored you to the spot. He looked at his boots, stuck out in front of him, and imagined roots emerging from his heels like the tentacles of some giant octopus, twisting and writhing and thrusting down into the soil.

He closed his eyes and leaned his head against the tree. When he opened his eyes again he felt his spirit leap up into the branches high above him. He was a squirrel, a darting bird, he could look down on all the lowly life of the woodland floor. All those creepy, crawly bugs and worms and pathetic little earthbound humans.

It was great. He loved the country. He'd always liked nature programmes, but when he first moved out of the squat and began travelling, he found the silence and the hugeness of the space beyond the site almost frightening. Definitely frightening, if he was honest. If Hopi hadn't let him lodge in her trailer, he probably wouldn't have stuck it out.

A pale, soft muzzle thrust itself under his hand. Misty had been ignored far too long. Terry wrapped his arms around her broad neck and rested his cheek against her fur. She responded by pressing the wet bump of her nose into his ear. A sense of wellbeing spread through him like warmth. He hadn't minded Hopi telling him to move on. It was only to be expected. People always shoved you out in the end. Even his gran couldn't cope any more when she got ill. You couldn't rely on people, not really. Misty was different. Misty would never turn away from him. Right from the start the bond had been there between them, and nothing could break it. It was unique.

Hugging Misty, he realised that his spine had detached itself from the tree trunk after all. He realised also that he could use a cup of tea, or coffee.

Vague swirls of leaves billowed and eddied across the woodland path. Terry was aware of the solidity of his hands and feet, great lumps of flesh hanging off the ends of his body, and the press of the shovel handle on his shoulder, but his mind was separate from all of that. His mind felt weightless, at liberty to shift and dance with the leaves.

He'd never experienced anything like this before. It was as though he'd been walking in a black tunnel all his life and had suddenly stepped into bright sunlight. He wondered if perhaps he was having what people called a mystic experience, or if – a still more incredible thought – this might be what other people meant when they talked about happiness.

But even as he noticed the sensation, it began to slip away.

Now he was coming back to reality, the reality of the site, and a stranger walking through it. No, not a stranger. Misty was bounding up to the girl and wagged a generous welcome. It was the one who had visited a few days before with Lydia. She stooped to fondle Misty's pale butterfly ears and her fair hair flopped over the pink blush spreading across her cheeks. She smiled at Terry shyly.

'Hello,' she said, her eyes resting briefly on his face then glancing quickly away again. 'I brought a couple of books for Saul. They're old ones of mine, actually, but I don't need them any more. He doesn't seem to be around.'

'No,' said Terry, 'I haven't seen him either.' He remembered now that her name was Suzie.

'Oh dear.' She was obviously flustered by her failure to locate Saul. She said, 'I thought I might give them to Hopi. For Saul, I mean. But I can't see her either.'

'Did you look in her caravan?'

'I don't know which it is.'

'I'm going there.'

Suzie wasn't sure if this meant he would look, or whether it was an invitation for her to accompany him, or what. After a brief silence, she said, 'Can I come with you?'

'Sure.'

'That's terribly kind of you. I do hope I'm not being a dreadful nuisance.'

Terry made no reply to this for the simple reason that he couldn't think of one. He led the way to the caravan, and Suzie and Misty followed him. The act of talking had made him aware of how desperately he needed a drink.

He went into Hopi's caravan and Suzie, standing on the step, peered inside and said, 'Oh dear, she's not here.' She shifted the two books from one arm to the other, as if they had suddenly become an enormous burden, and said, 'I don't suppose . . . I mean, would you mind awfully giving them to Saul for me? There's no need to say they're from me, or anything like that. I just wanted him to have them. I mean, he might as well.'

'Sure.'

'Oh, thank you so much. That's frightfully kind of you . . .'

Once again Terry didn't answer. He'd never been exposed to

such an onslaught of politeness and gratitude, and the thought did occur to him that she might be sending him up. But she didn't look like the sending-up type. Since the kettle was now on the hob, he asked, 'Like a cup of tea?'

'Wow, that would be brilliant. I mean, if you're sure that's not too much trouble.'

'It's OK.' He had emptied the dregs of their morning tea outside the door. 'You can come in if you like.'

She didn't enter the caravan exactly, but hovered in the doorway. She was trying to take in every detail of its interior without wanting to appear nosy.

After a while, she said, 'It's very homely in here, isn't it? Is this your place?'

'No, it's Hopi's.'

'Oh.' Terry heard the disappointment in her voice, but couldn't imagine its cause.

'I'm her lodger.'

'Oh.' Even deeper disappointment.

'I'm getting my own place soon.'

'Oh.' A neutral, tentative 'oh'.

Terry handed her a mug of tea. The bag was still floating on its surface and the milk was not altogether fresh, but she continued to act as if he was doing her a huge favour. It was odd, because she had one of those television-type voices that usually gave him the horrors, reminding him of school teachers and officialdom generally, but Suzie, maybe because she was so much younger than him, and so obviously lacking in confidence, was beginning to make him feel rather self-assured, and special.

Despite the odd sensations still lurking in his head from the night before, Terry managed a wan smile.

'We can sit in the sun if you like. And drink our tea together.'

'That's lovely.'

'I expect Saul will be pleased with those books,' said Terry. 'It's good to help little kids with their reading, isn't it?'

'Oh yes,' said Suzie, 'I do so agree. I mean, it's absolutely vital.' When Terry looked at her with those almond-shaped eyes, Suzie would have agreed that the moon was made of blue cheese, if that was what he thought.

*   *   *

Some time at the beginning of October a sea change came over Saul which took everyone by surprise. The other two children on the site had settled into school life straight away, but it was some time before Briarswood's most reluctant scholar allowed himself to be seduced by the pleasures of education; when he did so, it was with the suddenness of a love affair. Neither Ann Robertson, wise and experienced teacher of infants that she was, nor Lydia, who had recently begun helping at the school for two afternoons a week, allowed themselves much credit for this transformation. Though both had tried their best to help Saul adjust to the alien environment of the classroom they knew the change was due entirely to the fact that Saul had fallen head over heels in love.

Not with any of the self-assured little girls in their white blouses and uniformly blue jerseys, but with the Wendy House.

His attendance during September had been sporadic, at best. On the rare occasions that Mal persuaded him to join the rosy-cheeked village children, he remained resolutely on the fringe of activities. A furtive, skulking outsider, he circled the classroom like a cattle-thief spying out a likely herd, only occasionally executing a small raid to carry off a crayon, or toy. This caused outrage, or grief on the part of the owner, but for the rest of the time the children tended to leave him to his own devices, apart from occasional taunts and attacks in the playground or after school.

Saul endured it when he had to, and resisted the adults' well-meaning efforts to interest him in learning. He preferred to lie low in the reading corner, or next to the sandpit when it wasn't being used. Once or twice he had strayed towards the large, plywood construction at the far end of the classroom. Its child-sized doorway and painted walls fascinated him, but the gloomy interior, usually containing a pair of bustling small girls, was alarming to a child so wary of new experiences. Then, one afternoon, Lydia couldn't see him when she looked up. Fearing that he had made yet another attempt to escape academic life, she was about to alert Ann Robertson when she heard a familiar adenoidal muttering coming from within the Wendy House. She approached obliquely, so he would not see her coming, pulled up a diminutive chair, and sat down.

'Put this here . . . no one can see . . . now this goes there . . . and this is mine, you can't touch it, you bloody won't have it . . . set this out like that . . . here's the chip pan . . . make some chips . . . that's good . . .'

Lydia smiled. Lost inside the twilight womb of the Wendy House Saul believed he was invisible, and thus completely safe. For the whole of that first afternoon he was left undisturbed. From time to time he peered out through the little window and surveyed the bright, noisy world of the classroom. He could observe, without having to take part. He had his plastic cooker and his pots and pans and some other toys that had been abandoned there earlier in the day; he could be a badger in his lair, a bear in his cave, a soldier in his castle. He was safe. He was still there when Brent and Jasmine, the older children who also lived on site, came to collect him at three thirty.

The next morning he arrived promptly, and immediately set off at a run across the classroom to lay first claim to the magical little house. To his immense chagrin, just past the nature table, he was waylaid by Mrs Robertson who had been giving the matter some thought. Kindly but firmly she explained that time spent in the Wendy House had to be earned by time spent sitting at one of the tables and doing 'busy work' like the others. Saul's desperation to regain the sanctuary of his den was so acute that he agreed to this arrangement with less fuss than she had anticipated. He had learned already that the soft-voiced, grey-haired woman, despite her gentle manner, was a formidable opponent. He hastily copied out a row of shapes she had drawn in his work book, then slid off his chair and disappeared once more. It wasn't much, thought Mrs Robertson, but it was a start. Later that morning she sat by the tiny doorway and persuaded him to read her one of the books he had found on the cooker. She was pleased to discover that he had a fair grasp of simple words already.

At lunch break she was confronted by a delegation of outraged small girls, among them Sandra's chubby daughter Naomi, who demanded in no uncertain terms to be allowed back into *their* Wendy House.

'Tomorrow,' she promised them, 'but just for today, we'll let Saul have it all for himself. Tomorrow will be a sharing day.'

She hoped. Still, she felt a faint optimism. She had discovered a means of luring Saul into the classroom orbit, and Ann Robertson had always much preferred the use of carrots over sticks.

An evening of low cloud and occasional sleeting rain. In Briarswood, home owners turned up their central heating and were thankful they had proper homes, not just a caravan or a converted lorry. At the Hollows, Hopi, Kate and Mal were glad of the logs they had collected from Rose Cottage, and any vehicle with smoke coming from its chimney quickly filled with people seeking shelter from the cold.

An evening for domesticity. An evening for mothers and daughters to talk.

Suzie, returning from school through the rain-chilled dusk, found Caro had baked apple scones as an autumn treat. Also, that she had been thinking about half term.

'Did you have a good day at school, darling?'

'Fine, thanks, Mummy.'

'Did anything interesting happen?'

'Not really.' Suzie frowned. Knowing that some uncontroversial information concerning her education was required at this point, she added, 'I got the sides fixed on my work box. Mr Beasley was really pleased.'

'Your work box?'

'You know, for CDT.'

'CD what?'

'Craft Design and Technology, Mummy. I've told you about it before.'

'Really? It just doesn't sound like proper school, I suppose. Anyway, never mind about that now. I've been meaning to tell you, I phoned Jean this afternoon. She said she and Mina would be simply thrilled to have you stay with them at half term.'

'Why did you phone Jean?'

'To ask if you could stay, of course. I knew you'd like to. Much better to spend half term with friends your own age . . .' Her voice faded. There was a brief silence while Caro and Suzie silently completed the sentence with, 'instead of moping about here on your own doing nothing'.

'But I wanted—'

'What, dear? If you've made other plans already, I do think you might have let me know. I'm going to look jolly silly if I have to phone Jean back now and say you can't come after all.'

'It's not that, Mummy, it's just . . .'

'Just what? I thought you'd be over the moon, Suzie. Jean said Rupert would probably be around then too.'

'I don't mind, but—'

'That's settled then. I'll give her a ring and make the arrangements.'

'No. Let me do that, Mummy. It makes me seem such a baby if you always do all the arranging.'

Caro opened her mouth to say nonsense, she would do it, Suzie was bound to get into a muddle over dates and times, but then she realised that this was absolutely the wrong approach with someone as unsure of herself as Suzie, so she closed her mouth again firmly, simply making a mental note to check her daughter's arrangements with Jean nearer the time. Suzie was frowning furiously: she really did seem to be taking this all terribly seriously, for some reason.

They finished their tea and apple scone in thoughtful silence, and Suzie slipped away 'to do some homework' as quickly as she could without igniting her mother's suspicions. The dreadful thought had just occurred to her that Caro might have somehow got wind of her two visits to the Hollows. Maybe the phone call to Jean had been part of an elaborate plot to remove her from Briarswood at half term in order to keep her away from the travellers.

The very hint of such a disaster was enough to pitch Suzie into turmoil. Without a doubt, that second visit to the Hollows had been the most amazing and brilliant hour of her life so far. She had sat with Terry on the steps of Hopi's trailer – two boxes side by side, actually, but they made perfectly good steps, or seats. They drank their mugs of tea. Terry offered her a roll-up but she said no, so he smoked one on his own. They chatted. He said they'd had a party the night before to cheer Lydia up. Suzie said one or two things about herself, though she thought her life must be horribly dull compared to his. Once or twice Terry turned his gaze to look at her face; his eyes had the most enormous dark pupils she had ever seen, and each time he looked at her Suzie felt as though an earthquake was taking place inside her. The clashing of tectonic plates on the San Andreas fault was as nothing compared to the lurch and tug of what must surely be her heart. Then Lydia had turned up, looking somewhat pale and haggard, as did most people on the site except Terry because of his wonderful sun tan, and told Kate that their logs were being delivered to Rose Cottage that afternoon and all thanks to Suzie. Though it was nice to have everyone being so friendly and grateful, Suzie found that suddenly being the centre of attention brought on all her wretched shyness, so she made her excuses and departed as soon as she could.

Since then, she had relived the events of that hour a thousand times. Every word and gesture of her conversation with Terry, his gentle smile as he handed her the mug, his obvious kindness to Misty, the sight of his long fingers tangling with the dog's pale fur, the glimpse of brown flesh through the rip in his jeans just above the knee was to be savoured again and again in the privacy of her room . . . Occasionally, Suzie allowed herself to imagine those long brown fingers touching her own hair, maybe even stroking her cheek – and each time she experienced such an overwhelming gust of pleasure it was a wonder she didn't faint clean away.

Suzie lay on her bed and listened to the radio chattering to Caro as she cooked the evening meal. Suzie had simply heaps of homework but she couldn't even make a start: her present situation was far too complicated. Obviously, she would have to go to Mina's at half term; a change of plan now would activate all the parental antennae, and that was the last thing she wanted. But she had been counting on paying a visit to the Hollows one day soon, if she could find a reason that didn't seem too impossibly trumped up. It was going to look odd if she kept on taking books down to Saul, but she thought she might just pop down to see how he was enjoying them. Somehow or other she had to find a pretext for revisiting the Hollows. If she didn't see Terry again soon, life simply was not worth living.

Equally unbearable was the possibility her mother knew: to

think of the most perfect occasion of her whole life coming under Caro's scrutiny was enough to make Suzie sick with horror. Like having the inside of her brain exposed and trampled on, like having her inmost self being made cheap and horrible. It wasn't that Suzie wanted to be deceitful or anything like that. Only that in this business of visiting the Hollows, there really wasn't any choice.

A little later that same evening, Hopi struggled through the sleety dark to the public phone box near the bus shelter. In her pocket was a phone card, her monthly gift from her mother, Zita. Years ago mother and daughter had hammered out an agreement: Zita promised never to worry about Hopi on condition that she phoned home on the first Friday of every month. A couple of years ago Hopi had forgotten: the police had turned up on site two days later, sent by Zita to make sure her daughter was unharmed. Hopi had not forgotten again.

'Hi, Mum.'

'Hello, Hopi. How are things?'

'Fine. We're still in Briarswood. We've got a great supply of logs and the farmer is still OK about giving us water, so that's good. How's Jack?'

A non-committal grunt at the mention of her husband's name, then, 'His breathing's giving him a lot of trouble. And he gets down because he can't help with the work. I tell him to enjoy a life of leisure while he can, but that just makes him worse.'

'Poor old Zita. Sounds like he's driving you crazy.'

'Well, what with the goats and the chickens and the cats, they're doing a pretty good job of it.' About ten years ago Hopi's parents had bought a ten-acre smallholding on a windy Welsh hillside. They were endeavouring to be self-sufficient.

'Do you want me to come and help out for a bit?'

'Not yet. I'll tell you when I've reached breaking point.'

'Do me a favour Mum, let me know before that, OK? It's easier in the long run. How's Blossom?'

'Your sister Joan – I take it that's who you mean. Joan goes from strength to strength. She's been promoted at work and her boyfriend, guess what, has been asked to join the Rotary Club.'

'Oh, no, how terrible—'

'I know, but there was nothing I could do. I wash my hands of the pair of them, I really do.'

'I don't know how to break this to you, but I'm thinking of going into business.'

'What?'

'Yeah. I've got this really brilliant old sewing machine, one of those treadle ones. I'm going to cut up old shirts and dresses from charity shops and turn them into new clothes. Sort of recycled designer wear. I can sell them at festivals and things next summer.'

'Sounds brilliant. Just don't go turning into a tycoon on me, OK?'

'Not much chance of that.'

'Oh, and by the way, Hopi—' Her mother's deliberately off-hand manner immediately raised Hopi's suspicions. 'I had a call from Colin. He was asking where you were. I told him I wasn't sure.'

'Is Colin back from Spain then?'

'A couple of weeks ago. They're parked up somewhere in Kent, I think.'

'Did he have a good time?'

'Colin would never admit to having a good time anywhere, you know that. The sun was too hot, the people were crap, the food was poison—'

'Sounds familiar.'

'Shall I tell him where you are?'

'Of course. Why keep it secret?'

'You know how I feel about Colin. He's bad news, Hopi. You're better off without that kind of psycho in your life.'

'He's not a psycho, he's just got a few problems, that's all. He can be wonderful at times.'

'It's the other times that worry me.'

'Don't fuss, Mum, I can handle him.'

An ambiguous 'hm' from down the line. Then Zita said, 'Why bother? I can easily tell him I don't know where you are.'

'That's daft. Don't worry, we'll work something out.'

But later, when she had put the receiver back in its cradle and wrapped her muffler around her face to keep out the wind, and was trudging back down Briarswood's main street to the turn-off for Ted Sedden's farm, Hopi felt a growing apprehension. Colin could be funny and charming and pathetic; he could make her feel the most special person in the world. Sometimes. When he felt like it. Or he could be cruel and dishonest and destructive, and cause more trouble in a day than most people do in a year.

Hopi would never dream of turning her back on someone who needed her, but . . . But she couldn't help wishing Colin had found someone to turn to while he was in Spain. She consoled herself with the thought that he might have just been asking Zita about her for old time's sake. He might not bother to make the trek to Briarswood. He might not come back into her life.

14

A bright morning towards the end of October, and Lydia sensed
the difference as soon as she approached Haddeley Hall: the
whole house was being groomed for Wyndham's return, and
all was buzz and bustle, flap and flurry. In his haste to do ten
different jobs at once, Mark barely had time for more than a
brief, 'Hello, Lydia,' as he dashed through the house, talking
into a mobile phone. This morning his face was nearly as brightly
coloured as one of his vibrant ties. A balding florist, with two
assistants and enough flowers to keep the average barrow boy
happy for a week, was creating vast edifices of botanic extravagance in which globe artichokes and strange-looking orchids
played a significant role. Miguel was supervising activity in the
kitchen, and the construction noises coming from the orangery
had assumed a new urgency. Women she had never seen before
were helping Mrs Miguel with the polishing and shining. Lydia
wandered bemused through all the activity. Haddeley Hall was
being transformed into the most scrubbed and polished construction site in England. Like royalty assuming their realm always
smelled of fresh paint, Wyndham must believe his home had a
natural odour of beeswax and wet flowers.

Slightly smugly, Lydia reflected that work in the steward's
room was right on schedule. With Hopi's help, all the preparation
had been finished the previous week. The wood panelling,
stripped of its layers of heavy paint, was palely beautiful, and
ready for waxing. The ceiling had been painted an old-fashioned
off white which would harmonise perfectly with the walls when
they were done. All that remained was to finish the two sample
sections of blue-green paint on the walls, so Wyndham could

choose between them on his return. For the last couple of days, Lydia had worked alone and this morning, while the household hummed and bustled around her, she was especially glad of the solitude. She had not thought about Wyndham much in the three weeks since his departure, but she did so now.

He was due to return the following day. Although he had insisted there was no ulterior motive, she doubted whether he had employed her simply because of her decorating skills, of which he after all had known nothing. Had he invited her to have dinner with him when he passed her on the driveway the better to discuss limewash and pigments? Highly unlikely. She did not believe she was flattering herself unduly by guessing that Wyndham Sale was interested in more than just a working relationship, and she felt the need of a strategy.

The complicating factor, she had to admit as she stirred the heavy paint, was that she found Wyndham Sale surprisingly attractive. Surprisingly, because he was not at all the kind of man she had ever thought of as 'her type', and she could think of little that they had in common, apart from an interest in the decoration of old buildings, hardly a sound basis for an affair.

Ridiculous, she scolded herself as she dipped the large brush into the pot of paint, an affair is the last thing you need right now. Being distemper, the paint had a particularly satisfying texture, and she applied it with increasingly emphatic strokes as she mentally talked herself into rejecting any overtures Wyndham might make on his return: slop, thwack – just as you've managed to escape from Gordon, what's the sense of getting entangled again? One of the spin-offs from the ceremony at Raven's Beacon was that she had spent a whole evening writing a long letter to Gordon explaining why their marriage was finally and irrevocably over. Thwack, slop, admittedly she hadn't yet posted the letter, but that was an oversight, a mere detail. Slosh, slosh, the whole point of being in Briarswood was to be alone, to have space, to get sorted. Whack, slosh, slap, thwack – at least she wasn't one of those feeble women who needed a man around just to feel complete. Thank God for that, she didn't need Wyndham in the slightest, she didn't even like him that much. The whole idea was simply preposterous, she'd finish this room

and be off, leave Briarswood entirely, there was nothing for her
here . . .

'It looks better than you described it.'

'Wyndham!'

'Did I startle you?'

'You're not supposed to come back until tomorrow.'

'My London meeting was cancelled. I came straight down.'

He was laughing. He looked enormously happy, a schoolboy
with an unexpected half-holiday. Skilled though he was at hiding
anger or pain, he appeared to have no defence against genuine
pleasure and it made him look suddenly younger than his years,
pink-cheeked and tousled with exhilaration. This was not the
Wyndham Lydia had been expecting to see the following day.
He was carrying a large white box, which bumped against her
hip as he touched her cheek with his own. She stepped back,
unsettled, and more than a little annoyed.

She said, 'If you'd given me warning, I could have got both
the sample sections finished in time.'

'Never mind, it has to be the greener blue. It's obvious.'

And of course, the moment he said it, it was obvious, which
for some strange reason only increased her annoyance and sense
of being wrong-footed. She said, 'I'll be finished in a few days.
You won't—'

He seemed not to have heard. He said, 'I've booked us a table
at the Mulberry Tree for tonight. It's not quite as amazing as
all the hype, but it's still far and away the best place near here.
Have you been?'

Lydia had turned away and was thoughtfully using up the
paint that remained on her brush. Swish, swish, now was the
perfect moment to nip this non-romance in the bud, all that
corny candle-lit dinner business, Wyndham lording it over the
waiters so she could see what a big-shot valued customer he was,
spending yet more money just to get her into bed. She'd been
through that process too many times in the past and she wasn't
about to launch into it all again, not yet, not with this one.

'Wyndham,' she began.

But once again he interrupted her. 'Stop working for a minute,' he ordered, 'and look—' He had set the white box down on
a trestle table and lifted the lid to reveal layers of tissue paper. 'I

had to guess your size.' He raised up a length of red silk, which flashed in the sunlight like flame. 'Let's see if I was right.'

It was the length of silk she had admired on the occasion of her first visit to Haddeley Hall, when she had draped it across her shoulder like a banner and had stopped feeling like Mrs Gordon Fairchild and unavailable to other men. Now it had been snipped and stitched into a short, straight-cut dress with a dramatic diagonal neckline, one shoulder exposed, a ruffled flourish highlighting the other. It was garish and wonderful, and Lydia knew at once that she could carry it off in style. She was still annoyed with Wyndham for catching her off-guard, and intensely aware that her hair was unwashed and spattered with paint and that she had been working in the same clothes all week. But she set down the brush.

No longer smiling, Wyndham held the dress in front of her, his fingertips resting lightly on her shoulders. 'Perfect,' he said, 'I congratulate myself. Eastern Promise Silks is launching a line of evening dresses in the spring, and this is one of the prototypes. I had to hunt all through the factory for a girl with your build, but I think I succeeded. Will you wear it tonight?'

It was the trace of uncertainty in his question that surprised her. He too was going through the motions of an ancient ritual, but he genuinely wanted her to accept. His eagerness to return to Haddeley Hall had been his eagerness to see her again.

'Careful,' she said, motioning him away, 'or you'll get paint on it.'

'Will you?'

Of course not, she thought. Already the man is telling me what to wear, this has gone quite far enough, time to draw a firm line.

She said, 'Yes. Thank you, Wyndham. It's beautiful.'

He smiled, as if he had known all along she would accept, his moment of uncertainty vanishing so completely that Lydia was left wondering if she had imagined it. He said calmly, 'You will look wonderful.'

Lydia felt a glow of excitement, the forgotten pleasure at being an object of desire, a wakening desire of her own. The uncertain prospect of adventure.

She said with a grin, 'Just so long as I can get the paint out of my hair.'

He glanced briefly at her dark curls. 'I've never had a speckled date before,' he commented lightly. 'It would be a novelty, anyway.' He was replacing the dress carefully in its white box. 'Tell Mark when you are ready to go home, he'll get one of the men to drive you. And be ready by seven thirty. I've booked us a table for eight.'

Peggy always felt uneasy when Mrs Cartwright came into the shop. Her natural way of gliding around in front of the shelves gave the impression that she was on castors. She often seemed unable to make a decision, as if she would like to stay and chat but didn't know how to begin. Usually she only bought a couple of postage stamps, or a small bottle of spirits, things she couldn't really need since Caro came in at least once a day to collect up bits and bobs for the Manor, but Peggy's efforts to draw her into conversation always failed utterly.

'Good morning, Mrs Cartwright, colder today, isn't it?' Peggy asked in her easy-going Birmingham voice. She believed in being friendly to all her customers, and as she had a naturally outgoing personality, she expected them all to be friendly back.

Twinks, snug inside her voluminous tweed coat, seemed mystified by this remark. Turning her pale eyes towards Peggy, who was busy with the bacon slicer, she said vaguely, 'Oh, yes.'

As it was a Saturday morning, Ann Robertson was picking up her milk and papers and a quarter of a pound of bacon. The school teacher had a pleasant but unexceptional face, and her straight, greying hair was cut in a childlike style, with a heavy fringe. Noticing that Mrs Cartwright had silently floated towards the snack section she said, 'Are you getting in supplies for Halloween? Trick or treat has caught on very quickly, don't you think?'

'Has it?' Twinks merely looked puzzled at this, and drifted past a shelf of canned fish.

Peggy and Ann exchanged glances.

While she wrapped the bacon, Peggy asked the teacher, 'Staying home for half term?'

'Yes. I intend to be a lady of leisure and catch up with some gardening.'

Twinks had come to stand beside her. She held a half bottle of brandy in one hand and a very small packet of paper handker-chiefs in the other. Ann smiled at her warmly and said, 'There's always such a lot to do in the garden at this time of year, isn't there?'

Twinks set her purchases down on the counter. 'I'll just take these two,' her usually serene voice tinged with anxiety.

When she had left the shop, Peggy tutted and said how rude of her, but Ann was of the opinion that Mrs Cartwright must be growing absent-minded, or perhaps deaf, and said she hoped this didn't indicate the onset of some form of senile decay.

A month ago, Suzie would have been thrilled and excited, but on this late October afternoon, Mina's home was not at all the place she wanted to be. The train that rattled through the darkening countryside was taking her ever further from Briarswood, further from the Hollows. Further from Terry.

She had only succeeded in getting down to the Hollows once since that day a fortnight earlier when she had sat on the steps of Hopi's trailer and chatted with Terry. The previous Sunday afternoon, when Caro had popped up to the Manor to see to her parents and Jim had fallen asleep by the fire, Suzie had slipped out of the house and cut across the fields, all the time planning what she would say to Terry. On her arrival she was plunged in despair: he was nowhere to be seen. She didn't like to ask anyone where he was in case they guessed her real reason for coming. The visit was however saved from disaster by Hopi, who had invited her into her trailer. An old-fashioned sewing machine occupied the space where the mattress had been, so they sat side by side on the bed, surrounded by brightly coloured pieces of fabric and Hopi explained her dress-making scheme and showed her a long skirt she was making out of pieces of blue and yellow fabrics.

Suzie wasn't at all sure what to make of it, so she said, with scrupulous honesty, 'It's very original, isn't it?'

'I hope so,' said Hopi. 'All the materials are recycled and the sewing machine doesn't use any power, so it's a really environmentally friendly way to get new clothes.'

'Mm.' Suzie had noticed a small television sitting on a shelf at the end of the bed. 'But you must have electricity for the TV,' she said.

Hopi smiled, but without making Suzie feel a fool and answered, 'It runs off an old car battery. When it's charged. But I'm giving it to Mal, so Saul can watch the cartoons. I don't really watch much since Terry moved out.'

Terry had gone? Suzie careered to the brink of black despair. She fingered a piece of butter yellow cloth and said casually, 'Has Terry left, then?'

'Yes. He's moved into Biff's commer.'

'What's that?'

'A commercial vehicle. When Kate moved in with Biff, they decided to get a bigger place. They've found a small bus and they're doing it up now. It's going to be great. Terry's sold his car and he's paying Biff by instalments. It's brilliant the way Terry is getting himself sorted now, he's got so much more confident since he started travelling.'

Suzie was able to breathe again. She had recognised Hopi's big-sister tone, and she asked, 'Wasn't he confident before, then?'

'You wouldn't recognise him, now. He'd been in loads of trouble since his gran died. Joy-riding mostly. He'd never hurt a fly, but he had been pretty wild.'

'He seems very gentle,' Suzie ventured.

And Hopi had agreed.

When Suzie left she had noticed the newly-installed bus parked in the corner of the field. It was painted in diagonal stripes of purple and green: Wimbledon colours, she noted, and she wondered if Biff and Kate were perhaps tennis lovers. She envied them their old-new home to do up. She wondered how Terry was managing on his own in his commer. Perhaps he'd like some help making it homely. This thought led to a blissful sequence in which she was busy cleaning and painting and arranging and Terry was wildly impressed by her efficiency and artistic flair. She was sure there must be masses of stuff at the Lodge which could be requisitioned to make Terry's the most desirable residence on site. Caro would never even notice if she took some old curtains that hadn't been used in years from the airing cupboard . . .

And now here she was, lugging a suitcase full of fruitcake

and chutneys that Caro had insisted she pack for Jean across the pavement that led to Mina's house. She was beginning to wish Caro had made all the arrangements after all, since there had been no one to meet her at the station and she'd waited for nearly an hour before finally taking a taxi to Mina's house. She only hoped they were expecting her now and not next week, or last week, which would be terminally embarrassing.

She hadn't realised how worried she had been until Mina opened the front door. Her hair had been clipped short, and the little that remained had been bleached to the colour of buttermilk. She was wearing dark mauve lipstick and her pale skin was stippled with spots. She seemed neither surprised, nor especially pleased to see Suzie, merely greeting her with a laconic, 'Oh, hi there Sooz, how's things?' which hardly made up for the hour-long wait at the station.

Suzie set her suitcase down in the cluttered hallway. 'Thank goodness,' she said, 'it weighs a ton.'

Mina looked at the case suspiciously. 'What is it? Rocks?'

'No, actually, it's some chutney for Jean. And a cake Mummy made as a present.'

'Brilliant, I haven't eaten for ages.'

'I'll get it out when I unpack.' Suzie wondered if Mina was going to show her to her room.

'Hey, Rupe, Suzie's brought a cake.'

'Great,' a man's voice came from the living room, 'I'm starving.'

'Well, it's for Jean, actually. Don't you think we should wait until she gets back?'

'Don't be stingy, Sooz. She might be bloody days.'

'Really? Where's she gone?'

'Christ knows. Yorkshire, I think.'

'Wales,' Rupert's voice again. 'You know she said Wales.'

'Same difference,' muttered Mina, crouching down as if she intended to start unpacking Suzie's case right there in the middle of the hall.

'Here, I'll do it,' said Suzie, who had visions of all her neatly-folded underwear being exposed in the hall for everyone to see. She was mentally digesting the fact that she was apparently visiting a home without a resident adult. As she extracted both cake and chutney, she was not altogether sure that this was a good move. Especially when Mina scurried into the living room with the cake and began breaking bits off with her fingers and handing them round.

Suzie followed her. Rupert was stretched out on the floor, his bare feet resting in the lap of a girl with matted brown hair. He still looked just as she remembered him, tall and good-looking in that slightly faded, blond way which she had always found so attractive.

'Hello,' Suzie addressed the room generally. Rupert merely grunted. The girl, whose name Suzie never did learn, did not even look at her. Only the occupant of the armchair, a youth with a large head and bulbous features, was anything like welcoming.

'Hi, Suzie,' he said, 'I'm Arnold.'

'Oh, hello, Arnold.'

Suzie perched on the arm of an empty chair and watched the cake being dismembered and wondered what she was supposed to do now. There was a sinking ache at the pit of her stomach, a kind of foreboding that the week ahead was not going to be at all as she had expected. She couldn't help wishing Jean was going to be there, after all.

'After that I worked for a couple of years for an antique dealer. To begin with I just minded the shop when he was away, but after a month or two he trusted me to do some simple restoration work.'

'Why did you stop?'

'He was arrested for embezzlement. I've never been a very good judge of character.'

Lydia had decided that although Wyndham had never asked her a single personal question, it was high time he learned something about her. To do him justice, he was making adequate noises of interest. A captive, if not deliriously enthusiastic, audience was sufficient encouragement, especially after several glasses of champagne.

'Then I ran a health food store for about eighteen months. It belonged to a friend of mine, but she was suffering from ME.'

Wyndham smiled. 'Hardly a recommendation for her products, one would think,' he commented.

'She saw the irony too. Anyway, after a year or so I started to get ill as well. It's no life, you know, weighing out beans and pulses all day. And the profit margins are lousy.'

'I shall bear that in mind if I am ever tempted by the wholefood market.'

'All things in moderation.'

Lydia spoke with some feeling. After nearly three months of the simple fare of the recluse – a diet based around tea and toast and nothing that took more than fifteen minutes to prepare – the glories of *haute cuisine* were proving rather a shock to the system. The chef at the Mulberry Tree produced various minute offerings in addition to the scripted menu: tiny pizzas sizzling with basil and olives, and thimble-sized brioches stuffed with smoked salmon and caviar had been brought with their aperitifs; now the main course had been cleared away and two dainty goblets of cardamon-flavoured ice were set before them with a flourish. Lydia made a mental note to skip dessert.

She remembered the first evening she had gone out with Gordon: he had taken her to a film put on for doctors by a large drugs company where he had insisted on asking the presenter a whole barrage of questions about the drug which eventually forced her into admitting that, far from being the miracle cure she had been told, it had various unpleasant side effects and might, under some circumstances, prove fatal. The presenter had left in confusion and Gordon had been given a round of applause. Later, over supper in a small bistro where Gordon was well-known, he had expounded to her his vision of the media's role in preventative medicine. If Gordon had stage-managed their first evening to demonstrate his high standing and dedication, Wyndham was letting her know that he offered nothing but the best.

Truth to tell, after nearly three months of living like a hermit at Rose Cottage with only occasional forays to the Manor for diversion, nothing but the best was extremely tempting. The red dress fitted perfectly, and the knowledge that it had been made for her without her knowing was both intrusive and seductive. It was sexy and garish, and she loved it already. She had found a pair of high-heeled sandals, and her entrance into the restaurant had been satisfyingly dramatic. Wyndham was a highly civilised companion: a brief fling, she told herself, at this stage of her life was just what the doctor ordered. Well, not one particular doctor – she thought guiltily of the letter to Gordon telling him their marriage was over, which she had finally posted that same afternoon.

Afterwards, when they stepped outside into the frost-cold air of the car park, she wobbled momentarily on her high heels and Wyndham touched her elbow to steady her. It was almost the first time they had made physical contact since the first polite kiss of greeting, and Lydia felt a shiver of mingled apprehension and pleasure. Apprehension because there had been safety in her period of celibacy; pleasure because she was suddenly impatient to end it.

She paused, and turned to face him. His eyes were smiling, as if the evening was turning out just as he had expected. Lydia felt an urge to take control of events. 'Well,' she asked, 'is it time to do a Pepys?'

'It depends on what a peeps is.'

'It's not a what, it's a who.'

'Who, then.' There was a hint of indulgence in his smile, as he waited for her to explain.

'Our immortal diarist, of course,' she told him lightly, 'Samuel Pepys. And so to bed.'

He hesitated. 'Are you always so direct?' To her satisfaction she saw a flicker of annoyance move briefly across his face.

'Only when I'm flirted with. Besides, if you insist on dressing me as a scarlet woman, what can you expect?'

He relaxed suddenly, remembering their conversation that first afternoon in the steward's room. '*Touché*,' he said softly, 'I was about to suggest we talk paint samples over a glass of cognac, but it would simply have been a ruse to lure you back to Haddeley Hall.'

'Then you should be grateful to me, Wyndham, I've saved you the trouble.'

Wyndham was old-fashioned enough to dislike short cuts in these matters and he briefly considered driving her back to Rose Cottage and bidding her a brusque good night, but she had been looking extraordinarily desirable all evening, and never more so than now, with the rain beading her thick dark hair and that strangely haunting expression that could shift from defiance to vulnerability in an instant. For once, he decided, he could see the advantages of bluntness. He touched her cheek lightly with his fingers, then leaned forward and pressed his mouth against hers.

'Kissing in the car park,' he said when he drew away. 'It's a long time since I've done that. Very well, then, Lydia. Let us Pepys.'

His driver was standing nearby, and had discreetly looked in the other direction while they kissed. Now he opened the door and Lydia eased herself gracefully in. Leaning back on the pale upholstery, Wyndham silent beside her, she felt pampered and luxurious and aware of all the physical details of her own body that she had ignored for so long. Briefly, as the car turned off the road and began the slow drive to Haddeley Hall, Wyndham turned to her. He was frowning slightly, as though there were something he wished to say, but he merely took her hand and raised it to his lips, then wrapped himself in solitude once again. The car came to a halt at the front of the house, Wyndham bid good night to the driver and ushered her into the hall, where Miguel was waiting and took her coat. The manservant's behaviour was faultless, but Lydia could see disapproval revealed in every line of his body, as he walked swiftly away to the rear of the house, the arm which carried her coat extended slightly, as though he feared contamination.

Wyndham turned to Lydia and looked at her without speaking for some moments. She waited, aware suddenly of the hugeness and the silence of the house. He raised his hand and, very gently, touched her bare shoulder, allowing his fingers to slide a delicate line across the raised bones of her throat before his hand cradled the back of her neck and he drew her towards him and kissed her again, long and slow. Lydia felt the cold, hard skin of convalescence start to fall away and the sensuous heart of her which had been buried for far too long was beginning to unfold in warm layers of desire, when all of a sudden Wyndham drew back.

His hands still resting lightly on her shoulders, he smiled and said, 'My lovely Lydia. First there is something I want to show you.'

Annoyance flamed inside her, but she bit it back. Just as she had seized the initiative from him by her proposition outside the restaurant, so now he was manoeuvring to reclaim it. She had no intention of making that easy for him.

So she confined herself to a lazy, 'What is it?'

For answer he led her along one of the passageways and up a staircase at the side of the house. This brought them to a landing she had not seen since the day of her first visit. Wyndham pushed open a door that led into a small, octagonal room and from there he led the way up a narrow, spiral staircase. By the time they reached the top, Lydia was shivering, partly from the cold, as this part of the house was not heated, but partly from excitement: the journey felt like the start of a quest in a story. There might be a gateway to magic at its summit, or perhaps – and she giggled as another possibility occurred to her – the first Mrs Wyndham Sale, not dead at all, but mad and locked away from public gaze in her lonely tower room.

'You're cold,' said Wyndham, as they entered the small room. He slipped off his jacket and put it across her shoulders.

'I never knew this was here.'

'It's a private place,' was all the explanation.

The room was bare but for two wooden chairs and an enormous telescope, raised to point through one of the high windows which completely ringed the tower.

'It was designed as an observatory by Alexander Fletcher about a hundred and fifty years ago. He was an amateur astronomer of some repute. I believe a comet was named after him. This telescope is almost identical to the one he used, apart from a couple of modern refinements. It arrived a couple of weeks ago.'

Wyndham stooped to peer through the lens. 'It's trained on the Pleiades at the moment. Do you know which those are?'

Lydia went to the window and looked up at the night sky. 'I'm a city girl,' she told him. 'Passing jets were the only lights I grew up with.'

When he had pointed out the cluster of stars visible with the naked eye, he said, 'Also known as the seven sisters, named for the seven daughters of Atlas. Now look.'

Seeing the same point in the heavens through the telescope she was astonished to see not seven, but dozens of bright stars.

'What a shame,' she said lightly. 'They'll have to rename it. I never knew you were an astrologer.'

Wyndham had gone to stand by the window. 'Astronomer,' he said, 'I don't see fortunes in the stars. Quite the contrary.'

'So what do you see?'

'Oh, just the infinitesimal smallness and futility of our existence. A great many of those stars burnt up thousands of years ago, but their light is only reaching us now. It's good to be reminded how petty we are.'

'How very gloomy.'

'Not at all. It is a release.'

'From what?'

He did not answer. Lydia bent down to look through the lens once more, then tried to angle the telescope to another part of the sky. 'It doesn't move,' she said.

'It does, but it's a complicated process,' he told her. 'You can't just wave it around like binoculars.'

'I'd like to see a different star.'

'Another time.'

Lydia straightened. Wyndham was leaning against the window sill, his arms folded across his chest. She could tell that, deprived of his jacket, he was beginning to feel the chill of the little room. She went to stand beside him and gazed out into the high brightness of the sky, and the inky black of the park spread all beneath them.

'Shall we go down?' he asked.

'It's lovely up here,' she said. 'But I can't help wondering why you want to be reminded of how futile we all are.'

He was shivering now. He said, 'Because it makes the present moment that more precious. Not because it means anything at all. But because it is all we have.'

'I still think that's depressing.'

'Only because you haven't understood,' he said, and kissed her. 'That's enough stargazing for one night. I'm bloody freezing. You can stay here if you want, but I'm going down for a brandy.'

'What an excellent idea. Here, have your jacket back. I never realised you were cold.'

On the landing, Wyndham turned to her and said, 'There's

brandy in the dining room or in my bedroom. Which would you prefer?'

'Same kind of brandy?'

He nodded. 'Champagne cognac. The best.'

'Oh, of course. Then which is warmest? You're still shivering.'

'The bedroom.'

It was lit only by the embers of a log fire, glowing red against the darkness. When Lydia went to switch on a lamp, Wyndham stopped her. 'No, leave it.'

She remembered then that this was one of the only rooms in the house which had been decorated before Annabel was taken ill, and she was suddenly very conscious of the dimly-perceived furnishings and pictures. Wyndham put a couple of logs on the fire and poured two glasses of brandy from a decanter on a small side table. As he handed one to her he said, 'Let's drink to the present moment.'

'I'll drink to that.' She sipped a mouthful of the brandy, then set her glass down. 'Is there anything else you want to show me?' she asked.

He shook his head. He was watching her very intently. She took the glass from his hand too and set it down beside her own. 'Then kiss me,' she told him.

He leaned towards her and touched her mouth caressingly with his own. She put her arms around his back and her lips parted on a sigh as she struggled to control her desire until she was sure of him, until she could be certain he would not move away from her again. When he did move, it was only to step out of his trousers and slide on a prophylactic; she began to go towards the bed, but he said, 'No, here,' and pulled her down to kneel in front of him, easing the red silk up over her thighs and rolling on to the soft rug with her. He pushed himself into her with a ferocity which both startled and excited her, but still she was wary of abandoning herself to him, so that her pleasure, when it came, caught her by surprise, as if she were fighting against her own body, as well as his. Even now their love-making retained a battling edge; sensing he was nearing his climax, she rolled swiftly over so that she was astride him when he ejaculated, and the waves of his pleasure pulsed through her, answering her own.

For a moment he lay stunned, as though sleeping, while the energy drained from him. Then he opened his eyes and looked up at her, setting her down beside him as he raised himself on one elbow. He put his hand on the hem of her skirt, but then bent to kiss the bare flesh of her hip bone before tugging the silk back over her legs.

He put his arms around her and held her for a moment, then stood up and looked down at her, smiling. 'Thank you, Lydia,' he said. Then, 'Come, and so to bed,' as he led her towards the heaped up pillows in the enormous, shadowy four-poster.

15

Caro burst into tears.

'I can't take it back because I've worn it twice already.' She spoke through her sobs. 'And the shoes. Oh, I knew I shouldn't have spent so much, I knew it!'

'Then why the hell did you?' White with shock and rage, Jim glanced again at the figures on the credit card statement. 'And over a hundred pounds on lunch. How can two people spend over a hundred pounds on *lunch*, for God's sake?'

'That's what I said! I mean, I simply couldn't believe my eyes. We hardly ate a thing, it's outrageous.'

'I don't give a damn how much you ate, Caro, only what it bloody cost.'

'They ought to put their prices up outside the door. It's not fair, luring people in like that, it's a kind of blackmail.'

'Oh, balls. No one forced you to go there.'

'I just wanted to give Polly a treat,' Caro sobbed, stung by Jim's bad language. 'I hardly ever see her.'

'Polly? Polly's a walking bank roll, she doesn't need you to give her treats. Caro, we simply do not have this kind of money.'

'Oh, it's all my fault, I know it is, I'm so hopeless at anything to do with money. It's all ghastly, I wish I'd never gone.'

'So do I,' said Jim grimly. 'But you did. And now we have to pay for it. How on earth are we going to do that?' Jim had done a few quick calculations. 'Do you realise you spent more than half our entire month's income in a single day?'

'Really?' There was genuine amazement in the tear-swimming eyes. 'Is that possible?'

'Of course it's bloody possible. Look for yourself.'

'No, I can't bear it. I believe you. I'll just never go to London again. It's London that does it. I'll cut right back.'

'Really?' Jim was still fuming. 'Do tell me how.'

Caro hated it when Jim went all supercilious and cold on her, even the swearing was better than that. She struggled to find some way of proving to him that she was totally sincere in her determination to spend less money, but as their expenses were already pared to the bone, as far as she could see, no obvious solution sprang to mind. After a while she said, 'I know. I'll use the Metro instead of the Range Rover. It's fuel efficient, you said so yourself.'

'Brilliant. That must be good for about ten pounds a month. What else?'

'And . . . oh, I don't know. I'll think of something.'

'In the meantime, Caro dearest heart, you have landed us well and truly in the shit.'

'Stop it, Jim, I can't bear it when you talk like that.'

'Then for God's sake stop crying. It never solves anything.'

'No, I'm sorry. I'm trying . . . I know, Jim, I'll get a job in a pub or – or somewhere. There must be something I can do. If I had a job—'

Jim groaned. The vision of Caro bravely pulling pints behind the bar at the Bird in Hand was hardly inspiring. Besides, they had already slotted into a well-worn track: all the hundreds of times he had berated Caro for spending too much came back to him in a wave, and he was overwhelmed by futility and rage. Once, years ago, after a particularly bitter wrangle involving bedroom curtains, she had found herself work cleaning for the wife of one of his colleagues. The job had lasted two days, the misery and humiliation for months.

Caro covered her face with her hands, and her shoulders pumped with sobs. 'I'm only trying to help.'

Jim hated to see Caro crying like that. There was something indecent in a woman of her age and build carrying on like a schoolgirl. If it was intended to elicit sympathy, then it was definitely counter-productive. Suddenly afraid that his fury and exasperation might push him into saying something he would later regret, Jim stood up. He flung the bill down among the residue of their half-eaten breakfast – one of Caro's 'proper' breakfasts, poached eggs and freshly-pressed orange juice and marmalade in a porcelain pot – and snapped, 'I'm going out. Maybe when I get back we can talk this through sensibly. If you're capable of ever doing anything remotely sensible, that is.'

He slammed the back door on the renewed sounds of Caro's misery and narrowly missed Bumpkin's tail as the dog, determined not to miss a walk, no matter what the cause, squeezed out after him. Man and dog set off briskly and, without a second thought, followed the road towards Rose Cottage.

Lydia had awoken just before it grew light, but already she was alone in the bed. Damn, she thought, she had intended to be the first to rise, the first to say thanks, and see you some time. Already she was certain that in her dealings with Wyndham the least committed would always keep the upper hand. She had a further instinct that the upper hand was going to be important. Besides, she had no great desire to sit, still in her scarlet-woman silk dress and strappy sandals and endure a morning-after breakfast in the sombre dining room, served by a disdainful Miguel.

She sat up and pushed her hair back from her face. It was strange, waking in what had so obviously been Annabel's bedroom, almost as if she had caused Wyndham to be unfaithful, though since his wife had been dead for nearly a year that was clearly ridiculous. All obvious traces of her, any photographs or personal items, had been removed, but Lydia could sense her influence everywhere – in the muted, tastefully patterned wallpaper, and the curtains and carpet that picked out the soft pinks and greens, in the sprigged lawn sheets and the ivory silk lamp shades and the water-colour views in their velvet frames. Though remembering Wyndham's account of how decisions were reached in his marriage, maybe this conventionally feminine room illustrated his preferred taste, not his wife's. In which case he must secretly hate what she was doing in the steward's room.

Good, thought Lydia inconsequentially, serves him right. But the thought was without rancour. This morning she was feeling well disposed towards Wyndham, if slightly mistrustful. Their love-making had been a surprise. Perhaps she and Gordon had grown too used to each other over the five years they had been together; she had forgotten the exhilaration of exploring uncharted territory, of revealing herself afresh. And Wyndham too had been not at all what she had been expecting. All the more reason, she decided, to remove herself promptly now.

In the bathroom she showered, then wrapped herself in an enormous white towelling robe, while debating whether to put her poppy-coloured dress back on or whether to ferret around for something more neutral of Wyndham's. Before she had made up her mind, she heard his voice in the corridor, 'I'll take that now, thank you, Miguel,' and he came in bearing a large tray laid with breakfast for one and coffee for two. He was washed and dapper and efficient, and looked as if he had been up for hours.

'I heard the shower,' he said. 'I thought you'd prefer breakfast up here.'

'How very considerate of you.'

'Of course. Sorry I left you in the lurch just now. Jet lag. I've been up since five.' He poured coffee into a cup and handed it to her.

'God, when do you sleep? Just coffee for me, that's fine.' Cradling the coffee, she went to stand by the window and looked out over the familiar view of parkland and trees, with Raven's Beacon visible beyond in the morning light. It was a slightly different perspective from the one she had grown used to in the steward's room, but already it was a view that she loved. She said, 'I want to get back to Rose Cottage. And I'm sure you're busy.'

Wyndham came to stand beside her. He was only a couple of inches taller than her, and in this unforgiving morning light, the tiny lines on his skin were accentuated . . . but even now his pale, slightly flat face, with its delicate features remained attractive. His mother had probably been beautiful, she thought, yet there was nothing effeminate about him. Quite the contrary in fact. She said, 'I can feel myself turning into a white mouse with every passing moment.'

'OK,' he said easily, 'I'll drive you.'

'Thanks. My sandals aren't much use for walking.'

Wyndham glanced down at her bare feet, then asked, 'Tell me Lydia, why do you have bile green toe-nails?'

'Designer colours, Wyndham. They're all the rage. Just like your walls will be.'

'They look revolting.'

'You didn't complain about them last night.'

'No.' He hesitated, no longer looking at her feet, but at the shadowed flesh where the lapels of her robe met just above her breasts. He said smoothly, 'Last night, my dear Lydia, there was absolutely nothing to complain of. Last night was . . . very special.'

'I'm delighted to hear it.'

'And you?'

'Of course. No complaints. Absolutely none.'

'Good.'

He set his hands about her waist and kissed her. It was intended, she was sure, as a courteous kiss of thanks, nothing passionate or romantic, and she kissed him lightly back. He drew away, looked at her intently for a moment, then seemed about to speak. Instead, he loosened the belt of her robe, slid his hand against the warm skin beneath her breast, and kissed her again, purposefully. The way his controlled façade dissolved in an instant was just one of the things that made Wyndham such an attractive proposition.

Lydia stepped back. 'I'll get dressed,' she smiled. 'It'll only take me five minutes.'

A fleeting moment, and he was once again remote. Lydia sensed that he would have been displeased had he allowed himself to be deflected from whatever schedule he had planned for today. He returned her smile coolly. 'I'll wait for you downstairs.'

He left the bedroom at once, closing the door noiselessly behind him, and Lydia twisted the corner off a croissant and ate it, thoughtfully, as she dressed.

'Arnold is OK, Sooz, apart from he's got this really twisted sense of humour. Actually he can be totally sick at times.'

'Oh?'

'Yeah. Like spiking people's drinks. That kind of crappy trick.'

'To make them get drunk?'

'The worst was when he dropped some acid into this young

kid's shandy – the boy really flipped out, he was in intensive care and then they had to put him into some kind of bin. It's worse when you're not expecting it, you know. It was pretty scary. The police were hassling everyone for ages.'

'Didn't Arnold get into trouble?'

'He got a shock, that's for sure, but no one fingered him. After a bit he even started boasting about it. Like I said, he's got a weird streak. But he can be good fun. And he's got a brilliant cash point card, which is more than most of the jerks I know. His dad's some kind of famous actor, a police hero on the box, or something like that. Arnold doesn't see him much, but he gets a mega allowance. Actually, I think Arnold's a bit hung up really because girls never seem to fancy him much. Not a load of sex appeal, that one.'

'Oh.' Suzie thought this was an understatement, but was too charitable to say so. Rupert's friend Arnold had an oversized head shaped like an avocado and a lugubrious, hang-dog face. She glanced down at her mug of instant coffee. Its pale, grey-brown surface glinted menacingly up at her. She and Mina were sitting at the pine table in the basement kitchen. Somewhere upstairs Rupert, and maybe several other people – Suzie had lost track of the comings and goings the previous evening – were still sleeping. She pushed the mug away, its contents untouched. She was aware of being very hungry: since the remains of her mother's cake and a couple of cups of tea the previous evening, she had eaten nothing.

'Tell you what, Mina,' she said casually, 'why don't we go into town and look at the shops?'

'If you like.' Mina sounded fairly apathetic at the prospect.

'We could maybe get a sandwich and a cup of coffee some-where,' Suzie added, and then, fearing her motives might be too obvious, she said, 'You get to miss cafés in Briarswood.'

'OK, but it'll have to be your treat. I'm bloody skint until Jean gets home,' here Mina frowned, '—and probably afterwards as well.'

'That's OK, I've got my half-term money. I could buy a few groceries too, if you like.'

'Great.' Mina was brightening. 'And there's this really wicked nail varnish I want to get.'

'But you haven't any money.'

'We'll nick it. Nail varnish is easy. I can get you some too if you like.'

Suzie wasn't at all sure what to make of that.

For some reason the extravagant meal at the Mulberry Tree, with only a mouthful of croissant and coffee on waking, had left Lydia ravenous. As soon as Wyndham had dropped her off at Rose Cottage – he showed no sign of wanting to come in, and she did not invite him – she pulled a heavy sweater over her dress and made a pot of tea and some toast. Just as she had sat down to enjoy herself, Jim arrived. She fetched another mug and made him sit down opposite her at the rickety table in her living room. He looked in a pacing mood, and she did not want her breakfast ruined by moody pacing.

'Have I done something wrong?' she asked, as he glowered at her over the toast.

'Not that I know of, why?'

'You look about as cheery as the Grim Reaper.'

'Sorry.' He attempted, but with only partial success, to modify his expression. 'Financial worries.'

'Ah. Then please keep them to yourself.' She assumed an Oscar Wildish voice and said lightly, 'I cannot abide worries of any kind, especially not financial ones, on a Monday morning.'

'Hm.' He glared at the toast.

'Do you know the joke about the actress and the porcupine?'

'Sorry?'

Lydia sighed. From the look of him, Jim was not to be deflected from his misery by mere banter. First Suzie and wood, now Jim and money: what was it about being a single and unemployed female that made one such a magnet to misery on Monday mornings?

She said, 'That bad, eh?'

'It's bad enough, now I'm on a reduced pension. And there's no prospect of any extra in future.'

Lydia said nothing.

'God, it's such a bloody cliché, that's what gets me down most,' Jim went on. 'Paterfamilias gets all heavy-handed regular as clockwork every time the damned credit card statement arrives. Sometimes I feel like a caricature of a stern Victorian husband.'

Still Lydia said nothing.

'But I honestly think that Caro will one day make us bankrupt.'

Since Jim had brought his wife's name into the conversation, Lydia asked, 'Can't her parents help out?'

'Not a chance. George explained to me years ago, man to man, of course, over a couple of his gin and tonics, that he would never undermine my position in my own home by interfering. Which was code for not helping out under any circumstances.'

'Can't Caro explain things to them?'

'She did ask them for help a couple of times. Twinks once gave her fifty pounds out of her dress allowance. And then last year George let us come and live at the Lodge, which was good of him. But for Caro especially it's a great let-down, having to return to the parental home.'

'Presumably it's only temporary. She's sure to be well-off eventually.'

'Her brother William gets the lot. Of course, we'll be able to stay on at the Lodge.'

'Sounds bloody unfair to me. Poor Caro.'

'She doesn't see it that way.'

All at once, Jim's anger had evaporated. He was ashamed at having complained about Caro to Lydia, ashamed at having made Caro cry to no purpose, since nothing would be changed. Most of all he felt ashamed at not providing the kind of income which might have accommodated Caro's occasional lapses. He had only to look at her brother William's friends to see that George and Twinks must have been expecting a son-in-law with very different career prospects from those of an impecunious assistant lecturer in a new university with no family money to back him up.

Lydia watched Jim as she finished her second piece of toast and peanut butter. Suddenly she understood how deeply these financial anxieties hurt him. Beneath his anger, which was passing, she saw his humiliation at having reached retirement age still unable to balance his household budget.

She said, 'I'd have thought the university gave you a decent pension.'

'Depends what you call decent. It certainly doesn't cover Caro's shopping extravaganzas with Polly. Oh, to hell with it, I'll go and rob a bank or something.'

'Oh, brilliant. I can just see Caro queuing up to visit you in Wormwood Scrubs.'

'Better than having her work as a barmaid.'

'Is that what she's planning to do?'

'She was muttering about getting some kind of job.' Suddenly Jim didn't want to talk about Caro any more. He gave Bumpkin a crust of toast and said, 'Never mind, it'll pass. How about you?'

'Me? I'm fine. Rather well, in fact.' Lydia had stood up to put more hot water in the teapot.

Jim peered round the edge of the table and observed, 'Nice skirt. Sandals too. Not very seasonal though.'

'I was out last night.'

'Oh?'

'With Wyndham.'

Jim was digesting the fact that she was still wearing clothes from the previous evening. Lydia, watching his expression, sat down again and said with a sudden smile, 'As a matter of fact, Wyndham dropped me off just before you got here.'

'Oh.' Jim paused and then added rather stiffly, 'I hope you had a good time.'

'I most certainly did. And thank you, Jim, for your concern.'

'I didn't realise you were so thick with him.'

'I wasn't. He only got back from the Far East yesterday.'

'Our Mr Sale is a fast worker then.'

'Quite pushy, actually. He had this dress made for me while he was away. It fits perfectly. Look.' She stood up again and lifted the sweater. Arms crossed above her head she turned around slowly. 'He's got silk factories all over the place. And now they're branching out into their own range of clothing. Designer stuff.' Her voice came out muffled from behind the layers of wool.

'Very nice, Lydia. You can sit down now.'

She sat. 'You don't like him, do you?'

'Not much. Do you?'

'I'm not sure.' She contemplated the question for a few

moments, before saying slowly, 'I enjoy being with him, for a short while at least. I wouldn't say that I trusted him particularly.'

'I'd have thought that was important. Trust.'

Lydia smiled at the huffiness apparent in his voice. Then she said, 'What worries me about being with Wyndham is that I start playing all those terrible games. I've always hated that way of carrying on, haven't done it since I was a teenager, but the odd part is that with Wyndham I seem to enjoy it.'

'Games, what sort of games?'

'Oh, you know, trying to make a move before he does, staying one step ahead. Pretending to play hard to get.'

'Not that hard to get, by the sound of it.'

This time even Jim heard the pique in his tone and, noticing Lydia's amusement, he broke into a grin.

She put her hand on his. 'Dear old Jim, I do believe you're jealous.'

'Don't you dear old Jim me. I've enough on my plate right now without being treated like some doddery old fossil. And of course I'm bloody jealous. I don't suppose your Mr Sale has heart failure every time he opens a statement.'

'I expect he finds other things to fret about.'

'Good. May he get ulcers.' Jim removed his hand from under hers and stood up. 'Meanwhile, I suppose I'd better go home and work out yet another financial plan. Which will last all of six weeks. Probably less, with Christmas due. What are you doing today?'

'I don't know. I think I'll skip decorating at Haddeley Hall for a day or so, and it's half term, so there's no infants' reading. I might go down to the Hollows for a bit. You could come with me if you like, meet them for yourself.'

'No thanks. Why do you want to go anyway?'

'Because I feel like it. And after the luxury of the Mulberry Tree and Haddeley Hall, a nice cup of tea with Hopi and her friends will be very welcome. It's a contrast, like cardamon ice.'

'What?'

'A palate cleanser.'

'Slumming,' said Jim firmly. And then, in his mangled French, he emphasised the point, '*Nostalgie de la boue*.'

'You're bloody hard to please, Jim. You don't like my rich friends and you don't like my poor ones either. What am I supposed to do, sit around here all day and wait to be invited to dinner with you and Caro once a month?'

'At least Caro ought to be pleased. One of her more successful matchmaking efforts.'

'Well, tell her not to get too carried away just yet. It's probably just a brief fling.'

'Do you think so?' And at that prospect Jim looked genuinely cheerful, for the first time that morning.

By the middle of that afternoon Suzie still didn't know what to think. She had been Mina's devoted adjutant for so long in the past that it required a tremendous mental turnaround to start being critical of her now. Besides, it was undoubtedly exhilarating to jump off the bus while it was still moving and without paying their fare, and to run down a side street while the conductor yelled after them. And she couldn't help but admire the skill with which Mina's fingers tripped across the rows of lipsticks and nail polish and selected precisely the one she wanted, while her attention seemed to be on something else entirely and Suzie knew she was actually keeping a sharp look-out for shop assistants and store detectives. But when Mina suggested they leave the café where they had their coffee and baked potatoes without paying because the waitress was busy with the espresso machine and would never notice, Suzie said no, it was all right, she really didn't mind paying, and she left a generous tip, as if to compensate. And then, when Mina offered her a couple of eye shadows, saying she had plenty more at home, Suzie pretended that they weren't her sort of colour. It would have made her sound like the most dreadful prude if she said she disapproved, but she knew she didn't want to be a receiver of stolen goods. Even that was proving difficult. On the way home, they dropped in at a small supermarket. Suzie bought a few sensible items like milk and eggs and bread and cheese, but when she got outside she found Mina had added several bars of chocolate and a tin of creamed rice pudding, none of which had been paid for.

All the way home, Suzie was in a terrible panic, expecting

the heavy hand of the law to descend on her shoulder. Mina, however, was jubilant.

Caro didn't allow herself to cry for long after Jim had slammed out of the house. Someone might come to the door, and the last thing she wanted was to be found with swollen eyes and a blotchy face. Besides, she knew that Jim had good reason to be angry, and she wanted to have a sensible plan worked out for when he got back, so they could sit down and sort this out between them, as they had often done in the past. So she went upstairs to the bathroom and washed her face and put on fresh make-up and gradually began to feel calm again.

But all the while there was an ache of despondency at the pit of her stomach. Not that she blamed Jim for a moment, she knew it had been her fault entirely, but it did seem terribly unfair that even at her stage in life she couldn't have a relaxed day out with her eldest daughter without ending up feeling like a criminal. The streets of London were full of people, much like her and Polly, who seemed to be spared these sordid worries. Of course, she ought never to have bought the aubergine dress, even though it had been amazing value, considering how perfect it was, but all the rest had stemmed from that, as she now saw: the shoes and the silk scarf to go with it, and then, because she had spent such a monstrous amount on herself, it was only fair to buy a little present for Polly. And she could hardly go back to Briarswood without presents for Jim and Suzie. But obviously, it had all added up horribly. It just seemed so dreadfully unfair.

Sometimes Caro felt a twinge of bitterness towards the university for not having recognised Jim's talents; more often she blamed herself for being such a nincompoop about money, but mostly her sense of injustice was random and unfocused. 'It' wasn't fair – but she had never paused to analyse exactly who or what 'it' was.

Still, there was no time to brood over what could not be changed. Caro had a wealth of experience at being firm with herself, and this morning was no exception. She had caused this mess, and it was up to her to find a solution. While she cleared away the breakfast things she realised it had been silly to pretend she was going to be a barmaid, small wonder that had only made Jim crosser. But there must be something she could do.

There was a depressing catalogue of activities that could be dismissed right away. In the past, at similar moments of crisis, she had launched various enterprises which had always ended up costing more than they earned. She knew from hard-won experience that she could not supplement their income by mending antique china, nor by doing freelance journalism, nor by taking in foreign students. There was, however, a recent change in her circumstances: for the first time in nearly thirty-five years she could contemplate some kind of job outside the home. Suzie would be sixteen next year, Jim was around a good deal of the time and the housework would just have to be slotted in somehow. The only question that remained was: what sort of job? Before her marriage she had worked, briefly and without glory, as a secretary. Nowadays the skills she had learned were hopelessly out of date, but she was sure there were courses you could do to catch up. She would need a computer, of course, to practise on . . .

No. Absolutely not. No computer. She corrected herself sternly. This time she was determined not to spend a penny on anything. The object was to make money, not find new ways of parting with it. She'd have to practise on Jim's when he wasn't using it. She might become a medical secretary, or work in an office. Or maybe she could type manuscripts for people from home.

The sound of the back door opening and closing, and Bumpkin lolloped muddy footprints across the floor. She hardly noticed.

'Jim, dear, is that you? I've been thinking.'

'So have I.'

He came into the kitchen and Caro felt ashamed at how tired and careworn he looked, and, thank heavens, no longer angry at all.

'Sorry about the row,' he said.

'It was my fault,' said Caro. 'You were right to be cross.' She put her hands nervously on his shoulders and, after only the briefest hesitation, he leaned towards her and gave her a small hug. She said, 'Sit down, and I'll make us some coffee. I've got a plan.'

'Have you?' Jim sat down at the table and prepared to listen, but he didn't hold out much hope.

'Yes,' said Caro, 'I think you'll be surprised.' She was feeling quite cheerful now. These after-row discussions at the kitchen table were often the best conversations they had together. They always made her aware of what a strong team they were, and gave her a sense of pulling together. Occasionally, it had even led to a daytime session in the bedroom, though by the look of Jim now, this was not going to be one of those days.

'Not too much coffee for me,' said Jim, 'I've already . . . no, that's OK.' Suddenly he felt guilty about his visit to Rose Cottage, not because of the visit itself, but because he had moaned about Caro to Lydia. Awareness of his disloyalty made him feel uncomfortably tender towards his wife, as well as exasperated, and he listened with quiet attention to her plan to become computer literate. Her sincerity and devotion were apparent in every word, and he could hardly pour cold water on her hopes, so he kept his doubts to himself.

Years ago, before Suzie was born, he had wondered what life would be like if he had a partner with whom he could talk on equal terms. A partner who understood the finer points of eighteenth-century agrarian policy, or even the political squabbles of his department. Nowadays, he found it unsettling even to imagine such a scenario, especially since Caro was always so steadfastly loyal. Never once had she even hinted that her life might have been happier had she chosen to marry a wealthier man.

16

Malcolm shunted the metal trunk around so that it fitted snugly against the foot of Saul's mattress, then sat back on his heels and scratched his head. He was in a quandary. He couldn't decide whether to put the bookcase on the right or the left of the cupboard. Neither position was quite right. The fundamental problem, he could see, was that there just wasn't enough space in the lorry. It had only been manageable during the summer because he and Kate and Saul had spent most of their time out of doors; he had thought that at least one of the advantages of her departure would be that they'd have more room. But that was before Hopi gave him her television, before Saul started collecting toys, school uniform and art work, before Mal brought home an old school desk and chair from the junk shop where Hopi had found her sewing machine. Despite the clutter and the lack of space, the interior of the lorry was acquiring an air of cosy domesticity it had never possessed in Kate's time. The wall above Saul's bed was festooned with work brought back from school: the inevitable collage of autumn leaves, a couple of potato prints and, Mal's favourite, a painting entitled 'My House'. Confronted with this challenge, Saul had drawn a traditional rectangular house with windows each side of the door, pitched roof, chimney and garden path. In addition, his house had four wheels along the base, like a supermarket trolley. This struck Mal as an excellent compromise between conformity and realism.

When Lydia found him he had installed the bookcase to the right of the cupboard and was about to move it back to the left for the third time, so he was heartily glad of the interruption.

'What do you think?' he asked.

'I think you need a bigger lorry,' was Lydia's reply. She was sitting on Saul's tiny chair. 'A bigger lorry with room for some grown-up chairs. I feel like Goldilocks.'

Mal grinned. 'I'm mobile,' he said, 'not upwardly mobile. A bigger lorry sounds a bit materialist to me.'

'I'm all in favour of materialism,' Lydia said, then added ruefully, 'I just don't seem to have got the hang of it yet. Where's Saul?'

'He's gone with Hopi to get a pumpkin. They've got some at the shop. He's a real pain at the moment, complains ten times a day about not going to school.'

'Ann Robertson's delighted at the way he's settled in.'

'What about the other kids?'

'He still doesn't have much to do with them. But he blends in more now he's got a uniform.'

'Odd, isn't it?' said Mal. 'I never thought I'd approve of uniforms, but there you go. It seems to be more democratic for Saul, somehow.'

Mal was rolling himself a cigarette. For the first time, Lydia noticed his hands, their long, tapering fingers and perfectly oval nails. Saul's hands, but on an adult scale. Sensitive hands. She examined his face, the thin nose and deep-set eyes, the full lips pressed lightly together in concentration. Odd, she thought, how she had never before observed that Mal was really quite attractive beneath his shaggy hair and irregular beard and several frayed sweaters. More the sort of man that she had been attracted to in the past than was the smoothly pink and brown Wyndham Sale. Lydia wondered what Mal would look like were he the new owner of Haddeley Hall. It was surprisingly easy to imagine him in an expensive suit, his well-shaped hands emerging from the cuffs of a hand-made shirt. A decent haircut and neatly-trimmed beard, and Mal would be an impressive figure, no doubt about it. She imagined him picking her up in the silver car and taking her to the Mulberry Tree, the waiters bobbing attendance. She imagined Twinks offering him a glass of sherry. 'So nice to have sympathetic neighbours,' Twinks might say.

Mal looked up, suddenly aware of her scrutiny. His eyes appeared to darken as he registered at least some of what was going through her mind. He shifted slightly. 'Like a roll-up?'

'No thanks.' Lydia smiled lazily. She had observed the phenomenon before, the way that when a period of celibacy ended one became more, not less, aware of the sexual potential of other men. She had often wondered whether Sleeping Beauty, after all those years in a catatonic stupor, was satisfied by the Prince alone.

Mal shifted again. He said, 'It's good that we're settled here for the winter. At least it means Saul can get the basics sorted at school.'

'Will you leave in the spring?'

'I expect so. Ted hasn't said anything, but, still, you get restless. You know, time to move on. Though it's getting so difficult to find anywhere to park up these days – and this place is great.'

Lydia felt a twinge of envy. 'The lure of the Open Road,' she said.

'Except it's not so open any more. All the old stop-over sites are getting blocked off, which makes it harder. And I worry more about the hassle, you know, people lobbing bricks through the windows.'

'Does that happen?'

'From time to time, sure it does.'

'Can't the police do anything?'

He laughed. 'I did complain, once. I'd been stopped by them for not having a tax disc. We were only moving off the site because a bloody great rock got hefted through Biff's window. "Where were you when we needed you?" I asked him. He said we should forget it, any problems we had were our own fault for living the way we do.'

'That's outrageous.'

'Common, though. Ask anyone. Not that I mind for myself, particularly, it's Saul I worry about. My schooling was a bit of a mess really because we kept moving house all the time. I don't want Saul to get mucked about like that, but then in lots of ways this is a brilliant life for a kid. I've been thinking about it a lot recently. Having a kid changes you in all sorts of ways – oh.' Mal broke off, suddenly remembering the reason for the wake.

All Lydia said was, 'I guess it does. Maybe I will have that roll-up, after all.'

Hopi returned, scandalised by the cost of the pumpkin. 'Peggy gave me fifty p off, but even so, it's a scam. They're so easy to grow.'

'Peggy?' queried Lydia. 'Since when did you get on first name terms with the local shopkeepers?'

'I don't know. Once she realised we weren't going to lift all her stock, I guess. We're valued customers, now.'

'Hurry up,' complained Saul, jigging impatiently from foot to foot. 'Where's my pumpkin man, then?'

After Lydia had gone, Mal helped Hopi with the pumpkin and Saul interfered and slowed them both up. Mal grew irritated when Saul fooled around and threw soggy pips in the air, but Hopi seemed to have infinite patience.

'Don't waste those pips, Saul,' she chided. 'We can dry them and make a necklace, or even keep some and grow our own pumpkins next year.'

For Mal, the narrow space in the lorry had retained some residue of sexual energy that Lydia had left behind her. He had always liked to watch Hopi when she was engaged in a task, her calm, steady movements, her dark eyebrows drawn closer in concentration. When the work was finished and the pumpkin face had been set down on top of the television and a stubby candle placed inside ready for the evening, Mal put his arm across her shoulders and said, 'That looks great, Hopi.'

A faint flush of pleasure began to spread across her cheek. Suddenly Mal wanted very much to kiss her.

Saul butted his way between them and demanded, 'Light it now.'

A bubble of anger was swelling under Mal's ribs, but Hopi said, 'OK, Saul, it will be dark soon anyway.' As she reached forward to blow out the match she added, apropos of nothing in particular, 'Colin's back from Spain. My mother gave him the address here. He could turn up any day.'

'Oh.' Mal sat down on Saul's little desk and his son wriggled between his knees to contemplate the Halloween face. 'I thought he might stay in Spain all winter.'

'I wondered about that too. But he doesn't seem to have got on all that well, didn't think much of the Spaniards, anyway.'

'I can imagine.' Mal smiled ruefully.

As Hopi made her way back to her own trailer, she reflected that Mal was probably scared of Colin, and with good reason. Colin could wipe the floor with Mal, any day. Which was a shame, a real shame.

For once Saul consented to an early night. A fresh stub of candle had been placed inside the pumpkin and its eyes and sharp-toothed mouth were lit from behind to wonderfully ghoulish effect. Mal had blown out all the other candles because he never left Saul alone with them, but he had agreed to make an exception for the pumpkin man just this once. When Mal went outside for a last smoke, the opening and closing of the door had made the orange light leap and flicker all over the inside of the lorry. It was scary – Saul wriggled deeper under the duvet and thought of shouting out for his dad – but then he decided that this kind of scary was almost fun. Not like the terror of falling asleep which lay behind his frequent refusals to go to bed and left him with dark circles under his eyes in the morning. That was the fear not of sleep itself, but of the dreams that lay in wait for him when he could no longer fight them off. Bittersweet dreams of being back in the flat with his mum and baby sister; suffocating dreams where he was shut up in a grey box, nightmares in which he was being thumped for no reason.

But now he was safe in the lorry with his pumpkin man, and his dad was sitting on the step outside and chatting to Biff as they had a last roll-up together. He could hear a couple of dogs barking and a radio playing, high-pitched laughter which sounded like Kate, but that was OK because she had gone away from his lorry and wasn't a threat any more. Then shouting, but it wasn't angry shouting, and even if it was, it didn't bother him much because he was safe.

Safe. A kind of mantra was repeating itself in Saul's head as he fixed his position at the essential heart of the world. Safe . . . under my duvet, safe in my bed, safe inside my lorry home, on the site, in the field, on the farm, in the village, on planet earth, middle of the universe . . . Safe.

*   *   *

In an attic bedroom in Mina's house, Suzie lay sleepless. She felt sick with exhaustion, but each time she felt herself drifting towards sleep, she forced herself to remain awake. Every nerve in her body ached for the vast silence of Briarswood nights and the privacy of her own bed. It wasn't the traffic noise that bothered her – that could be quite soothing – it was the voices and footsteps inside the house.

Wide-eyed and taut with anxiety, Suzie tried to keep track of who was where and doing what, but with so many people coming and going all evening, that was a desperate task. Rupert and a girl – she thought it was probably the shaven-haired girl named Gail – were asleep in the room next to hers. She assumed they were now asleep. At any rate, the awesomely embarrassing squeaks and groans and gasps which had begun almost as soon as their footsteps climbed the stairs, had ceased. There had been some giggling and pattering of feet, and since then, nothing. While the squeaking and grunting had been going on Suzie had been worried that they didn't realise she was in the next door room and that somehow that had turned her into an eavesdropper. She wondered if she ought to have begun whistling when she heard them first, like sitting in a loo with no lock, just to let them know she was there, but it was soon too late for that. Maybe they didn't care. Now that it was quiet again, she was troubled by how deeply unattractive the noises had been. Nothing tender or romantic or loving, nothing like her secret imaginings. She thought there must be something wrong with her, to have reacted this way.

She wondered where Mina was now. They'd hardly spoken to each other all evening, not since Cass had turned up. Cass was at school with Mina and had arrived in floods of tears because she'd been thrown out of home after a fight with her stepfather who was a psychologist. She'd brought a nearly full bottle of Southern Comfort with her, and she and Mina had drunk most of it watching videos through the evening. Cass was probably sleeping in Mina's room.

That left an ex-girlfriend of Rupert's who was anorexic or bulimic, Suzie wasn't sure which, whom no one seemed to like much, and a couple of boys who had wandered into the house and settled down in front of the television after the pubs had closed. And Arnold.

'Is it all right if Arnold crashes in your bed?' Mina had asked her casually that evening.

'Where will I sleep?'

'You can sleep in there too, of course. Oh Sooz—' and here Mina had given her a superior smile, 'sharing a bed doesn't have to mean sex or anything. Just somewhere to sleep. Rupert and I share with friends all the time. It's just, well, friends.'

'I'd rather he didn't,' said Suzie.

'Well he can hardly sleep on the floor. You're not the only guest in this house, you know,' said Mina, swishing off in a huff.

Now Suzie hoped with every ounce of hope that Arnold was sleeping on the floor, and she didn't care how hard and uncomfortable it was. Every time she heard water running in the bathroom or footsteps on the landing below she tensed in anticipation of the door swinging open, Arnold's large and deeply unattractive face peering in on her. It wasn't that she was afraid of being raped, or anything like that. She might be a fifteen-year-old virgin but she knew enough to be able to fend him off . . . but it was the awful embarrassment of it that she dreaded. With his heavy, mournful features, Arnold was totally obnoxious and repulsive and even sitting near him when he ate a piece of toast was enough to turn her stomach. Mina herself said he was weird. Who knows what someone capable of spiking drinks might do? Maybe he could put something on the pillow that would render her temporarily unconscious, or unable to protect herself . . . it was all such a nightmare, she'd sleep in a chair if she thought there was an armchair somewhere in the house that didn't have someone in it already.

An eerie silence had descended on the house. In the distance a church clock struck four. Suzie was hungry and her stomach rumbled, but it was impossible to battle against sleep any longer. She was sliding—

Slow footsteps on the stairs. A thump and a muttered curse. Arnold's voice. Suzie pulled her nightdress down below her knees and rolled to the furthest side of the bed, by the wall. He was in the room. She could hear him stumbling around, removing shoes and trousers, then the bed sagged as the weight of another body toppled down beside hers. Suzie, curled in a ball facing away from him, had a pain in her upper chest from not breathing properly. Arnold flopped about once or twice like a large fish in the bottom of a boat, and Suzie bounced helplessly beside him. 'Oh, fuck,' came a voice by her ear. A cold hand landed on her hip. Suzie prepared to shout, scream, leap from the bed, punch him in the nose . . . but her limbs had set like concrete, no sound emerged.

And then he snored.

A slow, ragged, gabbling snore.

Now Suzie dared not move for fear of waking him. After what seemed like a lifetime of not moving, she heard the clock strike five, another lifetime and it struck six. Only one more hour and she could get up. Get up and find some excuse to leave.

The clock was striking nine.

In an agony of stiffness from lying in one position so long, Suzie forced herself to uncurl with infinite care so as not to wake the still-snuffling Arnold. His hand, warm now, had slid down to her thigh. When she was standing up and putting on her clothes, she could still feel the hand print on her skin. Her head felt as if it might rattle if she shook it. However, the day might be just bearable if she could begin with a shower.

The basin in the bathroom was rimmed with what looked horribly like vomit. Someone had made a half-hearted attempt to clear it away. Susie was going to finish the job, but then she noticed that the taps also were smeared. Gagging, she retreated to the kitchen.

And there she found Jean, calmly drinking tea and thumbing through a large pile of post.

'Hello, Suzie,' she said amiably. 'Look at this, nothing but bloody bills and circulars. How are things? Caro said you might be dropping round.'

'I'm fine, thanks,' Suzie answered automatically. 'When did you get home?'

'About five minutes ago. Ron's got a conference in London and he dropped me off on the way through.'

'Oh.' Suzie had no idea who Ron was. She glanced uneasily towards the sink where several days' worth of washing up was balanced precariously. But Jean seemed oblivious to the unwashed dishes and the debris on the floor, nor did she raise an eyebrow at the sounds of reviving life form in the sitting room as the chair-sleepers lit cigarettes, came in for mugs of tea or instant coffee, and returned to switch on the television.

When Mina wandered in an hour or so later she glanced nervously at her mother and said, 'Oh, hi Mum. You should've let us know you were coming back, we would have cleaned up a bit.' She moved across to the sink and began stacking things on the draining board.

'That's OK, you can do it now while I catch up on some sleep. I feel wrecked.'

'Me too,' said the anorexic-bulimic girl who had crept in behind Mina and poured herself a glass of water.

Jean cast her a glance of sympathetic contempt. 'You always feel wrecked,' she said. Suzie found a tea towel and joined Mina at the sink. Considering Jean was taking it all so well, she didn't understand why Mina was looking so anxious.

'Oh good,' said Jean, 'plenty of milk. I'm taking a tray up to my room. I'll see you all again later.'

'OK, Mum.'

Just as Suzie was being handed the first mug to dry, there was a piercing yell from Jean. 'Who's bloody pinched all my evening primrose pills? And the Vitamin Es! You know I need those, you all just help yourselves and never consider me. You're all just a bunch of freeloaders and take whatever you want and leave me with bloody NOTIIING!'

It was like a switch being tripped, Jean carried on at full throttle for a good five minutes and the two youths and the ex-girlfriend melted into the background. The front door could be heard opening and shutting several times. Mina was hunched over the sink, scrubbing furiously, so that Suzie had a job to keep up with her. She looked so frightened and miserable that Suzie whispered to her, 'It's OK, I can get some more of those health pills with my half-term money.' But Mina just muttered, 'Bloody cow,' and scrubbed more than ever.

Jean's tirade only ended when Rupert shambled into the room and swore and yelled back at his mother even louder than her. Jean stopped shouting at once, gave him an affectionate hug and put the kettle on for coffee.

'Let's all do something special today,' she beamed. Mina flung the washing up sponge into the water and sat down opposite Jean and began rolling a cigarette.

'Let's go out for hamburgers,' she said.

'No money, love.'

When Caro phoned to talk to Suzie they were all arguing about what film to go and see. As Suzie picked up the receiver in the hall, the last of the night's visitors, Arnold, loped past her to the front door.

'Better split,' he said, jerking his bulbous head in the direction of the kitchen, and then, with a half-hearted grin to Suzie he added, 'See you around, then.'

'I hope not,' thought Suzie, and then, in answer to her mother's questions she said out loud, 'Oh, we've been doing all sorts of things. Shopping, going out, you know. And Jean says she'll take us to the cinema later. Yes, Mummy, of course I'm fine.'

She had been intending to tell her mother that there'd been a change of plan and she was coming home that afternoon, but with Jean right now emerging from the kitchen, what else could she say?

'Suzie's having a wonderful time with her friend Mina. You remember Mina, don't you Mummy? She's that nice girl whose father worked with Jim for years. They've always been as thick as thieves. Such a lively girl, and so good for Suzie.'

'That's nice, dear.' Twinks was sitting very upright in her wing chair, as always. Her pale eyes were fixed on her daughter, as if she was listening, but Caro was beginning to have doubts on this score. Twinks had never really been the sort of mother you could confide in, now she sometimes didn't even seem to hear what was being said to her. Yet Caro knew she was not deaf. It was all very puzzling.

Caro said cheerfully, 'It's good for her to get away on her own a bit.'

George, who was reading about a new system for keeping pigeons away from crops, glanced up and said, 'Can't think why you didn't send her to a proper school. No good keeping them hanging on your apron strings.'

'Jim believes in state education, Daddy.' This argument had

rumbled on for years and neither had the energy any more for anything but the briefest of ritual exchanges. As usual, Caro loyally repeated Jim's argument and never mentioned the deciding factor, which was that private education was beyond their means.

'Your school was the making of you, Caro,' said Twinks.

Caro had a brief memory of boredom and bad food, chilblains and bickering girls and said vaguely, 'I suppose so, Mummy.' Then, more briskly, she went on, 'By the way, I've been investigating a computer course I can do. It sounds jolly exciting.'

'Computers? What for?'

'Interest, mainly. One feels such a dinosaur not knowing anything about them. And you can't get any kind of work these days unless you're computer literate.'

'You don't want a job,' Twinks pointed out.

'I might do. Suzie will be leaving home soon and I'll need something to keep me occupied.'

Twinks stared at her blankly. George said, 'Why? You can't fit everything in as it is.'

'Well—'

'Besides,' said her father, 'ridiculous, no one will employ you, not at your age, Caro. Young blood, that's what people want these days.'

Caro blinked. Her eyes were prickling and painful. Sometimes she felt she was eighteen years old still. She said despairingly, 'Oh well, I don't suppose anything will come of it. But I'd better give it a try.'

Twinks gazed into her empty glass. 'So long as you leave a bit of time for us, now and then.'

After Caro had gone, George said, 'Odd girl, Caro. Can't see what she wants to get fussing with computers for, she'll never get the hang of them. She doesn't seem to be satisfied with what she's got, not like us, eh Twinks?'

Twinks murmured a vague reply. No, she thought, not like me at all. I've always been perfectly content with my life. How could it be otherwise? A fine husband, a lovely home, no worries. I have been a happy woman all my life. A rippling arpeggio strayed through her mind, accompanied by a jolt of acute pain. She remembered, with relief, that there was some cooking sherry tucked away at the back of the larder, and she stood up abruptly.

It was beginning to rain as Caro drove the short distance from the Manor to the Lodge. Big drops of rain spattering against the windscreen and smearing into the grime as she put the wipers on. She felt horribly deflated by her parents' reaction to her latest plan, and had half a mind to give up before she had even begun. Except that the woman at the IT centre had been so friendly and welcoming and she had only mentioned it to George and Twinks because she was genuinely looking forward to starting.

Partly this was because she was missing Suzie, much to her surprise. She had spent so many years waiting for the time when she would be a free agent that this brief taste of future independence had been rather a shock. She was afraid she had been a mother for such a huge chunk of her life that it was now too late for her to be anything else. It might have been easier if she and Jim did more together, but though they were of course absolutely devoted to each other, they didn't actually share very many activities. Caro was beginning to count the days until Suzie's return. Someone to fuss over and chat with across the kitchen table.

Anyway, it didn't matter if George put the dampers on, she simply had to try and bring in some money. Jim's pension never seemed to stretch and one had to keep up appearances somehow. She would never dream of telling her parents they couldn't manage on their income. It might look like a criticism of Jim, and that would never do.

The rain announced itself at Rose Cottage as first of all a gentle pattering on the roof of the lean-to kitchen. Soon, all too soon, this was embellished with a counterpoint of sharp 'plunks' as the water penetrated the several points in the glazing that were not waterproof. Lydia fetched bowls and pots and set them at strategic spots around the kitchen, then returned to the letter she was writing to her friend Charlotte in Minorca.

'*Skate for the sceptical* sounds like a great addition to your Marine Menu. And I'm glad you liked my idea of Octopus for the Orderly – a neat lattice of tentacles would work brilliantly.

I'd be delighted to come and help you get the place decorated and ready for the spring, but I'll have to wait and see how things turn out this end first. I'll definitely let you know by Christmas, so as not to mess you around. That's a promise.

Since I last wrote to you there have been several developments. I somehow got involved in a rather weird New Age sort of ceremony with some travellers who had moved in round here. Not at all my sort of thing, but oddly effective in its way. It happened on the day your godchild would have been born if he/she hadn't decided to skip over this whole messy living bit. Most important of all, though, and I'm sure you'll approve, I finally got round to writing and, what's more, actually posting, a letter to Gordon telling him the marriage died with the baby, for me at least. God knows how he'll take it – I should think he's heartily fed up with me by now anyway – but at least it's done. And I seem to have begun some kind of relationship with the local tycoon – do you remember I told you I had been working on one of the rooms in his house? (A stately home to you and me.) I hate to sound mercenary, but it is a definite pleasure to be wined and dined in style after months of virtuous abstinence. As well as what your mother used to refer to as 'carnal knowledge', which he seems to excel at as well. And now an enormous bunch of orchids has just been delivered to my door. They must have cost a small fortune. Beautiful though they are, I can't help thinking that the money might have been better spent on a workman to fix the roof. Probably a new roof would cost about the same. I can see there's more to this kept woman business than I thought at first. Anyway, I'm sure this whole romance will just be a nine-day wonder, so I'll be winging my way to help you decorate Seafood Selection before the orchids have faded. Better book me a Latin lover to fix my broken heart.

See you soon,
Love,
Lydia'

Suzie had had enough.

Jean had slept all morning and then gone out as soon as she got up. 'Chasing after that creep,' said Mina angrily. There had been no further mention of hamburgers or a trip to the cinema. After sitting around all day, Mina and Rupert and Gail suddenly decided they wanted to go out, so they phoned Arnold, who was the only person they knew with money and a car, and told him to come round for them. It was assumed that Suzie would be tagging along, and so she did. Until now.

They were in a vast club, dark and very hot; Mina, Rupert and Gail had instantly disappeared into the mass of scantily-clad dancers, leaving Suzie and Arnold hovering uncertainly by the entrance. Already the relentless bass thump of the music was hurting Suzie's ears.

'Great place!' shouted Arnold, putting his hand on her arm, and then, 'Are you OK?' he asked. The question sounded almost kind.

'Fine,' she responded automatically, at the same time edging away from his hand. Then she said, 'Actually, I'm feeling quite tired.'

Arnold fished in the pocket of his shirt and brought out a small packet. 'Here, have one of these. You'll be dancing into the middle of next week.'

'No thanks.' She wished refusals didn't always sound so prim and proper. Arnold probably thought she was a hopeless wimp. And then suddenly she no longer cared. She didn't care if she was the only teenager in Great Britain who hated this sort of place and this amount of noise. She didn't care what anyone thought of her, she just wanted to be away from here, away from Arnold and Rupert and Gail. Even away from Mina.

She said, 'If you really want to know, my head hurts and I feel awful. I'm going back to Mina's. Can you tell the others for me?'

'Are you going?' It was hard to hear what was being said over the pulsing music.

She nodded.

Arnold looked around, then said, 'You're right, this place is crap. Let's split.'

Suzie was about to protest that one of them ought to find Mina and Rupert and tell them what was going on, but then she realised that this was an entirely superfluous courtesy. Also, that she had no idea where the club was or how to get back to Mina's house. She remembered too that there had been a number of quite scary looking people on the pavement outside the club.

'It would be brilliant if you didn't mind driving me home,' she said.

'No problem.' Arnold draped his arm over her shoulder and steered her towards the exit.

Once they were in the car, Arnold drove with great slowness and concentration and told her in detail all that was wrong with his life. The sadder his story became, the slower he drove, until Suzie became anxious that they might be arrested for curb-crawling. He told her he was lonely and miserable, his mother was a complete slag and had never done anything for him and his father just threw money at him and told him what a useless prat he was all the time.

Just as Suzie was trying to think of a tactful way of suggesting that things were only going to improve when he stopped feeling sorry for himself and did something positive for once, the car stopped.

'Here we are, sweetie,' he said.

'Where?'

'Home.'

'But this isn't—'

'I have a bachelor pad on the first floor. Very stylish. Come on, I'll show you.'

In the orange glow from the street light, his large face, attempting a seductive smile, looked more than ever like that of some jaded hound.

Suzie began, 'That's awfully kind of you, Arnold, but I thought you were going to drop me off at Mina's.'

'This is better.' His bulbous face was looming closer. Suzie felt the back of her head touch the passenger window as she edged away.

'No,' she said, as firmly as she could. 'I want to go back to Mina's. Now. Please.'

'Oh, Suzie—'

'Stop it.' But before she could say 'Please' again his face had collided with her own and he had begun mumbling all sorts of embarrassing endearments.

Suzie began to tell him she didn't want to hurt his feelings but she really wasn't interested, when his wet lips bumped against her mouth and she felt such a shock of revulsion that she jammed the palm of her hand against his chin and shoved with all her strength. Despite his weight, he offered no immediate resistance and his shoulder slewed into the steering wheel.

He swore viciously and clutched at his jaw. 'Bloody cow, what was that for?'

'Because you weren't listening,' she said, and her voice surprised her with its firmness. 'I don't want to kiss you and I don't want to see your flat. I don't want to see you again, ever. I'm going back to Mina's. Leave me alone.'

She found the door handle and let herself out of the car. She was afraid he might try to stop her, or follow, but as she slammed the door shut behind her, she heard him begin to sob. She couldn't remember ever having made anyone cry before, and for a moment she almost weakened and turned back to comfort him. A picture of misery, he was huddled over the steering wheel. She wavered, then began to walk resolutely away.

As it was half term, Sandra was just taking the children over to her mother's when the stranger pulled up beside her. She recognised him as soon as he began to speak.

'Can you tell me the way to Rose Cottage?'

The newcomer had a broad, handsome face and a mass of

dark hair. In his early forties, he looked strong and purposeful, the kind of man you'd trust to lead an expedition across rugged terrain. But it was the voice, rich and sonorous and with just enough of a Scots accent to be distinctive, which gave his identity away. That, and the fact that he was asking for Rose Cottage.

Sandra patted her hair and wished she was wearing her high-heeled boots, rather than wellingtons. 'You must be Dr Gordon Fairchild,' she said. His face, which was framed by the car window, relaxed into a warm smile.

'Indeed I am,' he said. 'How clever of you to recognise me.'

'We don't get that many celebrities in Briarswood.'

His smile deepened slightly at the word celebrity. Naomi, who was standing beside her mother said, 'Why are you talking to the strange man, Mummy? I thought you weren't supposed to talk to strangers.' Sean was hunting for conkers. Afterwards, Sandra thought it was a shame it was half term and she had the children with her. Otherwise she might have said, 'Rose Cottage? It's hard to explain exactly, but I can jump in and show you if you like.'

As it was, Naomi started demanding sweets at the shop and Sean was about to get muck all over his clean trousers, so she had to give the directions as best she could. Dr Gordon Fairchild smiled his appreciation, then he nodded in the direction of Sean. 'I think your little boy may have put something in his mouth,' he said. 'Best to check. Always the danger from choking.' Then, when she had dutifully made sure Sean had nothing in his mouth and signalled this fact to the famous doctor, he drove away slowly. Watching him go, Sandra was somewhat surprised to see that he was driving a none-too-clean six-year-old Renault estate. Only a year younger than Dave's Astra and not so well looked after. She would have expected something more stylish for a Radio Doctor.

Gradually the darkness beyond the train window began to pale, the sky in the east was brightening, and then suddenly the countryside was flooded with light. Suzie watched it with a sense of awe, as if she were seeing the sunrise for the very first time. She felt she was a different person from the girl who had made the reverse journey only two days before, her suitcase weighed down with chutney and fruitcake.

It had taken ages to walk home. For the first half hour she'd been so relieved to escape from Arnold that she hadn't worried too much about where she was going, and then she found herself near the point where she and Mina had jumped off the bus the previous day. By the time she reached Mina's house, her feet felt as though they had swollen to twice their normal size. The house had been in darkness and she'd had to climb in through one of the downstairs windows. It appeared to be empty – at least there did not seem to be anybody awake. She had packed and phoned for a minicab and left a note for Mina and Jean saying something had cropped up and she had to go home. She waited in the eerie night-time world of the station until she could catch the first train back to Edleston.

She had no idea what she was going to say to Caro, but she knew she would think of something. She would probably go to Rose Cottage and have a coffee with Lydia so that she wouldn't get home too early – if Caro knew she had caught the earliest train, she would be extra suspicious. To her amazement she felt not the least bit worried or upset, or even cross about what had happened – only a kind of floating triumph. For as long as she could remember, Caro had supervised her every meal, insisted on a balanced diet and early nights. Suzie had always assumed that total bodily collapse would inevitably follow any deviation from this strict regime: after all, even when she stuck to it, she felt tired and ill most of the time.

Now she had endured two nights with hardly any sleep, and had not eaten a proper meal in days. She felt dirty, sick and exhausted, but she was still functioning. What's more, she had acted decisively, maybe for the very first time in her life. She felt as though from now on she could cope with anything, anything at all.

The florist's bunch of red roses lay on Lydia's flimsy table. Above them, in the only vase in the house, Wyndham's orchids effortlessly asserted their milky-white and speckled superiority.

'Roses, Gordon, how lovely. I'll put them in water.'

Gordon seemed unable to wrench his eyes away from the orchids. 'Just roses,' he said. 'Nothing special.'

'Nonsense, you know how I love roses.'

'You've found someone else.'

'It's a bit early to say that.'

'An admirer, anyway. I won't ask if you're sleeping with him.'

Lydia made no attempt to hide her annoyance. 'You just did,' she said.

'Did I? Well then . . .'

'You were right the first time. You shouldn't have asked.'

Gordon nodded. 'That means you are,' he said, imperturbably. 'I only hope you're not getting involved in something you'll end up regretting. I can't help being concerned about you Lydia.'

Lydia did not answer straight away. Her fingers picked at the stems of the roses. She did not look at him. At length she said, 'I meant what I said in my letter, Gordon. I'm not coming back.'

He took a deep breath. 'There's no need to talk about that, not yet. And of course, you mustn't do anything you're not comfortable with. You're a free agent, always have been.'

'I know.'

'I realise now that I was probably crowding you. All I meant to do was help you get over the miscarriage, but obviously that was something you had to do on your own.'

'Yes.'

'Sometimes, I've even wondered if you blamed me.'

'You? Why should I blame you?'

'Maybe subconsciously you thought that I would be able to keep you safe, because I'm a doctor. I wanted to, I really did, but it didn't work out.'

His analysis suddenly seemed a little close to the bone. She asked cautiously, 'How about you, Gordon? How have you been?'

He frowned. A frown had always been his way of indicating that he took the questioner seriously. 'I can't say it's been easy, Lydia. But I think I can safely say I'm through the worst phase of grieving. The rage and the disorientation.' There was a silence while Lydia tried to digest this statement. Just possibly, she could imagine Gordon in a rage. He would have read somewhere that anger was an important stage in the process, and so he might have kicked a wastepaper basket and said 'Damn!'. Gordon disoriented was harder to swallow. He said gently, 'I hope I've begun to accept what happened.'

'So you haven't been missing me too much?'

'I was referring to the baby, Lydia. Of course I still miss you, how can you ask? I've thought about you every day.'

'Oh yes, of course.'

'I've been frantic with worry, not knowing where you were. You might at least have trusted me enough to tell me where you'd gone.'

'I meant to. I just kept putting it off.'

His frown relaxed into a warm smile. 'That sounds like my Lydia,' he said fondly. 'Never do today what you can put off until tomorrow, eh? You haven't changed a bit.'

Like Alice when she swallowed the 'Drink me' potion, Lydia could feel herself begin to shrink. She said, 'As a matter of fact, I've changed quite a lot.'

He smiled at her. He was on the verge of saying, 'However much you change, you'll always be my Lydia,' but then some instinct of self-preservation warned him this would not be a good line to take. In the silence, Lydia's eyes narrowed. She was waiting for him to say, 'Whatever happens, you'll always be my Lydia' in which case the conversation could have been terminated before it had properly begun.

Instead he asked, 'What have you been up to all this time? It must be horribly lonely for you.'

'Not at all,' she lied. 'I've always liked my own company, and I've made some good friends.'

'All the same, you must get bored.'

'You'd be amazed what a lot there is to do in the country.'

'Really?' he smiled at her indulgently. 'Don't tell me you devote your time to making pickles and helping out at the church bazaar.'

'Not far off. I've been helping with the infants at the school and . . . oh, other bits as well.' She had no desire to mention her work for Wyndham Sale.

Perhaps because of this omission, she glanced once more at the spray of orchids, and Gordon's gaze trailed after hers. He said, 'Of course, we must not forget the mysterious supplier of orchids.'

Lydia shrugged.

'If you have found someone you care for,' said Gordon, and there could be no doubting his sincerity, 'then I am only too happy for you. I just hope you know what you're doing. You've been hurt so badly in the past, I'd hate to think that might happen again.'

'Oh, I'm much tougher these days.'

This time his smile was wistful. 'You look terribly vulnerable to me. Almost the way you were when we first met.'

Quite unexpectedly, Lydia felt her eyes fill with tears. In retrospect their first encounter had been unbearably romantic. She had been drifting about on Hammersmith Bridge, with no serious intention to throw herself into the river, merely a hopeless wish that such a straightforward option were available. A particularly long and messy affair had just ended and as her ex-lover had also been her ex-boss, she was out of work, pretty well homeless, and low on funds. From time to time, as she wandered up and down the bridge, she had indulged in some futile tears. Enter dark stranger, a jogger, but a jogger who just happened to be a well-known doctor with a weakness for women in distress, especially dramatically dressed and attractive ones. He had produced a handkerchief and offered support. They had adjourned to a pub where Lydia had told him her sad tale. The next day, he had sent her red roses.

'Lydia, I know it's wrong to put pressure on you, but have you really considered what you're doing? How can you simply throw away five years of happiness because of one tragedy?'

Lydia could feel herself weakening in the presence of Gordon's massive certainty. 'I don't know,' she said. 'It seems crazy, doesn't it?'

Suzie had noticed the unfamiliar car parked in the lane. Before ringing the cowbell, she glanced in through the low window and saw Lydia wrapped in the arms of a strange man.

Now what am I going to do? she wondered. It was far too early to return to the Lodge but she did not want to have to drag her suitcase all over Briarswood.

She had used the last of her holiday money on a taxi from Edleston and besides, the car had already driven off. Suddenly glad of the chance to prolong this in-between moment, Suzie tucked her suitcase in the woodshed behind Rose Cottage and took the track that led up to Raven's Beacon. It was a beautiful morning, and Suzie felt almost possessive towards it, having watched its progress from the very first glimmer of light seen from the train.

She was no longer aware of being particularly tired, and she hardly noticed the climb up the old sheep track to the summit. She found a patch of grass that was comparatively free of rabbit droppings and sat down to look at the view and think. The countryside had taken on the soft colourings of autumn: Haddeley Hall with its huge park, the Manor with its gardens, all the scattered houses of Briarswood and the church with its two great cedars. Suzie felt sure that it was much easier to get things in perspective from a vantage point like this, and just at present she had masses to think about.

After a few moments she decided she could probably think just as well, and in greater comfort, if she lay down. Within seconds she was fast asleep.

Lydia sniffed, and eased herself away from the shelter of Gordon's encircling arms. 'I'd better put these in water,' she said.

'Oh Lydia, it's no use pretending with me. I can see how miserable you are.'

'Honestly, Gordon, I'm not miserable and I wasn't pretending. I don't know what's come over me. I was fine until you turned up.'

'I suppose I've stirred up emotions you didn't want to have to deal with yet.' He had followed her into the kitchen. 'Don't you think it's better to face things?'

'I don't know what I'm supposed to be facing. Damn.' The milk jug, which stood on the floor near the sink, had succeeded in catching such a copious amount of rainwater during the night that when she picked it up, some of the water slopped on her shoe.

Gordon looked around him in bewilderment. 'Why are all these pots and pans full of water?'

'The roof leaks. When it rains a lot I need an umbrella just to make a cup of tea.'

'That's outrageous. Who's your landlord? I'll get on to them right away.'

'No. Please don't. It was a joke about the umbrella. This house belongs to an elderly couple who happen to be parents of a friend. They've let me have this place for hardly any rent.'

'Oh Lydia, my dear Lydia. This accommodation is totally substandard. You're letting yourself be exploited again. You'll get ill. How are you feeling? Any aches and pains? Sore throat?'

'No, Gordon, I'm fighting fit.'

'I thought you were looking rather pale when I came in.'

'Honestly, I'm fine.'

Her health having failed him, Gordon turned his attention to the kitchen roof. He tapped and tutted and finally declared, 'A half-decent roofer could get this fixed in no time. It's not a major job. Some of the weatherstripping has perished, that's all. Where's the nearest builders' merchants? I might as well do it for you myself, while I'm here.'

'Gordon, no.'

'It's going to need a couple of cross pieces. Do you have a measuring tape? Better to do a proper job.'

'Gordon, I told you, I don't want you to fix the roof. I'd rather sit here and catch pneumonia. I'd rather drown.'

'Oh Lydia,' Gordon smiled down at her benignly, 'what nonsense you do talk sometimes.'

'I just know I don't want you to mend the roof.'

'There's no one in the world can be perverse quite like you – it's quite adorable.'

'If you carry on talking as though I'm some kind of fluffy pink bear, I think I'm going to scream.'

'Why? Because I've offered to help? Try looking at it from a different perspective. If you don't let me mend your roof, I'll just worry about you more than ever. Can't you let me do it for my sake, if not for yours?'

Lydia screamed.

She also dashed the jug of red roses to the ground where it broke into a satisfying number of fragments.

'There,' Gordon smiled, 'I knew you must have been under the most frightful strain. Now the tension is beginning to show. I've been so worried about you all this time, on your own. Suffering. You need someone to look after you. You can't—'

'No, Gordon. I do not. That's the whole point. That's why I left. I didn't understand it properly until now, I guess that's why I never wrote to tell you where I was.'

'That's OK, darling, no one was blaming you.'

Lydia shook her hair slightly, the way spaniels do when they want to get water out of their ears. She said, 'I knew I had to get away, but I didn't really understand why. Now I think I do.'

'You were grieving for the baby, darling.' Gordon explained this patiently. 'We both were. I thought we'd be able to comfort each other but—'

'No, that's just it. You wanted to comfort me. Never the other way round. It wasn't fair.'

'Dearest heart, do stop, you're not making any sense.'

'Shut up, Gordon. I am making sense. I'm trying to make sense, at least to me. Maybe you won't ever understand, but I've got to try to explain.'

'Of course.' That attentive frown again. 'You know I'm listening.'

'Are you? I wonder. Anyway, when we first met, I admit, I was at a bit of a low ebb.'

'Rather an understatement, don't you think?'

'All right, rock bottom, if you insist. I needed a crutch. You were wonderful. You were kind and understanding and supportive and altogether magnificent.'

'Darling.' He moved to put his arms around her, but she stepped back and put her hands up defensively.

'But then I got better. At least, I tried to. You wanted to carry on being a crutch. You're doing it now, trying to convince me that I'm lonely and miserable and need a new roof.'

'It leaks, Lydia, of course you need a new roof.'

'But that's not the point. It's almost like you need me to fall apart so as you can be superman and do everything all the time. Anyway, it's over. I meant what I said in my letter. I'm not coming back.'

He began to smile away her statement, but Lydia added, 'Never, Gordon.' And her voice had a new coldness in it. He looked completely baffled.

A moment or two passed before he rallied and said, 'Darling, I hope you're not making a terrible mistake.'

'Oh, I expect I am,' she smiled wryly. 'I usually do, don't I?'

Frowning, as though still completely mystified, Gordon bent down and began picking up the pieces of china and the roses. 'I'll do that,' said Lydia, squatting down beside him. He half turned towards her and suddenly they were very close, forcing her to remember all the tiny details she had tried so hard to forget: the way his brown eyes were flecked with gold, the bump on the bridge of his nose, the broad sweep of his jaw and its thick crop of stubble. And the faint trace of something – self-doubt or uncertainty or a kind of questioning unease, she would probably never, now, know what it was – which lay beneath the confidence and the unceasing care for others. He was a good man, Dr Gordon Fairchild, a genuinely good man, though she had mocked him recently, and a year ago she had thought he was the man with whom she wanted to spend the rest of her life. Since she came to Rose Cottage in July she had only allowed herself to remember his negative side, her reasons for leaving him. Now she was reminded of all she was losing: the pleasure of falling asleep beside him at night, his particular smell and the pressure of his arms. She remembered how she had loved to plough her fingers through that thick dark hair and force his head back so she could kiss him.

She said, 'I'm sorry, Gordon, truly I am. I never meant to hurt you.'

For a moment, he wavered, but then he hauled himself back to the superior ground of his own invincibility. 'Oh, I'll be all right. It's you I'm worried about.'

'I know,' said Lydia, 'and that's why I had to leave.'

'You never used to talk in riddles,' he said.

'You see, Gordon,' she said, 'I have changed, after all.'

In Suzie's dream someone was attempting to erase her features with a harsh wet sponge. She put her hands up to protect her face and found a fur coat. She opened her eyes and was staring into a large, pale, canine muzzle.

'Misty, what are you doing here?'

'Are you OK?' A familiar voice. Suzie looked up and saw Terry looming over her. Dazzled by the sun, she couldn't make out his features, only the way his dark hair was fringed with gold where the light touched it. And that the sky behind was an intense and radiant blue.

She struggled into a sitting position, embarrassed at being found fast asleep in a public place. 'I must have nodded off,' she said.

'I thought maybe you'd gone unconscious or something.'

'No, just too many late nights.'

He smiled, and sat down beside her. 'I bring Misty up here quite often,' he said. 'It's brilliant, isn't it? This is where we had the ceremony for Lydia's baby. We planted a holly tree but it doesn't look too happy. I think it may be dying. Do you want a roll-up?'

'No thanks.'

'Sorry if I woke you up.'

'Just as well. I shouldn't really be here.'

'Bunking off school, are you?'

'No, it's half term. I went to stay with a friend, but she's changed a lot and she seems to know some really odd people. Or maybe it's me that's peculiar for not liking them. I can't really work it out.'

'What sort of odd?'

'Well, mixing things in people's drinks and thinking it's a joke. Taking stuff without paying for it.'

Terry nodded. 'Kids go through that,' he acknowledged. 'I was pretty reckless myself until recently.'

'Really?' Suzie didn't like to enquire too deeply; she remembered what Hopi had said about the joy-riding.

'Yeah. Got into all sorts of trouble. But I've changed a lot since I got settled.'

It struck Suzie as funny that he should describe himself as settled considering that he lived in a van, or lorry, or commer, or whatever it was. She said, 'Well, I'm glad you feel settled now, anyway.'

'It's Misty really. I've got her to think about now.'

Misty raised her ears at the mention of her name. She had especially beautiful ears, pale and feathered, the ears of a ghostly butterfly and she manipulated them with all the skill of a semaphore expert.

'She's a lovely dog,' agreed Suzie. And then, because she had been longing to know for ages, she asked, 'It's such a pity about her leg. What happened? Was she in an accident?'

Terry's face darkened. 'No,' he said. 'She'd been kept in a shed. Her owner used to tie her up with wire instead of a proper lead and she'd got it wrapped around her foot. The bastard went away for a couple of days and just left her there. She was hardly more than a puppy. The wire had dug so deep under the skin, and then poison set in, the vet had to amputate the foot. The animal welfare people wanted me to be a witness in the prosecution, but it was a bit awkward, so I couldn't really. If I ever met the bastard who treated her like that, I know what I'd say to him.'

'Wow.' Suzie was wide-eyed with admiration. 'You rescued her. That's wonderful.'

'It worked out,' Terry acknowledged modestly. To himself he thought, as he often did, that he and Misty were two of a kind, and that was how they had come to be so close. People were always saying how beautiful Misty was, but that hadn't prevented her from being maltreated and abandoned. No one had even bothered to take care of her, until he came along.

Suzie was fondling Misty's ears thoughtfully. Terry stroked the dog's neck. Misty half-closed her eyes, revelling in the attention. Suzie and Terry's hands were quite close to each other in the pale fur, but they did not touch.

After a bit Suzie asked, 'How did you know she was in that shed? Had you gone there specially to rescue her?'

Terry was gazing across the elegant roof tops of Haddeley Hall to the line of hills at the far side of the valley. 'Not exactly,' he said. 'It was kind of awkward. That's why I couldn't be a witness.'

'Awkward? Why?'

'Well,' he frowned, struggling with the urge to make up a good story, but unable to find one that would have been convincing, he gave up. 'I used to break into people's sheds now and then. Not all the time, but just every now and then. I thought there might be something there I could sell, tools, or something like that. And then I found Misty.'

'Wow.'

'That was when I was still quite reckless.'

'Yes, I see.'

As Suzie's initial shock faded, she began to picture the scene and the more she thought about it, the more the humour of it appealed to her. The thief becoming the rescuer. Everything was upside-down. A giggle escaped her, like a small hiccup.

'I don't see—' Terry turned to her angrily, his face rigid with injured pride.

Suzie made a valiant attempt to hide her giggles, and had almost succeeded, when Terry's face began to relax into a smile. 'I suppose it does have its funny side,' he admitted. 'I just never saw it like that before.'

Trying not to laugh had only made Suzie want to laugh ten times more. Her laughter erupted with such irrepressible spontaneity that it was infectious, and after a few moments Terry found that he was grinning too. Clutching her stomach, Suzie rolled onto her back and laughed up at the brilliant blue of the sky. Still grinning, Terry watched her for a little while, the way her fair hair was fanned out round her like the tail of some exotic bird and her pink, young girl's mouth opened with the laughter, and before he knew it, he had lain down on his back beside her, and was laughing too.

18

'We propose a traditional Victorian ambience for the library,' said Miranda Foley in her clipped and faintly bossy voice. 'These swatches indicate the effect we've been endeavouring to achieve.'

With an artful flourish, she opened the folder in front of Wyndham, making a fan in sombre greens and russets of the wallpaper pieces, fabric and carpet.

Lydia had to lean across the table in order to see. 'Nice,' she said, 'but maybe a bit safe?'

Miranda Foley's exquisite nostrils became slightly pinched, but she gave no other indication that she had even heard Lydia's remark. She said to Wyndham, 'The lighting would be muted, naturally, with directional lights for readers. Leather furniture, we thought, Mr Sale, a few well-chosen traditional pieces.'

'And hunting prints on the walls?' asked Lydia.

Two spots of colour appeared on Miranda Foley's cheeks. 'We thought perhaps a series of botanical illustrations. The room, obviously, speaks for itself.'

Wyndham examined the samples then glanced across the table at Lydia, who raised one eyebrow, fractionally.

'What do you think, Lydia?' asked Wyndham.

'It's OK, but it would just end up looking like every other boring library in a big house. Why not try something different?'

'Such as?'

'Um . . .' She tilted back in her chair. 'How about Art Deco, for instance? A huge carpet with irregular geometric patterns, those weird lights that look like giant sweets, armchairs in bright colours.'

Miranda Foley smirked her relief and addressed Wyndham, 'In a period house of this calibre it is of course vital to remain attuned to its essential nature. Haddeley Hall is a near perfect example of Jacobean architecture.'

'So?' asked Lydia. 'I'm not suggesting ripping down the walls or putting in picture windows. Nothing that would be structurally different. And anyway, who says Victorian pastiche is more in keeping with a seventeenth-century house than Art Deco?'

Miranda Foley nudged the folder a little closer to Wyndham. He already had several others splayed out in front of him. 'You might care to absorb these at your leisure, Mr Sale. I think you'll find several ideas we can usefully build on.'

Wyndham gathered up the folders and shunted them across the table. 'It all depends what Lydia thinks,' he said equably, 'I find her opinions invaluable.'

Miranda Foley looked so irritated by his statement that Lydia felt almost sorry for her. This morning's meeting had been by way of a compromise. While Wyndham claimed to be delighted with the steward's room, now virtually complete, he pointed out that at Lydia's present rate of progress it would be three years at least before even the upstairs rooms were finished, and he was no longer in the mood to wait. He wanted to pick up the threads that had been snapped when Annabel died, and see his ambitions for Haddeley Hall realised. So he persuaded her to come to a meeting with an interior designer who had been recommended to him when Annabel first became ill. 'Just give your opinion,' he told her. 'See what you think.'

Lydia did not need asking twice. Having seen a fragment of the house transformed by her handiwork, she felt a jealous love of the place. It astonished her, this feeling, since she had never even cared much about her own homes in the past, let alone someone else's. But now she found that she minded passionately what happened to Haddeley Hall. She could imagine how it might be reborn. How, with imagination and hard work, the quirky beauty of the house could be complemented and enhanced. She wanted to be a part of that process. Of course she agreed.

After Miranda Foley had left and as it was a fine morning, she and Wyndham took the two spaniels for a walk along one of the rides in the park. It led to an area of marshy ground which had once, so Wyndham had learned from the old records of the house, been the site of an ornamental lake. Felix and Zoe, his two young spaniels, plunged around in the reeds until they were both coated with thick mud, totally ignoring Wyndham's commands. He grew annoyed, but Lydia, who had heard them many times on their twice daily walks with Miguel, told him, 'I think the problem might be that they only understand Portuguese.'

'Do you think so?' Wyndham looked momentarily baffled. 'Then how the hell do you say "Get out of the mud you filthy animals before I come over and kill you both" in Portuguese?'

'I've no idea. Maybe we should just try calling their names in a Miguel-sounding voice.'

'Go on then.'

Wyndham watched while Lydia, trying as hard as she could to sound like Miguel, shouted 'Felix! Zoe!' several times. The dogs raised their heads and eventually trotted over to join her.

'Amazing,' said Wyndham, 'I'm a foreigner in my own home.'

He was thoughtful for a while before saying, 'I've been in touch with some landscape contractors. They begin work in the new year. By next summer there'll be a lake here again and the place will start to look as it should. I want to have most of the work inside the house finished by then too.'

'Poor Miranda Foley,' said Lydia. 'She didn't take kindly to me shoving my oar in. I suppose a non-resident mistress doesn't have much status when you're trying to get clients to make up their minds.'

'Her error,' said Wyndham brusquely. 'Of course, there is a simple solution to that one.'

'Which is?'

'Become my wife.'

Lydia was so startled, she stumbled, almost tripping over her own feet. 'What?'

Wyndham took her elbow, to steady her, but merely said, 'You heard what I said.'

'Any more jokes like that, and I could break a leg.'

'And if it wasn't a joke?'

Lydia only hesitated fractionally before saying, 'You're safe, anyway. I won't take it seriously. For one thing, I happen to be married already.'

'I was under the impression the doctor had been dispatched.'

'Not legally. Besides, I'm rather off marriage just at present.'

'That's that, then.' Wyndham put his hands in his pockets and looked away, across the reedy hollow and the wide sweep of grassland to the line of trees that bordered the road. Then he said, 'How about a weekend in Paris instead?'

'Is that the bonus you promised when the work on the steward's room was finished?'

'Not especially. I'd like to go to Paris with you, that's all.'

'Fine. When can we leave?'

Later, as they were walking back towards the house, Lydia asked, 'Supposing I had said yes to marriage, what then?'

Wyndham's impassive face never altered. 'A long engagement, I suppose. And of course, an enormous ring.'

Alone at Rose Cottage again, Lydia was surprised by the way the idea of marriage to Wyndham had wedged itself in her mind. She assumed his remark had been some kind of testing of the water, rather than a sincere proposal, but she found the very thought of it disturbingly attractive. She gave herself up to savouring the many pleasures of her present situation. It was not the spending of money that so drew her to the challenge presented by Haddeley Hall: it was the chance, for once in her life, to do a job properly, to create precisely the atmosphere that the house demanded. She knew Wyndham was not prepared to wait while she did every stage of it herself, and, now that she had worked on one room, she was more than happy to delegate most of the actual labour to others. It was like being given an enormous canvas, and all the materials she could ever want to paint the most important picture of her life. That, and an occasional trip to Paris every now and then – no wonder she was feeling happier than she had done in months.

When Wyndham returned to his panelled office, he found Mark looking through Miranda Foley's samples.

'What do you think?' Wyndham asked.

'Excellent. The woman has brilliant taste. I love her ideas for the library.'

'You don't think they're rather safe? Boring, even?'

'Not at all. Classic, I'd say. Timeless. Understated elegance.'

'Like your tie?'

Mark grinned. He fingered the acid green knot at his throat and said, 'La Foley was highly complimentary.'

'Then I definitely don't want her doing up my house. I might let Lydia take charge.'

Mark was wise enough not to comment. He disapproved of Lydia, who he thought exerted a bad influence on his employer in all sorts of ways. 'That reminds me,' he said, not quite changing the subject, 'I've got hold of a copy of the lease on Hazel Farm.'

'Hazel Farm?'

'The one Sedden's son-in-law rents. It's up for renewal. It would be perfectly straightforward to refuse it on a technicality, if you wanted to put in a new tenant.'

'Why would I want to do that?'

Mark hesitated.

'Ah yes,' said Wyndham, 'pressure to get rid of the travellers. Who's been knobbling you, Mark?'

'Everyone wants them to move on.'

'Everyone? They do have some allies, you know. Don't do anything just at present. I want to keep my options open for a bit.'

Mark did not argue. He was prepared to bide his time until his employer came to his senses. He did not think he would have to wait long. Had he known of Wyndham's proposal of marriage that morning, he might not have been so sanguine.

Wyndham had been only half-joking when he spoke of marriage, half-trying it out to see what the idea felt like. He recognised that he had not begun to emerge from the grey shadows which had followed Annabel's death until Lydia appeared on the scene. For a few months he had stopped functioning properly, but now he was recovered and impatient to get on not just with the work at Haddeley Hall, but also with the whole process of living. He had been single long enough to know it did not suit him. Lydia, on the other hand, did suit him. Besides, he was tired of inhabiting a home where even his own dogs did not respond to the English language.

Her refusal did not bother him in the least. He enjoyed the whole process of negotiations and he found that a dramatic opening bid was often a good way to start things rolling. He was reasonably confident of eventual success, and in the meantime his only concern was that Lydia did not have suitable clothes for the weekend ahead.

'Don't waste a moment longer, Lydia. You must snap him up at once. He's a brilliant catch: wealthy, unattached, presentable. He doesn't have any strange personal habits, does he?'

'Like what?'

'You know what I mean,' said Ann Robertson darkly, then she brightened, 'He's every woman's dream. I'm only sorry I didn't get to him first.'

'You? What about Mr Robertson?'

'What about him indeed? I often wonder. The man is a complete dead loss.'

'You don't believe that for a moment,' said Lydia, grinning. Anyone hearing the schoolteacher talk about her husband would gain the impression that divorce was imminent, yet Lydia had observed the way her face lit up with delight when he called unexpectedly at the school and she had spied them, only the previous Saturday, holding hands near the freezer cabinets in Edleston's Marks & Spencer. She had no idea why it suited Ann to talk as if they only remained together through grim necessity.

'Try me,' said Ann firmly.

Lydia held up a piece of cardboard and examined it critically. 'Is this palm tree good for another year or should we start again from scratch?'

'All it needs is a fresh coat of paint.'

They had stayed on after school to sort through the props and scenery for the Nativity play. Now that half term was over, Halloween and Guy Fawkes behind them, the collective attention of the Briarswood infants class was firmly fixed on Christmas. Though Ann prided herself on keeping abreast of all the latest trends in educational theory, the start of each November found her transformed into an immovable traditionalist. When challenged, she maintained that there was little point in staging a multicultural celebration in a village where inbreeding had only recently stopped being a serious problem. Besides, it wasn't just the fact that the children loved it, the annual Nativity play had become part of the fabric of Briarswood life.

'He's invited me to go to Paris with him,' said Lydia, examining a battered star. 'This one is beyond redemption.'

'A second bite at the apple. Excellent news. Make sure you extract another proposal out of him, and don't fluff it up this time.'

Lydia sat back on her heels. 'How do I make him propose?'

'I don't suppose I can teach you anything about that. All the usual *femme fatale* tricks. Lots of sexy underwear, that kind of thing. I suppose it's too late to suggest playing hard to get?'

'Just a little.'

'Never mind. A couple of diaphanous negligées should get him hooked.'

'You make him sound like a fish. Besides, I'm not certain I want to hook him.'

'Don't be ridiculous, Lydia. Wyndham Sale is a very fine fish. A grade A top of the market fresh salmon. Not a herring or a sprat.' Here she added meaningfully, 'Not like some men I could mention.'

'Was sexy underwear responsible for the snaring of Mr Robertson?' asked Lydia. Like a character from a Jane Austen novel, Ann always referred to her husband by his surname, and Lydia had fallen into the same habit.

Ann pulled a face. 'Bedsocks and pyjamas. Utterly pedestrian, needless to say. And a wedding night shared with two hot water bottles in Scarborough.'

'In that case it must have been true love.'

'Nothing of the kind,' insisted Ann, 'practically a marriage of convenience.'

Lydia grinned. Her growing friendship with the schoolteacher was one of the unexpected bonuses of her part-time work with the infants. So wise with regard to the children in her charge, Ann Robertson had a blind spot over what she referred to as 'matters of the heart'. Her opinions and advice might have been culled from the pages of an Edwardian woman's magazine. Perhaps because she herself had been a plain and hardworking teenager, she saw love and romance as luxuries that occurred in other people's lives, and nothing at all to do with the deep affection and companionship she and Mr Robertson had shared for over twenty years.

'I don't have any negligées, diaphanous or otherwise,' said Lydia. 'In fact, now I come to think of it, lack of suitable clothes is a bit of a problem.'

'Send to Dulwich straightaway. You must have masses of alluring outfits back at home.'

Lydia giggled. 'Actually, no. Nothing that would do for a wicked weekend with a wealthy Wyndham. And I never want to go to Dulwich again. I told Gordon to give everything away.'

'Sounds to me as if you're still half in love with him.'

'Good lord no.' Lydia frowned as she scraped a blob of paint from a palm frond with her thumbnail. 'I think maybe the trouble is that I never was in love with him, just pretended to be.' Casting around for a way to change the subject she said, 'What about Saul? Are you going to risk giving him a part in the play?'

'Every child always has a part,' said Ann firmly. 'I've never been defeated yet. Saul has made brilliant progress this last month, but he is still uneasy when he has to work too closely with the other children. I can't just mix him in with the angels or the sheep.'

'He'll never be a herd animal will he?'

'And that terrible scowl. No talent for worship, so shepherds and kings are out.'

'A lone camel?'

'I thought I might try him out as the innkeeper. It would be like being in the Wendy House for him and we could utilise his natural aptitude for shooing people away.'

It was the most peculiar sensation.

Twinks had pulled her small white car to a careful halt outside the village shop and applied the handbrake. She turned off the ignition. These days, with the terrible whiteness closing in on her, she performed every action with scrupulous care lest she make some foolish mistake. She opened the car door and swung her feet round and on to the concrete prior to getting out. And then she stopped.

A strange-looking young woman had just emerged from the

shop carrying a bag of groceries. She had a great many very peculiar plaits hanging down like little snakes on her shoulders, and earrings where no earring ought to be. But it was not these aberrations that held Twinks' attention: it was her flowing and brightly-patterned skirt.

It was like no skirt Twinks had ever seen before, and yet it was oddly familiar. Some of the fabrics used in the patchwork reminded Twinks of other times and other places: that delicate lawn with the misty drifts of blues and greys was exactly the same as the dress she had worn when William's youngest son was christened. And that buttery, flower-sprigged cotton was an identical pattern to a shirtwaister she had bought at the same time. Just looking at it brought back the haunting sound of a nocturne she had played on a summer afternoon not so many years before.

Twinks placed a pale hand on her chest, as though to still her suddenly pounding heart: her life was passing before her eyes. First the narrowing of her vision to the point where almost all the world was wrapped in ghostly blankets, and now this.

The young woman had gone, striding away in heavy boots and that extraordinary, disturbing skirt, but it was some little time before Twinks had the strength to leave her car and walk the few yards to Peggy's shop.

The first run through of the Nativity play later that week was only a partial success. Saul listened attentively as his role was explained to him, then retreated behind the plywood screen that represented the inn. Sandra's daughter Naomi was to be the Holy Mother. A stocky and placid girl, she could be relied on to rise above such minor problems as a Joseph who placed three fingers in his mouth and mimed vomiting every time he was asked to hold her hand. They stumped up to the inn door and knocked. Saul could be heard nasally muttering to himself behind the screen. They knocked again.

The door opened a fraction and a furious face peered out. 'Yes?'

'Can we stay here tonight?' asked Joseph. 'Mary is expecting a baby and—'

'You just bugger off away from my inn,' said Saul menacingly.

'Oh Saul!' Ann Robertson threw up her hands in dismay, 'You still have to be polite, even though they can't stay at your inn.'

Saul frowned harder than ever as he tried to grasp this. Then he said, 'OK miss.' He scowled once more and said, more gently this time, 'Please bugger off away from my inn.'

'That'll do for now,' said Ann, while Naomi remained standing in the middle of the stage and Joseph joined the sheep and angels who were giggling at the side. 'I think we're going to need a written script for some of this.'

'Method acting,' she explained charitably to Lydia after school the following day. 'The lad was throwing himself heart and soul into the role, and it seemed a shame to have to tell him off.' She looked across at the work Lydia was doing. 'I don't like to have to say this, Lydia, but your palm tree is much too beautiful. It shows mine up. People will think the children did this one.'

'I won't tell anyone.' Lydia had just finished painting a small monkey at the top of her tree. 'Are these banana palms or coconut palms?'

'Palm palms. By the way, I've found something for your trousseau. It was in the charity shop in Edleston, so you don't owe me a penny. Look, isn't it beautiful?'

Lydia opened the package with some dread, but her exclamations of delight were genuine enough. Nestling in its bed of tissue paper, though neither of them ever guessed its provenance, was the oyster silk negligée which had caused Sandra and her husband such mirth when passed on a couple of months earlier by Mrs Cartwright.

'Just one glimpse of you in that,' declared Ann triumphantly, 'and our Mr Sale will be down on his knees in an instant.'

'Definitely diaphanous,' said Lydia, holding the sliver of silk up against her chest and executing a little dance around the classroom while Ann watched in admiration. Lydia couldn't help thinking how much simpler life would be if it could be lived by the advice Ann loved to give, but never followed herself.

'You read it me.' Saul thrust the book at Terry's ribcage. 'Read it like she does.'

'Some other time, Saul,' said Terry, 'I'm busy right now.'

'No you're not,' said Saul, accurately enough. 'You're not doing nothing. Read me the book.'

'I told you, I'm busy.'

'You were just reading it.'

Terry snatched the book and flung it with sudden fury across the van before striding out into the fresh air. His face was flushed and his heart was pounding. He imagined his thoughts must be transparent, that everyone who watched him pass must know what was in his mind. He was burning with an evil mix of fear and rage and shame. True enough, he had been looking at one of the books Suzie had brought, but he hadn't been reading it. Not much of it anyway. He couldn't.

Terry's failure with the written word had caused humiliation and secret misery for as long as he could remember. All his memories of school were of panic and evasion. He had developed endless strategies to hide his secret, even resorted to injuring his right hand rather than reveal the truth. He was shouted at and mocked. He was called lazy and stupid. He skipped classes, skipped school altogether.

When Suzie brought the books and began reading them to Saul, Terry's old nightmares were rekindled. At the same time he was fascinated. He found that when he was sitting near the two of them, he could follow some of the words. Some, like 'Cottontail' and 'Mr McGregor' were a jumble, but when he heard the way Suzie said them, he thought he might one day master even those. Occasionally he allowed himself a faint hope that it might be possible to make up for the missing years. But his optimism was tempered by the possibility that Saul or Suzie or anyone might stumble on the truth. Just a hint that someone might guess the grotesque failure at the heart of him made his brain feel as if it were bubbling and hot inside his skull.

He wanted to be able to hold his head up and get respect. He wanted to cut a way through the dark jungle of the adult world. But how could he even begin when he couldn't read the words on the simplest of forms, let alone begin to fill one in? The gulf between his ambitions and his present abilities was so vast that he could only leap it in imagination. He would show them all what he was capable of. They'd all be amazed. He'd become a disc jockey or a TV star, a famous race horse owner or a film producer or a musician. He'd applied once to work in a burger bar. You wouldn't think you'd need to read or write to slap circles of beef on to round buns, but there had been an impossible hurdle called induction: a whole page of company policy to be memorised and repeated. He'd told them he was vegetarian and working there was against his principles. They'd yelled at him for wasting their time.

He sat in his car. Misty scratched at the door and demanded to be let in too. She scrambled on to his lap and licked his ear and neck. His anger suddenly gave way to enormous misery. What was the point of pretending, he was never going to amount to anything, he couldn't even read a kid's book about a dumb bunch of rabbits. He was pathetic and useless, all those teachers and people who had taunted him had been right all along. He buried his face in Misty's dense fur and hugged her so tightly she began to wriggle. As he released his grip, she turned and licked the tears off his cheek.

There was a gentle tapping on the car window.

'It's only me,' said Hopi. 'Can I talk to you a minute?'

'Sure. Jump in.'

'Are you OK?' she asked as she climbed in on the passenger side.

'Fine. I think I might be getting a bit of an allergy to dog fur.' He kept his arms around Misty's broad neck.

Hopi was about to recommend a herbal remedy, but then she decided his explanation was probably a cover up so she didn't bother.

'Suzie was here again this morning,' she said.

'Yeah. She brought some books for Saul.'

'It's the second time this week.'

'She seems to like it here,' agreed Terry. 'Her and that friend of hers, Lydia.'

'You don't think it might be something else as well?'

'Like what?'

Hopi turned to see if Terry really was unaware of what she was driving at. His dusky and always handsome face showed no deception. She sighed.

'I think you might be part of the reason she keeps coming down here.'

'Me?' His surprise was genuine. Also genuine was the distaste with which he responded to her suggestion. 'Why me?'

'Well, you are attractive, Terry. You must know that.'

'Oh.' Terry hunched his shoulders like a sparrow in the rain and sank a little deeper inside his jacket. He wasn't flattered by Hopi's statement: attractive to him was not a reason for pride. It meant people noticing you for all the wrong reasons. As a child he'd been called Gypo and Paki among a hundred other names, but no one had ever complimented him on his looks. Sure, there'd been no shortage of unwelcome attention, from men as well as women, but he always assumed that was because he looked like an easy touch, like someone who couldn't protect himself properly, someone with no real family to look out for him.

'I think maybe Suzie's got a crush on you.'

'Oh.' Terry hunched even more miserably inside his coat. Again, he didn't really believe Hopi. Suzie had never acted like someone who wanted something from him: he could smell that a mile off. Still, even the thought was depressing. He'd grown quite to enjoy Suzie's company; she seemed gentle and unthreatening. But at the back of his mind loomed the spectre of how completely she and Hopi and everyone else would despise him if they knew he couldn't even look in a paper and tell them what was on TV.

Hopi sensed his distress, but had no way of divining its cause. She said, 'It's not your fault, Terry. No one's saying that. But we need to be careful, that's all. I've seen it happen before. Young kids from posh homes start hanging around the site and the next thing we get accused of leading them off the straight and narrow.'

'We can't stop her coming down, though,' said Terry. 'After all, it's a free country.'

'Depends what you mean by free,' said Hopi with a wry smile.

The inside of the car was beginning to steam up, so neither of them was aware of the new arrivals until there was a thump on the passenger door. Hopi rolled down the window, gradually revealing a man peering in at them. He had large grey eyes, a sensitive and nervous face, several rings in each ear and a blond ponytail.

'Hello, Hopi,' said the man. 'How's it going?'

Misty had leapt on to Hopi's lap and was barking excitedly. The disturbance was brief, but sufficient to deflect the man's attention from the way Hopi's expression clouded briefly before she recovered herself and said warmly, 'Hi Colin. Great to see you. What kept you so long?'

The party that followed Colin's arrival went on into the small hours. He had arrived with two friends, Barney and Flea, he had met up with in France. Colin had brought Hopi a beautiful silk shawl from Spain and he told her how beautiful she looked in it until she almost believed him.

After four months apart, they had loads to talk about, and Colin was so funny and entertaining and warm-hearted and generous that Hopi, in a daze of happiness and excitement, was soon wondering how she could have lived without him all through the summer months.

19

'Isn't this just jumping out of the frying pan and into thc fire?'

'Only if you want to call Gordon a frying pan. Hardly a very flattering description, I'd have thought.'

'But you'll settle for Wyndham as fire?'

'I don't have to answer that one.'

'OK then, but how much do you actually know about Wyndham Sale?'

Lydia pretended to give serious consideration to Jim's question. 'Hm, that's a toughie. Let me see now. He has more houses than anyone I've met before. He likes Schubert, hates Mahler. Can't stand cigars. Likes malt whisky and loathes cocktails. He wakes unbelievably early and catnaps at least once during the day. How am I doing so far?'

'Trivia, mainly. How does he make his money?'

'Fast.'

'But how?'

'Silk works in the Far East, among other things.'

Jim remained silent, as though oppressed by the weight of knowledge unspoken.

Lydia said lightly, 'So far as I know he did not murder his wife. Nor is he laundering drugs money. Nor does he torture little old ladies in his spare time. What's your problem, Jim?'

'You seem to have got in deep with him remarkably quickly, that's all.'

Lydia laid down the shirt she was mending and looked across the table at Jim. He returned her gaze, but his smile was uneasy. He understood books and ideas, she thought, but knew almost nothing about people, and what made them act in the ways that they did. She said, 'Wyndham and I happen to be going away together for three days. To Paris. For one weekend. Hardly cause for a full-scale inquisition.'

'Just making conversation.'

'Then try another topic. How is your work coming on?'

'Fine. I should have a first draft ready when you get back. If you're interested. Are you flying by private jet?'

'I don't think he has one. But first class, definitely.' She broke the thread between her teeth and unreeled some more. 'What conclusions have you drawn about eighteenth-century outlaws?'

'The usual. Necessary safety valve, society's ambivalence, famous outlaws simultaneously rejected and idolised. Where will you be staying?'

'Some smart hotel. Wyndham told me, but I can't remember the name. What do you plan to work on next?'

'I thought I might develop a biography of one of the more attractive villains, someone called Jem Whitby of Lincolnshire. Are you planning to see the sites or will the glamorous hotel room suffice?'

'Give it a rest, Jim. You're supposed to be telling me about your work, remember.'

'Sorry. I seem to be more interested in your play.'

'It's none of your bloody business!' Suddenly she was angry. Jim opened his mouth to retaliate, but was interrupted by some vigorous clonking of the cowbell. The front door swung open and four warmly muffled figures came stamping in from the cold. Lydia's face lit up at the sight of her visitors, just as Jim's settled into gloom.

'Hi everybody,' said Lydia with delight. 'This is Jim Lewis. Jim, meet Hopi, Malcolm, Terry and Saul. Saul is the small one.'

Jim nodded vaguely in their direction. 'Pleased to meet you,' he said, formal and cold.

'Is this a good time?' asked Hopi earnestly. 'We didn't know you had company. We can do the roof tomorrow morning if you'd rather.'

'The roof?' Jim turned to Lydia.

'They've offered to patch up the leaks. Each redundant drip-catcher earns one bath point per person.'

'The barter system,' explained Mal helpfully.

Jim turned to look at him more closely. He was not impressed by what he saw. Lank dark hair, a narrow face, several layers of woollen sweater. Jim began to stand up. 'I was just going anyway,' he said, but Lydia pushed him firmly back in his chair.

'You haven't had your cup of tea yet, Jim. And I've been wanting to introduce you to this lot for ages.'

Jim began to say, 'Some other time, perhaps . . .' but Lydia interrupted him with, 'Jim's a historian. His special field is eighteenth-century agrarian unrest, also the role of outlaw in society. Isn't that right, Jim?'

'Not entirely; for one thing I've retired, and for another—'

Mal had sat down in Lydia's former chair. 'I am a great admirer of the writings of Gerard Winstanley,' he said earnestly. 'He was a man ahead of his time, don't you agree?'

Jim sighed. 'What about that tea, then, Lydia?'

Saul had planted himself four-square in front of Lydia. In his toy fog-horn voice he declared, 'You be Joseph and knock on my door.'

'What?' asked Lydia, who had missed recent rehearsals at the school.

The volume on the fog horn was turned up slightly as Saul repeated his command. Lydia glanced a query at Mal who told her, 'Just say knock knock. It saves time in the end.'

'Knock knock,' said Lydia recklessly.

Saul thrust his chin forward defiantly. 'What do you want?'

Lydia turned to Mal and whispered, 'Well, what do I want?'

Hopi intervened. 'My wife is expecting a baby,' she said gently, 'and we are far from home. Can we stay for tonight at your inn?'

'I'm sorry,' Saul said this bit with intense concentration, 'but there is no room at my inn.'

'Oh dear.' Hopi again, 'My poor wife is very tired. Is there nowhere we can stay?'

'Well, there is a stable at the back. There's a ox and a camel there, but you can have a bed in the straw.'

'Thank you very much,' said Hopi.

'Don't mention it,' said Saul, with a modest shrug of the shoulders. Then he turned to Jim. 'Do you know what that was?'

'I think I could probably guess,' said Jim with a smile.

'I'm the innkeeper,' explained Saul anyway. 'Innkeeper's a very important thing to be. I have to learn the words off exactly because it's so important to say it right. Shall I say them again?' This question was addressed to Jim, and then, as a special favour he offered, 'You can be Mary and Joseph this time. You start off with knock knock. You can do the knocking on the table if you like.'

Jim's face had broken into his gentlest and most delighted of smiles. He said, 'That's extremely generous of you, Saul.'

'Not again, Saul, please,' begged Mal, grinning, 'we've heard nothing else for days.'

'So? I have to get the words right.'

'Mrs Robertson at the school gave him his own script,' explained Hopi. 'Usually she lets them improvise, but Saul came a bit unstuck on improvisation.'

'So I heard,' said Lydia.

Saul bristled. 'I was not fuckin' unstuck,' he declared.

'Exactly,' said Lydia.

Mal told his son not to swear.

Jim didn't leave for over an hour, by which time Terry, Mal and Hopi were debating the best way to reduce the leaks on the kitchen roof.

'You see,' said Lydia as she followed Jim out of the cottage to have a few words with him in private, 'I knew you'd come round once you met them.'

'I never said I wouldn't,' said Jim. 'Tell me, what does lover-boy make of your colourful friends?'

'Wyndham? He's never met them.'

'So you're not trying to persuade him to get chummy with them too?'

'No, only you, Jim. I can hardly see Wyndham inviting Hopi to be matron of honour, can you?'

Jim's attention narrowed. 'Matron of honour? Are we talking weddings, here?'

'You know I'm hopeless at telling fortunes.'

Jim, who had been gazing at the wood pile for some moments, now asked, 'Has someone been pinching your wood, Lydia? There ought to be much more than this.'

'I don't think so,' she said, deliberately vague.

'Then you must have been burning it round the clock. I thought you didn't bother much with fires.'

'Oh yes. Well . . . Now I come to think of it, I may have given a few logs to Mal and Hopi. No need to mention it to Caro, though.'

Jim grinned. 'I wouldn't dream of it. I don't think Caro would appreciate the irony of Wyndham's precious logs ending up down at the Hollows after all. Good-bye then, Lydia. I suppose I ought to say I hope you have a good time in Paris, but that would be impossibly hypocritical of me.'

'Say it anyway.'

'Have a good time. In Paris. Lydia.'

Peggy checked through the column of figures for the third time. Still the same total. She scanned a second list and found here also that her original total had been correct. For once she wished she wasn't blessed with such relentless accuracy. The two sums showed without doubt that her losses from theft were more than double what they had been for the same period the previous year. With losses on this scale, she could be out of business within months. A certain amount of shoplifting was sadly inevitable, even in a small village shop like this one; the intimacy of the deception made it all the harder to bear. Which of her smiling customers, with whom she exchanged gossip and platitudes, was all the time undermining her efforts to make ends meet?

Almost against her will her thoughts turned to the newcomers at the Hollows. When they moved in at the beginning of September she had been in half a mind to ban them from her shop altogether, and had received no shortage of well-intentioned advice on the topic. Her compromise policy of only allowing two in at a time meant that she could always keep a close eye on their activities, but recently she had begun to forget her rule. The travellers she had come to know, like Hopi and Malcolm and Kate, were as patently honest as any of the villagers, she was confident of that. But if it wasn't one of them, who was the culprit?

The door of the shop opened and closed with a jingle and a gust of cold air. Caro, wearing a waxed jacket and a brightly patterned headscarf, bustled in, throwing Peggy a more than usually busy smile.

'Gracious me,' she exclaimed as she whizzed round the shop selecting items and depositing them by the till, 'simply not enough hours in the day, are there? How I'm going to fit the course in on top of everything else I can't imagine. And I must not forget marmalade.'

'Doing a course are you?'

'Computers. Signed up for it yesterday. Looks absolutely fascinating. I would have started today but Mummy's a bit under the weather so I've been up at the Manor all morning.'

'Anything serious?'

'Touch of flu, I think. And half a bottle of brandy, please. Mummy's hell bent on making a Christmas cake, though I told her I'd already made three. There's no arguing with the elderly, is there?'

Caro and Peggy were settling in for one of their periodic chats about the tribulations of the elderly – Peggy's mother had lived with her as long as anyone could remember and, although frail, was fundamentally indestructible – when the bell jingled once more and Kate and Biff strolled into the shop. Caro rolled her eyes at Peggy and said, 'I won't distract you, I can see you've got your hands full,' and made a hurried exit, almost colliding with two tall thin dogs who were loitering by the litter bin.

Caro hurried into the safety of the Range Rover. She thought it was outrageous that she couldn't even have a five-minute chat in the village shop without being interrupted by a couple of scruffy outsiders. She was full of sympathy for poor Peggy, who had to deal with them practically every day.

Hopi laid the section of stripy fabric over the chequered material and pinned them carefully. She worked with steady concentration, and a growing sense of satisfaction. As her dressmaking skills increased, she was becoming more ambitious, but this was the first time she had tried a jacket. It was to be a loose-cut man's jacket for summer in a patchwork of stripes and checks. Not exactly Savile Row, she would have been the first to admit, but the finished garment was sure to be unique.

It was peaceful in the trailer. Colin was sitting cross-legged on the crocheted bedspread and fingering his guitar. He played like an angel, and it was his music-making which had attracted her first. He had spent nearly two years at music college before dropping out and Hopi remembered her first glimpse of him one summer's afternoon at a festival. He had been sitting on the ground, his body curved over the guitar and he was so utterly absorbed in what he was doing that he had not noticed the small crowd that had gathered. She had been struck by his surrender to the music; then she had noticed his sensitive, delicate features and the huge grey eyes. When the music ended there was a moment of silence, then someone at the rear of the circle began to clap, and others followed. Colin had looked up, blinked, seemed surprised, then smiled shyly. His gaze settled on Hopi . . . She began to fall for him in that moment.

She slid the two pieces of fabric under the foot of the sewing machine and began to work the treadle. With a contented whirring noise the needle bobbed up and down and a row of stitches appeared behind like a comet's trail.

Colin banged his fist on the guitar and swore viciously. 'How the fuck can I concentrate with you making that bloody racket? You've ruined it!'

Hopi stopped at once. 'Sorry, Col.' She knew the only way to prevent his flashes of ill humour from escalating into a full-scale row was through appeasement, the sooner the better. 'I'll do this bit later. Carry on love, it sounded great.'

'Bloody hopeless now.' He pushed the guitar away from him. 'I'd nearly got that bit right too.'

'Sorry.'

'Make some tea then.'

Hopi left her sewing and went to put the kettle on. She was annoyed at having to stop in the middle of her work, but she told herself it must be difficult to be so sensitive to sounds as Colin was. You were always hearing about artistic temperament, and she could understand how infuriating it must be to have machinery hammering away while you were trying to work out a complex piece. All the same, she couldn't help worrying about when she was going to find the time to do the necessary machine sewing. Since his return, Colin seemed to sleep for quite large chunks of the day, so it would be mean to disturb him then, and most of his waking hours were spent sitting on the bed with the guitar across his knees.

When she had made the two mugs of tea, Colin patted the space beside him. 'Come and sit with me, Hopi,' he said. No one could smile with their eyes quite the way Colin could.

'In a minute. I'll just finish that bit of sewing while you have your tea.'

'Fuck the sewing!' His anger had blazed up again. 'All those stupid bits of stuff. Bloody waste of time, all of it.'

'Oh.' Hopi stood uncertainly in the middle of the trailer. She pushed back a strand of dark hair. 'I'm making a jacket,' she said, 'a man's jacket. I thought you might like to wear it.'

'Me? You must be joking. I'd never be seen dead in the crappy thing.'

'Don't be so bloody mean!' Stung to anger by the attack on her handiwork as she never was by attacks on herself, Hopi said vigorously, 'I've been working really hard on this. I'm going to sell things in the summer, get a little business going. It's not fair to be so rude about it, it's taken me loads of work.'

Colin slid off the bed and came over to where she was standing. He slid his hands around her waist. 'Don't be cross with me, Hopi,' he pleaded. 'Please. I can't stand it when you're cross. It's going to look great. I was only joking, I've always wanted a stripy-check jacket. Kind of camouflage, isn't it? Like a zebra. Will you still fancy me when I look like a zebra?'

Hopi smiled, her anger evaporating. Colin's hands had moved up under her sweater to caress her breasts. She closed her eyes. He began kissing the line of her jaw, then her mouth. This, even more than the guitar playing, was the part of Colin she had missed while he was away through the summer. Most of the time she felt jerked up and down by his moods, helpless as a yo-yo on a length of string and unable to gather her thoughts together long enough to work out how to deal with him. He could provoke her to screaming pitch in no time at all and then, just when she was on the verge of calling it quits, he found a hundred different ways to diffuse the tension, each one more delicious than the last.

'Hang on a minute, Colin,' she said, as her mind began to fog. 'Let me bolt the door first.'

'Expecting visitors?' Colin frowned suspiciously.

'Only small ones,' said Hopi, slotting the bolt home.

Just in time. As she was pulling off her jeans there was a thump of small fists against the door and an unmistakable voice shouted, 'Knock knock. You can be the Virgin Mary if you want.'

'Not if I can help it,' said Colin with a grin, crouching down to kiss the warm flesh of Hopi's stomach, and then, when the beating at the door grew more insistent he added, 'if that brat carries on I'm going to break both his arms.'

'Come back later, Saul,' Hopi shouted, 'I'm busy just now.'

A small boot kicked the door in disgust, but then Saul went away. When their lovemaking was over and Hopi was lying beside Colin in a daze of physical contentment and wondering how to piece together the rest of her day, he said, 'You're great, Hopi. I'm glad I came back. D'you want some vodka?'

'Vodka? Since when did you have the money for vodka?'

'I got some when I went out this morning.'

'I thought you were skint until your Giro got sorted?'

'Ways and means, Hopi, there's always a way.'

'Oh Colin, you haven't been nicking stuff from the local shop have you? Peggy's been really good to us.'

'Yeah, yeah,' Colin interrupted, 'no need to make a meal of it. You know me better than that. I'd never take anything from our own patch. What do you think I am, some kind of petty thief? Here, have a swig.'

Hopi was about to refuse, but already the harmony of their love-making was beginning to fray and she didn't, right now, have the energy for a row, so she said, 'Just a bit then. And promise me you won't go pinching stuff from Peggy's.'

'Scout's honour,' Colin grinned. 'Who the hell's Peggy anyway?'

'When I get my first wages,' said Caro firmly, 'you and I are going to have a proper shopping expedition, young lady. Those trousers are an absolute disgrace. Aren't they the ones we bought last spring? You look as though you'd gone through a hedge backwards.'

'Hm,' Suzie adopted a deliberately vague expression as she took her place at the breakfast table. She had dedicated a whole afternoon to giving her jeans an authentically care-worn look and she was secretly delighted with the result.

'I can't think how they've got into such a state.' Caro leaned across to examine the rip just above Suzie's knee. 'They're past invisible mending I'm afraid. Haven't you got any others you can wear?'

'I like these,' said Suzie. 'They're comfy.'

'Well you certainly can't wear them in the village,' said Caro firmly. 'People will think you're one of those New Agers.'

Suzie turned away and muttered, 'Oh Mummy, don't fuss.'

Jim, who had been opening his post, said mildly, 'I met some of them the other day. They seemed all right.'

Round-eyed Suzie stared at her father. She was so stunned by his remark that she did not even notice that her mother had inserted her index finger into the largest of the holes in her jeans and was tutting vigorously.

'You met some of the travellers?' asked Suzie, coming back to life, and then, 'Mum, don't. That tickles.'

'Yes, at Lydia's. You know she's friendly with them.'

'That woman,' Caro broke in, 'anything to be difficult.'

'But that's the point, Caro. They were really quite jolly.'

Suzie had to remind herself to keep breathing. She said in what she hoped was an offhand manner, 'What were they like, Daddy? Did you meet many?'

'Just three of them. And a child. He's got a part in the school play, dead chuffed he was. Quite entertaining, in fact.'

'Did they have odd names?' asked Suzie.

'The girl did. She was called Hopi. I think the man was called Malcolm. I can't remember the lad's name. He didn't say much. Good looking, though.'

'Really, Daddy? What did he look like?'

'Dark hair. Usual display of ironmongery in ears and nose—'

'Rings in his nose, ugh! Don't put me off my breakfast,' exclaimed Caro. 'It makes me feel ill just thinking about it.'

'I don't see why,' said Suzie. 'I mean, you don't go on about it when it's ears, how can it be OK for one part of the body and not others?'

'Don't be silly, Suzie, it's not at all the same thing.'

'I must say,' said Jim, who had just seen the interest that had been added to his credit card bill in the past month and felt that needling Caro was forgivable this morning, 'you can't help seeing the attraction of their way of life.'

Having noticed the envelope from the Visa company among the post, Caro restricted herself to a noise of vague dismissal, and went to fill the teapot.

Jim leaned back in his chair and continued amiably, 'No worries, no bills, none of this endless flap about keeping up appearances. Lots of fresh air and company. Always plenty to do. A very immediate, hands-on kind of life.'

'Yes, Daddy, you can really see why some people like to live like that, can't you?'

Jim regarded his youngest affectionately. 'Maybe we should just jack it all in and opt for the simple life, eh Suzie? A nice shiny bus and plenty of room for my books, a quiet pipe in the evening – what more could one ask for? And just look what we'd be leaving behind!' He lifted the pile of envelopes and let them fall randomly through his fingers.

Suzie giggled. 'I'll come with you any time you like,' she said.

'Now look what you've done,' Caro fussed. She knew Jim was annoying her deliberately but was unable to resist the bait. 'It's all a joke to you, but poor Suzie is taking you seriously. I wish you'd think before you said things like that.'

'Maybe it wasn't a joke. I could imagine being very happy with much less. What does one need after all? Somewhere warm and dry in bad weather, friends and a change of scenery whenever you get bored – it really is very tempting.'

'How could anyone be happy without even a decent bath? Every sane person wants a proper roof over their heads.'

'That surely depends,' said Jim, 'on the price of the roof.'

'Besides,' Caro went on, 'it's just going backwards, living like that. It goes against everything civilisation stands for. We might as well all slide back into the Dark Ages.'

'Speaking as a historian,' said Jim, 'I must point out that there were no credit cards in the so-called Dark Ages.'

Caro flushed, defeated in an instant, and began clearing away the breakfast things.

Suzie said, 'I bet it's quite healthy though, living like that.'

Caro banged the stacked dishes down on the draining board. 'It's their parents I feel sorry for,' she said. 'You'd die of shame if one of your own children started living like an animal.'

'Would you?' Suzie's question was almost inaudible.

Jim shrugged. He was bored with baiting Caro, an activity which always left him feeling out of sorts and irritated with himself. He glanced at the kitchen clock. 'I'd better get a move on if I want to catch my train.'

'Train?' Suzie had been hoping to have a few private words with her father in his study.

'Daddy's got to go to London today,' Caro spoke in the slightly deferential voice with which she always referred to her husband's work. 'He has some research to do.'

'I'm going out to Collindale,' said Jim. 'It's a pig of a journey so I may be late back. I'll ring and let you know.'

'More outlaws, Daddy?'

'In a manner of speaking,' said Jim. He felt it unnecessary to explain that the villain he was interested in today was not in the least historical. This villain was nothing if not contemporary.

Dear Charlotte,

You know those moments when everything is so perfect you know it can't last but you want to stop the clock and stay in that moment for ever? Well, this is one of those. It's ten o'clock in the morning of our second day in Paris. The first surprise has been that Wyndham has a flat here, one of those beautiful nineteenth-century ones in the *sixième*, all wrought-iron balconies and enormous double doors and long corridors. There is even a cook/housekeeper whose job most of the year must be just to keep it all looking perfect on the faint offchance that he might turn up for a night or two. If I wasn't otherwise occupied, I think I might apply for the job. Wyndham is off doing whatever it is Wyndhams do at this hour of the day – dreaming up new and still better ways for us to spend his money, perhaps.

Shopping, by the way, is different for the Wyndhams of this world. No trekking round antique shops or poking through racks of stuff and disappearing into changing rooms for us. No, the antique dealers phone him up to tell him what they've got, and sometimes they bring it here for him to look at.

Clothes are even more fun. Before we left London, Wyndham had arranged this amazing woman who brought the clothes to us while we sat in a private suite and had coffee and champagne and checked through what she found. At first I thought we were going to have our first ever row. The wretched woman kept bringing all these dismal outfits that Wyndham loved. I got more and more fed up and depressed and the two of them were making me feel like a spoilt child complaining about her Christmas presents, but then I finally got through to her that my taste doesn't change just because I've got more money, so she started ferreting out some amazing stuff. Then it was Wyndham's turn to look cheesed off, but he soon perked up when I started trying them on in different combinations. In fact the whole exercise became something of an aphrodisiac and we raced out of the shop and back to his flat and nearly missed the plane. Why are money and clothes so wickedly sexy? Char, am I a totally hopeless case? Nothing like this has ever happened to me before, and I have no intention of examining the teeth on this particular gift horse, not yet, anyway. Besides, Wyndham has beautiful teeth.

And the odd part of all is that I'd be with him without all of that. One of the things I most like about him is that he has an even lower boredom tolerance than I do. For instance, last night we went to what may well be the best restaurant in the world, how am I to know, and he'd been telling me about it all day. He really enjoyed all the stuff at the beginning, the menu and the ordering, but he started to get fidgety in the first course and by the end of the second course he was pawing the ground with impatience to get on to the next thing – nightclub, moonlit stroll beside the Seine, uniquely special bar – the point is, it doesn't matter what the next thing is, so long as one is always en route to something else. For the first time ever I'm the one who'd sometimes like to stay a little longer. Maybe this means he'll get tired of me, before I get tired of him. I hope not, I'm enjoying myself too much. Charlotte, I think maybe you're going to have to find someone else to help you decorate your fish restaurant after Christmas. I'm having too much fun being wined and dined in other people's.

I hope you are writhing in envy, Char my dear, yours in a daze of lust and lucre,

Lydia

20

'I met your dad the other day.'

'At Lydia's?'

Terry nodded. 'We went over to fix the roof of her lean-to.'

'I wondered if it was you. He said he'd met Hopi and Mal, but he couldn't remember your name.'

'He was OK, your dad.'

'He liked you all. He told us so at breakfast. Mummy got quite upset.'

'Why?'

'She wants everyone to think you're all absolutely frightful, same as she does.'

When Suzie saw the way Terry's eyes clouded with hurt she wished she hadn't been so brutally honest, so she popped in a small lie, to make up. 'Daddy thought you seemed really intelligent.'

'Yeah?' Terry's habitual caution battled with his desire to believe her statement. 'He said he thought I looked intelligent?'

'Yes.' Not wishing to wade too deep into untruth, Suzie was hunting for a way to change the subject. It was Sunday afternoon and they had brought the dogs to the top of Raven's Beacon. Bumpkin and Misty, having conquered their initial rivalry, were sociably investigating the copse that had been planted near the summit. From where Terry and Suzie were sitting Misty fluttered pale as a snowy moth, Bumpkin was a more solid blob of yellow. Suzie said, 'It's a shame about Lydia's holly tree.' When she and Terry had observed its brown leaves the previous Sunday Terry had said maybe it was just autumn and Suzie had gently mentioned about hollies being evergreen.

'Hope it doesn't mean bad luck for her,' said Terry.

Suzie giggled. 'I don't see how it can. Right now she's enjoying a holiday in Paris with Wyndham Sale. If that is bad luck then I could use a bit myself.'

'Fancy him, do you?'

'Wyndham Sale?' Suzie found herself blushing at the question, and blushing was something she hardly ever did any more, at least not when she was with Terry. 'Of course not. He's so *old*. But Paris must be brilliant.'

Terry was on the point of saying he'd been to Paris himself a couple of times for holidays, which was totally untrue but the sort of thing he often did say to make up for the fact that he never seemed to have been anywhere or done anything, but then he found he couldn't be bothered to lie to Suzie. He wasn't sure why not. He remembered what Hopi had said to him about Suzie having a crush on him and how it was important not to encourage her, but he thought for once Hopi had got it wrong. Suzie seemed more like a little sister than a potential girlfriend, and Terry had always thought it would be great to have a sister, someone you could watch out for, someone who was on your side. Besides, he hadn't planned this meeting: it just seemed to work out that on weekend afternoons they both took their dogs up to Raven's Beacon – and surely there was no law against people bumping into each other on a walk?

He asked, 'What does your dad do?'

'He's retired now, sort of. He still does articles and research sometimes. He used to teach at the university. Well, it was a poly and then it was a university.'

'That must be an interesting job.'

'I suppose so.' Suzie's uncertainty was due to the fact that most of her memories were of her father complaining about administration and paperwork, and her parents' anxiety about money.

'I wouldn't mind doing that,' said Terry. 'I should think teaching people is a really good job.'

'I don't think it pays all that well. My grandfather was in business and he made heaps of money. Of course,' she added vaguely, 'there's job satisfaction to think of as well.'

'Business would be OK,' said Terry. 'I wouldn't mind being a businessman, or something like that.' His imagination began to colour in a series of scenes: Terry walking into an office building and people watching him with respect and admiration; Terry pulling up at the Lodge in an expensive German car and Suzie's father coming out to say hello; Terry carrying a briefcase full of documents and books. He said to Suzie, 'How about you? What do you want to do later on?'

'I haven't the first idea,' said Suzie truthfully. A phrase from one of her teachers came to mind. 'I don't think I have any especial aptitudes.'

'You mustn't say that,' Terry protested. 'How about being a teacher like your dad? Not students, but little kids like Saul. He thinks you're brilliant. He's doing really well at school since you started bringing him those books.'

'That's wonderful.' Suzie glowed quietly for a moment before saying, 'It's a funny thing about Saul, but I don't think I've ever seen him laugh. Or even smile – not what I'd call a proper smile.'

Terry shrugged. 'I don't suppose he had all that much to smile about before he came to live with Mal. It can be pretty tough for little kids these days.'

'Isn't he happy now?'

'Sure he is, but Hopi said these things take time. He's still afraid he might get sent back to his mum.'

'I'd love to see him smile, just once. A proper, happy smile.'

That night Terry had a dream which weighed heavily on him long after he woke up next day. In his dream he was standing at the foot of a sheer cliff, a vast stretch of smooth rock towering above him, higher than any cliff he had ever seen. He felt compelled to climb to its summit, something lodged at the top that he had to reach, or someone he must join, though he wasn't sure who the someone was. It might have been his gran, or Suzie, or it might even have been Misty; all he knew was he had to reach them. But when he stretched up, the rock was smooth as polished marble. He started to climb anyway, clinging to the surface the way animals do. His toe found a crevice, his hand gripped a ledge, he began to haul himself slowly upwards. But then the rock crumbled and he slithered back to the ground, his palms and knees grazed and bleeding. He began again.

The dream pressed so heavily on him all morning that eventually he went in search of Hopi. She was chopping some wood, not far from her trailer. To Terry's relief Colin was nowhere to be seen. Hopi had already stacked a good pile of logs and was more than happy to pause a while for a roll-up and a chat. The air was damp, as though it might rain, but it was mild enough for them to enjoy being outside.

'That friend of Lydia's,' he began casually, 'did you know he used to teach at university?'

'Suzie's father? Yes, I think Lydia did mention it.'

'I reckon you have to be dead clever for that job. Pass loads of exams.'

Hopi looked at him closely, but his expression betrayed nothing. She said merely, 'It's a lot of work.'

'It might be hard to know where to begin, I mean, if someone was thinking of getting on.'

'There's courses,' said Hopi. 'My mum did an Access course. She was really doing well, but then my dad got ill and she had to stop. There's one of those Learning Centre places in Edleston, I've been past it a few times. Anyone can go there.'

'You can see how it might be interesting,' said Terry, still avoiding her eye. 'But then again, we don't need any of that, living the way we do. I mean, we've got all we need right here. You'd have to stop in one place for ages and live in a house or a flat. We're better off the way we are.'

'Perhaps,' Hopi said with a smile, 'but wait and see how you feel about life in the open air come February when it's been chucking it down with rain and freezing for weeks.' She caught sight of a figure near the gate and her smile faded. Automatically she stood up. 'Time to be getting on,' she said, as Colin began to cross the field to join them. 'Hi, Colin,' she greeted him cheerfully, 'can you give me a hand with these logs?'

'What did he want?' Colin jerked his head towards Terry, who had nodded a brief hello before heading off to his own van. From under his favourite floppy hat, Colin's face peered out anxious and wide-eyed while Hopi gathered up as much wood as she could carry.

'We were just chatting,' she said. 'How did you get on in Edleston?'

'Waste of bloody time. Stupid tossers had lost my file. So they said. Come back in a week – what the hell am I supposed to live on till then?'

'Never mind, Colin. We'll manage OK.' Her eyes smiled their reassurance over the pile of logs she was carrying, but Colin was too agitated to notice. When she had placed the wood neatly on some corrugated iron under her caravan, she was about to return for the rest when Colin caught hold of her arm.

'What were you two talking about?'

'Nothing much, I can't remember. Look, I can get the rest of the wood later. Why don't we have a cup of tea and you can tell me what happened in Edleston?'

Colin followed her up the two boxes that formed the steps to her caravan. 'I don't like him hanging round you all the time,' he said.

'He doesn't hang round.'

'You're always talking to him.'

Hopi made soothing noises while she made them each a mug of tea. Colin was bristling with insecurity, she could see that, and that was why he was so prickly and could be difficult at times. He couldn't bear to share her with anyone, which was of course flattering, but also a real nuisance.

Saul came to the door demanding that she go through his new reading book with him. She said, 'Later, Saul, I'm busy right now,' and when Saul began a nasal whining, Colin let rip with a volley of threats.

'You shouldn't talk to him like that,' said Hopi when Saul had retreated, muttering a few curses of his own. 'It only makes him worse.'

'So? He's not my problem, is he? And when did you get all lovey-dovey with someone else's kid? What went on between you and Mal while I was away?'

'Don't be daft, Colin. Mal's just a friend.'

'Everybody's "just a friend". You've got too many bloody friends. And what about this woman you've got so matey with? What's going on with *her*, eh?'

'Lydia?' Incredulously, Hopi burst out with a laugh, 'You surely can't be jealous of *Lydia*?'

Too late, Hopi realised Colin had offset his disappointments

over his Giro with another bottle of vodka and that even a hint
of mockery was salt on his wounds. Too late she realised also
that his infinite jealousy extended even to the sewing she had
spent hours doing.

'I'm not fucking jealous!' he bellowed. 'You're the one has
to be queen bee and have everyone think you're so bloody
wonderful. It's you can't leave stuff alone. Look at this mess,
all this crap just messing the place up—' He reached past her to
grab the jacket she had been working on that morning.

Instinctively Hopi said, 'Hey, don't do that,' and leaned across
to retrieve her work, but he barrelled her out of the way. She
fell sideways against the corner of the sewing machine, crying
out in pain and shock as her shoulder struck the metal. There
was a sharp tearing noise. Colin had ripped the jacket from neck
to hem.

'Stop it, you maniac!' Once again she tried to seize the patchwork from him, but, almost casually, he administered a savage
whack above her ear, knocking her to the ground, then carried
on ripping and tearing until the jacket was in fragments.

In the silence that followed, Colin stood trembling from head
to toe in the centre of the trailer, while Hopi gasped and held
her head.

It was Colin who eventually spoke. 'Now look what you
bloody made me do,' he breathed. 'You just don't know when
to stop. You just wind me up, you do . . .' As if to emphasise his
point he picked up his mug of tea, which had not been drunk
at all, and flung it against the far wall of the caravan. 'There!'
He was panting. 'Don't say I didn't warn you!' He banged open
the door and stormed out.

Too distraught to notice who or what was in his way, he
strode past Mal who was standing not far from the caravan.
Mal had noticed Colin arrive and Terry depart, he had seen
Colin and Hopi enter the trailer and then Saul come away,
rebuffed and furious. He had heard raised voices and the smash
of crockery. His anger at Colin's treatment of Saul was magnified
hugely at the idea of anyone shouting at Hopi. There was a
darkening behind his eyes and a tightness in his upper chest,
but when he found himself in the caravan with Hopi and
saw her still crouched by the sewing machine, holding her

head and drawing in long painful breaths, his rage gave way to concern.

'Hopi, are you OK?'

'I've been better,' she admitted. 'Colin was in a state. His money didn't come through. He's had a bad morning.'

'Doesn't mean he has to take it out on you. He didn't hit you, did he?'

'I'm all right Mal, honestly.' She managed a weak smile and, trying to avoid looking at the torn pieces of fabric, she knelt down and began to pick up the chunks of china. 'What a bloody mess, eh?'

Mal crouched down to help her, then picked up a scrap of material. 'What's all this?'

'It *was* that patchwork jacket I was making.'

'Colin?'

She nodded, but did not trust herself to speak.

'The bastard!' Mal sat back on his heels and stared. 'After all your work.'

Hopi shrugged and scooped up a pile of scraps. She sniffed. Mal reached out a hand and touched her shoulder. 'The bastard,' he said again. 'I don't believe it. I was just outside, too. I should've stopped him.'

Still on his knees, Mal shuffled forwards and put his arm around her shoulders. For a second Hopi leaned her cheek against his woolly shoulder, but his support felt tentative and unsure. Like her, he was shaking. Perhaps with fear. She eased back and pushed him gently away.

'It's OK, Mal. I'm all right now, really I am. You'd better push off, it only makes him worse if people come in. He'll be fine now for a bit, I know Colin.'

She stood up.

Mal said, 'Let me help you get straightened up.'

'No. I won't bother with it now.'

'What are you going to do?'

She considered for a moment. Her head was throbbing and she felt sick and deeply shaken. From some residual urge to protect Colin, she did not want Mal to see the extent of her distress. She wanted to get away from the caravan, away from the site altogether. She wanted to put as much distance between herself and Colin as possible, not because she was frightened of his anger, but because she couldn't face his remorse, not yet. What she really wanted was to be home with her mother for a little while, but that was obviously not an option. She said, 'I think I'll go to Lydia's. She should've come back from Paris last night and she still owes me a bath. I'll be OK, Mal. You mustn't worry about me.'

'Colin's a bloody maniac,' Mal was not at all convinced. 'I don't know why you stick with him.'

Hopi said nothing. Time was, she had been ready with all manner of excuses for Colin: he was insecure, he was highly strung, he couldn't help it, he had a lot on his mind – but he had never hit her before. He had pushed and shoved and broken things, he had shouted and sobbed and driven people away and made grotesque scenes. But he had never hit her. No one had ever hit her in her life before, not like that. She felt chilled and very dirty. She needed to get away from the site and have that bath at Lydia's. She wasn't going to be able to think straight until she had soaked off the horror of the last few minutes. So all she said was, 'It's OK, Mal. It'll all work out.'

But she felt that some kind of boundary had been crossed and she was confused and frightened, so that her voice, usually so reassuring, came out wavering and unsure.

Lydia had only dropped back to Rose Cottage to collect her post. She was not officially living at Haddeley Hall yet, but she had slept there the previous night because it had been late when she and Wyndham returned from Paris and it seemed to both of them an opportunity to extend their holiday by a few hours more. She was going to stay there again tonight because he had suggested a working supper in order to finalise the first stage of work to be done on the house. Lydia had revised her suggestion of Art Deco in the library in favour of something more austere. In fact the more she thought about it the more certain she was that the whole house wanted to follow the romantically minimal style she had achieved in the steward's room. The following day she would be travelling with Wyndham to London because he happened to have two tickets for Covent Garden and had invited her to join him for a couple of nights at his flat overlooking Hyde Park. And when they returned she would probably stay another night or two at Haddeley Hall because they had decided on a dinner party, a small gathering, but even so one intended as a declaration of their changed relationship and the beginning of Haddeley Hall's transformation from mausoleum to living home.

But, Lydia insisted, as much to herself as to Wyndham, Rose Cottage was still her real base.

Already, however, the cottage had absorbed a faint aura of neglect: it was nothing tangible, more a mood, a hint of reproach, as though the place was jealous of the attention being lavished on Haddeley Hall.

'Well,' Lydia defended herself to the silent air, 'at least I tried to get your roof fixed.'

There was a letter from Gordon among her post, as she had known there would be. It was full of anxieties for her welfare and said nothing of his own needs or activities. Yet she thought – half-dared to hope – that there was a new detachment in his tone. His concern was remote, impersonal almost, the solicitude of a doctor for his patient and she thought to herself: I wonder if he has found someone else to worry over. She realised then that her unkindness had not been in leaving him, but in waiting so long to tell him it was final.

She was just settling into reading a long letter from Charlotte about the antics of her Minorcan builders when Hopi arrived. Damn, thought Lydia, as the familiar homely face appeared in the doorway, just when I wanted a few minutes to myself. Her dismay stemmed from more than a craving for solitude. The mental adjustment required to get back on to Hopi's wavelength after a weekend of champagne-fuelled pampering with Wyndham, suddenly felt excessive. Lydia would have been horrified if anyone had accused her of abandoning old friends simply because she had taken a step up in the world; it was merely that she didn't feel like making the necessary effort this very minute. Perhaps in order to compensate for this, she was effusive in her welcome.

'Hello Hopi, come on in. How are you? You're lucky to catch me in. I'd offer you a cup of tea but—'

'Thanks, but it's the bath I'm after.'

Somewhere at the back of her mind Lydia registered the fact that Hopi was not her usual placid self, but she dismissed this and said brightly, 'Oh dear, there's hardly any hot water right now. I can put the immersion on if you like but—'

'Yes please,' said Hopi, for once ignoring Lydia's obvious reluctance.

Again Lydia dismissed the hint of something not quite right in Hopi's manner and said, 'Sure. I owe you at least two. Can I get you a drink while the water heats up?'

'Do you have anything alcoholic?'

'Sorry.'

'That's OK then. You carry on with what you were doing.'

Lydia tried to. She left Hopi flipping through a magazine she had picked up at the airport and busied herself in the kitchen. She might even have succeeded in ignoring Hopi's distress altogether, but at the very last minute, as Hopi began removing her layers of woollen clothing in the steam-filled bathroom, Lydia remembered there were no towels in there. As she pushed open the door she caught Hopi examining the bruise on her shoulder, then move swiftly as if to hide her action.

'That must have hurt a bit,' commented Lydia, handing over the towel.

'Mm,' said Hopi noncommittally. She caught Lydia's eye for a fleeting moment before she unhooked the dark hair from behind her ear and shook it forward to conceal a second bruise high on her jawline.

Lydia stood very still, a chill spreading through her, banishing grammar. 'Hopi, did someone *do* those bruises to you? Not Mal, surely.'

'Jesus, no, Mal would never harm a fly.'

'The returning boyfriend, then?' Hopi did not answer, but hugged herself protectively. Lydia drew in a deep breath and said, 'Bloody hell, Hopi, I thought I was a bad judge of men, but even I draw the line at violence. OK, I'm sorry, I'm not about to give you a lecture. At least have your bath first. A proper, pampering bath. Here . . .' She peered into the cobweb-hung cupboard and fished out a small bottle of bath essence and a new bar of soap. 'Luxuriate. Take as long as you like. I'm not in any hurry.' And with that, Lydia retreated.

Hopi stayed in the bathroom for over half an hour, and when she came down she had the pink and puckered look of a small child ready for a bedtime story. Lydia, however, had had plenty of time to reflect, and was not in the mood for bedtime stories.

'That was great, Lydia, thanks a million. I know you're busy so I won't stop—'

'Oh yes you will. You're not leaving here till you've told me what's going on. I can be just as stubborn as you, so don't bother arguing. Besides Hopi, I *owe* you, remember? And I don't mean the roof. I owe you for that weird ceremony at Raven's Beacon. Well, now it's my turn to bully you. What's been going on?'

'Colin got upset, that's all. He's very highly strung—'

'That's a new word for it.'

'Oh, he never meant to hurt me,' Hopi began earnestly, but then she paused and said after a moment or two, 'Hell, I don't know. Maybe he did. Maybe I'm just making excuses for him.'

'Kick him out, Hopi.'

'I can't.'

'Why not?'

'Because . . . God, I don't know. Maybe I feel sorry for him.'

'He'll manage.'

'And also . . .' Hopi was frowning as she rolled her cigarette, 'also I worry about what he might do. I know he wouldn't hurt me but—'

'Hopi, he just did.'

'I mean, he'd never do anything really violent. He just stirs up trouble. It's hard to explain really, he's so unpredictable. I just can't imagine how he'd react.'

'How do you mean?'

'Well, since he and his friends Barney and Flea came back from Spain the whole atmosphere on site has changed. Everyone used to get on really well, now there's arguments and hassle all the time. It's just not the same any more.'

'You'll have to get together and make them leave.'

'We can't. There's no organisation, things just happen. We believe people must be free to come and go as they like.'

'Hopi, that's crazy. You must have some kind of control over who comes on the site.'

'No, 'cause then we'd be just the same as all those people who keep trying to kick us out, don't you see that?'

Lydia shook her head. 'Not if the alternative is you staying with a man who knocks you about.'

'He's never done it before.'

'Once is enough.'

As Hopi walked back to the site she was inclined, much against her will, to agree with Lydia. However, identifying the problem was only half the battle, acting on it was likely to prove far more difficult. She knew that by now Colin would be so charming and repentant, she'd need a heart of stone not to kiss and make up. As elfin child and little-boy-lost he was almost irresistible, at least to Hopi who regarded herself as plodding and ordinary, and never saw the warmth and humanity that others were instantly drawn by. She thought it would be a wonderful way out if Colin decided he wanted to move on without her, but until that happened she could see no alternative but to make the best of the present situation.

21

Since the food had been chosen by Wyndham and was being prepared by Miguel and his wife, Lydia was free to devote her energies to preparing the setting for their dinner party that evening. She was not entirely surprised to discover that this was the first entertaining that had been done at Haddeley Hall, though she was not sure whether this was because Annabel had fallen ill almost immediately after they moved in, or whether they had simply chosen to keep to themselves. The result, however, was that the dining room had never been used – Wyndham preferring when he was on his own to eat in the breakfast room – the best china and glass was still deep in packing cases, linen, cutlery and vases all had to be tracked down and made ready. For Lydia, it was the best of treasure hunts.

'You should get Mrs Mig to do that,' said Wyndham. He had emerged from his study to find Lydia in the hall, dusting off an enormous Chinese pot.

'And spoil my fun?' responded Lydia. She had in mind a precise picture of the impression she wanted her guests to have from the very moment they entered the front door and were drawn into the softly-lit romance of the house.

'It's only Jim and Caro,' Wyndham pointed out.

'And George. And Twinks,' she added. Because the supper was intended as a public declaration of their changed status, they had decided to replicate the dinner at which they met first, though it had not occurred to either that Suzie had also been present on that occasion.

'All the same,' said Wyndham.

'You don't understand,' said Lydia, 'I'm not doing this for your guests. I'm doing it for the house.'

Wyndham was about to continue on his way to collect some papers he had left in his dressing room, but he paused a moment to watch Lydia in her work. She shifted the pot about three inches to the left, stood back and gazed at it intently, bobbed forward once more and turned it forty-five degrees on its axis, stepped back and looked again, then licked the tip of her finger and rubbed off an invisible mark. She was wearing a pale sweater tucked into cropped jeans, and flat shoes. Wyndham approached her and placed his hands on her hips.

'Marry me,' he said.

Lydia shook back her hair and grinned. 'What, now?'

He tugged her a little closer to him. 'This afternoon. As soon as possible.' He kissed her forehead, the bridge of her nose.

'I can't.'

'Damn. Come to bed with me then, instead.'

Still smiling, she leaned back a little way. 'Isn't it amazing, the adoration that is inspired by housework?'

'What?' He was kissing the hollow at the base of her throat.

'Even in these liberated times nothing turns a man on as much as a glimpse of his beloved with a duster in her hand. If I ever do get married again I intend to have a wedding dress made entirely of dusters and tea cloths. It will cause a sensation.'

Wyndham was beginning to say something crude and quite unconnected with housework which made Lydia forget all about Chinese pots and her vision for the house that evening, when there was an awkward movement in the shadowy recess near the small sitting room.

'You'd better have a look at this fax that's just come in from Milan,' said Mark in the slightly belligerent tone of an interloper. It was a puce tie day, always a bad sign.

Wyndham paused in his explorations long enough to mutter, 'Bugger off, Mark, can't you see I'm busy?'

'Bobo says there's been a hold-up with the new dyes,' Mark persisted.

Wyndham swore, and released Lydia with obvious reluctance. 'Bloody fools. OK, Mark, I'll be right there.' And to Lydia he said, 'Promise me you won't go away. Apart from anything else, I wanted to show you the latest set of drawings the garden contractors have delivered.'

Lydia smiled happily and turned back to her pot, moving it a full ninety degrees and discovering another smudge of dirt. 'Don't worry,' she said, 'I wasn't going anywhere.'

Colin was not simply apologetic for having hit Hopi, his remorse threatened to take over their lives. He was so genuinely shocked and appalled that Hopi, as he wept in her arms that evening, almost convinced herself his violence had been a unique, never-to-be-repeated aberration. He swore that he would rather die than ever hurt her again, that she was the only woman he had ever cared for, the only woman who had ever understood him and that if she turned her back on him now he would either die of grief or kill himself. Hopi was not entirely convinced by this argument, but she was far too soft-hearted to resist the appeal of those huge, tear-filled grey eyes. But after a day or two his determination to make amends became such a nuisance that Hopi several times begged him to forget it had ever happened. This Colin was quite unable to do. Racked with guilt at having destroyed her jacket, he decided to help her start another, and, while she was getting water from the farm, he ruined several more pieces of fabric by cutting them into crazy-paving shapes. His desperation to please was so intense that Hopi could not bring herself to tell him these were fit only to be thrown away.

She had no scruples, however, about taking advantage of his new mood of repentance when she discovered a half bottle of rum with a price tag on it from Peggy's shop.

'You never paid for this, did you?' she demanded sternly.

His pale eyes expressed amazement that she could even contemplate such an eventuality. 'Where am I going to get that kind of money from?'

'You promised, Colin. You promised you wouldn't take stuff from Peggy.'

'Don't be like that, Hopi. I only took it to give you a little treat. After all you've been through.'

'I'm taking it back.'

'Don't be stupid.'

'I'm taking it back, Colin.' There was no doubting her determination.

'You won't get me into trouble will you?'

Hopi sighed. 'No, Colin, I promise. I'll put it back on the shelf when no one's looking.' It was the best compromise she could think of. Then she smiled. 'Kind of thieving in reverse, isn't it, trying to put stuff back without being caught?'

Gaining confidence from her smile, Colin ventured, 'Why don't we have some of it now? If I promise not to take any again, that's almost the same as you taking it back, isn't it?'

'Not quite, Colin. Not really the same.'

As Hopi concealed the bottle of rum in one of the deep side pockets of her jacket she realised that as far as Colin was concerned she was just making a pointless gesture.

A couple of times on the way into Briarswood Hopi had to force herself not to turn back. Her compromise solution had seemed reasonable enough while talking to Colin in the trailer, but now it felt desperately risky. Presumably you were as likely to be caught trying to replace items without being seen as you were when trying to remove them. And then what was she going to say to Peggy? She had promised not to get Colin into trouble, but it would be perfectly obvious that someone had been nicking the stuff, and their reputation was bound to suffer. But Hopi was so fed up at people always assuming they were a bunch of thieves that she was determined to put matters to rights now. No good protesting her innocence if she knew her caravan was being used for stolen goods.

Peggy was in her usual spot behind the counter, and she gave Hopi a cheery 'Hello,' and then carried on listening to Ann's account of rehearsals for the Nativity play. The only other customer was a lady Hopi had seen once or twice before: tall, straight and very elegant, she had white curls and a face that must have once been beautiful.

'Hi,' said Hopi and gave the old lady a friendly grin. Her only response was a slightly startled step backwards. Hopi picked out a bag of crisps and then moved nonchalantly towards the wines and spirits.

'We were all getting along fine,' said Ann, 'until my best sheep was bitten on the foot by an angel.'

Hopi slipped her hand into her pocket and it closed around the smooth surface of the bottle. She heard Peggy say, 'Will that be all, Mrs Cartwright?' in the overemphatic tone reserved for the elderly, deaf or incompetent. She glanced around to make sure none of the other three women was looking her way, hunched close to the shelf where spirits were displayed, and pulled out the rum.

'Great heavens above, just look at that!' Peggy's voice rang out across the shop. 'I simply don't believe my eyes!'

Cheeks aflame with humiliation, Hopi let the bottle fall back into her pocket and spun round, mentally preparing to make a full confession. She was just wondering whether to take all the blame herself, or whether to give a version of the truth, when she realised she could have replaced a whole caseload of spirits and no one would have noticed.

Peggy and Ann were both staring at the old lady. Twinks stood between the till and the half-open door. Her pencil-thin legs were placed wide apart and she was swaying slightly, as though in danger of being toppled by the draught from outside. On the floor by her feet lay a scattered assortment of goods: a couple of tins of salmon, a quarter bottle of brandy, a packet of licorice and some powdered soup.

'If that doesn't beat everything,' said Ann, incredulous.

Twinks, as upright and apparently composed as ever, was frowning in the manner of someone trying to remember a telephone number. As she stood there, hardly moving, there was a faint tearing noise and a small bottle of gin fell from under the folds of her coat, and joined the other items on the floor.

Peggy's voice was almost awed as she said again, 'I don't believe it.'

Twinks smiled at her benignly and murmured, 'So kind of you. Thank you so much. Would love to stay and talk but . . . Mustn't stop.' She began a slow drift towards the door.

'Just a minute, not so fast,' began Peggy and then, as Twinks continued her stately glide towards the exit, she roared, 'For God's sake, one of you, stop her!' and struggled to emerge from behind the counter before her quarry escaped.

Because of the layout of the little shop, it was Hopi who reached the door first, closing it firmly behind her as she turned and said to Twinks, 'Sorry, but I think Peggy wants to talk to you.'

Suddenly the old lady's smile was no longer condescending. Something cold and hard seemed to freeze in her eyes. 'Really, this is all most tedious, I can't think why you leave all these things lying around on the floor, someone might trip over them, you know.'

By this time Peggy had come round the end of the counter. Deference and long years of being polite to customers no matter what the provocation was battling against a growing sense of outrage at her eroded profits.

'If you don't mind, Mrs Cartwright,' she began, and then, with a sudden lunging movement she pulled open Twinks' coat to reveal a large tear near the hem of her lining. The other side still bulged with mysterious shapes. Peggy stepped back in amazement and said for the third time, 'I simply don't believe it!'

'Have you finished?' Twinks enquired politely. 'This is all frightfully inconvenient, you know.'

For a moment Hopi thought Twinks' cool disregard for the evidence was going to carry the day. Peggy and Ann were both staring at her as if she had just sprouted a second head, but they appeared to have no idea how to deal with this situation. Twinks turned once more to Hopi and said, 'Now, if you would please excuse me, I am expected at home.'

Peggy blinked and could be seen to give herself a mental shake. 'Just a minute, Mrs Cartwright. You can't just go off like that and pretend it didn't happen. What about all that other stuff? Let's have a look at what else you've got stashed away in there.'

'Oh dear, all right then, if you must.'

Twinks stood stock still with an expression of long-suffering patience on her face while Peggy removed further bottles and tins within the left-hand lining, and set them down on the counter.

'Please hurry,' said Twinks, 'I haven't got all day.'

'I'm sorry, Mrs Cartwright,' Peggy began, 'but it has to be done.' And then, as the booty piled up on the counter, she began to realise how ridiculous her apology had been. 'Though why in God's name I'm the one to say sorry, I can't imagine.

Have you any idea how hard I have to work just to cover the overheads on this place? You sail in here like Lady Muck and help yourself to whatever you fancy, and it's not as if you couldn't pay for it perfectly well. More spirits! Quite a little cellar you've been getting, haven't you? And all at my expense. Well, it's not right, I don't care who you are, I treat all as I find and if you've been thieving, then I'm telling the police. I'm not running a bloody charity for distressed gentlefolk, you know. I've got competition from the supermarkets and business rates and God knows what. I'm phoning the police right now.'

At this second mention of the police, Twinks began to tremble violently. Hopi's initial surprise had faded and she was beginning to feel sickened at the sight of the frail old lady's distress. Instinctively she put her arm out to steady her; she was shaking so badly she seemed about to fall over. Twinks' pale hands gripped her fiercely.

'Just a minute, Peg,' said Ann, 'don't do anything in a hurry. Are you sure you want to involve the police straightaway?'

'Bloody right I do. God only knows how much has gone missing. Why should I put up with it?'

'I'm not saying you should. I just think you should talk to Mrs Cartwright's family first. I'm sure they'd want to make up to you for any losses, but it might be best for everyone to deal with it quietly. I know it's unfair, but it's sure to look bad if it came to court, you know. Little old lady victimised by ruthless shopkeeper, that sort of thing.'

Peggy swore. 'There's no justice,' she said. 'Lord knows how long this has been going on.' She turned to Twinks. 'How much have you taken, Mrs Cartwright? How long having you been thieving?'

'I believe,' said Twinks, 'that I may have removed one or two items in error. Please allow me to pay for them now. If you will just tell me how much I owe you . . .' She began to pat her arm and waist as though searching for her handbag. 'Oh dear, I seem to have left my purse at home. I hope you will accept a cheque.'

'Brazen,' said Peggy, 'downright brazen.'

Ann was more thoughtful. 'Might as well let Mrs Cartwright go home now, Peggy. I reckon your best bet is to have a talk with her daughter. She's a customer of yours too, isn't she? In my opinion, Mrs Cartwright needs help.'

As a description of her present state, this was clearly accurate. Even when Peggy had grudgingly agreed to let her go, Twinks was unable to walk to her car unaided; driving it was out of the question.

'Now what?' exclaimed Peggy in exasperation. 'I'm not leaving the shop to see her home. I've lost enough already thanks to her.'

'I'd take her,' said Ann, 'but I can't drive. And I don't think she could manage the walk.'

'I'll phone her husband. Let him sort it out.'

Twinks started violently. 'No! Not him! Don't tell George.'

By now Hopi was feeling so sorry for Twinks that she was regretting her own part in preventing her escape. 'I can drive her home,' she offered.

Peggy and Ann turned to look at her. 'What a good idea,' said Ann warmly.

'Might as well,' said Peggy, 'I'll phone Mrs Lewis.'

Twinks began to say, 'How very kind of you,' to Hopi in a serene voice, but was unable to finish her sentence for violent shivering. Hopi was suddenly horribly aware of the half bottle of rum still nestling in the pocket of her own jacket, and was on the verge of declaring her guilt.

'You'd better go with them, Ann,' said Peggy. 'Mrs Cartwright's about to collapse, I reckon.'

The keys to the little Peugeot were in the ignition. Ann sat in the back and Hopi and Peggy helped Twinks into the passenger seat and did up her seat belt. She was unresisting, but so obviously overwhelmed by all that had happened that they began to feel a sense of real urgency. 'It's all right, Mrs Cartwright,' said Ann, 'you'll be home in a jiff.'

Hopi was so used to driving lorries and ancient cars with faulty gearboxes that it took her most of the distance to the Manor to adjust to the smoothly precise controls of the little hatchback. Under different circumstances she might have suggested taking a longer route in order to enjoy the drive, but as it was they pulled to a halt on the gravel sweep in front of the Manor in less than five minutes.

George opened the front door. He had a copy of the *Countryman* in his hand and was less than overjoyed at the interruption. Especially when he was confronted by the spectacle of his wife, supported on either side by a strange woman. He became outraged when he saw that one of the strange women was one of the unspeakable harpies who had invaded the Hollows.

'What the devil have you done to my wife?' he roared.

Ann had been fully intending to explain the situation to Mr Cartwright but, as she said to Peggy ten minutes later when she reported back, 'I just couldn't do it. He looked so fierce and unreachable, I felt quite sorry for the poor woman, no wonder she was in such a state. He could have been making her life a misery for years and no one would ever know what went on tucked away in that great house of theirs. Anyway, I'm sorry, Peggy, but suddenly it just seemed like telling tales out of school.'

'So what did you tell him?'

'I just said she'd been taken ill in the shop and you'd asked us to bring her home.'

'I'll phone her daughter,' said Peggy.

'It's Peggy from the shop,' said Jim, conveying this information to the outside of the bathroom door. 'Shall I tell her to ring back later?'

'Please, darling.' Caro's voice emerged hazy with warmth and steam.

'Damn.' A few moments later the phone was ringing again. It seemed to Jim that ever since Suzie had been persuaded to terminate her vacuous conversation with Mina, the wretched thing had barely stopped. Jim hurried down the stairs, only to return a few minutes later with fresh news for the bathroom door.

'That was your father,' he announced. 'He said Twinks won't be able to make it to Haddeley Hall tonight. She had some kind of funny turn at the shop and she's gone to bed.'

'Oh dear, poor Mummy. Is she all right?'

'She's fine, by the sound of it. George says she took one of those pills she's got and now she's fast asleep. He wanted you to go and sit with her so he could go out this evening. Don't worry Caro, I told him not to be such a selfish old goat and to take care of her himself for once.'

'Oh Jim, you didn't!'

'I may not have used those exact words, but that was the gist of it.'

'Poor Daddy wouldn't know how to look after anyone if he tried. We'd better pop in on our way to the Hall, just to make sure they're all right.' Wet thrashing noises from the other side of the door indicated that Caro was planning to cut short her bath in order to go to the aid of her parents.

'Don't fuss, Caro. Suzie can go, can't you Suzie?'

'Um?'

Suzie was sitting on the corner of her bed, but she had left the door of her room open. She was still digesting all the news she had just heard from an extremely excited Mina. Jean had been away again for a few days, during which period Rupert had been expelled from his crammer for selling drugs to a couple of Japanese students, Arnold had written off his car, and Mina herself had celebrated the ending of a recent pregnancy scare with a feast of magic mushrooms and had thought she was turning into a set of bongo drums.

'How about you, Sooz?' Mina had ended up after talking without pause for more than half an hour. 'Is life as boring as ever?'

'Just about,' Suzie had answered happily. In fact her days were most deliciously filled with thoughts of Terry. So long as there was always a chance of seeing him again with the dogs at the weekend, she could imagine no greater bliss.

'Poor old Sooz,' Mina had ended up, sounding practically sympathetic for once, 'nothing ever happens in Briarswood, does it?'

Caro was wearing the aubergine wool dress she had bought when she went shopping with Polly. Jim had remarked on how nice she looked, which was sweet of him, and encouraging. She hoped this was a sign that he had forgotten the unpleasantness caused by its purchase. She felt almost justified in having bought it, since it was such a help to be able to dress smartly for a place like Haddeley Hall. Unfortunately, however, what with all the worry of the last few weeks and too many autumnal puddings, she seemed to have developed a few extra bulges around the middle and had to keep remembering to hold herself in, especially while standing, which was rather a strain.

Lydia of course had legs a mile long and not an ounce of surplus fat anywhere. Caro tried to be pleased that Lydia had so obviously fallen on her feet, but she thought it might be easier to be public-spirited if Lydia was about two stone heavier and not quite so radiantly attractive. Presumably Wyndham was buying her clothes these days – no more tatty lace vests and tight jeans – though the cropped trousers and black silk matador jacket she was wearing were not exactly what Caro would have chosen were she invited to play hostess at Haddeley Hall. Still, the parts of the house that they had seen so far were looking very beautiful, the food was excellent and the wine flowed freely. In fact, some of the wine seemed to be flowing a little too freely in Jim's direction: his features had taken on that blurry pinkness which often heralded one of his rare attacks of nastiness.

She smiled at him uncertainly across the cluster of candles in the centre of the dining table. He gave her a conspiratorial wink. This struck her as an ominous sign.

'I went to that adult learning place in Edleston this morning,' she said brightly, since there seemed to be something of a lull in the conversation. 'I've started a computer course. I couldn't help noticing, Wyndham, that you've got all sorts of computer equipment in that office of yours, but the whole business is absolutely new to me. Still, I've made a start. Today I conquered the mouse.'

For Lydia this conjured up an image that was irresistible, and she smiled as she asked, 'Are you going to type Jim's work for him?'

'Oh, I don't think he'd like that, he can't bear me interfering,' said Caro, with one of her disarming flashes of honesty. 'I was thinking of trying to get some part-time work. Every penny helps these days, doesn't it?'

Wyndham nodded, but he was clearly puzzled by this question.

Jim was wondering why the hell Caro had to bash on about their straightened circumstances in this present company. If he hadn't known her better he might have thought she was doing it deliberately to bate him. His irritation was growing into an itch of anger that he had to deal with somehow. It wasn't that he envied Wyndham his obvious wealth, far from it. He had no wish to live in a place like Haddeley Hall or jet-set around the world doing deals, or whatever it was Wyndham did. Jim was truly content with his books and his study and family life at the Lodge. What he resented, bitterly and furiously resented, was the effect Wyndham's money had on the women for whom he cared. Here was Caro fawning like an adolescent. Worse, just look at Lydia, even now casting adoring glances across the dining table at this utterly mediocre man.

Lydia continued to encourage Caro. 'How very enterprising,' she said. 'Didn't you find it a bit alarming, just walking in off the street?'

'Terrifying,' agreed Caro, 'and they really do have a complete cross section of society there. I even saw one of those New Agers hanging round outside this morning, but he never went inside, thank heavens.'

'One of the ones from the Hollows?' asked Lydia. 'What did he look like?'

'Goodness knows, they all look the same to me,' Caro said with a little laugh. Lydia looked faintly annoyed, but obviously decided to let it pass. If he hadn't been so irritated, Jim would have been pleased to see the two women making such strenuous efforts to get along. He had always hoped they might be friends, though he could see they did not have much in common. Or had not had until now. Suddenly the conversation had switched from adult learning programmes to matters decorative and they plunged with obvious delight into a discussion of various suppliers of antique French fabrics and wallpapers. He heard Lydia say she intended to study with a well-known garden designer, so she could do the grounds at Haddeley Hall justice.

So, he thought, she is going to stay. He felt a cold hand close over his heart. Years ago Lydia had been his protégée; he had expected great things of her. And now this. A professional spender of a rich man's money. Through a haze of anger and disgust, he became aware that Wyndham was watching him.

Wyndham smiled sardonically. 'The quest for the perfect pelmet. Still, if it makes them happy . . .'

Jim felt a sudden loathing for the man. To Wyndham Lydia was an ornament, nothing more. Even her rare intelligence was only of value because it reflected well on the man whose wealth had gained her affections. Or so it seemed to Jim.

Wyndham nodded to Miguel who stepped forward and refilled Jim's wine glass. Wyndham leaned back in his chair and surveyed the scene with satisfaction. 'I'm a lucky man,' he said. A meaningless phrase, a platitude to fill the time or even a compliment to Lydia herself, but to Jim, as he drained his glass, it seemed the last word in complacency and intended deliberately to goad him.

'If it is luck,' sneered Jim, and then wished he had not spoken at all. He had not meant to bring the topic up now, but to talk to Lydia about it in private some time. And then he thought, to hell with it, he was glad he had spoken after all.

'What else could it be?' asked Wyndham mildly.

'It must help if you don't play by the rules, for one thing.'

Wyndham was silent for a moment, fingering his glass and watching Lydia's animated face. Then he asked, 'Meaning what, precisely?'

'You know damn well,' said Jim.

'. . . Even using the original wooden print blocks,' Lydia was saying, but Caro had stopped listening. The two women broke off their discussion and watched the men in silence.

'Tell me anyway,' insisted Wyndham.

'The Collet report for one thing.'

'Isn't that rather out of date?'

'Apparently not,' said Jim. 'Sources I spoke to last week said the situation is virtually unchanged from seven years ago. The operation has merely introduced extra middlemen to distance the company, a perfect example of reaping the benefit without taking the responsibility. Or so the evidence implies.'

'Jim, darling, what on earth are you talking about?' Caro asked, though she instantly knew she didn't want to hear the answer.

'What's this all about, Wyndham?' asked Lydia.

'Your friend Jim has been acting the sleuth, apparently. He's itching to tell you what he's found, aren't you, Jim?'

'Jim?' Lydia turned to him. Her expression indicated that he'd better come up with something that merited all this fuss.

Suddenly Jim found that he was enjoying himself. He snapped his fingers at Miguel and waited while the fresh wine was poured. He grinned. 'Child slavery,' he announced, and allowed a dramatic pause before continuing, 'Eastern Promise Silks, owned and run by our friend and generous host, Wyndham Sale, was exposed some years ago as one of the few remaining Western-controlled companies still employing large numbers of under-age labourers in the Far East. Children as young as five years of age working a sixteen-hour day. At least one eight-year-old girl is reported to have been beaten to death by an overzealous supervisor. And all for a few lengths of beautiful silk.'

The silence that followed was broken only by the muffled sound of the door closing behind Miguel as he made a discreet exit. Lydia's hand had flown up to touch the lapel of her jacket, a jet black, heavily-grained silk. Caro was desperately struggling for a way to salvage the situation. Eventually she said, 'Heavens above, Jim, what a dreadful time to start talking about business, of all things. Right in the middle of this lovely dinner. I'm quite sure there's a very simple explanation for everything. It's so silly to go jumping to conclusions and ruining everything—'

'Is there?' Lydia broke in with sudden intensity. 'Can you explain, Wyndham?'

He was stroking his chin with the tips of his pale fingers. 'I would have thought you knew me better than that, Lydia. I have no intention whatsoever of discussing my work with any of you. Ever.'

'Ha!' Jim banged his glass down in triumph. 'I knew it!'

'Oh for God's sake, shut up, Jim,' snapped Lydia.

'Oh dear,' Caro was all of a flurry. 'I'm sure we can discuss this like rational adults. No need to get in a tizz about it. I suggest we simply change the subject altogether. We're none of us really experts, are we, except Wyndham of course and he quite sensibly has other things to talk about.'

'Stop bloody wittering on,' Jim told her.

'There's no need to be rude, Jim,' said Caro valiantly. 'I just think we should all try to get on and enjoy this lovely dinner that Wyndham and Lydia have taken such trouble over and—'

'Too late,' said Wyndham with a dangerous little smile. 'You see, I'm curious to know what has motivated Jim's sudden interest in my business affairs.' He paused for a moment. His smile was not at all pleasant. 'It's Lydia, isn't it, Jim?'

'Me?'

Wyndham ignored her. He spoke with the deadly quietness of a skilled attorney. 'I would suggest Jim, that you don't give a damn about working conditions in the Far East. You are motivated purely and simply by sexual jealousy. You hate seeing Lydia happy with me, because she used to be your mistress and you still regard her as in some sense your personal property.'

'Good heavens,' exclaimed Caro. 'Now this is just getting silly!'

Still without raising his voice Wyndham continued, 'You still lust after her, Jim. It must have been serious, then, not just a brief fling. It probably came close to wrecking your marriage. Am I not right?'

'You lying bastard,' said Jim.

Wyndham smiled.

'This is all too much,' said Caro decisively. 'You've had your little revenge, Wyndham, and made up I don't know what. And I really can't imagine why . . .' Her voice trailed to a halt as she absorbed the massive stillness growing up between Lydia and Jim, both white with shock.

Lydia felt as though a huge pit had opened up before her and she was about to tumble in.

'You told him,' Jim accused her.

Falling, falling, falling, Lydia protested, 'No! No, he must have guessed.'

'What do you mean?' Caro asked Lydia.

Lydia looked away.

'I don't believe it,' said Caro.

There was absolute silence. Then Caro made a strange roaring noise and pushed back her chair. Moving heavily, she stood up and gazed all around her with panic-stricken eyes. She looked liked someone who has forgotten where she was, who had mislaid the script and did not know what she was supposed to do next.

'It's not true,' she panted. 'You must tell me it's not true.'

Jim opened his mouth to speak, but no words came out. Lydia swore vividly.

Caro seemed to be aging by the minute. Her face was rigid. Staring with hunted eyes at Jim she managed, 'Is it—? Did you—? And she—?'

Jim lifted his hands in a helpless gesture. 'It was so long ago, Caro. Before Suzie was born. I can explain everything. Please.'

'Oh!'

'Caro, love. Wait.' Jim stood up and took a step towards her, but she screamed, a small, involuntary scream, and bolted towards the door.

'Don't. Leave me alone. You're disgusting. Don't come near me. You're a monster. You—' Her voice was rising to a shriek. She rammed her fist against her mouth to silence herself, and fled from the room.

Wyndham had not moved. He was still smiling. 'Shall I ring for coffee?' he asked.

'You total fucking bastard,' said Jim, sinking back into his chair. 'Why the hell did you do that?'

Wyndham shrugged. 'I should have warned you never to attack me without being prepared for the consequences. I always make it my business to hit back harder. Coffee, Lydia?'

She flung the side plate at his head with such ferocity that he was obliged to duck quickly. The china shattered against the far wall. Her wine glass quickly followed. She stood up very straight and tall.

She said, 'Caro never deserved that.'

'Luckily,' said Wyndham, 'we none of us get what we deserve.'

'You're not human,' said Lydia with disgust. She turned to Jim. 'Aren't you even going to see if she's all right? Jesus, you're both such shits.'

'And you, Lydia,' asked Wyndham, 'are you entirely blameless?'

He watched her as she walked from the room, but he made no attempt to follow.

*　　*　　*

Caro's coat was still in the cloakroom, but the front door was wide open and she was nowhere to be seen. Cursing under his breath, Jim went out into the November darkness to search for her. His rage against Wyndham had been replaced by the certainty that the events of the previous ten minutes had already changed his life for ever.

'Caro! Caro, where are you?'

He stood quite still, straining his ears for the sounds of muffled sobs, or retreating footsteps which would guide him to her. He would put his arms around her and do whatever was necessary to comfort her. For more than thirty years he had always found a way to bring her round. He felt a sudden rush of tenderness for her. Poor Caro, she had not deserved that. Damn Wyndham. Damn, damn, damn him to hell.

'Caro?'

Inside the house someone was closing the front door quietly behind him. Outside, all was silence, and the immense darkness of the night.

'Caro!'

The car was still there. She must have decided to walk home. He calculated that she could not have got very far in so short a time. Even if he drove slowly he was sure to catch up with her before she reached the road. Caro had always been uneasy on country lanes at night, so she would be relieved to be picked up. It would be necessary to plead and comfort and explain. He would have to apologise a hundred times and then a hundred more. He might as well begin now.

He walked over to the Range Rover and his legs were rubbery and strange. He wished he had not drunk quite so much of Wyndham's poisonous wine. He wished Wyndham a violent and painful end. As he flung the car into a clumsy three-point turn he heard a crashing noise behind him and hoped that something irreplaceable had been destroyed. He glanced up at the house and saw a light come on in an upstairs room. No doubt Wyndham was explaining to Lydia exactly why she should ignore the Collet report and she would allow herself to be convinced and would live with him in miserable luxury ever after. Their future was of no interest to him. At this precise moment he was in danger of losing Caro who had been the fixed point in his life for over thirty years, and the prospect was suddenly terrifying. Something malignant and ugly which had been growing and festering inside him for weeks had, quite suddenly, vanished. Nothing was left except a primeval terror of loss.

He released the clutch and set off slowly down the drive.

Caro heard the Range Rover's familiar engine and, with no very clear idea of why or what she was doing, she left the gravel safety of the driveway and set off at a run across the open grassland. There was a burning pain in her upper chest and she seemed to be hounded by a strange animal sobbing which clung to her like a foul smell and which she was unable to shake off. Only gradually did she realise it was her own gasping breath that made the noise.

'Caro!' Jim's voice, calling over the noise of the Range Rover's engine, was so hateful that she clapped her hands over her ears to shut it out and the tears gushed from her eyes. Her foot plunged into soft ground and she fell forward into mud and brambles. The effort to rise again was suddenly too great. If she only stayed here she might die and escape it all. Lydia and Jim, Lydia and Jim . . . her own crushing, blind, shaming stupidity. For fifteen years her marriage had been a lie and her whole life had been a disaster and she was utterly alone. While Jim and Lydia, Jim and Lydia . . . Her whole being revolted against the words and she was violently, agonisingly, sick.

After a while, she struggled to free herself and stand up. She was weak and trembling, but horribly, cruelly indestructible. She walked on. There was a ditch, and a hedge that tore at her clothes, she tripped and fell twice more and lay against the earth and howled her misery, knowing that no one would ever hear. She wished the ground would open up and swallow her and make a proper job of it, but deep down she knew it never would. She was Caro. She was to be forever denied the luxury of going to pieces or giving up. She struggled to her feet and walked on. Even at this worst and blackest moment of her life her choices were, inevitably, limited to a single one. She had to go home. She had to try to deal with this somehow. She had to make decisions and find a way to cope with the pain. There were others to think of apart from herself. There was Suzie. There were her parents.

People who needed her. She could not go against the grain of so many years of being dependable, not for long.

And so, at a little after midnight, she arrived back at the Lodge and pushed open the door that led into the kitchen. She could hear Jim's voice, talking on the telephone in the hallway, but it was Suzie, in dressing gown and pyjamas, sitting at the kitchen table, twiddling a strand of fair hair and holding a mug of cocoa, who saw her first.

'Mummy! Where have you been?'

Suzie's relief at her mother's return changed instantly to horror. Scratched and muddy and dishevelled, her aubergine dress ripped, her tights in shreds and her shoes destroyed, Caro was almost unrecognisable.

'It's all right, darling,' Caro managed, 'you mustn't worry. Mummy's fine.'

And then she collapsed.

22

'How did you guess?'

'It was obvious that first evening at the Manor.'

Pacing restlessly over the boards of the steward's room, Lydia absorbed this without comment. When she quit the dining room, she had been hoping, against all reason, to find Caro and somehow comfort her, but there was no sign of her in the hall, nor on the driveway. She could not face returning to the dining room. Her footsteps led her here, to the one room in this massive house that felt like hers. She heard Jim's voice calling his wife, and then a little while after the engine of the Range Rover had faded into the silence of the night Wyndham had joined her. Arms folded, watching her impassively, he stood near the door as though ready to leave the moment she requested him to do so.

When she still did not speak, Wyndham said quietly, 'My mother and father coexisted in a state of permanent, but heavily disguised, warfare. Their frustrations were invariably deflected on to me. I understand it now; as a child I learned to detect the smallest signs. I learned to observe and give nothing away. Perhaps I should be grateful to them. In my work it helps always to know more about others than they can ever know about me. It has become a habit.'

'A very destructive habit,' said Lydia. She registered somewhere that Wyndham was talking about himself for the very first time. She wondered if it was an appeal for her sympathy, a plea for her not to judge him too harshly. She had paused by the window and stood there for a moment, looking out into the darkness. Now she turned and traced a line along the wall with her finger.

'You know I'm leaving, Wyndham, don't you?'

'You would have left anyway,' he replied. 'I had nothing to lose.'

She turned to him with genuine surprise. 'Why do you say that?'

His eyes never left her face. 'Because we've been playing, you and I. This whole business has been an elaborate masquerade. I guessed as much this afternoon when I saw you making the arrangements for the dinner. And then again when you were discussing fabrics with Caro. It was real for her, same as it always was for Annabel, but you were simply acting out a part. The odd thing is that I realised I've been doing the same thing. Doing up this house, being part of country society, fussing over trees and lakes and dogs – it's just a game.'

'We have that much in common then,' said Lydia. She felt he was pushing her away, and though she had made up her mind to leave, she did not care to be pushed. 'And I do love this house,' she added. 'That was real.'

'It would not have been enough, though, not for long.'

Lydia continued to move around the room, touching the objects that she and Wyndham had chosen together, the paint that she had so lovingly applied, the wood panelling that she had worked to a dull shine. Wyndham had sat down on the edge of the bed. He leaned back against the headrest and watched her. His face was as impassive as ever. Or perhaps there was a hint of weariness around the pale eyes, a downward tug of defeat in the faint lines about his mouth.

'You're really quite profound, Wyndham,' she said lightly. 'I think I must have been underestimating you all along.'

'It's a common mistake.'

'But useful in business?'

'Sometimes. In this case I'd say it was tragic.'

The word 'tragic', so softly uttered, stopped her in her tracks. She turned to examine his face, took a step towards him, stopped once more. She wondered suddenly why she had been so convinced that this was the end of all that had been growing between them. There had been no real quarrel. There had been an ugly rumour, he had lashed out at Caro – poor, defenceless well-intentioned Caro – but did that outweigh all the good things they had shared?

'What about that report of Jim's? Was it true about the children?'

A slight movement of his hands dismissed her question. 'That's irrelevant. If you wanted to stay with me, then I could explain the situation to allay your concerns. But since you wish to go, you will assume the worst.'

'So cynical.'

Again, that almost imperceptible gesture of the hands.

She asked, 'What makes you so sure I'll go? Because I said so?'

'No. Because it's what you do, what you've always done. Don't ask me why. You expect a man to be infallible. At the first sign of weakness, you're off. It's what you did with that doctor husband of yours. It's probably what happened with Jim, though why you were attracted to him in the first place is a mystery.'

'He was my teacher,' she told him, preferring to talk of Jim than to linger on his analysis of her character. 'What the Americans call a mentor. I had escaped from home, from parents I despised. He represented a world where books and ideas and truth were all-important. I thought he believed in the things that really mattered. In those days he cared passionately about people and causes – he's changed since then. I thought he could teach me how to live. I was besotted with him.'

'Until?'

'He turned out to have feet of clay, just like everyone else. I was supposed to be the great love of his life, he was going to give up everything so we could be together. And then his wife got pregnant. Three teenage daughters and Caro had to get pregnant. I often wondered if she knew, deep down, and the pregnancy wasn't quite the "accident" she claimed it was. Jim went to pieces. He just didn't know how to handle it. This man who was supposed to know the answers to everything fell apart like a schoolboy, it was pathetic. So I left. I left him, left the university. I even left the country for a while.'

'Fairly comprehensive leaving.'

'You must be right, Wyndham. Leaving is what I do best.'

For the first time since he had come into the room, Wyndham

smiled. Lydia stood very still. She felt as if she were seeing him properly for the first time. The magnetism that she had found so attractive right from the start when they had met at George and Twinks' dinner was in no way diminished. Besides, the sexual pleasure they had found together gave the lie to his claim that it had all been a charade. Now that the gulf between them was widening by the moment, she desired him more forcefully than ever before. Perhaps for her the unattainable was always going to be the most attractive.

She said, 'Morning is the time to leave.'

He nodded. Slipping off her shoes, Lydia crossed the room and knelt beside him on the bed. As she leaned forward to kiss him, she had the brief impression that his face was spinning away from her lips, becoming infinitesimally small. She closed her eyes and kissed him, demanding his response. She wanted to anchor him to her body, but only for a single night.

In the morning she would leave. But she was in no hurry for morning to come.

Caro woke at six thirty with the sensation of not having slept at all. There was an huge emptiness beside her in the bed; Jim had slept in the spare bedroom, almost for the first time in their married life. As she hauled herself from the bed, forced herself to wash and dress as usual, her face felt heavy and drugged with misery. From now on, for the rest of her life, she must rise each morning to the leaden certainty that her husband had been unfaithful and that for the fifteen years of Suzie's life, her marriage had been riddled with deceit. When she came into the house at midnight she had been too demented to do more than push away Jim's demands that they talk. But at some stage during the remorselessly long night, as her mind picked over the details of her marriage, she recalled that Lydia had left the university, suddenly and for no very obvious reason, at some stage during her final pregnancy.

Should she have been suspicious at the time? Had she been horribly naïve in this as in so many other matters? Never for a moment had she contemplated the possibility of Jim's infidelity. It was such a cliché of campus life, the lecturer bedding his bright young student, but she had believed that she and Jim were immune from those hazards. Theirs had always been a marriage of opposites – Jim with his great cleverness and his humble background had been attracted to Caro, who had never considered herself clever at all, but whose upbringing went some way towards weighting her side of the marital scales. And Caro had understood that despite his radical ideas about many topics, he was fundamentally a traditionalist in the home: it mattered to him that she was a proper housewife and mother. She had believed he was content.

For over fifteen years she had been wrong. Grotesquely, shamingly, stupidly wrong.

As she lay awake all night, as she went down in the morning and routinely made the breakfast she knew she had no appetite to eat, as she went back upstairs and folded clothes and made the bed, she had ample time to begin the task of realising just how pathetically wrong she had been. Every picture, every scene, had to be taken out and dusted down and injected with a lethal dose of poison before being set back in place. She remembered now that when she told Jim of her fourth pregnancy he had been appalled. He had even – she had forgotten this fact until now – asked her to consider a termination. She had always assumed his concern had been for her health and wellbeing, just as she had assumed, all through that period when Lydia had been a peripheral part of her life, that Jim was under pressure at work – all those departmental wrangles that she had never somehow managed to disentangle, though of course she had always been totally supportive. Now she saw that concern for his wife must have been the last thing on his mind. Stupid, blind, deluded Caro. Another image: Caro handing Jim the baby and telling him to smile for the photograph. The picture that resulted was on her dressing table – the proud father. She glanced at it now as she did every morning while tidying the bedroom. His smile did not look proud any more: reluctant, deceitful, tortured with regret . . . She took the photograph from its frame and began cutting it up with her nail scissors. She was sobbing with rage. The cutting up was over far too soon. Keeping hold of the scissors she crossed to the wardrobe and took out one of his shirts. Still sobbing, she struggled against the longing to slash it into shreds. The door opened. Jim looked at her across the expanse of their double bed. 'Caro,' he said, 'we've got to talk.'

His face was grey and haggard. A moment's weakness, and Caro would have gone to him. Bitter rage pinned her to the spot.

'Talk? You want to tell me more lies? How can I listen to you? How can I ever believe you again?'

'Please, Caro—'

'Liar,' she said, 'liar, liar, LIAR!'

'Caro.'

He took a step towards her. She raised the nail scissors and, if he had come within reach, she knew she would have plunged them into his heart. If it is possible to kill a man with nail scissors, she could have done murder at that moment. The knowledge was terrifying.

He said, 'I know how you must feel—'

'Get out of here!'

He was about to speak, but then Suzie's bedroom door opened and a shadow crossed the landing to the bathroom. Swearing under his breath, Jim went out and she heard the murmur of conspiratorial voices on the stairs. She flung the scissors into the corner and dragged herself back from the brink of some precipice beyond which lay murder and black hate.

When their footsteps had gone down the stairs, she went to the bathroom, washed her face and dabbed on some make-up. Then she glanced in the mirror and a freshly-painted cadaver stared back at her, so she scrubbed most of it off again. She went downstairs. The door to Jim's study was almost closed, Suzie was alone in the kitchen and looked up at her with wordless anxiety. Caro formed the words, 'It's all right, darling, not to worry, Mummy's just a bit upset,' but then couldn't bring herself to say it out loud.

'Can I make you some coffee, Mummy?'

'Not now, thank you,' was all Caro could manage.

She moved around the kitchen, picked up a cloth and wiped down the draining board, then put the cloth down again because the action was so futile. What was she supposed to do now? There must be some activity that would help her survive this first morning of a lifetime of knowing her marriage had been a sham, but just at present she could not imagine what. She opened the freezer and took out three pork chops to defrost for their supper that evening, and then she thought, how idiotic, she could never eat a chop while her mouth was filled with the taste of dust.

Her head throbbed and there was a burning ache in her chest. The hurt was so appallingly physical: maybe it was possible, after all, to die of a broken heart, and this was how it began. Ridiculous, she wasn't going to die. Suddenly she felt brisk and confident: obviously it was pointless to remain and suffer this agony. Much better to accept the fact that her life with Jim was at an end. She would have to leave him. She must find herself somewhere to live, get a job, live an independent life. She could see the future quite clearly: Caro in a smart London flat, going out to work each morning to a well-paid job and building a new life for herself. Caro self-sufficient and strong. Caro with a fresh circle of friends, independent women with full and interesting lives and the occasional admiring male. Briefly the image flared up, then watered into nothingness. The bitter truth was that she would be lonely and miserable and poor. She might as well stop deluding herself and admit that life without a husband, even Jim, would be unbearable. In that case she ought to talk to him. She must be understanding and try to forgive. This was the chance to prove that her love was strong enough to survive even this most deadly blow.

She set down the pork chops and went to his study door, but paused before pushing it open.

'Caro?'

A huge lump of disgust rose like seasickness in her throat. A torrent of all the vilest swear words she had ever heard and never yet uttered began clamouring to be spoken. She wanted to batter on his door and shriek obscenities. But there was Suzie to consider. Always there was someone else.

Hurriedly she pulled on coat and boots and went out into the crisp morning air. She wanted to talk about the past, but not with Jim. Not yet. As soon as she stepped out of the front gate the thought came to her clear as air: the person she wanted to talk to now was Lydia.

Surprisingly, her hostility was directed against Jim, not Lydia.

She could remember quite distinctly the young woman who had been, for a few months, a frequent visitor to their home. Hardly older than Polly, and in those days far less sophisticated: she had guessed that Lydia was one of the students who developed a passing crush on their young lecturer, and she had never blamed the young girls for being attracted to her husband: she still was herself. Never for a moment had she thought he would act on that attraction. It was Jim she blamed, not Lydia.

And now it was Lydia who was likely to tell the truth about the affair. Unlike Jim, Lydia had no reason to lie to her.

She took the track that led to Rose Cottage.

'Are you looking for Lydia?'

Hopi emerged around the side of Rose Cottage from the woodshed at the back where she had been sitting having a roll-up with Mal. When she had awoken that morning she had stepped outside her caravan only to find that the last of her log pile had vanished during the night. She guessed at once where the wood had gone. There was a tell-tale plume of smoke rising from the chimney of Flea and Barney's lorry, though only yesterday they had been complaining about their lack of fuel. She had had one row with them the previous week when the same thing had happened. Barney and Flea had retaliated with such vicious abuse that she was in no hurry to repeat the exercise. She noticed that Mal also was looking at the empty crate where his wood had been stored, and she went over to commiserate.

'Barney and Flea again?' she asked.

'I'm sure of it.' Mal spoke in the tight voice that always meant he was reining in his anger. 'The bastards. They're ruining everything.'

'Dead right they are. No point having a go at them though, just makes it worse. They love a fight, those two. I know, why don't we take the handcart down to Lydia's and get some more? She said we could any time.'

Even as she made this suggestion, Hopi was mentally calculating that Colin was unlikely to wake for at least two hours – plenty of time for her to get the wood with Mal and be back before he awoke, thus avoiding the risk of another jealous outburst. Similarly, when the wood was safely loaded and Mal suggested a smoke before going back, she agreed because there was still plenty of time. Her days had become full of these cowardly calculations: she hated herself for them, but did not know what else to do.

'It's great here, isn't it?' Mal had said as they sat side by side on the makeshift bench and contemplated the rough patch of grass and the tangle of shrubs and brambles that constituted the garden of Rose Cottage.

'Would you like to have a place like this?' asked Hopi.

Mal debated this for a while. 'It'd be a good base, somewhere to park up for the winter. Great little garden for Saul. But come the spring you'd get restless.'

'Sometimes I think I'd like to settle,' said Hopi thoughtfully. 'Sometimes I get fed up with people turning up and wrecking a site, like Barney and Flea.'

And Colin, Mal added inside his head. Out loud all he said was, 'I know what you mean.'

'It'd be different if you had your own space.'

'I've been wondering, since Saul came on site, whether we don't have to think about the sort of people we want to share with. I mean, we're adults, and we know what we believe in, but as far as Saul's concerned, they represent our values just as much, say, as Biff and Kate. I think I want to bring him up in a place where I can control who he mixes with.'

'I know a few sites like that. The trouble is, you'd end up just the same as all those miserable types who don't want us messing up their pretty little corner of England, with Keep Off notices all over the place. I was talking about this with Lydia. She thought we were mad to let just anyone come and go.'

'She's got a point.'

'Mm.'

'Where is Lydia, anyway?'

'Haddeley Hall, I suppose.'

There was a sound of footsteps at the front of the cottage. The door rattled, the cowbell clonked, then an elegant female voice was heard to say, 'Oh, hell and damnation. Where is the bloody woman now?'

At first Hopi did not recognise the middle-aged woman in her navy jacket and boots as being Suzie's mother. Just as Caro found it difficult to tell the travellers apart, so Hopi had trouble distinguishing between the ladies of the village.

'Are you looking for Lydia?'

Caro turned with a gasp of surprise. 'What are you doing here?' she demanded.

'It's OK,' Hopi soothed. She had no problem identifying Caro's suspicion since she had come across it so often in the past. 'I'm a friend of Lydia's.'

'Oh, I see.' Caro's hostility deflated in an instant. 'I've come to talk to her.'

'She's not here.'

'Oh, I see,' said Caro again. All her energy had been concentrated into steeling herself for this encounter. Thwarted, she looked bewildered and lost. Helpless tears began to trickle out of her eyes. 'I'll just go then,' she said.

'Hang on a minute,' said Hopi, responding automatically to Caro's distress. 'Let's go inside. Lydia usually leaves the key under a stone at the side. I'll just get it. She's bound to be back soon and I'm sure she'd want to see you.' Hopi chattered on, a bland babble of comfort while she found the key, pushed open the front door, steered Caro towards the one easy chair and went into the kitchen to put the kettle on. She had no idea why this unknown woman was so upset at not finding Lydia, but, being Hopi, she immediately assumed responsibility for her until she was calm enough to decide what to do next. As she came out of the kitchen, she heard Caro give a little cry of alarm. Mal had appeared at the front door.

'Who are you?' Caro wanted to know.

Hopi grinned. 'This is Mal. It's OK, he's a friend of Lydia's too.' And then, guessing that Caro might prefer female company only for a bit, she said to him, 'Why don't you take the wood back? I'll hang on here and see if Lydia turns up.'

'Wood?' asked Caro. 'What wood?'

'Lydia said we could use her wood whenever we wanted it,' said Hopi, as Mal retreated from the scene, and then, because the sound of her voice seemed to be vaguely soothing, she chattered on unthinkingly, 'it's quite funny really because this grouchy old man took the wood off us in the first place, even though he didn't want it himself, and then it got to Lydia and she's been giving it to us. Ironic, isn't it?'

Caro had a sudden memory of reversing the Range Rover into a heap of rotting logs. 'Not very,' she said crossly. 'That grouchy old man you referred to happens to be my father.'

'Ah. Yes,' said Hopi, simultaneously smothering a giggle and telling herself off for putting her foot in it. Pointlessly she added, 'Well, that's nice, isn't it?' And then turned her attention with relief to the kettle which had begun to boil. 'There doesn't seem to be any fresh milk. D'you mind just tea?'

Caro told herself that the situation was rapidly becoming quite ridiculous and it was high time she pulled herself together and did something sensible instead of lolling about here. But when she tried to rise from the armchair she felt as though all the bones and muscles had been removed from her body. She blew her nose and said, 'Just tea's fine.'

While Hopi was pouring the tea she pieced together the fact that the grouchy old man who had chased them away from their logs was the same as the grouchy old man who had opened the door at the Manor the previous afternoon when she had taken the elegant elderly shoplifter home. She thought she now understood the reason for Caro's anguish: she must have been hoping to discuss her anxieties about her mother with Lydia.

'It's your parents that live at the Manor then?'

'That's right,' agreed Caro listlessly.

'Yours is the blue mug. It's only ordinary tea. I've been on at Lydia to get in some Earl Grey, but she can be very stubborn. It must have been a terrible shock for you, finding out.'

'Yes,' said Caro, only half-listening, though somewhere she registered the fact that Hopi, despite her uncouth appearance, had a gentle, soothing manner. Although her body was drained of all strength, her mind had launched itself into overdrive: she was struggling to decide what to do next, while at the same time going over incidents from the past in endless detail and wondering what she was supposed to do with the remainder of her life. With the fraction of attention that was left she noted that this conversation had shot off in a fairly surprising direction.

'My friend's mum was caught shoplifting once,' said Hopi in that flat and oddly reassuring way of hers. 'The shop went ahead and prosecuted her, but then she had psychiatric reports and it turned out there was some dark and terrible secret in her life that no one had ever dreamed of. It was all dead dramatic at the time, and now I can't even remember what the secret was. It goes to show how important things seem and then a year or so later it's all kind of blurred over and you can't think what all the fuss was about. Still, I can see how it must have been a terrible shock. For you, I mean.'

Shock? thought Caro vaguely. How does she know? And then she told herself not to be ridiculous, she couldn't possibly know. But because she was aching to unburden herself to someone, anyone, even a woman with strange hair and terrible clothes, she responded to the sympathy and said wearily, 'Some shocks you never get over.'

'Mm,' Hopi agreed, but doubtfully. 'Maybe.'

'You just have to find a way to live with it.'

'But there's always reasons,' suggested Hopi. 'If you know the reasons it's much easier to know what to do about it.'

'Reasons! Excuses, more likely. God, just the thought of having to listen to a whole string of pathetic excuses makes me feel absolutely sick. Don't talk to me about bloody reasons!'

'I think you ought to try to be a bit more understanding,' Hopi was beginning to feel quite sorry for Twinks. 'She seemed really upset about it all. I'm not even sure she knew what she was doing,' and she added to herself: not like Colin, who most definitely did know right from wrong and who seemed to have got away with it yet again.

'Of course she damn well knew. Lydia may be a two-faced bitch, but she's not stupid.'

'Lydia, why bring Lydia into this?'

'I thought . . .' Caro stared at Hopi for a moment. Both women were sitting up very straight in their chairs. 'I assumed you were talking about Lydia.'

'No.'

'Then who?'

'Your mother, of course. Mrs Cartwright.'

'My mother? Why on earth bring her into it?'

'Peggy caught her trying to nick stuff from the shop yesterday. I thought you knew.'

'No. There's been a mistake.' But even as she spoke Caro remembered Jim's voice outside the bathroom the previous evening. Peggy had phoned to talk to her, back in the time when she had been content in her stupid delusions. And then the earthquake had obliterated her familiar world and she had forgotten it entirely. 'Are you sure?' she asked in a faint voice.

'Positive. Peggy caught her red-handed.'

'How do you know?'

'I happened to be in the shop. Your mum was about to leave when the lining of her coat ripped and all this stuff fell on the ground.'

'Good heavens, I can't believe it.'

'Mrs Robertson told Peggy to contact you.'

'Oh lord, was the whole village there?'

'Only me and the teacher. We had to take her home. She was in too much of a state to drive.'

'My mother . . . I can't really take it in.'

'Well, it's bound to be a shock. Peggy said later she thought she must have been at it for months. She had all sorts of things hidden inside her coat. But as I say, she didn't look as if she really knew what she was doing.'

'No,' said Caro, 'I see.' She remembered now that Twinks had been 'unwell' the previous evening and so the dinner party for six had become a foursome. If George and Twinks had been there, would Jim have risked causing trouble by asking Wyndham about his business? And would Wyndham then have struck back by saying he and Lydia had been lovers? And did she wish it had never happened or was it after all better to know the truth, however ghastly? And what in heaven's name had been going through Twinks' mind then, and what was she going through now?

'Are you all right?' asked Hopi. 'You're shaking.'

Caro was on the point of saying, as always, that she was absolutely fine, just a bit of a shock, she'd be herself again in a minute, but then she found herself saying instead, 'Actually, I don't think I've ever felt this bad in my life. I'm the absolute bloody opposite of all right. This is the most frightful day of my entire life and I think I may go stark staring mad' – and all at once she felt a very slight lifting of the spirits.

'I am sorry,' said Hopi, 'I thought you knew.'

'No,' said Caro, 'I never knew anything about anything. I have been a complete fool.'

'Oh, you mustn't blame yourself.'

Caro made a contemptuous noise, then said, 'My mother's antics are only a fraction of my worries. My life really is an absolute bloody shambles.' Caro giggled slightly to hear herself swearing so much and Hopi smiled at her encouragingly. For a moment Caro was tempted to pour out all her great woes to this thoroughly understanding stranger with the warm smile and the sympathetic eyes and the low, soft-spoken voice. She wanted to allow herself to sob and be comforted – but there was the little difficulty of the several earrings in each lobe and the strange hairstyle and tatty coat to surmount, so instead she gave herself a little shake to pull herself together and said briskly, 'Listen to me going on. Heigh ho, time to stop moping about myself and think about my poor mother. I can't imagine what she's been up to. Do I look the most dreadful fright?'

'Your mascara's run a bit,' said Hopi.

'I'll go and freshen up. It's all right, I know where the bathroom is. This is Daddy's house, after all.'

'Yeah. I'm sorry I called him a grouchy old man.'

Caro smiled, and Hopi suddenly caught a glimpse of her kindness and shy charm. 'Don't lose any sleep over it, my dear,' said Caro. 'It's nothing to what he called you.'

'I can imagine.' Hopi's answering smile was rueful.

For a moment the two women hovered on the brink of friendship, then Caro performed another of her mental shakes and said briskly, 'Right then, time to go and repair the old face and then see what my mother has been up to.' Suddenly she dreaded the thought that Lydia might return: she couldn't imagine why she had ever wanted to talk to her. Just being in the same room as her would be unbearable. And now there was her mother to think of. 'I still can't believe she's been stealing. Do you think it might be Alzheimer's? Oh God, I can't think which would be worse. Thank you for the tea, by the way, you've been most kind.'

Suddenly Caro's eagerness to express gratitude reminded Hopi of Suzie and she was on the point of saying, 'You must be Suzie's mum!' but then she checked herself. Most probably Suzie had kept her visits to the Hollows a secret, and Hopi had already been outspoken enough for one morning. So she merely said, 'It was good to meet you. Don't worry about this place. I'll wash out the mugs and lock up before I go.'

'That's wonderful. You've been a real Good Samaritan.'

That's me, thought Hopi as she rinsed and dried the two mugs and put them away. Brilliant at sorting out other people's worries. She worked quickly because she realised that Colin might well have woken up while she was talking to Caro. If she wasn't there when he woke, there was a strong chance of him being in a foul mood all day. She wished her own problems were as easy to sort out as other people's.

'What was that about?'

Jim had emerged from his study while Caro was on the phone. She set the receiver back in its cradle and sat down heavily on the stairs. She felt as if the smallest thing would be enough to trip her over the edge and into hysteria, but Peggy was on her way and she needed all the calm she could muster to deal with the coming interview. She said flatly, 'Mummy's been taking things from Peggy's without paying.'

'Twinks? Shoplifting? Are you sure?'

'Of course I'm not sure. It's probably just an old age thing, absent-mindedness. But it's bound to be unpleasant.'

'Poor Caro. What bloody awful timing.'

'Oh, I don't know.' Caro threw him a brief and bitter glance, 'At least it takes my mind off everything else.'

Jim had never heard her sound so bleak and hopeless. He said with genuine tenderness, 'I am sorry it's happened now.'

'Yes, well . . . ' Caro tried, and failed, to hide the tremor in her voice. 'That's how it is.'

'Do you want me to help out with Peggy?'

She shrugged. 'You might as well. God knows what one is meant to say. I suppose I'll have to try to persuade her to hush it up, not to involve the police.'

'The police?' It was Suzie, wide-eyed with amazement, who joined them in the hall. 'Is Granny in trouble with the police?'

'Oh, for God's sake,' snapped Jim. 'Can't I talk to your mother for an instant without you barging in all the time?'

'Don't worry darling,' soothed Caro, 'I expect it's just a mistake.'

'And why the hell aren't you at school?' demanded Jim.

'I overslept.'

'It's my fault,' said Caro. 'What with . . . everything, I didn't get her off in time.'

'Nonsense, she's not an infant. Surely she can get herself to school once in her life!'

'Oh, shut up, both of you!' wailed Suzie. 'I'm going, so you can both be as beastly to each other as you damn well like!' And she slammed out of the house, narrowly followed by Bumpkin.

'Poor Suzie,' murmured Caro. 'Everything is ruined.'

'She's all right. What about us? We've got to talk without being interrupted all the time. We've got to – Oh, hell.' A gentle knocking at the front door signalled Peggy's arrival.

Caro flung Jim a stricken glance. 'Do I look a fright?'

Jim examined her ashen face with the bright spots of blusher on her cheeks only emphasising the shadows around eyes puffy with weeping, and at that moment he would have given almost anything not to have caused such pain. Touching her for the first time in what seemed like an age, he brushed a thread of hair from her shoulder. She winced slightly but did not step back. He said, 'Don't worry, Peggy will assume it's because of Twinks.'

'Oh God, isn't it shaming? I keep forgetting all about poor Mummy.'

She went to open the door.

Suzie intended going to the Hollows. She was fuming mad with both her parents and never wanted to set foot in the Lodge again. If she ran away from home, then they'd be sorry. She'd take masses of drugs and do all the most dreadful things she could think of and serve them right for making such a mess of everything and telling her to go away. They were both loathsome and mean and she despised them utterly.

But anxiety was a magnet, tugging her home. She'd never seen her mother upset before, not in that deep down, fundamental, through and through sort of way, and it made her stomach feel sick just to think of it. They'd better hurry up and sort it out and get back to normal again. But maybe that wasn't going to happen, ever. Something to do with Lydia and Daddy, she had gleaned that much, though they tried to keep her in the dark as always. Maybe her mother had found Daddy and Lydia kissing. She couldn't imagine them having sex together, Daddy was far too old. She thought of the noises she had heard Rupert and that girl making . . . no wonder Mummy was so upset. And now Granny was going to be arrested, it was enough to drive her mother to a total nervous breakdown. Suzie's picture of a total nervous breakdown was of someone running around stark naked and screaming wildly and being generally mad. The prospect of sensible Caro acting like that was so horrifying that before Suzie knew what she was doing she had followed the path round in a loop and was back at the Lodge. She still thought she would never be able to forgive Jim for being so hateful, but obviously her mother was going to need loads of support to prevent a complete nervous collapse.

Peggy, Caro and Jim were seated around the kitchen table, but their conversation froze to silence the moment Suzie walked in. 'Well?' she demanded. 'What have you decided to do about Granny?'

Peggy flung Caro a questioning glance, but Jim intervened, 'We're just sorting that out now, Suzie. Obviously there must be some financial recompense, but meanwhile Peggy has agreed that if Granny doesn't go to the shop any more, she won't involve the police.'

Suzie ignored him. 'Poor Mummy. What a shock this has been for you.' Then she said to Peggy, 'Are you absolutely sure there's no mistake?'

'Not a chance, I'm afraid. Just what Mrs Cartwright thought she was doing, heaven alone knows. Ann Robertson said she thought it might be a cry for help.'

'Why would Granny cry for help?'

'That's what we need to find out,' said Jim. 'Dr Bell will be able to say if she needs psychiatric help.'

'Has Granny gone mad, then?'

'Not mad, dear,' Caro said, then added uncertainly, 'at least, I don't think she has.'

Suzie was thinking. 'Is shoplifting often a cry for help?' Suddenly she remembered the intense expression on Mina's face as she slid the make-up into her pocket.

'Ann Robertson said there's all sorts of reasons,' said Peggy. 'Sometimes people just work out the risks and decide it's worth it. She says some children don't even know it's wrong and have to be taught that.'

'Granny certainly knew it was wrong.'

'Yes, my mother has always been the most upright and law-abiding person,' said Caro.

'That's what makes it so strange,' said Peggy. 'But there you are. Whatever the motive, I lose just the same,' she added, not wanting her own losses to be overlooked.

'Are you going to tell Grandpa?'

'We hadn't got to that one yet,' admitted Jim. 'For the time being, though, Peggy, we'd be grateful if you'd keep this to yourself. Of course, it's up to you, but . . .'

Warmed by the promise of a handsome lump sum and by the family's obvious distress, Peggy said, 'Don't worry, I won't make a meal of it, but it's a job to keep anything secret in a small place like Briarswood.'

Suzie asked again, 'But what about Grandpa?'

Caro covered her eyes with her hand. 'I just don't know,' she said wearily.

Jim frowned, but said nothing. Peggy began to look awkward, and sipped the last of her coffee. Into the silence Suzie said firmly, 'Granny would die if Grandpa ever knew she'd done that.'

Another silence, then Caro said, 'Yes, Suzie, you're right. We'll have to try to keep him in the dark.'

'He's been in the dark all his life,' muttered Jim, earning furious looks from both wife and daughter.

Peggy decided it was time to leave.

'I'll pop up and see Mummy right away,' said Caro, once the front door had closed behind Peggy's tapping high heels.

'I'll come with you,' said Jim.

'No,' said Caro with sudden firmness, 'I'd rather be alone for a bit.'

'I'll make some soup for your lunch, Mummy,' said Suzie. Her father could starve to death before she'd condescend to feed him, but Caro obviously needed looking after.

Jim followed Caro into the hall. Suzie could be heard banging around self-importantly in the kitchen.

'We've got to talk, Caro. Without being interrupted all the time.' Jim's voice was low, but urgent.

'I know. But later. Not now.'

'When?'

'Oh, sometime. I don't know.'

'Mummy,' Suzie's voice came from the depths of the freezer, 'which would you prefer, mixed veg, or cream of mushroom?'

'You decide, darling.'

'This is crazy. We'll have to go somewhere we can be private.'

'Oh dear.' Caro was tormented by hating Jim so much and wanting to be with him at the same time. 'Where can we go?'

'I'll arrange it.'

'What about Suzie?'

'I'll arrange that too. You deal with Twinks, Caro, and I'll sort out all the rest.'

'Goody,' said Suzie, 'there's cream of parsnip.' Jim, she knew, hated parsnips.

Caro's voice seemed to be arriving inside Twinks' brain from a great distance away. She was able to distinguish that she was no longer to frequent Peggy's shop, also that some money was going to be necessary to smooth things over, also, and most important from her point of view, that George was not going to be told. And there was a vague reference to doctors.

'I'm quite well, Caro,' she said sternly.

Caro's voice babbled on. Twinks smiled patiently, but hoped her daughter would finish soon, and go. Waking up had become increasingly difficult throughout the autumn, and this morning had been such a struggle that Twinks was left feeling the job was only half done. The previous evening, having felt horribly bothered by that unfortunate incident in the shop, she had taken several of the useful little pills that kind doctors had given her over the years, and when it came to bedtime she had forgotten how many sleeping pills she was supposed to take in an emergency and had helped herself to one or two extras just in case. They had all worn off at some stage during the night and she had woken with a headache. Luckily, she had some good strong headache pills, but when she hunted around for a little something to wash them down, George woke up demanding to know what she was up to, so she had had to make do with a couple more pills, chosen quite at random and washed down with a little water.

This morning an all-over sense of ill-health combined with the memory of Peggy's accusing stare disturbed her so much that she had taken several of the pills she had accumulated for different nervous afflictions and had, at last, found a small bottle of rum tucked away in the bottom of her sewing basket. The rum did not clear the fog that surrounded her, but it did make it just about bearable.

'Are you feeling all right, Mummy?'

Twinks heard the question because Caro had repeated it, slowly and very deliberately.

'Of course. I'm fine. No need to worry about me.'

That's what I always say, thought Caro wretchedly. Why can't we for once in our lives just tell each other how miserable we are? And then she wondered if perhaps this new, fallible mother was a person she could learn to confide in. If someone didn't listen to her woes soon she was likely to go mad.

She tried it out. 'I'm not, Mummy. I'm not fine at all. I've never been so miserable in all my life. I've just found out Jim had an affair when I was pregnant with Suzie. I think I might leave him.'

Shocked at having said so much, and to her mother of all people, Caro glanced away out of the drawing room window, to where her father was standing beside the long border, a bag of bulbs in his hand, which Mr Gee was planting under supervision. Hamish watched them, his chin resting on dark paws. When Caro looked back, her mother was still smiling serenely.

'I do hope Jim is better soon,' said Twinks. 'Run along now, you must be so busy.'

While Caro was droning on about goodness knows what, Twinks had remembered she had prudently concealed a small brandy bottle in the Scrabble bag only last week, and she was impatient to be left in peace.

23

November rains and the approach of winter revealed the Hollows' many shortcomings as a site. On frosty nights mist formed over the stream and spread rapidly across the low ground so that by morning all the vehicles were blanketed in grey dampness. When it rained the field, which always had a tendency to be waterlogged in winter, rapidly degenerated into a quagmire of mud clinging to boots and wheels like brown glue. The rough grass, no longer green, developed an intricate veining of planks and stepping stones, but these were often slippery. One overcast morning Saul, to his indignation, missed nearly an hour of school when he slithered off a board placed across the churned-up mud by the gate and had to be wiped down and dressed in clean clothes before he was able to set off once again. Mal spent a good deal of time exploring the feasibility of various drainage schemes, and when all those turned out to be impractical for one reason or another, he began planning his ideal winter site. This was to be south-facing and sheltered from the prevailing winds, but above all it would have to be on porous, well-drained soil. It was, he knew, the last kind of site they were ever likely to be offered.

Friday morning. The rain clouds had rolled away in the night and the sun shone from a radiant blue sky. The mud sparkled and the puddles reflected blue. Mal had just flung wide the door of his lorry and was wrapping Saul's Christmas present when Kate interrupted him with a breezy, 'Can we come in? Lydia needs a cup of tea and I saw your fire going.'

'Sure.'

'Cheers,' said Kate. 'We're out of gas. Biff's going to get some later.'

Mal was sceptical. Kate and Biff had become the merrily feckless couple on the site. Always running out of gas, batteries, tea, tobacco, always borrowing and seldom paying back, they would have been a nuisance to their neighbours but for their unending good company and willingness to help out.

'Come on in, Lydia,' Kate spoke as if the lorry were still her home as her muddy boots clumped up the steps. 'Don't worry, Mal, I'll put the kettle on. Where d'you keep the tea? Your place is so tidy these days I can't find a thing.'

Mal grinned. 'Hi, Lydia. Tea's in the tin behind the corn-flakes. I have to keep it straight or Saul can't find his kit in the morning. We single parents don't have it all easy, you know.'

'What's that you're wrapping?' asked Lydia.

Mal held out the Celtic World colouring book for her scrutiny. 'It's for Saul. I got him some new felt tips as well. I'm trying to get him interested in Arthurian legend, but at the moment he prefers rabbits.'

'Rabbits?'

'All those Beatrix Potter books Suzie keeps bringing him. He thinks they're great.'

'So why the Celtic art?' teased Lydia. 'Are you hoping he'll become a Druid?'

Instantly she saw her question had not been far off the mark. 'We can learn a lot from the Celts,' he was trying to hide his annoyance. 'They lived in harmony with their environment. A lot of modern day problems can be traced back to the introduction of Christianity.'

Kate was in no hurry to hear Mal's analysis of the origins of present day problems; she remarked quickly, 'Isn't this weather great? All that rain last week really got me down. I had a bad house-attack.'

'What on earth is a house-attack?' Lydia was intrigued.

'You get them sometimes on site, at least, I do. It's when you start wishing you were back home with your mum. With a sofa and a bath and a thirty-six-inch tele.'

'Baths is the only bit I miss,' said Mal.

'That's what I came to tell you,' said Lydia, 'I still owe you a bath, Mal, for the work you did on the roof. You'd better collect your debt this weekend. Why don't you have one too, Kate? I'm leaving Rose Cottage in a couple of days.'

'Moving into the big house, are you?' asked Kate, who had heard of Lydia's affair from Hopi.

Lydia shook her head. 'That's over,' she said, wondering, as she spoke, how it had ever begun. 'I'm leaving Briarswood for good.'

'What are you going to do?'

'God knows. I've got to get some money together for the fare, then I expect I'll go to Minorca. There's an old friend of mine wants me to do some murals in her restaurant. I shall probably spend the next three months painting giant squid and tuna in all sorts of exotic poses.'

Kate sighed. 'It must be brilliant to be artistic,' she said, with the genuine admiration of someone who finds even matchstick figures an impossible challenge. 'You are lucky.'

Lydia didn't feel especially lucky just at that moment. She felt battered and guilty and as if everything she began only led to disaster. She said, 'It's a living, sometimes, but it can be terribly frustrating too.'

'How?' asked Mal.

'Nothing ever turns out how you expect. You start off with a clear idea of how you want it to look, but when you try to get it down, the ideal picture keeps moving away. It's always just out of reach. In the end you just hope the finished product isn't too grossly different from the idea you started with. But it always ends in disaster, no matter how hard you try.'

It occurred to her as she spoke that she was describing more than her artistic failures. In her despondent mood that day, it seemed as if she was detailing the pattern of events since her arrival in Briarswood. She had imagined the village would provide her with a sanctuary, a blank sheet of paper where she could redraw her life anew. Now she was leaving, off once more on her wanderings, and yet again leaving devastation in her wake. Lydia did not like herself much that Friday morning.

Jim had to keep reminding himself that this was no time to show impatience. This whole exercise was supposed to be the beginning of a well-planned marital salvage operation. He had booked rooms for two nights at a hotel in Devon where he and Caro had once spent a pleasant weekend. With some difficulty he had cajoled Polly into coming down to stay with Suzie while they were away. Now he must resist the temptation to prize Caro away from her home and daughter by brute force. He was so totally and abjectly in the wrong that he could not, just at present, foresee a time when he would ever again be in a position to criticise his wife for anything.

Caro, however, without the spur of even a muttered 'Oh, for God's sake get a move on!' seemed quite incapable of leaving her youngest daughter. And Suzie, as far as Jim could see, had exploited her parents' present disarray by failing to get to school for the third day in a row.

'Take the lamb out of the freezer tomorrow,' said Caro. 'It must thaw out completely. Polly will cook it on Sunday. We'll be back that evening.'

'Yes, Mummy. I know.'

'And Polly will be here at tea-time. Oh dear, I hate leaving you in the house on your own like this, but she promised to come down as soon as she finishes her fitness thing. And you must phone at once if anything goes wrong, or if you're worried, or—'

In the end it was Suzie who chivvied her mother through the front door and into the waiting Range Rover. It seemed odd for Suzie to be telling her mother what to do, but then everything was so peculiar just now and she couldn't wait to see the backs of them both. Her protectiveness towards her mother had been blunted by Caro's failure to eat any of the delicacies Suzie had dished up, or to be the least bit cheered by Suzie's efforts. In fact, Suzie was thoroughly fed up with both of them and the muddle they had created and just wanted them to go away and leave her in peace. If either had bothered to tell her what was going on, she might have been more sympathetic, but as it was, her disillusion was intense.

Still, she managed a cheery smile and a wave as the Range Rover departed down the road, and then, with a sigh of relief and a sudden lowering of the spirits, she returned to the house, where the phone was ringing.

'Hello?'

'Oh, Suzie. Is Daddy still there?'

'Hello, Polly. No, they've just gone.'

'Damn. Oh well . . . listen, Suzie, something's come up and I can't make it down after all. I've tried Emily and Kate and they're both tied up too. What you must do is go and stay with Grandpa and Twinks. They'd love to see you, I know they would.'

Suzie's heart sank. 'I know what,' she said. 'I could always come to London and stay with you.'

'Out of the question, sweetie,' said Polly, who was tidying her flat following her husband Angus' departure for Amsterdam and preparing for an unexpected weekend with Simon, 'I'd explain, but there's not time. Promise me you'll phone Twinks the moment we finish talking?'

'OK. I promise.'

When she put the phone down, Suzie was in half a mind not to do anything of the kind. 'Oh God,' she said out loud to Bumpkin, 'aren't they all absolutely despicable? Nobody ever bothers to ask about what I want, oh no. I'm just a pawn in their game.'

She was rather taken with that last phrase, and began to cheer up at once. But still, a promise was a promise, so she dialled the Manor's number. Her grandmother answered. Suzie explained the situation.

'I'll be up later on,' she said finally. She was definitely not going to waste a whole precious afternoon when she should have been at school with her grandparents. 'Probably around tea-time.'

Her grandmother said something like, 'I know, Hamish, we must get you a treat,' and hung up.

'Just listen to that, Bumps.' Suzie held the receiver close to his golden ear so he could hear the dialling tone. 'Not even the courtesy of a good-bye.' Then she contemplated the fact that her mother was on the verge of a nervous breakdown, her father might very well be an adulterer and her grandmother was developing criminal tendencies.

'My family would never get me a place at Crufts, would they Bumps?'

He wagged his tail. Suzie was suddenly inexplicably and guiltily happy. 'Oh, drat the lot of them,' she said, 'let's go for a walk.'

The afternoon stretched ahead – blissful, empty hours of freedom.

'Is it safe to visit Hopi now? I want to see her before I go.'

Kate peered out of the open door of Mal's lorry. 'No sign of crappy Colin yet,' she said. 'He goes nuts if you wake him up. The stupid sod,' she added with easy-going contempt.

'Hopi bears the brunt of it,' said Mal.

'I can't think why she puts up with him,' said Lydia.

Kate, who did not have an analytical turn of mind, suggested that she must like him, but Mal, remembering the tangle of hate and fear and desperate need which had bound him to his parents throughout childhood, said, 'It's difficult for her. She wants to believe the gentle, musical Colin is the real Colin and will win out over the vicious one. What she doesn't realise is it's all him, all mixed up together.'

'I think she's scared of him,' declared Kate. 'He can be a right bastard.'

Mal looked startled. 'Hopi? Scared?'

'Just a hunch. There she is now.' Kate leaned forward and roared through the door in a voice that could be heard from one end of the site to the other, 'Hopi! Come and say good-bye to Lydia!'

Hopi glanced across at them with a smile, then picked her way through the mud to Mal's lorry. She was dismayed to hear that Lydia was leaving both Wyndham Sale and the village. 'What a shame,' she said. 'I enjoyed working at the Hall. I don't suppose I'll ever get a chance to work in a house like that again.'

'Nor me,' said Lydia.

'What went wrong? Was he a total bastard?' asked Kate. 'Did you get dumped?'

Lydia grinned. She was going to miss Kate's unerring directness nearly as much as Hopi's sympathy. She said, 'You could say it was a mutual decision. Also, I think he did turn out to be a bit of a bastard too.'

'Typical bloody men,' said Kate.

Mal, who was tying the ribbon on Saul's colouring book in an elaborate bow, glanced up, startled. 'What?'

'Are you upset about it?' asked Hopi.

'I suppose so, in a way. It's like snakes and ladders, one moment I'm flying first class to a luxury flat in Paris, then I'm stony broke again and no idea what to do next.'

'You ought to come and live like this,' suggested Kate.

'Really?'

'Yeah. Why not?'

Lydia glanced through the open door at the site which had come to look like a First World War battlefield. 'I don't like to be rude, but why on earth would I want to do that?'

Kate was undaunted. 'Loads of reasons.'

'You're seeing all the disadvantages now,' said Hopi. 'Just wait till spring. We'll be miles away, a new place, a fresh start. It can be really great.'

'It's hard work,' said Mal, 'but you wouldn't mind that. You're hardly ever bored on site.'

'And you're never lonely,' Hopi and Kate said in unison, then grinned at each other.

For a moment the vision was almost tempting. Lydia thought she might be able to scrape together enough money for an old car and a caravan of sorts, or maybe a commercial vehicle she could turn into an unusual home. All the problems of where to live and what to do solved at a stroke, with a family of friends to help her through the adjustment and the bad times. But then she thought there must be more to life than scraping a living and chopping wood and chatting over cups of Earl Grey tea. Precisely what more she had yet to discover; once again her efforts to find herself a place and a purpose had failed horribly, but she was not yet ready to give up the attempt.

Hopi saw her hesitation. 'You'd know if it was right,' she said.

'I think I'm more of a house nomad,' said Lydia. 'I like soaking in hot baths too much to give it up. You'd better get the rest of the wood before I go.'

'Wood, right,' said Hopi, remembering. 'This woman was at your place yesterday. I think it must have been Suzie's mum.'

'Caro?'

'She said she wanted to see you. She seemed pretty upset. I thought at first it was because of her mum stealing from Peggy's shop, but she didn't know anything about it.'

Lydia, who had heard nothing of Twinks' law-breaking, was amazed and Kate wasted no time in bringing her up to date. 'Mrs Psycho-Gramps turns out to be a light-fingered old bat,' she gloated. 'I bet her old man's been on the fiddle too. So much for the criminal classes. You could get away with bloody murder coming from a house like that.'

Mal grinned. 'Maybe she started out as a cat burglar.'

Kate burst out laughing. 'The whole family's probably bent. I bet they've got bloody diplomas in breaking and entering.'

'Oh, don't be so mean, poor old dear,' exclaimed Hopi, but even she was beginning to giggle.

Lydia stood up abruptly. 'I'd better go.' She felt sick at heart. She knew Twinks' family too well, and had contributed enough to their unhappiness; she did not enjoy their humiliation. 'I've got to pack and start cleaning up. Can you say good-bye to Terry and the others for me?'

They agreed cheerfully, but their good-byes were casual, and Lydia felt a sense of anti-climax as she walked away. In their strange way, Hopi and her friends had been an important part of her life for nearly three months, but they treated her departure with no more ceremony than if they were to see her again the next day. In the ever-changing constellation of their lives people appeared and vanished again with such frequency that they made the best of whoever happened to be around, but did not waste time on those who had gone.

She heard Kate's uninhibited cackle, and her rough voice declare, 'Just you wait, they'll send Suzie off to an academy for young lady pickpockets,' and a loud burst of laughter.

And then Lydia could hear them no more.

At last, Suzie had something of interest to tell Terry.

'My family,' she declared, 'is falling apart.'

She expected her present desperate situation to strengthen the bonds between them; from the little she had gleaned concerning his background, Terry's own family had been falling apart steadily since the day he was born, but to her chagrin, he did not appear very interested.

'Oh yeah?' he asked, glancing across at her briefly. 'That's a shame.'

He did not particularly want to hear about the woes of Suzie's family. He much preferred to believe that she had stepped out of a story-book family, or one like the advertisements where Dad smokes a pipe and grins a lot and Mum worries about washing stains and gravy. He had never in his life come across anyone remotely resembling these mythical figures, but it was important for his picture of the world that they existed somewhere. If even Suzie's family couldn't get it together to keep themselves sorted, what hope was there for everyone else?

As usual they had walked to the top of Raven's Beacon and were enjoying the last of the day's sunshine, while the dogs busied themselves in the bramble thicket.

Suzie said, 'My parents have gone away for the weekend. I think it must be a last attempt to save their crumbling marriage. My sister was supposed to come down, but now she can't and I've got to go and stay with my grandparents.' Just in time she remembered that Twinks' misdeeds had to be kept secret, so she ended up, 'And they've got troubles of their own right now, so they're hardly going to want me around. It's all such a ghastly mess.'

She hadn't even known she felt sad about it until that moment, but now the tears spilled out and rolled down her cheek. Terry did not even notice. She hugged her knees and sniffed.

He said, 'It was your gran who was nicking stuff from the shop, wasn't it? Hopi had to drive her home.' He turned and saw her swimming eyes. 'Hey, don't cry.' Automatically he put his arm across her back. Suzie ducked her head and let her cheek rest on his shoulder. She could feel the pressure of his hand against her back; it was like the warmth from an electric fire. Everything had changed in an instant and she felt totally and deliriously happy.

'I still can't believe it,' she said, but now she was just speaking to keep the conversation going. Her grandmother could have been declared a mass murderer and she wouldn't care. Not so long as Terry's arm remained across her back and her cheek was resting against his shoulder.

'Grandmothers are a funny old lot,' said Terry. 'My gran could be really weird sometimes, but she was all right, really.'

'She must have been very kind,' said Suzie. His grandmother

was the only member of his family Terry had ever talked about, and his voice mellowed whenever he mentioned her. Suzie imagined a kindly, grey-haired old lady, not elegant like Twinks but round and friendly in a flowered apron and soft slippers. She liked to think that this cosy, warm-hearted old body had been the fixed point in Terry's obviously most unusual childhood. Terry was thinking of his grandmother too, but the woman he remembered had waist-length hair which was usually auburn. She wore tiny skirts and high heels and died of cirrhosis of the liver just before her fifty-fourth birthday. She had always done what she could for little Terry; it had never been nearly enough.

'She was great.' Terry was beginning to feel awkward with Suzie's weight against him. 'It was all down to her that I got Misty.'

'I thought the rescue people gave her to you.'

'No chance. Not a kid with no home and no job. But my gran saw how much I wanted her, so she spun them some yarn about how the doctor had told her she had to go for long walks every day for her health. She had them all eating out of her hand in no time. Then, as soon as she got Misty, she passed her straight on to me. The next day she had to go into hospital. I never saw her after that. I never realised she was so ill. No one said she was dying. I was just thinking about Misty.'

'Heavens, how sad. Aren't families strange?'

Terry was quiet for a while. The sun had just gone down in a fairly unremarkable sunset, and already the air was chilly. He was watching Misty, who had paused to relieve herself against the base of a tree.

'It's kind of weird,' he said in a changed voice, 'but sometimes it doesn't feel like my gran's dead at all. When I'm with Misty, I often think she's still close. Like she's keeping an eye on me, through the dog. Does that sound crazy?'

'Oh no, not at all,' declared Suzie, a little too emphatically, because in fact the concept did strike her as somewhat peculiar. She tried to imagine Twinks' spirit living on in Bumpkin's rangy body, and had to suppress a giggle.

But the next moment, almost as if she had understood the meaning behind Terry's words, Misty came bounding over the grass and parked herself in front of them. Her tongue lolled from her mouth at a rakish angle, and she raised her golden eyes to bestow on him a gaze of uncritical and absolute adoration.

Saul ran most of the way back from school and then swaggered into the lorry, puffing out his chest like a self-important little bird.

'Look,' he ordered Mal, 'look what I've got.'

Saul extracted from his pocket a yellow envelope that had been folded in half. He smoothed it carefully, then drew out a sheet of lemon-coloured paper that was printed with violet balloons and announced, 'I've got an invitation.'

'Great, Saul.' Mal was trying to find a wrench in the tool-box which was kept in the space above the driver's cab, so did not look round straight away.

'I'm going to Naomi's party,' said Saul.

'Brilliant,' said Mal. And then he turned, and saw the child standing in the doorway. Saul's narrow face was lit up by a smile of such radiant happiness that for a moment Mal felt more astonished than glad. Never before, in all the months they had spent together, had he seen that expression on his son's face. Sullenness and rage, fear and mistrust and a kind of stoical acceptance of his fate, but never this spontaneous and irresistible joy. Mal felt a lump rise in his throat as he remembered the traumatised boy he had first seen in Angie's flat. The child clutching the invitation in his small and grubby hand had rosy cheeks and bright eyes. This child's delight overflowed into a huge smile.

'Wow,' said Mal, sitting down on the edge of his bed. 'Your first invitation, Saul. This is a special day.'

Saul nodded his agreement. For ages now the girls in his class had talked of little apart from Naomi's party: who was to be invited and, even more importantly, who was to be excluded. Naomi herself had extracted the maximum benefit from this brief time of power and had not finalised the guest list until the last moment. Saul and most of the other boys had remained aloof from these negotiations, but the spectre of being one of the few social outcasts not to be admitted to the magic circle of games and presents hung over all the children like a threat of doom. Saul was more aloof than most, since he had no expectation whatsoever of being chosen, so that when Naomi minced up to him during dinner break and handed him one of the treasured lemon-coloured envelopes and informed him, 'Here you are, Saul, you can come to my party,' he had at first suspected a trick – an empty envelope or some such cruelty. But gradually his delight and excitement had grown. Never having been to a party before he was unsure what to expect, but his imagination came to the rescue of experience and he now envisaged an occasion of fairy-tale splendours. Suddenly, the next few weeks were brimful of excitement: the Nativity play, the school Christmas party, and now this. No wonder his mouth refused to stay in its usual drooping position and kept spreading into this most unaccustomed smile of joy.

'Not everybody got one,' said Saul, anxious that his father understand the honour bestowed.

'You did, anyway. Can I see it?'

Saul did not release the precious paper, but held it where Mal could see and pointed out the important words. 'See here, that's my name – Saul. And this bit says: you – are – invited – to – and that word written in there is Na – omi,' he pronounced the name carefully because he had seen her anger when addressed as 'Naymee'. 'And that's the day and that's the time.' He stabbed at the bottom of the paper and then danced off across the lorry. He was still beaming.

'I'm going to Naomi's party!'

He danced out of the door and down the steps.

'Hey, where are you off to now?' called Mal. 'Take your school clothes off before you play!'

'I'm going to a party!' Saul sang back. 'I'm going to tell Hopi!'

'Wait a minute! Don't go over there!'

Colin had been in a foul mood all day, ever since he woke up and discovered Hopi was enjoying herself with Mal and Kate and Lydia. His period of remorse had expired the previous day, and had been replaced with a conviction that Hopi was not only out to run his life for him, but was also determined to make him feel bad about perfectly reasonable errors like helping himself to items he was unable to afford, or getting upset when pushed beyond the limits of endurance. As well as thinking she was trying to control his every move, he was also outraged that she squandered so much time on others, when he desperately needed all her attention for himself. On that particular day his mood of angry self-pity was magnified by a vicious hangover. However, as luck would have it, he had dropped over to visit Barney and Flea for a few minutes when Saul skipped over with his invitation, so Hopi was alone in the caravan. She had seized the opportunity to machine stitch the seams of a smock she was making for her mother's Christmas present out of a variety of spotted and plain cottons. She was finding the patchwork effect was much more satisfying if she restricted the choice of materials either by pattern or colour.

Frowning, she glanced up from her work as Saul announced his presence at the door of the caravan. Her annoyance at being interrupted vanished as soon as she noticed the expression on his face. Seeing the sparkle of sheer happiness in his dark eyes, she saw that he was going to look very like Mal, and be just as handsome.

'I'm going to a party,' he announced.

'Amazing,' said Hopi, her eyes reflecting back his pleasure. 'A party, you are lucky!'

'Two parties,' corrected Saul. 'The Christmas party at school and Naomi's party at her house. Not everyone is invited to Naomi's party but I am. Look, I've got my very own special invitation.'

When Hopi had examined the lemon-coloured paper sufficiently and admired its violet balloons, she gave Saul an impulsive hug. Normally wary of any physical contact, he consented to be embraced by Hopi. Apart from Mal, Hopi was the only person Saul really trusted on the site and he thought her kindly face most beautiful. He also thought Mrs Robertson was beautiful, but most beautiful of all in his opinion was Suzie. With her pale hair and her toothy smile, her gentle voice and her exaggerated solicitude, Suzie was to remain Saul's image of ideal female beauty for years to come.

Saul was nestled against Hopi's knee when Mal appeared at the doorway. Mal was grinning, but said firmly, 'No running off in your school clothes like that. Come back and get changed. I spend enough time at the launderette as it is.' In his determination that no one should ever have cause to taunt his son with being either dirty or smelly, as tended to be automatic with traveller children, Mal devoted a good deal of time to his son's schoolwear.

'Hang on a minute, Mal,' said Hopi. 'I found this for Saul. It was going to be his Christmas present but I think he's going to need it before that, what with all this wild social life.'

Since starting her patchwork enterprise, Hopi had become a frequent visitor to the charity shops in Edleston. On her most recent trawl she had found a child's sweater about Saul's size. It was a fetching shade of orange with a row of black and white pandas strung across the chest. She dug it out from the bottom of a carrier bag and held it up against his chest.

'Perfect,' she decided, 'just your size.'

Saul peered down at his stomach. 'I like the dogs,' he said.

'They're pandas,' Mal corrected him. 'Pandas are a kind of bear.'

'I thought they were dogs,' said Saul, not minding the correction. 'I'll put it on.'

Hopi helped him wriggle out of his school sweater, but the panda one turned out to be tightly knitted at the neck.

'Hold still, Saul,' said Mal, coming over to assist in the process, 'Hopi's just stretching it for you.'

Saul squirmed, half joking, half panicking inside the noose of stitches; Mal and Hopi were grinning as they tussled with little limbs and unyielding wool.

'Don't worry, Saul,' laughed Hopi as the boy's red face finally emerged puffing into the daylight, 'I'll put a couple of buttons in the shoulder seam. There now, you're certainly going to wow them all in that outfit.'

'What the fuck's going on here?'

Colin's lithe figure had appeared in the doorway. He was quivering with rage. He saw Mal and Hopi squatting each side of the beaming child; he saw their pleasure in which he played no part; he saw his space overrun and his security threatened; he saw betrayal and deception in their happiness.

Flushing swiftly, Hopi said, 'Look Col, it's that sweater I got for Saul. Doesn't it look great?'

'It looks bloody spastic,' Colin sneered. Saul's smile vanished, replaced in an instant by the stony defiance Mal remembered from their first days. Seeing how the child's fragile happiness had been crushed, Mal felt a slow fuse of anger begin to burn in his chest.

He said, 'Come on, Saul. Let's go. Some people just don't understand fashion, I guess.' Forcing himself to remain calm, Mal moved forward to take Saul's school jersey from Hopi.

'Get the fuck out of my caravan. And don't come nosing round here again,' snarled Colin.

'Oh Col,' protested Hopi, 'it's only a kid's sweater.'

Saul was plucking at the pandas on his chest, as though suddenly ashamed of them.

Mal said carefully, 'This happens to be Hopi's caravan, Colin. She's free to invite friends in if she wants.'

'Not while I'm bloody here,' said Colin. 'Go on, get out. Move!' And he reached across to bundle Saul out by force.

'There's no need to be mean about it,' said Hopi, reaching across as if to protect Saul. Colin shoved her out of the way and grabbed Saul by the shoulder. Saul squealed in outrage. Mal felt a white light burst like a firework inside his brain and all the rational, peaceable things he might have said were forgotten as he sprang forward and smashed his hand down on Colin's arm, forcing him to release his hold on the child. Whirling around in surprise, Colin lashed back at once, and his clenched fist pounded into the side of Mal's face, causing his glasses to spring down on his nose. Mal put his hands up to protect himself, as Hopi reached out to get hold of Saul who was in danger of being crushed between the two men. Colin's second punch at Mal caught her squarely on the cheekbone and she fell back with a cry of pain. Mal let out a roar of rage and pounded Colin twice with such force and purpose that his opponent crumpled in fear and stumbled towards the door; but Mal was too incensed to let him get away so easily and he pushed and pummelled him until Colin lost his balance on the top step and toppled down into the mud with a yell of fear and hurt pride. The soft ground broke his fall, but his struggles to right himself only resulted in his becoming covered from the top of his head to his feet in thick mud. Already there was a fair crowd of onlookers to see his fall, dogs leaping round and barking.

'Help me, then, someone. He bloody wants to kill me!' yelled Colin.

'Damn right I do.' Breathing heavily, Mal stood on the top step and gazed down with loathing and contempt at the sludge-covered figure squirming below. He was battling against the temptation to jump down and finish the job off.

Hopi appeared in the doorway behind Mal. Her face was grey, though whether because of the fight or the pain of her injury it was impossible to say. 'Oh, Colin,' she breathed, and began to push past Mal to reach him, but Mal put his hand on her arm.

'Leave him,' he pleaded. 'He had it coming, Hopi, just leave him.'

Hopi made a noise that was close to a sob, and she gazed down on Colin with a stricken face, but she remained where she was. Barney and Flea had appeared on the edge of the group that had gathered to watch the fight. Reluctantly they moved forward to help Colin to his feet. He pushed them away with flailing arms, covering them in liberal clods of mud.

'Come on then, Hopi. Don't just stand there like a bloody statue,' Colin was whining now and his large blue eyes were filled with tears. 'Get that bastard out of there and come and give me a hand. I think he's broken my jaw. Do something, you useless bitch.'

Hopi was shaking. Almost imperceptibly she shook her head. 'Mal's right,' she told him. 'Sorry, Col, but that's it. I've finished with you. It's over.'

Mal turned to her with astonishment. 'Are you sure, Hopi?' he said, and then cursed himself for having given her a chance to go back on her decision. 'I mean—'

'I'm sure,' she said.

Mal's grin mirrored his son's earlier, as he put his arm across her shoulders and said, 'Good decision, Hopi.' Then he spoke to Colin in a voice that allowed no contradiction, 'Get out of here. Now. You and your friends. No one wants you around any more. You've blown it.'

In a cloud of abuse, Barney and Flea helped Colin to leave the now hostile crowd.

Saul wriggled between Mal and Hopi and said approvingly,

'Wow, Dad. You fuckin' showed him, didn't you? That was brilliant!'

'Don't swear, Saul.' Hopi and Mal corrected him in unison as they watched Colin disappear into a far trailer with his friends.

'Sorry,' said Saul meekly.

Barney and Flea's bus crawled off the site just before dark. Colin was with them, and no one was sorry to see them go. Hopi had stayed away as Colin returned to her trailer to gather up his kit, and he and his friends had been gone for some while when smoke was observed escaping from her window. By the time the alarm had been raised and the Briarswood fire engine had found its way down the rutted track to the Hollows, the blaze was out of control and, besides, the nearest hydrant was beyond reach of their hoses. No one knew if the fire had been accidental or deliberate, but the destruction was complete. By morning Hopi's caravan was a twisted shell. Her books and her home-made wines, the pot of scented geranium and the crocheted bedspread and all her patchworks were destroyed. Only enough remained of her precious sewing machine to remind her of what she had lost.

24

Terry and Suzie walked slowly down the hill in the fading light. Exhausted by the company of the younger dog, Bumpkin walked stiffly just in front of them, while Misty, still full of energy, raced ahead. Her feathered tail streamed behind her as she ran, and in this dusky half-light Suzie found it less fanciful to imagine her as some kind of guardian spirit, keeping watch over the handsome youth who walked beside her.

As they drew closer to the road and the outskirts of the village, Suzie unconsciously slowed her pace: she was in no hurry to exchange Terry's company for the stilted conversation and formality of her grandparents.

'Oh well,' she sighed finally as she stooped to attach Bumpkin's leash to his chain collar, 'I suppose I'd better go and face the old people.' Now that she was about to part from Terry she was again angry that Jim, Caro and even Polly had made their weekend arrangements with no thought for her wishes. She added, 'I expect Bumpkin and I will be walking this way again tomorrow. If it isn't raining.'

'We might see you, then,' said Terry. They had reached the point where the narrow country lane joined the main road into Briarswood; here their paths divided. Terry pulled a piece of string from his pocket and whistled to Misty. A self-preserving attitude towards road traffic was not among the dog's many virtues, and on several occasions it was only the skill of country drivers which had prevented disaster.

'Misty! Here, girl!'

Misty had been patrolling the far side of the road. She lifted her head at the sound of her master's call, waved her tail like a white banner and bounded into the road. Straight into the path of a small white Peugeot which was rounding the corner at frantic speed.

'Misty! No!'

Twinks was returning from the supermarket on the outskirts of Edleston where she had purchased two bottles of gin and a bag of roasted peanuts. Now that Peggy's shop was effectively out of bounds, she had been obliged to go further afield for her requirements, especially as George's monthly order to his wine merchants was no longer adequate. She assumed he must be growing mean in his old age: it did not occur to her that her own consumption was rising all the time. Anyway, it was all a frightful nuisance, because she had never felt really comfortable about driving, but she had taken a couple of little pills before she set off to help with the anxiety, and then, as always in her long life, there was no alternative but simply to get on with it. The journey into Edleston had gone without a hitch, and she had managed to get round the supermarket quite nicely with one of those small trolleys they provided for the elderly, but on the way home bands of anxiety began tightening around her chest. She was tempted to pull over to the side of the road and dip into one of the bottles of gin, but she knew that drinking and driving were liable to lead to even greater bother than forgetting to pay for goods at the village shop. Above all calamities, she dreaded losing her licence: if she no longer had the freedom to drive herself around in search of what she needed, then life would be altogether unendurable. So she forced herself to concentrate as hard as she could on the drive: once back at the Manor she would reward herself with a decent drink. She was so absorbed in her task that she gripped the steering wheel between pale hands and leaned forward so that her chin was almost brushing against the wheel. The most vexing part of this return journey was that it was getting increasingly difficult to see the road. She tried wiping the inside of the windscreen with a small sponge kept specially in the glove compartment, but that was no help – mainly because despite the early dusk she had omitted to switch on her headlights.

Once safely off the dual carriageway and approaching Briarswood, she began to relax but, more than ever eager to be home, she did not reduce her speed. When a large pale shape suddenly rose up in front of her she assumed it must be a stray calf, or an enormous sheep. She pressed her foot down hard on what she thought was the brake, but the car leaped forward faster than ever. Something solid thumped against the bonnet, like hitting a wave in a small boat. Twinks' feet flew off the pedals. While struggling to locate the brake, she lost control of the steering and the car screamed to a halt with its nose in the hedge, just a few short feet from where Suzie, Bumpkin at her side, was standing on the verge and gazing at her grandmother with undisguised horror.

'Granny you maniac, you nearly hit us! And you could have killed Misty!' Suzie's fright had been replaced by a surge of rage. Twinks opened her mouth to speak, but Suzie shook her head and, clutching Bumpkin's leash, she raced down the road to where Misty, miraculously, was still standing. Terry knelt by the dog's side, his arms around her neck. Misty's tail was slotted between her legs and her back had an oddly slumped look. She was whimpering. Terry did not respond when Suzie asked, 'Is she really all right?'

When she repeated the question, still with no reply, Suzie checked over the pale body with her fingers as best she could. Although Misty was clearly shaken and in considerable pain, Suzie could see no obvious injury.

'Heavens above,' she said, resting a comforting hand on Terry's shoulder, 'and I thought it was cats who were supposed to have nine lives. She's been amazingly lucky.'

Terry was fondling Misty's thick fur: he seemed hardly aware that anyone else was there. 'Oh Misty,' he said, 'I thought you'd had it.'

'We'd better see if she can walk,' said Suzie, realising that she would have to take charge of the situation. Terry released his grip on the dog's neck long enough for Suzie to coax her into taking a couple of obviously painful steps. Her ears drooped in misery and her haunches sagged. Suzie told herself to stay calm. 'We must get her to a vet straightaway. She might have a broken bone or something that we can't see.' And she thought: oh God, I hope it's not her back.

They were about half a mile from the site, much too far for Terry to carry such a large animal, and it was out of the question for her to walk more than a couple of steps.

Terry wiped the tears from his cheek and said, 'You stay with her then. I'll run back and get help.'

'Too slow,' said Suzie, who was beginning to think that Misty might be more badly hurt than she looked. 'We'll have to use Granny's car. We'll drop her off at the Manor and then go on from there.'

'Isn't there a vet in Briarswood?'

'No, I think the nearest one is the other side of Edleston, but there might be one closer. We can phone from the Manor to make sure there's someone there. Can you carry her to the car?'

With great gentleness, Terry gathered the large dog in his arms. She yelped and licked his hand, pleading with him not to hurt her. Legs braced against the dog's weight, he moved slowly down the road while Suzie, with Bumpkin following quietly, stroked the pale head and told her it was going to be all right. When they reached the car Twinks was still sitting just as Suzie had left her.

'Granny, we've got to borrow your car to take the dog to the vet.'

'I refuse to give up my car!' declared Twinks.

'You must. You were driving much too fast and you might have killed Misty. It was your fault. You've got to let us use the car.' She opened the rear door and helped Terry settle Misty on the back seat.

Twinks was becoming agitated. 'That dog could have caused an accident,' she said.

Speaking in a low voice, so as not to alarm the injured dog, Terry said furiously, 'You're a bloody liability, you are, didn't even have your lights on. You're not fit to drive, you're a danger to everyone, you're—'

'Oh don't Terry, please don't make it worse.'

Twinks had heard the words 'not fit to drive' and somewhere deep in some still-functioning part of her mind she knew that this uncouth boy was speaking the truth. She gazed up at Suzie and her eyes filled with tears. 'It's the end of the road, then, for me,' she said, in blank despair.

'Oh heavens above, Granny, don't be so melodramatic,' said Suzie, misunderstanding. 'And stop fussing about yourself all the time. You've just gone on to the verge a bit and you're practically home.' Suzie turned to Terry. 'She's much too upset to drive. Can you do it?' And to her grandmother she said, 'Here, I'll help you out. Terry will drive us home.'

Luckily, George was on the telephone and so did not observe the fact that his wife was being returned to him by a barbarous stranger for the second time in three days. Deposited on the front step by her granddaughter, Twinks walked straight past her husband and went carefully up the stairs to her room, the carrier bag clinking merrily at her side.

Suzie gestured to George that she needed the phone urgently, and when he waved her away she told him fiercely to finish his conversation at once. George, who was talking to Wyndham Sale, was about to get very angry with her indeed, but then the words 'injured dog' and 'vet' worked like magic. He became extremely solicitous, believing at first that Bumpkin was the affected animal.

'No,' said Suzie, 'Bumpkin will have to stay with you. It's a friend's dog that's been injured. A collie.'

'Oh dear,' said George, with genuine concern, 'fine dogs, collies.'

Five minutes later Suzie had established that the nearest available vet was in a practice in Arnchester which used to be a small village but was now little more than a suburb of Edleston. It would knock about ten minutes off the drive.

Clutching the hastily written instructions, and growing seriously alarmed at the length of time it was taking to get help for Misty, Suzie went out to the car. She had not bothered to tell George they were taking Twinks' car: what her grandfather did not know about, he could not forbid.

'There's a Mr Davies, just this side of Edleston,' she said as she got back into the car. 'They're expecting us.'

'Look.' Terry was twisted round in the driver's seat and his face was ashen. 'There's blood on her mouth.'

Suzie felt something plummet inside her. For the first time the words 'internal injuries' came into her mind. She said resolutely, 'Don't worry Terry. I expect she's just cut her lip or something.

Still, the sooner we get her to the vet the better. I've got the instructions here. I'll sit in the back with Misty and see that she's all right.'

'OK then.'

'We need to go along the dual carriageway for a bit, but we don't go as far as Edleston. Keep a look out for the Arnchester turn-off.'

Terry drove in silence. The sky just above the western horizon was still stained with light, but trees and houses were black shapes in the darkness. His shoulders were hunched with misery and panic. The Arnchester turn-off. How was he ever going to know which that one was? The headlights of the car picked out a large road sign on the left of the dual carriageway – one arrow pointing straight ahead and another pointing to the left. Two lines of letters, black on white. He struggled to make sense of them before they vanished from view. It was impossible. How was he supposed to know where to go?

Suzie was squashed into about six inches of space on the back seat. She kept up a low murmur of talk to soothe herself as well as Terry and the dog, as she stroked Misty's head and fondled her ears.

'Is it far?' Terry's voice was choked with tension. 'I don't want to miss it.'

'You'll see the sign,' Suzie was crouched over Misty's warm body, 'you can't miss it.'

'You look too,' said Terry desperately, 'just to be on the safe side.'

Suzie wasn't listening. Her hand was suddenly spotted with warm, sticky liquid. 'Oh, hurry, Terry, I think Misty's been sick.'

'I'm going as fast as I can.'

Suzie sniffed her hand. No, not vomit. Saliva, maybe. She smothered a cry of alarm. Blood. Blood was oozing out of Misty's mouth.

'It's all right, Misty.' Her words came through her tears. 'We're taking you to someone who can help. Don't worry, Misty. Don't . . .'

She had been aware that they were travelling much too fast. But she did not care. Now, suddenly, the car slammed to a halt and it was all Suzie could do to stop Misty from pitching forward on to the floor.

'Why have you stopped?'

'Red light.'

'But . . .' Suzie looked up and saw the streets lined with shops, the garage and the pub. 'But this is Edleston, we've come too far!'

Terry swore and, seizing the chance of a gap in the traffic moving forward on a green light, he swung the car round and began heading back the way they had come. Glancing through the rear window, Suzie was dazzled by the headlights of an enormous lorry, its front picked out in white bulbs like a Christmas tree and its horn blaring furiously.

Dear God, thought Suzie, we're going to be killed.

The lorry was only inches away from their rear bumper. Then Terry saw a chance to overtake the car in front and they rocketed forward.

'Oh, do be careful!' Suzie begged.

'You look out for the sign!' said Terry furiously. 'This time you look out too.'

'OK.' It wasn't just Terry's tone of voice that made Suzie suddenly compliant. She no longer wanted to look at Misty. Her own hand was covered now with the thick warm blood. With her other hand she kneaded the dense fur on the scruff of Misty's neck, and her eyes strained to see through the darkness.

'Here!' she shouted. 'Pull over here. See, Arnchester is on the right.'

Terry cut across an approaching van which swerved to avoid them. 'Now where?' he demanded savagely.

'You've got to look out for Abercrombie Terrace.'

'You bloody well look for it!'

'But I can't see from – oh look, there it is. You've gone past it!'

Terry flung the car into reverse and turned into Abercrombie Terrace. 'Where is it?'

'It's called Meadowview, there's a sign apparently. It's a big house.' She bent over to smooth Misty's head. 'Nearly there, Misty. It won't be long now, there's a good girl.' She looked up. 'Why are we stopping here? This is the Health Centre. It must be further on. What's the matter? Why don't you—?'

Terry had pounded the steering wheel in frustration. 'Just fucking tell me where to go!'

'There, that must be it on the other side of the road. Oh, thank God.'

The car pulled to a sudden halt. Terry leaped out and opened the back door. 'We're here, Misty,' he said. 'Come along, old girl. You'll be all right now.'

As the interior light came on, Suzie glanced down at Misty's pale head and the seat stained with blood. She bent over the dog and wept.

'Come along,' said Terry, 'let's get her inside.'

'It's too late,' sobbed Suzie.

'What d'you mean?'

'It's too late. She's . . . look. Oh, Terry!'

Terry leaned forward and pulled the dog towards him. Her head rolled awkwardly over the edge of the seat.

'Come along then, Misty,' he said. 'We'll get you sorted.'

'But—'

Ignoring Suzie, Terry gathered the dog in his arms once more and began walking with her to the lit doorway of Meadowview House. Just before they got there, he paused. His head bent forward and he raised the dog's body slightly. His shoulders were hunched and tense. Suzie watched him helplessly. He turned away from the door, but instead of returning to the car he walked a little way along the street, before he stopped and stood for some moments without moving. Misty's limbs were draped casually over his forearms, her pale head dangling as though her neck had been broken. A low wall bordered the pavement and there Terry sank down and curled his body over the ghostly corpse, as if his own warmth could bring her back to life.

Very quietly, Suzie walked over and sat down beside him. She touched the thick fur that already seemed cooler in the frosty night and she said, 'Oh Terry, I'm so sorry.'

He did not look up. Still clinging to the dog he began to rock backwards and forwards and said, 'It's my fault, it's all my fault. I've gone and killed her.'

Suzie was appalled. 'Oh no, you couldn't help it. Granny didn't even have her lights on. You said yourself she wasn't fit to drive. You mustn't blame—'

'It is my fault!' he interrupted her furiously. 'We should have got here sooner.'

'You drove as fast as you could.'

'We got lost. It's my fault we got lost.'

'But—'

In a rage he turned towards her. 'Because I can't bloody read!'

Suzie let out her breath, but could think of nothing to say. She was so startled by this information that it took a little while for it to sink in. She remembered the turn for Arnchester and the sign for Abercrombie Terrace. He must have thought she was torturing him.

She said, 'Oh Terry, I'm so sorry. I didn't know.'

'No one knows. I never told no one.'

She put her hand on his arm. 'It wouldn't have made any difference, you know,' she said gently. 'It was only a few minutes. With that kind of internal injury, there's nothing any vet can do.'

'I should have got here in time. I'm not fit to have a dog.'

'She was with you when she died. And she loved you, Terry. She'd have sooner been with you at the end than surrounded by strangers, I know she would.'

Terry looked away sharply. After a bit he said, 'Thanks, anyway.' He was still holding Misty against his chest, and shivering. Suzie put her arm around him.

'You did all you could.'

'Just wasn't enough, was it?' he said bleakly. He shrugged off Suzie's arm as he removed his jacket and spread it over the dog.

On the way back to Briarswood, Suzie sat in the front with Terry, while Misty, still under the khaki jacket, was laid gently across the back seat. As if to make up for their reckless drive to the vet's Terry drove with great care, conscious at all times of the burden he was carrying. Like a hearse. They did not speak at all until they turned off the dual carriageway and were approaching Briarswood. Suzie was thinking of the boys in the remedial class at school with their swaggering loudness and their primary school reading books; she was thinking about Misty and about Terry's gran. What Terry was thinking about she had no idea, only that his face, in the lights from the oncoming cars, looked desperately young, and vulnerable.

'What are you going to do now?' she asked.

'I don't know.'

'Will you take her back to the site?'

'No, I'm not going back there.' Instinctively he knew that going back to an empty van, with no Misty there for company, would bring home the horror of his loss, and he was not ready for that. Not yet.

Suzie thought for a moment. 'Do you want to come back to my house?' she asked. 'There's no one there. Sometimes it's good to be somewhere different. And then in the morning, we can decide what to do about Misty. Maybe Hopi can do something, like she did for Lydia's baby.'

Terry was willing to be gently bossed by Suzie. 'OK,' he said, 'if you're sure no one will mind.'

'They'll never know anything about it,' said Suzie with unexpected firmness.

There were times when Caro almost managed to convince herself that she had just been overreacting to the whole business. Lots of husbands had affairs, wives too, and it didn't mean the end of the world, or even, necessarily, the end of a marriage. During these calmer interludes, it seemed to Caro that it was pointless to make a fuss about something that happened fifteen years before; it was all over and done with and irrelevant to their present life together. Her need to talk about it all the time felt all wrong. As if she was one of those people who store up grudges and never know when to forgive and forget. As if she was trying to punish Jim for something that was so far in the past that he had practically forgotten all about it, and she hated to think she was harping on . . .

But then, oh! the pain of it! Just as she thought she was being calm and rational and dealing with it all absolutely brilliantly, a picture would spring up in her mind, a loathsome picture of Jim touching Lydia, Lydia with her long legs and her thin body and no clothes on at all, and it was as if a fire was lit inside her head and she was tormented worse than ever with rage and a hellish agony.

On the drive down to Devon they had, at last, talked. Like two captives in their prison car, chained together in endless torment, unable to be close and unable to leave each other alone, they had talked. Picking over and over the same deep wound. Hurting, but unable to stop.

How long had it lasted? Oh, not long. How long? A couple of months, maybe three. How had it begun? He couldn't remember, these things happen. Why? Had there been others? No, only Lydia, there had never been other affairs. What had he seen in her? Oh, she was pretty, and young and he had been flattered. Mid-life crisis, an aberration, he couldn't imagine it now, he must have been mad. How had it ended? The affair had just run out of steam, they both knew it wasn't going anywhere, he had come to his senses, thank God. Had they made love often? No, only a few times. And where? In her bedsit, he thought, never anywhere else. Endless questions, endless answers, again and again, and almost all of them lies.

Jim was tempted, very tempted, to tell Caro the truth. At the time he had longed for her to know; on several occasions he had been on the verge of breaking down and confessing all to his wife. He was desperate for her to know. He still wanted her to know, even now, after all these years. But how could he possibly tell her the truth? How could he tell Caro that he had never known what love was until he met Lydia? How could he tell her that for nearly a year Lydia Allen had been his life, his world, his universe, and not because she was young and pretty, though of course that helped, but because he could talk to her and she talked too. They talked about history and politics and the department and their families and ideas and books and causes; the infidelity had started with the talking: sex had just confirmed what they both already knew. He could never tell Caro that, he had already hurt her enough, that knowledge would be her death blow. So he had to lie and evade and bend the truth, because he had injured Caro enough already and he cared for her too much to want to inflict more pain. He had to lie to her, even though he despised and hated himself yet more for doing it. She was the woman with whom he had shared nearly thirty-five years and wanted to be with for the rest of his life. Besides, Lydia had turned her back on him fifteen years before, when Caro became pregnant and Jim was finally confronted with the hugeness of what he was intending to do. He had still hoped to break free and make a life with Lydia, but she had been disgusted by his indecision and guilt. She had wanted him to be always strong and knowledgeable, always the wise teacher, never the conscience-stricken husband. She had left him and he had stayed with Caro and in the end he had even convinced himself that he was glad it had turned out that way. He had pushed Lydia to the back of his mind, so much so that when he bumped into her on the Tottenham Court Road and learned of her present unhappiness, he had not hesitated to offer her the use of Rose Cottage, as he would have done any former student or colleague who needed a period of rural convalescence. But he had underestimated the power of old associations. The real discomfort had begun when Wyndham appeared on the scene, when he saw the younger man begin to fall under her spell just as he had done. In Wyndham's apparent success he saw his own failures magnified, and he found it intolerable. He had not been jealous of Wyndham for his great wealth, but for his freedom to make a life with Lydia, for the fact that her face came to life when she was with him, when she so obviously despised Jim. He had been jealous because he still cared.

None of this could be said to Caro. None of this would ever be said to anyone. His silence was both punishment and penance. The lies were for Caro's sake, not his.

It was dark when they arrived at the hotel. They checked in, went up to their room, washed and got ready for supper. There was an awkwardness between them, a shyness that was quite new. Caro had noticed with relief that the room had twin beds, but then when she went into the little bathroom to put on the skirt and blouse that she had picked out for the evening, she felt suddenly more attracted to Jim than she had done in months. Baffled by her body's demands, but seeing no reason to deny them, she went back into the bedroom, wearing only her pale slip and underwear and sat down beside Jim who had been idly looking through the information pack laid out on the bedside table.

'We might consider a walk tomorrow,' he said, peering at a leaflet which showed the moors in high summer, 'if it isn't raining.'

'Jim.'

He turned to look at her.

'Jim, will you hold me?'

'Of course.'

He put his arms around her and she laid her cheek against his. Their closeness felt strange, but neither would be the first to move away. Because Caro had never been very sure how to express her wishes, it was some little while before Jim understood what she was asking for, and then a little while more before he could provide it. And then, as their love-making reached its climax, she began to cry.

'What is it Caro? Do you want me to stop?'

'No, don't stop. Please go on, I can't help it, I don't know what's the matter with me.'

'Oh Caro,' he groaned, 'I do love you. I've never really loved anyone but you.'

It wasn't the whole truth, but it was true enough.

That evening at supper they ordered lavishly but ate hardly anything. The waiter observed that sometimes they seemed to have too much to say to each other, at other times, very little. Once or twice he thought they were having an argument, but during the main course he saw them holding hands across the table, and staring into each other's eyes like young lovers.

25

It was gone midnight when the fire engine left the Hollows and Ted Sedden returned to the farmhouse. Norma was waiting up for him, and she made them both a cup of tea.

'What a terrible thing to happen,' she said tentatively. 'Still, it's lucky no one was hurt.'

Ted took off his cap and scratched his head. 'I had a word with Malcolm,' he said slowly. 'They'll be leaving in a day or two.'

Norma was so surprised that she sat down suddenly and said, 'Oh.'

'He said there'd be no trouble about it.'

'Why? Because of the fire?'

'Partly. The hoses couldn't reach. How would I have felt if someone had been hurt? It's not a safe place. But that's not the real reason, Norma. I didn't tell you earlier because I didn't want to worry you, but Sale's assistant has been on to our Ben and Sally.'

'What?'

'Happened yesterday. Ben had been in touch with them about extending the milking parlour. Sale's man made it clear their lease was dicey unless Ben made sure we got the travellers off.'

'Can he do that?'

'A man in Sale's position can do what he wants. Oh, we could fight him, no problem. But it doesn't seem fair on Ben and Sally to make trouble for them.'

Norma was stunned. Her earlier misgivings about the travellers seemed a long time in the past. On the whole they had been a nice enough bunch and she had rather enjoyed the company.

'It's not fair,' she said.

Ted pushed his cap back on his head. 'When was farming ever fair?' he asked. 'Still, I'll be sorry to see them go. I've enjoyed some of my talks with Malcolm. But Sale's man is being a right bastard apparently. Won't even allow them time to find somewhere else to go. Says they've got to be out by the end of the week or he'll make sure Ben loses the farm. Sale's put it all in his hands apparently.'

Norma sipped her tea. 'It's blackmail,' she said, 'that's what it is.'

'Yes,' said Ted.

As Twinks had omitted to inform George that Suzie was to spend the weekend with them at the Manor, he was not in the least surprised when his granddaughter phoned to tell him that she was, after all, going to remain at the Lodge. She had been planning to tell him that a school friend was visiting, but as it happened, even this subterfuge was unnecessary.

'Your father phoned,' he said, 'they've arrived at that hotel place. Can't think why they want to go prancing off at this time of year. By the way, how's the injured dog?'

'Oh Grandpa, she died before we even got her to the vet. It was horrible.'

There was a brief silence at the other end of the line. Then George said, in a voice Suzie had never heard before, 'Terrible. Please give your friend my deepest sympathy. I've had eight dogs in my life and wept like a baby over each one. Always vow never to have another. Damned hard. Damned bloody sad.'

'Yes, isn't it? We'll bring Granny's car back. There may be some blood stains on the back seat but—'

'Never mind about that. Can't be helped. Only a damned car.'

'Yes, thank you Grandpa.'

A gruff noise at the other end of the line announced the fact that he was about to hang up. Suzie was aware that she had just had the first real conversation with George in her life. She felt she was seeing him in an entirely new light.

She found an old basket of Bumpkin's in the garage and folded a clean sheet inside it. Terry laid Misty carefully on the sheet and then covered her with a tartan travel rug. After some deliberation they placed the basket in the centre of the house, near the telephone table in the hall. Although neither said so, they could not bear the thought of Misty being remote from the human company she had always loved.

When they had parked the Peugeot on the gravel forecourt at the Manor, and Suzie had collected Bumpkin and some more sympathy from George for her bereaved friend – whom he never saw, since he was waiting outside in the darkness – they walked back to the Lodge. Suzie spoke once or twice, but she had the impression Terry was too sunk in his own thoughts even to hear what she was saying. She assumed he was grieving for Misty, but when they entered the kitchen he said suddenly, 'You won't tell anyone, will you?'

Suzie turned to him with surprise. 'About Misty? But you can hardly keep it secret.'

'About the reading.'

'Oh.' She thought for a moment, then followed Terry into the hall where he was crouched over the old dog basket and tucking the plaid blanket in around the sides. Bumpkin sniffed the mound cautiously.

Terry said, 'Promise me, Suzie, promise you won't tell anyone.'

'Of course I won't.'

'I'd die if they found out.'

'It's nothing to be ashamed of. I expect no one ever taught you properly.'

Terry's face was turned away. 'I'm stupid, that's all. Stupid and useless. I shouldn't have ever had a dog.'

'You mustn't blame yourself. And I know you're not stupid, anyone can see that. Maybe you're just dyslexic.' When Terry didn't answer, Suzie tried to think what Caro would do in a situation like this. She said, 'I'm going to light a fire in the sitting room. Would you like a drink?'

A little later Suzie was on the sofa, Terry in her father's armchair, in front of a struggling fire. Terry held a large tumbler of whisky, with hardly any water, and Suzie was on her second sherry. Terry was frowning into his glass. When it was nearly empty, he said in a low voice, 'Will you help me, Suzie?'

'How?'

'Help me read.'

'Oh Terry, I'd love to.'

It should have felt strange, sitting with Terry in her parents' sitting room and helping him go through the first chapter of *Pippa's Pony Holiday* which was the book they had selected together from the children's shelf in the spare room. Apart from words like 'martingale' and 'dressage' which she had to explain anyway, Terry was able to make out most of the words, especially as his confidence increased under the combined influence of Suzie's gentle prompting and a second generous portion of whisky.

'You read really well,' said Suzie, when they had got Pippa safely over her first five-barred gate.

'It's OK if I can take my time,' he said. 'Teachers used to yell at me and then the words just went into a nonsense pattern.'

'A bit of practice, and you'll do fine.'

He began to smile, but then he said in despair, 'Too late, though, too late for Misty. I couldn't read those road signs. I let her down, Suzie. She needed my help and I bloody let her down!' His voice cracked, and a great choking sob rose up inside his chest.

'Oh Terry, don't say that. Misty had such a happy life with you.'

But, 'I should have got there sooner,' he insisted through terrible, racking sobs. Suzie felt her own eyes fill with tears, and she flung her arms around him and held him tightly. Clinging to each other helplessly, they sat together for a long time on Caro's chintz-covered sofa, and wept.

The fog that had surrounded Twinks for so many months had shifted and solidified and formed a solid white wall in front of her, obliterating all future. Alone in her bedroom, she had drunk enough of the gin to dull the horror of her situation, but the facts remained hopeless. She no longer had the freedom to visit the village shop, nor to drive her car. George was sure to hear of her misdemeanours: nothing remained secret for long in Briarswood. And he would never understand. Why should he? She did not understand herself. Only that she was consumed by a terrible hunger, a yearning for something somewhere that would colour in the blank space that had opened up inside her when she lost her music. Giving herself little treats in the shop had helped for a moment or two. A small nip of a comforting drink every now and then was essential. Both were now denied her.

There was nothing left, only silence. Not even the faint echo of a musical scale to remind her of past contentment. Ahead there was only a flat white wall of oblivion. No way through. She no longer wished to find a way through.

She heard the television and the telephone and George's voice talking to Hamish. Far off sounds that no longer had any significance at all. Earlier he had called upstairs and she had told him she had a headache and was lying down. Already George was becoming an irrelevance, like everything else. She no longer had a life. The end of the road had been getting closer for a long time and she had not realised it until now. This was it.

She went into her bathroom with its pink paper and mushroom-coloured tiles. She removed several small bottles from the cabinet above the basin, and took them back to the bedroom, where she diverted herself for a while by arranging the differently coloured pills in rows and patterns on her bedside table. Every now and then she sampled one or two, or several, and had a sip of gin to wash them down.

After a little while she happened to glance up and catch sight of her reflection in the oval mirror near the bed. An elegant figure, she was, with her white hair beautifully cut and brushed, her three strands of pearls and her heathery cardigan, buttoned to the throat. But the features, the pale eyes and the nose and mouth that had once been so admired, these were already losing focus. Soon there would no longer be a Twinks.

Whatever would people think? How would they react, those friends and neighbours and family who had admired and respected her for so long? Oh Twinks, you're so wonderful . . . Such a marvellous lady . . . Why ever did she do it? She smiled privately to herself and shunted all the white pills into a small pile. She had swallowed a fair number of them, when her spine refused to support her weight any more and she felt herself slithering towards the floor. For a little while she lay with her cheek against the patterned Chinese rug. From this position she had a clear view of a hot-water bottle top that had somehow rolled under the bed and no one had noticed. She remembered she had been looking for it for ages. Really, Sandra had been getting very slap dash about the cleaning. She must have a word with her about it.

And then she could see nothing at all.

Some time in the silent heart of the night, Hopi awoke. She knew she was not in her own bed, but it took her a moment or two to piece together what had happened. It had been gone midnight when the fire engine left the site, nearly two o'clock by the time everyone drifted back to their own vehicles to sleep. Her caravan was a blackened and still-smoking shell. Everything she possessed had been destroyed. All the presents she had been collecting in readiness for Christmas. Even her precious little bottle of Rescue Remedy, just when she needed it most. Kate and Biff and Donna and all the others hugged her and promised comfort and practical help, but the truth was that she was still too shocked to take it in properly. Mal had offered her his own bed to sleep in, and she had accepted numbly. When they lay down together, they were both so shattered by the events of the day that they had fallen asleep almost instantly. But now he was gone.

'Mal?' Careful not to wake Saul, who was sleeping in his little box bed at the side of the lorry, she whispered his name in the darkness.

'Yes?'

'Can't you sleep?'

There was a sigh, a sound of movement, and Mal moved through the black to come and sit on the edge of the bed. 'I keep thinking about what happened,' he said.

Hopi shivered. She remembered seeing her caravan lit from inside like Saul's Halloween pumpkin, then flames reaching out through the windows, pandemonium all around and no one could do anything. 'Me too,' she said.

'I can't believe I attacked Colin like that. I know everyone says he had it coming, and I'm glad he's gone, Barney and Flea too. But I shouldn't have done it, not like that. I hate violence, I've always hated it, and now I'm just a bully and a thug, everything I hate most.'

'No you're not, Mal. You were defending Saul.'

'And you.'

'And me.'

Mal was silent for a while, then he said, 'But I enjoyed it, Hopi, that's what makes it so hard. When I hit him, it felt great. I wanted to smash his face to a pulp. I saw him lying in the mud and I wanted to jump down and kick his head in, I wanted to finish him off once and for all. And all this time I've gone on about non-violence and finding a way of living in harmony with people, and I'm just a hypocrite. None of it was true. I'm a bully boy, no different from my dad.'

Hopi reached out her hand and placed it over his; she stroked the smooth knuckles of his clenched fist. She said, 'You try to be different, Mal. It's the trying that's important. No one gets it right all the time.'

'But I always thought I was so bloody special,' he said bitterly.

'You are special. You're special to me.'

'No, just listen to me going on about myself. You're the one who's lost their home. And all I do is moan about my own worries.'

Hopi said again, 'You are special to me, Mal. I mean it.' She sat up in the bed and touched his shoulders. Feeling her way in the blackness, she touched his neck, and then his jaw, turning his face to meet her own. She kissed him gently. 'Very special.'

He did not respond. 'Because I beat your boyfriend up? We might as well be bloody cavemen. Besides, I wasn't just protecting you, Hopi. I hated Colin because I was jealous of him. I've been crazy about you for months.'

'Me?'

'Yes.'

'Why didn't you say?'

'Because of Kate. And then Colin came back.'

'I was glad when you hit him. I know what you mean. I always thought it was better not to be violent, but I wanted you to hurt him. Does that make us both cavemen, Mal? Anyway, I'm really glad he's gone. I don't know why I ever stayed with him so long. I thought I could change him, but I think he was beginning to change me instead.'

'I just wish I'd got him to leave without thumping him.'

For answer, Hopi kissed him again. When he still did not respond, she said, 'Don't worry about it, Mal. It's done.'

'I love you, Hopi.'

She was silent.

He went on, 'I don't mean love you the way people say it. I mean I've never felt like this before. It's the real thing, Hopi, for me. I don't want us just to get together and drift around and then go our separate ways when we get tired of it. Because I know I'm never going to get tired of you or want to be with anyone else. I want to take care of you and travel with you, learn things together and then one day, when we're ready, I want to have children with you. I love you now, Hopi, and I always will.'

There was a long silence. Mal gazed down at his hands and then, as Hopi still had not spoken he stood up and went to the wood stove, opened the door and put another log in. It was always better to wake up in the morning and find the fire still burning and besides, it was something to do.

Still sitting very straight in the bed, Hopi said in a low voice, 'I think I love you too, Mal.'

Mal was putting a match to the little night-light Saul liked to see burning when he woke up. 'Think?' He smiled at her gently. 'No, don't say it, that's OK, I'll make do with "think" for now.' He came back and sat down beside her on the bed and wrapped his arms around her. 'Just don't keep me waiting too long.' Releasing her, he said, 'We're going to have to leave this place. Ted told me this evening.'

'Why? Because of the fire?'

He shook his head. 'That feller of Lydia's is leaning on him somehow. Something to do with his son-in-law, I think. We've got to clear out by the end of the week. I said we'd go. You could see he felt bad about it.'

Hopi sighed. 'Oh God, Mal. Where can we go?'

'We'll find somewhere. But I've been thinking, I don't want any more Barneys and Fleas and Colins turning up and wrecking things for us next time. I want a site where I know everyone will look out for Saul, same as I would for their kids. What do you think?'

'We'll have to talk to the others about it.'

'But what about you?'

'I guess so. I'm just not very clear about anything, right now.'

Mal took her hands between his; they were icy cold. He said, 'You're freezing. Do you mind if I come back in bed with you?'

'I wish you would.'

She grinned, leaning back against the pillow. Mal eased himself down beside her, his head propped on his elbow. 'You're beautiful, Hopi,' he said.

She giggled. 'In the dark, maybe.'

'No, I mean it. I like the way your cheeks go when you smile.'

'You never stop talking, Mal, do you?'

'I know,' he said earnestly. 'People are always telling—' but the end of his sentence was smothered as Hopi pulled his head down and began kissing him fiercely.

'Never mind about all that,' she said, surfacing briefly for a gulp of air, 'just enjoy being a caveman for once.'

Suzie had made up the bed in the spare room and found a pair of Jim's pyjamas for Terry. While he took a bath, she changed into her nightdress. They had drunk quite a lot, and only eaten some toast and cheese, and she was feeling light-headed and strange. Partly that was because of all that had happened, but mostly it was because of the different way she felt about Terry: much closer to him than she had ever imagined possible, but at the same time a gulf was opening up between them, one which she knew was never going to be bridged. It wasn't the reading, because in many ways that had brought them together: Suzie had always felt so feeble and inadequate next to Terry, and now there was something she had to offer him. For weeks he had been the hero of her dreams, she had imagined a hundred different ways they might be together in the future. Now she knew those dreams were impossible, not because of background or education, but because of something inside Terry himself. While she held her arms around him on the sofa and they wept together, she understood that he was the most faraway person she had ever known.

Terry lay in the bath and tried to imagine he was floating

in a magic sea where nothing and no one could hurt him. There was a grinding pain in the very heart of him, an old familiar ache of loss, but it had been dulled by the whisky and being in a strange place: it was almost possible to believe that none of the day's events had occurred, and that Misty was not lying under a plaid rug in a strange hallway, but waiting for him back at the site. Here, everything felt unreal; it was not Terry who lay in this soapy water, not Terry who dried himself in a towel the size of a blanket, not Terry who put on those comical striped pyjamas and the slippery dressing gown with the squirls of purple and green. Never Terry who stepped out of the bathroom and was shown into an immaculate bedroom by this girl with the luminous eyes and the gentle, toothy smile.

But when he sat down on the edge of the bed and she went towards the door and said, 'Good night, Terry, see you in the morning,' waves of panic began rolling through his body. The unreal Terry was dissolving, and the real Terry underneath was shattering into a million fragments like a sheet of glass. Caring for Misty had held him together. Without Misty all the different bits of him were spinning wildly out of control. He was disintegrating.

In blind terror he cried out, 'Don't go.'

Suzie paused in the doorway. She said, 'I'll just be in the next room.' Then she saw that he was shaking horribly. She returned to the bed and sat down beside him. 'It's OK,' she said, 'I'm here.'

Beads of perspiration had appeared on his forehead. She smoothed his black hair. Downstairs the phone was ringing, but she barely registered the sound. Suzie stroked his shoulders. He did not draw away from her touch. She said, 'I can lie down with you if you like. It's OK, Terry. I'll stay.'

He was still shaking as they lay down together and Suzie pulled the duvet up to cover them. It smelled of the sachets of pot pourri Caro loved to buy for her linen cupboard. Suzie put her arms around him and soothed him until his shaking grew less violent. He curled his body up against hers and pressed his head against her shoulder.

'It's always so cold,' he said, though Suzie could feel that his skin was burning hot. After a little while his altered breathing told her that he was asleep.

She lay very still. The light was still shining on the landing and she could see all the details of the spare room quite clearly: the carafe with an upturned glass on top of it and the patterned tin for digestive biscuits on the bedside table; the chest of drawers and the ghostly mirror and the two views of highland scenery done in oils by one of Twinks' artistic forebears. The phone was ringing again. Never for a moment did she consider answering it. Briefly, she was even annoyed, fearing that its shrill sound would disturb Misty, peaceful and lonely under her plaid rug. Then she told herself not to be ridiculous.

Mina's words came back to her: it's just sharing a bed, Suzie, it doesn't have to mean sex or anything. Sex. Her breasts felt heavy and mature and she ached to feel the touch of Terry's hands on her waiting skin. Very carefully she moved her foot a little way so it was resting against his leg. His flesh against hers. Maybe he would wake and begin to kiss and caress her . . . she knew that would never happen. But this, even this, was wondrous and she did not want to waste any of it in sleep. She wished she might hold him in her arms for ever.

26

Alone in their separate hotel beds, Jim and Caro had just fallen into an exhausted sleep when the phone shrilled in the darkness. Jim groaned and reached out a hand.

'Yes?'

George's voice, but incoherent and strange.

'Hang on a minute, George, take it slowly. Just tell me what happened.'

Out of the babble of words Jim was able to make out, 'Twinks', and 'pills', 'doctor' and 'hospital'.

'What is it, Jim?' Caro struggled into waking. 'Is Suzie all right?'

'I think so,' and into the phone Jim said, 'get hold of Polly, George. She's staying at the Lodge with Suzie. She'll hold the fort till we get back.'

Jim snapped on the light. Caro heard him say, 'OK, George, now tell me very slowly: which hospital are you at?' and she had left the bed and was getting dressed before he had put the receiver down again.

He looked up at her with a rueful smile. 'Your family,' he said. 'The things they'll do to stop us having a weekend to ourselves.'

As always, Wyndham Sale was up long before dawn. He showered and dressed and then, as he often did, he walked around Haddeley Hall with a candle-lantern. At this hour, electric light seemed out of place; the house revealed itself more intimately by the flickering glow of a candle. It amused him now to see his house as layered, like an archaeological dig: there was the pre-Sale era, all heavy chocolate and green paint and dark papers;

there was the neo-Annabel period of elegantly conventional furnishings and fabrics and then, in the steward's room, there was early-Lydia: a cool wash of colour, but starkly simple and dramatic. He was trying to decide whether there was to be a fourth layer: the late-Wyndham era, or whether, after all, it was time to sell up and move on. He was undecided, and that in itself was a novelty of sorts. There was a strong temptation to escape from old ghosts, but he was beginning to think that he would have to stay and confront them after all. He had to stamp the house with his own presence before he would be free to leave it. Everything took so much longer than he had ever realised.

Annabel's was the ghost that haunted him, not Lydia's. Lydia, he saw now, had been a diversion, a pretence that it was possible to find a new partner as easily as the first one had disappeared. But that was not the case.

In the meantime he needed a fixed point and a focus. That would be provided by Haddelcy Hall. Still using his candle-lantern, he found the swatches of materials and paint samples that Miranda Foley had left for him. He would contact her in the morning. He had always thought that leather chairs and botanical prints would look very good in the library. Late Wyndham Sale, with a touch of Miranda Foley.

On the endless drive back from Devon to the hospital Caro and Jim talked. But this time they avoided the subject that had so absorbed them only the day before. Without consciously saying as much, both were working hard to forge themselves back into a team that could cope with this new crisis Twinks had supplied.

'When I think that I only spoke to her two days ago,' said Caro. 'I mean, she seemed a bit vague, but I never would have said she was unhappy. I keep thinking that I should have spotted something was wrong.'

'Why?' asked Jim. 'Why do you always have to feel responsible?'

'Well, I am her daughter. I should have known.'

'She's always been a very private person, Caro. She never let you get close.'

'Didn't she?' Caro had never thought of it like that before.

When they reached the motorway beyond Exeter, Caro chatted

just to help Jim to stay awake. The roads were nearly empty, and she dared not look at the speedometer.

'I never told you,' she said, 'but I met one of those traveller people the other morning. She was really very nice. Not at all how I had expected.'

Jim flashed her a sudden smile. 'Don't tell me you're thinking of life on the road, Caro.'

'Of course not. But I dare say it's fine for some people. I'm going to have a word with Daddy when all this has sorted itself out, and tell him to stop badgering Wyndham Sale to get them moved on. After all, they haven't done any harm at the Hollows, have they?'

'None that I know of,' said Jim.

When they got to the hospital, the doctor was more immediately concerned about George than about his wife. Twinks was in intensive care, and no one could do more than look at her through a plastic window, but they seemed to think there was a serious chance George might have some kind of collapse if he wasn't taken home and given some medication by his own GP.

It was still dark when Jim drove Caro and George back to the Manor.

'Where's Polly?' Caro had asked him. 'I thought you were going to get hold of her.'

'Polly?' George was confused.

'She's staying at the Lodge with Suzie.'

'Ah, yes. Never knew she had a dog. Collie, apparently. Terrible shame. And now this . . .' George's eyes filled with tears.

Caro put her arm around his shoulder and led him into the house. 'Poor Daddy. We'll stay with you until the doctor comes and then we'll go back to the Lodge. Polly can come up and stay with you for the morning. Thank heavens she's here. If Jim and I don't get some sleep soon, we're going to be no use to anyone. And you must try not to worry, Daddy: you know the hospital said they'd phone the moment there was any news.'

It was a new father, this frail and bewildered man who allowed himself to be led up to his bedroom to await the doctor's arrival. When the shock wore off he would no doubt regain all his old bluff and bombast, but for the moment he let Caro tend him, and was even grateful. Her solicitude felt strange to her: she had always thought she was caring for her parents by shopping and cooking and fussing. Never for a moment had she imagined removing shoes, helping him to lie down on his bed, offering reassurance.

As they drove the Range Rover the short distance to the Lodge, the sky was beginning to lighten over the eastern hills.

While she was caring for her father, Caro's own anxieties had slid to the back of her mind: now they absorbed her once again.

'Is Mummy going to make it, do you think?'

Jim frowned. 'I really don't know. They seemed to think she might, but then there's the danger of kidney damage. And her age is against her.'

'I want to be with her. Now. Let's not go home.'

'Later, Caro. Just get your head down for a couple of hours and then we'll go back to the hospital. There's nothing you can do now.'

'That's what's so dreadful, not being able to do anything. And all the while I could have helped, I just didn't know how unhappy she was.'

'Well, there's always the chance that it was an accident,' said Jim. But he didn't sound very convinced. There had been the gin, as well as the pills.

'Home again,' said Caro as they pulled up in front of the Lodge. 'Thank God.'

She was too exhausted even to notice that Polly's car was missing from the garage, too exhausted to do anything but push open the front door and stagger into the hallway. Bumpkin greeted her cheerfully.

'Hello Bumps, old thing,' she said gently. 'Have you missed us? Good heavens, what's your old basket doing here? And what on earth—?'

As she pulled back the plaid rug, revealing a dog's pale muzzle encrusted with dark blood, Caro let out a small scream of shock. Jim, who was following, dropped their case and put his arm around her.

'What's the matter?'

Then he, too, looked down.

'Oh Jim, it's dead! What's it doing in our hall? Oh!'

'Your father muttered something about Polly and dogs. I thought he was wandering.' He stooped and covered the white head once more. 'I've never seen the animal before. Where ever did it come from?'

'We'll have to ask Polly,' said Caro, recovering herself. 'Put the kettle on Jim, there's a dear. I'll go and wake her. I suppose she's in the spare room as usual.'

Bumpkin followed Jim as he went into the kitchen while Caro began to climb the stairs. To his surprise, Jim found he was suddenly remarkably cheerful. He could see that all these dramas created by Caro's parents were going to make his own ancient errors fade – not into insignificance, that would be too much to ask – but to a point where they became manageable. This crisis gave him the opportunity to show Caro his loyalty and support; the process of rebuilding would still take time. He must be careful and do nothing to antagonise her, but—

This time Caro's scream was loud and piercing. It reverberated round the house and went on and on. There were other voices, sobbing, and Caro's unending hysterical scream. Jim was up the stairs in a moment. A dark-haired figure, a young man who appeared to be wearing Jim's pyjamas, dashed past him and into the bathroom, and in the spare bedroom Caro was still standing and screaming at her daughter, while Suzie, crouched in her nightdress on the bed, sobbed and pleaded and made no sense at all.

Understanding the situation at once, and feeling a brief surge of revulsion that his youngest daughter, his baby, had betrayed them the moment their backs were turned, Jim strode into the spare bedroom and caught Caro by the shoulders.

'Shut up!' he shouted. 'Shut up! You're just hysterical and making it all worse. Shut up!'

Then he slapped her, once, but hard. Suzie burst into even louder sobs and flung her face against the pillow, but Caro had stopped screaming. She said to Jim, 'He was in bed, that half-caste was in bed with Suzie.'

Suzie looked up at them in horror. 'It wasn't how you think!' she wailed.

Incredulous, her parents stood side by side and stared.

'Where's Polly?' demanded Jim.

'She couldn't come.'

'So you lied to Grandpa and Twinks! How could you?'

Suddenly Suzie wasn't crying any more. A cold hard core of certainty was beginning to form inside her. She scrambled to her feet. 'Oh, what's the point? You're not going to believe me, no matter what I say,' and she started to push past them.

'Where do you think you are going?'

'I'm going to get dressed. Do you mind?'

At that moment Terry emerged from the bathroom. He looked dazed and frightened, but he was dressed in his own clothes again and he glanced briefly at Suzie.

'Thanks for helping me with Misty,' he said.

Jim began walking towards him, but Terry fled down the stairs. They heard the front door slam shut. Suzie had started to run after him but Jim caught her by the arm.

'Oh no you don't!' he told her.

'Let me go!' Suzie struggled free, and was about to run down the stairs, still in her nightdress when her mother's voice stopped her at once.

'Oh Suzie, you can't do this! Twinks has taken an overdose and she might be going to die. You can't do this to me, not now, after everything else.'

Suzie turned slowly. 'Granny?'

Jim nodded. Suddenly sickened by the whole wretched circus, he said, 'Get dressed, Suzie, and come downstairs. We'll tell you what's been happening. And maybe you'd like to tell us what's been going on here.'

'I'd have thought that was obvious,' said Caro. She was haunted by that image of the two heads on the pillow, one fair, one dark. It would haunt her for months to come.

'Why should I tell you anything?' asked Suzie. 'You've already made your minds up.'

'Try us,' said Jim.

The way he said it made Suzie suddenly hopeful, but when she had dressed and was going down the stairs, she heard Jim say something to Caro, something about calling the police.

'The police?' she exclaimed. 'What have they got to do with anything?'

Jim had already picked up the receiver. Suzie noticed that the basket by the hall table was empty, just a folded sheet and a couple of bloody stains. 'Sorry, Suzie,' said Jim, and she could see that he meant it, 'but your young friend has just stolen the Range Rover.'

Their car was found later that afternoon, about a hundred and fifty miles north of Briarswood. The Range Rover had been abandoned when it ran out of fuel. A young man answering Terry's description had been seen hitching along a country road a little distance away. Later in the week a farmer found the body of a large white dog in a shallow grave nearby. A clumsy attempt had been made to hide the pale corpse with bracken and branches, but of the dog's owner there was no trace, neither then, nor at any time.

Whenever she went to a large gathering, Hopi always kept a lookout for Terry's lithe form and dark good looks, but she never saw him. She went through his few papers, and followed up one or two leads, but they came to nothing. When Suzie finally had a few days in London with her sister, she escaped for as long as she could and hunted among the down-and-outs in shop doorways and huddled close to heating vents, but she never saw him. She became haunted by the despair that she saw in the weary eyes of the homeless – homeless and hopeless and rootless, a thousand Terrys, but none of them him. She never heard of him again, never knew the end of his story.

He had, quite simply, disappeared.

The worst part about leaving the Hollows, so far as Hopi and Mal were concerned, was telling Saul. At first he refused to believe that Jason Lawrence was to have the role of innkeeper in the Nativity play in his place. After all his work, he couldn't imagine how they were possibly going to manage without him. Nor could he accept the fact that his lemon-coloured party invitation had been rendered null and void: pass the parcel and lucky dips and jelly and custard were all to remain mysteries. He was utterly devastated.

Mal felt wounded on his son's behalf. It might not have been so bad, he thought, if Saul had grieved openly; what he hated was the way the child retreated into his sullen shell, as surly and uncommunicative as on the day Mal collected him from Angie's flat. All the progress of the autumn months seemed to have counted for nothing.

At the school, Ann Robertson did what she could to soften the blow; she was surprised at how fond she had grown of the difficult little boy in a short time, maybe because she had begun to consider him one of her successes. In spite of all the teacher's best efforts, Saul remained inconsolable.

And then even Saul's woes were forgotten in the pandemonium of getting the vehicles off the site. For half a day everyone became a motor mechanic as wheels whirred in the mud, engines sparked into life and then died again, batteries were charged and swopped and discarded. There was some debate about what to do with Terry's van, but the general opinion was that he would want to catch up with them sooner or later, so Kate agreed to drive it to their next resting spot. They all agreed that they'd look after his stuff until he came for it, but the fact was that his van was practically empty of possessions.

Ted Sedden, who still hated having offered them a place to stay only to snatch it away from them just as winter was beginning in earnest, gave them all the help he could. Norma baked large batches of scones for them to take with them. She stood in the farmyard as the strange procession rumbled past: lorries and vans, cars and caravans, each one more cheerfully ramshackle than the one before. She waved and smiled at them all indiscriminately; her sorrow at seeing them go was tinged with relief.

Biff was last, in his purple and green bus. As the best mechanic on the site he had waited until the rest had begun their journey, in case anyone needed his assistance. He turned to Norma as he bounced along the track beside the farm, and gave her a hearty grin and a thumbs up sign.

And then they were gone.

Lydia was waiting for the taxi that would take her to the station. Her parents had agreed to lend her a couple of hundred pounds so she could fly to Minorca; she had promised to pay them back from her earnings. She was looking forward to the work on Charlotte's mural; already she had made some sketches of elegant squid and mysterious looking tuna disporting themselves among seaweed and coral.

Rose Cottage was packed and neat and impersonal. No longer home. She was ready for the next stage.

In the lonely hours of tidying and preparing to leave, Lydia had had plenty of time to contemplate Wyndham's analysis of her character. Leaving was what she did best: that was true. Already she felt excited, and eager for what lay ahead. Where he had been wrong, she thought, was in his assumption that she left because her present man had let her down. He thought she required perfection in her partners, but it was only from herself that she required the impossible. She had a clear image of the kind of person she wanted to be. Perhaps a Mediterranean mural painter was the key she had been looking for all along.

She glanced at her watch. Well, why not? One more time. It would be difficult to catch the programme once she was abroad.

Gordon's voice: '. . . from their point of view.'

And then a voice that sounded extraordinarily like Suzie's: 'But they make me feel like such a criminal. And if I try to explain to them what happened, they say that only makes it worse because I'm lying, and then I get so angry but I can't—'

Lydia flipped the knob. It couldn't be Suzie. It didn't make any sense for Suzie to be phoning in to the wise and smooth-tongued Dr Gordon Fairchild. And if Suzie was phoning him, then Lydia certainly did not want to know about it. In her mind, Lydia had already left Briarswood far behind.

It was two days before the doctors at the hospital were able to assure the family that Twinks was going to pull through. There was some damage to the kidneys that might cause problems later, but the general opinion was that she had been lucky. Caro had confided all her anxieties to a young and sympathetic doctor. Since he firmly believed that every patient deserved to hear the truth, he explained to George that his wife had been not only suicidal, but most probably alcoholic and a kleptomaniac as well. George held on to this information for as long as he was able, and then rearranged it to make a more credible picture. His wife had been under terrible strain. She was not well. Though he would, of course, do anything he could to help out, she was altogether too much for him to deal with.

The days of Twinks' hospitalisation blurred into one long family conference. Caro's brother William came down from London with his wife Laura. Polly came down looking remarkably subdued with a grim-faced Angus in tow. Kate and Emily were summoned. George appeared to be quite unable to make a decision of any kind, Jim was still more concerned to save his marriage than make any suggestion not previously thought of by Caro, and William was so obviously out of touch that his comments were invariably ignored. Twinks had already made the transition to invalidity and would never be required to make a decision again. To Caro's amazement, everyone looked to her to take charge of the situation.

And so she did.

During one especially long and whisky-enhanced talk with her brother and sister-in-law, Caro finally confided some of her own worries to her elder brother.

'Why don't you send Suzie to private school then?' asked Laura.

'We can't afford it,' said Caro simply.

By midnight that evening, William for the first time had some idea of his younger sister's situation. After a brief discussion with Laura, who was so appalled at the prospect of having to take any responsibility for her husband's parents that her usual parsimony was forgotten, he decided that the Lodge should be permanently transferred to Caro's name and that George should be made to pay his daughter for all the work that would be involved in looking after Twinks once she was brought home. Guiltily aware that he was getting off lightly even so, William volunteered to pay for Suzie to attend a private school for sixth form. He was paying so many sets of school fees already, that one more for a couple of years would not make much impact on his finances one way or the other. Jim, when the plan was broached to him, was more than happy to agree to anything that would ease the burden on Caro. Suzie was not consulted.

Caro was finding it extraordinarily difficult to talk to Suzie at all. Each time she caught sight of her youngest daughter, an image flashed up in her mind of the two sleeping heads on the white pillow in the spare room and she felt a stab of betrayal and loss that was at least as deep as anything she felt over Jim.

'But Mummy,' insisted Suzie, 'nothing happened. He was just unhappy about his dog dying, and I'd been comforting him.'

It was the first time they had been alone together in what seemed like a year but had, in fact, been only five days. They were driving back to the Lodge after a brief visit to the hospital. Twinks was to come home the following day.

Caro glanced at her daughter. Suzie had always been a scrupulously honest child, but still . . .

'It seems very peculiar to me,' said Caro dubiously, 'two young people sharing a bed and not—' she braced herself, before saying firmly, 'not having intercourse.'

'Yes. Well. Maybe in your day. But Mina and her friends do it all the time. It's just sharing, you know. It doesn't have to mean sex or anything.'

'All right then, Suzie. If you say so, then of course I believe you.'

That was when Suzie started to cry. 'He was so unhappy,' she said, staring through the front window of the Range Rover as the tears streamed down her cheeks, 'and I loved him so much. I'll never love anyone as much as I loved him. And I knew it would never come to anything. I wanted him to make love to me, and I knew he wouldn't.'

'Oh Suzie.' Caro pulled over to the side of the road and stopped the car so she could comfort her daughter. Instead she found that she was crying too. heaven knows, there had been plenty to cry about, this last few days. She said, 'Suzie, I know it hurts now, but you'll get over it. Believe me, one can get over anything.'

She knew that much at least, from bitter experience.

Through her sobs, Suzie registered the truth of what her mother was saying, but found that it only made her present misery worse. She knew that she was 'only' fifteen, and that in years to come she would probably make a joke of the terrible things that had happened in recent days, and she dreaded becoming the person who would betray the Suzie she was now. She was just wondering how she could begin to explain this tangle to her mother, when she heard a rumbling, roaring noise, and the first of the traveller vehicles began thundering past.

*   *   *

'Oh look,' said Hopi. 'Isn't that Suzie and her mother?'

Mal peered down at the occupants of the Range Rover. 'Do you think they've broken down?'

'Well, we can't stop to help them,' said Hopi. 'We'd just hold everyone else up.'

Saul sat between them. His face lit up briefly as he caught sight of Suzie and he waved the small book he was holding in his lap. He grinned as the girl smiled and waved back to him. And then they had gone past.

Mal glanced at his son. 'Feeling better, then, are you?' he asked.

'Yup,' said Saul.

'We'll have our own party just as soon as we find a place to stop,' said Hopi. 'We'll get balloons and jelly, the whole works.'

'I don't mind,' said Saul, and it was true. Naomi and all the others might have the party to look forward to, but they were stuck in Briarswood all the time, they didn't have a brilliant home which moved around the countryside, free as a bird in a flock. Hopi and Mal had tried so hard to protect Saul from the downside of their eviction that he was convinced they were moving on to better things. He was wearing his orange panda sweater and had a bag of crisps in his hand and all the books about rabbits and fat little bears and piglets that Suzie had given him. Wedged between Hopi and his dad, high up in his lorry home, Saul felt contented as a king in his travelling realm.

'Good-bye Briarswood!' said Hopi and Mal together as they left the village behind them and turned towards the dual carriage-way.

'Good-bye Briarswood,' echoed Saul, and then snuggled more securely between the two adults on either side of him. 'Where are we going now?'